A RIGHT SHAMBLES IN YORK

A DI ADAMS MYSTERY

KIM M. WATT

For further information contact www.kmwatt.com

Cover design: Monika McFarland, www.ampersandbookcovers.com

Editor: Lynda Dietz, www.easyreaderediting.com

ISBN ebook: 978-1-067011-69-7

ISBN paperback: 978-1-991381-00-2

First Edition June 2025

10 9 8 7 6 5 4 3 2 1

CONTENTS

A NOTE BEFORE WE BEGIN

Lovely people, thank you once more for joining me on yet another foray into the wilds of Yorkshire, armed only with a duck and a very large stick.

I mean, *wilds*. We are in the city of York here, so let's not overstate things.

On the other paw, of course, York is not quite as it may seem. So perhaps *wilds* isn't all that misplaced after all …

Anyhow! I am going to assume you have arrived here after a meander through the previous books in DI Adams' series, but if not I shall reiterate my usual assurance that you won't be *too* lost if you haven't read the others (although questions about ducks and Yorkie bars may persist).

I shall also let Beaufort Scales readers know where this book fits into the series: between *A Toot Hansell Christmas Cracker* and *Coming Up Roses*, for if you're keeping track. The full reading order can be found on the website, should you be interested (www.kmwatt.com).

And now we know where we are (at least a little), I think we're ready to get a little lost, don't you think?

Step on in. And please mind the Wilfred.

Happy reading!
Kim

1

THIEVING DUCKS

"Ducks," Detective Inspector Adams said, her tone flat.

"Ducks," the man facing her across the scarred wood of the pub table agreed, nodding sagely. He had a drooping face, everything sliding down from the sparse hair at the crown of his head to his loose jowls, the skin mottled with broken veins. His hands were heavy and big-knuckled with arthritis and hard work, and one of them rested with easy familiarity around a pint glass, despite it being barely ten in the morning.

Adams looked at her notebook, lying open on the table in front of her, and wished she'd kept it on her lap. Everything was desperately sticky, and she was trying not to lean back in her chair, because she thought it might grab her jacket just as firmly as the table had grabbed her notebook. Even her boots were sticking to the old red carpet with its scars and faded patches, and though she could smell the strident notes of cleaning products in the near-empty pub, they were underlaid by a persistent funk of old beer and the ghosts of forgotten cigarettes. Spring sunshine filtered through the chunky mullioned windows, giving everything a warm glow that couldn't quite manage charming, and except for a couple of fruit machines humming quietly by the door to the loos, all was silent.

The only other people in attendance were the proprietor – a short, sturdy woman with pale blonde hair and a low-cut top stacking glasses behind the bar – and a tall, lean man propped against it with a mug of coffee in front of him. He was examining the coffee with as much doubt as Adams had regarded her own, and she had a feeling he was trying very hard not to meet her gaze. A large, dreadlocked grey dog sat on the bar itself, panting on the proprietor and making her look around in a puzzled way, as if feeling his breath but not sure where it was coming from, and two border collies stood close to the man's legs, gazes shifting between the selectively invisible grey dog and Adams.

She turned her attention back to the man across the table. "I thought you said you had a trophy stolen," she said.

"I did," he said. "It were the ducks as took it."

She looked back at her notepad, where she'd written very neatly the name of the pub, which was The Dabbling Dipper; the name of the man, which was Travis Fletcher; and the complaint, which was the aforementioned stolen trophy. She very carefully laid her pen on top of the pad, making sure it didn't roll off onto the table. She'd have to disinfect it if it did.

"Can you tell me why you suspect ducks?" she asked.

"They're up to things. Always sneaking around and acting cute. But I'm onto them." Travis didn't tap the side of his nose, yet he somehow gave the impression of doing so anyway.

"And that's your only reason?" She was trying very hard to keep her voice neutral, but he narrowed his eyes, taking a swig of beer.

"You don't believe me," he said, and the man at the bar gave a very small snort.

Adams managed not to glare at him, keeping her attention on Travis. "It's not that I don't believe you," she said. "It's just that I think you should be calling the RSPB if you've got a duck problem. Birds aren't really a police issue."

"I did call them," he said. "They reckon they can't do anything. They said if someone had stolen the *ducks*, they could help, but not if the ducks are doing the stealing, which don't seem right, does it? That's prejudice."

Adams nodded slowly, picked up her mug to have a sip of coffee, then decided against it. There was a nasty, greasy film on the surface and something caked on the handle, plus she thought she could see mysterious, drifting bodies in the depths. She set it down, removed her notebook from the table with some difficulty, and got up. "I can't arrest a duck."

"Can't you get rid of them, at least?" Travis asked. He drained the last of his pint and set it on the table, then, to Adams' horror, pulled the leg of his trousers up and showed her a very pale, very hairy calf. "They pecked me! Assault *and* thievery!"

"Um." She couldn't see anything on his leg from here, and she didn't want to take a closer look.

"I heal quick, but it's there. They're bloody menaces." He pulled his trouser leg down again, and looked at the woman behind the bar. "And there were your garden thingies as well, Belle."

Belle huffed, stretching to put a glass back on a high shelf. "It'll be kids," she said. "It's always damn kids. I really liked them, though."

"What's this?" Adams asked.

"I lost a little family of hedgehogs," she said. "Not real ones. Metal. Thought they'd look cute in the beer garden. They did and all." She thought about it. "Well, most of the time. Some divot was always moving them about, or putting them in compromising situations."

Travis made a sympathetic sound, but no one else spoke until Adams said, "I suppose that's always a risk."

"Idiots," Belle muttered.

"Could try the RSPCA," the lean man at the bar said. "Cruelty to hedgehogs." He was struggling not to grin, and Adams narrowed her eyes at him.

"They won't be any help. Not if the RSPB are anything to go by," Travis said darkly, inspecting his empty glass.

"So what happened to these hedgehogs?" Adams asked.

"I'm telling you, it'll be kids," Belle said. "They vanished the same time as his ridiculous trophy, so some little menaces probably took the lot. I remember we used to go about stealing those ceramic ducks and wire butterflies people had on their walls when we were that age. Nothing changes."

"No, kids are too busy on the Tic-Tac or whatever these days," Travis said. "They're not interested in hedgehogs and trophies. *And* it wasn't ridiculous." He went to the wall and took a framed photo down, turning around to show it to Adams. She didn't take it, not wanting to touch the grimy glass, but she had to admit it was a rather nice trophy. Instead of some cheap, generic cup picked up from the local sports shop it looked like an actual sculpture, thin, carefully folded metal blossoming into the form of an origami-style frog which shone even in the dull print.

"Very nice," she said. "What was it for again?"

"Marrow growing."

"It's a frog."

"I know," he said, petting the frame.

Adams decided against trying to make sense out of that. "Whose was it?" Because the man holding it in the photo definitely wasn't Travis, even if it did look to be a fairly old photo.

"*Mine*," he said, sounding aggrieved, and Belle snorted.

"She's a *detective*. She's not buying that. Travis here's never grown a marrow in his life," she added to Adams.

Travis huffed. "Alright, so it wasn't mine originally. But I came about it honestly."

"If you call hustling a card game honest," Belle said.

Adams pocketed her notebook and pen. "So it's not actually yours."

"I won it fair and square."

"Not for growing marrows, though," Belle pointed out. "And not from someone who was entirely sober either."

Adams massaged her forehead, where a small but persistent headache was forming at her hairline that had nothing to do with her habitual tight bun. It was better than the eye twitch she had to deal with every time she went to the village of Toot Hansell, with its problematic dragons and much more concerning ladies of a certain age, but she still wasn't a fan of it. Life in the country was proving much more stressful than London had ever been, and in entirely new ways.

She took a steadying breath. "Right. Was the trophy really stolen, then?"

"Yes," Travis said.

"No," Belle said, and they glared at each other. "You left it outside!" she said.

"And the ducks took it!"

"You're ridiculous."

"No one wants to admit the truth. Ducks are *trouble*."

Adams looked at the tall man at the bar, who was watching the exchange with a faint grin on his face. The border collies looked about as impressed by the smell of the pub as she was, and the big grey dog had helped himself to a barstool, perching on it comfortably. Adams scowled at the man, and he gave her a very small shrug, took a mouthful of coffee, and immediately looked horrified.

She allowed herself one small moment of satisfaction, then looked at Belle. "Do you want to report the hedgehogs stolen?" she asked.

"I don't know. I mean, my niece gave them to me, so I'd like them back, but how's anyone going to find them? I even looked at my little doorbell cam, just for interest, and there's nothing on it. It's a waste of time."

Adams agreed wholeheartedly, but she couldn't exactly say that. "If you're sure—"

"What about my trophy?" Travis demanded.

"Old Pat probably took it back," Belle said.

"Then that's thieving!"

"Thought you said it was the ducks," the man at the bar said.

Adams resisted the urge to tell him to shut up.

"That's because of the camera," Travis said.

"The one that showed nothing?" Adams asked.

"Not *nothing*. It went fuzzy, like something flew across the screen. A *duck*." He actually did tap his nose this time, nodding as well, and the other man snorted, then turned it into a cough. He set his mug on the bar, and the big grey dog gave it a horrified look, then jumped to the floor.

Travis crossed to the bar and set his empty pint glass down. "Set us up another one, would you, love?"

"Don't you *love* me," Belle said. "All this damn fuss, and you probably dropped the trophy in the water yourself. *And* my hedgehogs."

"I would *never*. I loved your hedgehogs."

Adams nodded, looking at the floor, and said, "Well, I can't arrest a duck, and if you're not making a complaint about missing hedgehogs, I think we're done here."

"Don't you want to check the doorbell footage?" the tall man asked, and she wondered briefly if it would be considered assault if she threw the remains of her very tepid coffee at him. Instead of doing that, she took a card from her pocket and set it on the bar. She couldn't slide it across because it immediately stuck in place, so she just tapped it and looked at Belle. "Send me the camera footage if you want."

Belle peeled the card off the bar and examined it. She had immaculate make-up, Adams noticed, and her nails were short but very tidy. Behind her, a clutter of cards and postcards were tacked to the wall, a litany of places seen and people loved, a lot of them featuring Belle with her arm around a younger woman who looked an awful lot like her. The niece, perhaps. "Alright," Belle said. "I might, at that. I miss those hedgehogs."

"Great," Adams said, without much enthusiasm. She headed for the door they'd arrived by, which opened onto a slightly ramshackle beer garden, dotted with leaning picnic tables and bordered at the bottom by a little stream. A path led around the side of the pub to the car park, but rather than follow it immediately she paused to examine the overgrown grass and shabby pots, not yet planted with fresh blooms. The sun was warm enough, but it wasn't trustworthy. Spring in North Yorkshire was a fickle beast, and it could be sunburn today and frostbite tomorrow.

Footsteps followed her, and she looked around to see the border collies running out ahead of the tall man, who had his hands tucked into the pockets of his waxed jacket, his shoulders broad and sharp and his stance relaxed. He gave her a grin that was almost apologetic but not quite. His name was Rory, and she had no idea why he'd dragged her out here, or, more to the point, why she'd agreed to come.

"Did you enjoy that?" she asked.

"I didn't realise it was going to be quite *that* bonkers," he said. "Travis seemed really reasonable when he said he'd been reporting a theft and the local cops weren't interested."

"You know I have my own cases? And this isn't even my patch?"

"Sure, but I thought it might be your area of expertise."

"Theft by duck?" she said, just as Travis emerged from the door, wielding a mop.

"There they are!" he shouted, and charged across the beer garden, waving his makeshift weapon wildly. "Give me back my trophy, you aquatic sodding Christmas dinners!"

A trio of ducks that had been gathered on the edge of the beer garden fled back into the water, feet and wings paddling wildly as they set up a chorus of outraged quacking. The big grey dog bounded into the shallows after them, and the border collies followed.

"Midge, Pinto, *heel!*" Rory yelled, but they ignored him entirely, and he scowled at Adams. "Is your bloody invisible dog leading them astray again?"

"No comment," she said, and watched Travis come to a staggering stop on the bank of the waterway, feinting with the mop as if he might still reach the birds.

"And bring back the hedgehogs!" he shouted. He spun, jabbing the mop across the garden to indicate the front of the building as he glared at Adams. "They were there! Really cute little critters, and now they're gone as well, and my trophy, and nobody will do anything about it!"

He swung back to the ducks, and Adams shouted, "Careful!"

She was too late. Travis yelped, his footing slipping as he staggered too close to the edge. He dropped the mop and windmilled his arms wildly, giving a little wail of fright. Adams lunged forward, but she was too far away. Rory was closer, but still not close enough. His fingers closed on air as Travis crashed into the shallow stream.

"Oh, bloody *hell*," Adams said, stopping at the water's edge and snatching up the mop. "Here, grab this," she started, reaching out to Travis with it, but Rory had already kicked his boots off and was splashing into the stream. It wasn't deep, but Travis couldn't seem to find his feet. He wailed, thrashing in the chattering water, lurching one way then the other and drenching himself thoroughly. The dogs had stopped their pursuit of the ducks and were standing in the middle of the waterway, watching with astonishment.

Belle emerged from the pub behind them. "What the hell is going on?" she started, then spotted Travis. "Travis, *for heaven's sake*, not again," she shouted, striding out to join Adams on the bank. "Are you chasing bloody mermaids again? Mermaids don't live in *streams!*"

Adams didn't know about mermaids, but she'd certainly encountered sprites, who seemed to come armed with swans and geese, which she wasn't keen on meeting. She checked the river, but only saw the ducks, who were watching with great interest from the far bank. They seemed like the least troublesome creatures in evidence, really. She stepped back as Rory hefted Travis to his feet and shoved him onto dry land, where he staggered in a circle yelling, "I want my trophy back!"

"And I want my hedgehogs!" Belle shouted. "But you don't see me jumping in the water making a spectacle of myself, do you?"

"You should arrest them," Travis said to Adams, pointing at the ducks. "You saw what they made me do!"

"Again," Adams said, "I can't arrest the ducks." She was mostly watching the large, dreadlocked dog, who might be invisible to everyone else, but was very much visible to her. He was looking up and down the river with interest, and she sighed inwardly. His invisibility didn't seem to extend to the water he was going to drag into the car with him, and the smell was very much discernible, she'd found.

Belle and Travis were still arguing, and Adams was just about to turn away from the scene when she caught a flash of movement in the shallow water. All three dogs looked toward it, ears pricked, and a woman's form melted out of the stream. She was sleek and scaled, the sunlight glistening on her silvery skin, and she scratched Dandy behind the ears while he wagged his tail eagerly.

"Who's a good beastie?" she said. "Aren't you a lovely scary monster?"

Rory turned, looked into the river, and said, "*Huh.*"

"You see her?" Adams asked.

"I see her," he said. "Still can't see your dog, though."

That tracked. The magical Folk of the world, such as the sprite, didn't seem to have any trouble seeing Dandy, but the only other human she'd found so far who could was one annoying journalist, which made him doubly annoying.

"What are you talking about?" Travis asked, peering at the river. He squinted, blinked his bleary eyes rapidly, then pointed at the sprite, yelling, "*You!* Did you take my trophy?" He didn't seem to notice Dandy, at least. The last thing she needed was to find someone else who could see the invisible dog, only for it to be a man obsessed with thieving ducks.

"Me?" the sprite asked, pointing at her own chest, one arm still hooked around Dandy's shoulders.

"Yes, you!" he shouted. "Stop splashing around in the river and bring back my trophy! And the hedgehogs!"

"Travis, you're cut off," Belle said. "You're seeing things again. You need to go to the damn doctor."

"I'm not *seeing things*. There's a woman in the river! She's got scales!"

"So now the invisible, scaly woman stole my hedgehogs?" Belle demanded. "I bet it was actually you!"

"Why would I steal your hedgehogs?"

"You probably bet them on something," she said. "That's what's happened, isn't it? You've lost your trophy in another game, then taken my bloody hedgehogs and lost them too!" She spun around, marching back to the door. "And if you walk into my pub dripping, you're never coming back again!" She slammed the door in her wake.

"*Belle!*" Travis yelled, then turned back to the sprite. She was already gone. He looked at Adams, eyes wide. "Get her back!"

"Don't know who you mean," Adams said. "You need to get dried off."

Travis was shivering, his already red face gone an even deeper shade. "No, I—"

"Come on, mate," Rory said, picking up his boots. "I'll run you home."

"But—"

The door of the pub opened in a manner that suggested someone had tried to throw it wide, but had been defeated by its heavy hinges. Belle stalked out, a towel in each hand. She threw one at Rory and another at Travis. "You're not getting bloody hypothermia in my beer garden," she snapped. "Get inside." She turned around and strode off again before anyone could respond, and Travis looked at Adams.

"I still think you should look into the ducks," he said. "You can't trust them." Then he tottered up the path, wrapped in the towel.

Rory picked up the other towel and sat down at one of the tables, pulling his sodden socks off so he could dry his feet. "Never-ending excitement with you, isn't it?"

"You're the one calling me out to look at thieving ducks." She whistled to Dandy, who gave a little bark, tipping his head expectantly at the water. "*Heel,*" Adams hissed at him, and he ignored her.

The sprite resurfaced, melting out of the water as if built from it. Maybe she was – she was a small, slight thing, but the stream still should've been too shallow to hide her. She smooched at Dandy, who flopped on his side so she could rub his belly, splashing water everywhere.

Adams winced, then called, "Excuse me? Have you got a minute?"

The sprite looked around at her, pale eyebrows raised. "Hi," she said, and tipped her head at Dandy. "He yours?"

"In a manner of speaking."

"He's cute. Not too keen on the red eyes, smells a bit of sulphur, otherwise he's pretty sweet."

"Yeah, I hadn't noticed the sulphur myself," she said. "But the eyes are a little unnerving, I agree. Haven't noticed any ducks stealing trophies or hedgehogs, have you?"

"*Hedgehogs?*"

"Metal ones."

"Oh, right." She looked past Adams at Rory, and waved her fingers at him. "He yours too?"

"Absolutely not."

"Harsh, Adams," Rory said, and waved back at the sprite.

"Were they his hedgehogs?" the sprite asked. "What'll he give me if I find them?" She winked at Rory, who grinned.

"They're not his," Adams said.

"Boring," the sprite said, and melted away again.

"No, wait—" But she was gone, and Dandy sloshed cheerily back out of the water, shaking himself off wildly as soon as he was on the bank. Adams fled, swearing, and Rory yelped as he was showered with a spray of invisible dog water.

"Dammit, can't he wear a bell or something?"

Dandy gave a short, disapproving bark.

"No, apparently," Adams said, and watched the border

collies splash across the stream to join them. "So this was a waste of time."

"Got you out of the books, though," Rory pointed out, grinning as he pulled his boots back on over his bare feet. He made a face. "Ugh. I need to go home and get some dry socks."

"I need to go and do some actual work."

"You said it was your day off."

"I've got overdue reports."

"Come on, this *could've* been something. Thieving ducks? Sprites?"

She frowned at him. Rory had proven himself singularly capable when faced with werewolves, but it didn't mean he'd suddenly become her sidekick, or whatever he thought was happening here. She was police, and he was some sort of penniless landed gentry. A civilian. He just *happened* to be one of the few people she'd met who both knew about the Folk world, the realm of sprites and werewolves and magic that moved within the human one, and who also had a handy, if patchy, library of esoteric books she'd been trying to work her way through. To be honest, the books' writing was even dustier than their pages, and she'd spent more time drinking coffee with Rory than reading them, but the intention was there.

She looked at the river again and said, "I suppose I can add to my pool of knowledge the fact that not all sprites are clinically depressed."

"What're you basing that on?" Rory asked. "Sample size of one?"

"Two, actually," Adams replied.

"You may need to meet a few more to really extrapolate that data. Fancy lunch?"

"I didn't agree to lunch. I came out on my very precious day off because you said you'd found a new book in your uncle's stuff, and now look at us. You've got wet feet and I've had to explain I can't arrest ducks."

"You still have to eat," he pointed out, and before she could say anything else her phone rang. She held a finger up to him as she took it from her pocket, and he wandered back to the pub with his towel in one hand.

There was no name on the display, and she didn't recognise the number. She hit answer. "Detective Inspector Adams, North Yorkshire Police."

"Detective Inspector," a woman's voice said. It was smooth and self-assured, with a deep warm timbre that made Adams think of bluebell glades in sunlit woods. "Heather from Ash & Yew, in York. We have a situation."

"Oh?" Adams said. "If you need the police, I'm Skipton, not York."

"This isn't a police situation, Inspector. This is a you situation."

And Adams stood there in the thin spring sunshine, watching the world grow clear, sharp edges, everything drawing into tighter, brighter focus as the familiar tingle lit in her fingertips.

It might not be a police situation, but it *was* a case. She could feel it.

2

A VERY PRECIOUS THING

ADAMS TAPPED HER TINGLING FINGERTIPS TOGETHER, watching the sun shattering on the surface of the stream. The ducks were still regarding her suspiciously from the other bank, apparently finding her more disturbing than Dandy, who was rolling in the grass.

"Inspector?" Heather said, her voice cool over the phone. "Have I lost you?"

"No. When you say it's a me situation—"

"You know exactly what I'm referring to." There was a touch of impatience in Heather's tone. "Do we really have to go through this?"

Adams supposed they didn't. Heather hadn't called her because she was police. She'd called her for the same reason Rory had thought she'd be interested in thieving ducks (or maybe not entirely, but there were shared aspects). As much as Adams wasn't quite sure how it had come about, or why, or what it meant, she seemed to have become the person who dealt with werewolves and sprites and, most recently, some really alarming revelations about the true nature of faeries and Christmas spirits. Her and her invisible dog. So it hardly mattered that York wasn't in the Craven district of North Yorkshire, meaning she had no reason to officially be called out there. For these sorts of cases, her police ID was worth rather less than her duck keyring and her really big stick.

"How can I help?" she asked, her voice level.

"Would you be able to pop up to the shop?"

The shop was a jewellers called Ash & Yew, tucked into the narrow streets of the Shambles, deep in the heart of York. Adams checked her watch. Coming out to visit Rory near Harrogate meant she was almost halfway from Skipton to York already, and late on a Friday morning the traffic shouldn't be bad. "I can be there in forty-five minutes or so. What're we talking here?"

"I'll explain when you get here," Heather said, and the phone disconnected.

Adams scowled at it, and hoped it wasn't more hedgehogs and thieving bloody ducks. She doubted it, though. She wasn't sure exactly what Heather was, but Adams suspected she wasn't entirely human. And, more to the point, human or not, Heather wasn't the sort of person to be jumping at shadows.

"Who was that, then?" Rory asked, emerging from the pub. Midge and Pinto ran to meet him, and he scuffled their ears absently.

"Work."

"You haven't quite grasped this day off thing, have you?"

"I need my car." She started toward the car park, wishing she'd driven from Rory's house, where she'd met him earlier. But three dogs in her VW Golf (even if one was invisible) had seemed excessive, so Rory's ancient Land Rover had been a better option.

"Are you heading back to Skipton?" he asked, catching up with her.

"York."

"I'll drive you. We can grab some lunch there."

She scowled at him as she hauled open the creaking back door of the 4x4, letting the dogs jump in. "This is police business."

"Not in York, it's not. That's way off your patch."

"Don't be difficult."

"By that, do you mean don't disagree with you?"

"I can arrest you, you know."

"Promises, promises." He grinned at her as he opened the driver's door. "But yes, I'll take you back to your car. Come on."

She sighed, shutting the dogs in and climbing into the front. At least Dandy could dry out on someone else's seats for a bit.

The old Land Rover groaned and rattled into life, and they pulled out of the car park with an asthmatic wheeze of exhaust, Adams wincing. "This thing couldn't make it to York anyway."

"Harsh." He patted the dashboard. "Don't you listen to the mean city lady, old girl."

"I'm not mean. I've just heard of a vehicle safety certificate."

"She's not that bad."

Adams raised her eyebrows and pointed at the footwell between her feet, where the rug had shifted. She could see the tarmac flashing past through a rusty hole not far from her toes.

"Alright, she might need a little TLC."

"Or scrapping."

"*Rude.*" Rory managed to coax the car up to the speed

limit, rumbling through the narrow lanes, green fields rolling away from them behind drystone walls. "So what's this emergency in York?"

"Work. I told you."

"Bollocks it is."

She sighed. "Alright, it's not work *exactly*. But why are you so interested? Do you really want to get in the middle of something like the werewolves again?"

He shrugged. "It's better than ignoring it, or being like my mum. Knowing the world wasn't the way everyone said, but not understanding how to navigate it."

Adams nodded at that. He hadn't told her the full story of his mother, just that she hadn't survived the disconnect between what her brain told her was real and what society told her to believe. Humans, for the most part, didn't see Folk. They believed the hidden part of the world didn't exist, so they simply looked past the horns and tails and strangenesses that surrounded them, blinded by their own conviction. And Folk preferred it that way. Humans had never been great with things they didn't understand. Rory had somehow muddled his way through, but his mother hadn't. Plenty of people who trod that line between the worlds simply slipped away, lost in the treacherous borders.

Aloud, she said, "There's nothing to tell yet. I just need to get up there and find out what's going on."

"Why don't I come along for backup?" he asked, and when she shot him a narrow look he raised one hand in acknowledgment. "Fine, for company, then."

"Best not." She didn't offer any explanation, and he left it, tapping his fingers absently on the steering wheel as he drove, the wind from the open window ruffling his dishevelled brown hair.

Rory was proving annoyingly useful. He'd acquired his crumbling country house via some complicated arrangement involving a deceased great uncle and various cousins who didn't want to take on the responsibility of the place, and while Adams wasn't sure he was excelling at the restoration work, given there seemed to be more holes in the ceilings and walls than there were intact areas, he'd been nurturing a steadily growing library with a distinctly arcane tilt. Many of the titles had surfaced out of unopened crates discovered in the house's warren of crumbling rooms, and she had an idea his mum wasn't the only family member who'd stumbled into the Folk world. He didn't talk about that, though, and she didn't ask. Not yet, at least. That could come later, and for now she found herself taking a reluctant comfort in the fact she wasn't navigating the unfamiliar landscape of this clash of worlds alone.

But she still didn't want him poking about in her cases.

At the house she took her car keys from her pocket, bouncing them in her hand as she climbed out of the Land Rover onto the patchy gravel. The righthand wing of the house, where Rory had done the least work, looked as if it had lost some more tiles. "Thanks for the duck-based diversion," she said.

"Sure. Let me know if you want me to do any research or anything like that."

"Will do." Adams swung into her car, not bothering to wait for Dandy to get in. He made his own way through walls and doors, and into cars. She wound down the window as a pre-emptive strike against wet invisible dog stink and started the engine.

A shout stopped her as she started to pull away, and Rory jogged toward her, leaning down to peer in the driver's window. His hair spilled over his forehead, the sun catching the first threads of grey, soft and luminous. "Be careful."

"That's normally my goal," she replied, examining him. His usual grin was absent.

He paused, then said, "Do you know York?"

"I've been there."

He nodded, looking down the drive with a frown tugging at the corners of his mouth. "Just watch yourself, alright?"

"I used to work in London. I think I can handle York."

"Sure. But you weren't dealing with this side of things."

She nodded slowly. "Not until the end. Why?"

"I think once you start seeing that world, it starts seeing you back. And it's not always friendly."

She managed not to shiver. She'd thought the same thing herself, more than once. "What do *you* know about York?"

He grimaced slightly. "I did some poking around after my mum died. She spent a lot of time there. It's not … it's not just a human city." He paused again, then added, "I'd like to go with you."

"I've got an invisible dog and a very large stick. I'll be fine." She put the car into gear. "Talk to you later."

Rory didn't argue, just stepped back and watched her go. She could still see him in the rear-view mirror as she headed down the rutted gravel drive with Dandy panting in the seat next to her and tension brewing in the pit of her belly. It was true, she hadn't known about that side of the world when she'd been in London, and it had just about devoured her when she stumbled into it. The encounter had sent her fleeing north, away from the city she'd been born into, whose salt and steel was still embedded in her bones, and sometimes she felt its absence as something physical, a gap in her centre. And it had all been for nothing, because she'd fallen into *other* things all over again up here.

But now she was prepared. She could handle whatever came out of the Folk world, because people were all the same, no matter their species. *Crime* was all the same. She just had to go up there, ask the right questions, and knock on the right doors. She'd manage. She always did.

So she ignored the twisting anxiety in her belly, and tried not to think of London, with its bridges and rivers and toasties and secrets. That was done. It was just another thing she'd had to figure out how to handle, and she had. That was what she did.

Instead she settled into the drive, focusing on nothing but the road ahead, which was as quiet as she'd hoped. It didn't take long for the folds of green fields with their stands of trees and scatterings of grey stone farms to begin slowly giving way to tarmac and villages and towns, spreading and expanding and melting into one another. From there the city bloomed in sprawls of housing estates and cul-de-sacs, rashes of bungalows and spring-startled parks, industrial areas and council housing. It didn't feel any different to Leeds or anywhere else, and she looked at Dandy, perched in the passenger seat with his nose lifted to the window.

"Have we got anything to worry about here?" she asked him.

He regarded her seriously, his red eyes mostly hidden behind the forest of dreadlocks, and whined softly.

"Helpful."

THE SHAMBLES, where Ash & Yew lurked, was a tangle of narrow lanes and alleys blossoming out from York's ancient centre, contained within what remained of the fortified walls. Its cobbled streets were endlessly packed with straggling tourists, while the old buildings and their exposed beams leaned gently toward each other over the twisting passageways, keeping eternal secrets. They shut out the sunlight, trapping the chilly air of the night gone, and the walls echoed with the footfalls of city explorers, chattering in a dozen different languages and accents, tourists and workers and scammers and guides.

The whole area was cluttered with little shops selling kids' clothes and fancy stationery and handmade fudge, all tucked under low ceilings and lit with soft, warm lighting. There were wine bars and craft beer pubs as well, and cafes advertising afternoon tea and vegan cakes. Adams parked right on the edge of the pedestrianised area, leaving her car in a delivery bay and sticking her permit in the windscreen before heading into the shadowed lanes. She caught a whiff of coffee as she walked past one of the cafes and detoured abruptly inside, eagerly trailed by Dandy, who immediately helped himself to a half-empty mocha that had been left on a table. She did her best to ignore the clattering cup as she ordered a triple-shot Americano. Dandy was hideously indiscriminate when it came to coffee.

She peered out of the cafe's window as she waited for her drink. The last time she'd been in York had been for her first … *ugh*. She hated to call it a *magical investigation,* because the word *magic* set her teeth on edge, as if it was all top hats and beautiful assistants, or wands and star-splattered robes. But *supernatural* made her feel like a YouTube ghost hunter, and *paranormal* made her think of crystal balls and fraud-sters. So mostly she thought of these strange, Folk-adjacent cases as simply *other.* She'd been here on her first *other* inves-tigation in Yorkshire, chasing down a stolen necklace. Ash & Yew was a jewellery shop run by Heather and Charles, a silversmith who had worked on the necklace in question. It had turned out to have once belonged to a sorcerer, and was a powerful and dangerous thing. Adams' pursuit of it had exposed her to more of the magical world than she'd realised existed, even given London and the distinctly less threat-ening but *endlessly* frustrating world of the Toot Hansell dragons.

Either way, the last time she'd been in York, it hadn't been like this. Or *she* hadn't been like this. She'd always been copper-aware, of course, noting those who moved a little differently, a little too fast or too slow, who smiled too widely or passed too closely to others, sharks in the pool. They were always there, in every city and every town, but now it wasn't all she saw.

There were the Folk, of course, even those who were human on the outside a little more sharp-edged and clear-cut than the average, as if more firmly set into the world. But as well as them, as well as stalking faeries and hurrying fauns and drifting dryads, as well as the others she couldn't name, with their wings and horns and tails and tentacles, now the actual city had rendered itself abruptly duplicitous.

Between the ice cream shops and the hat stores, the cafes and the pharmacies, had blossomed hole-in-the-wall pubs advertising gnome-made ale, photography studios special-ising in nocturnal portraits, and a herbalist with a two-for-one special on wart-casting charms. Directly opposite the cafe was a rather charming bookshop which had half its window display given over to perfectly normal volumes on the history of York and walking atlases of the Dales, and the other half full of titles such as *How to Raise a Kraken for Fun & Profit*, and *Banshee Wails for Beginners*.

Adams stared at the books, momentarily intrigued by the idea of keeping a Kraken and wondering if a bath was big enough or if one needed access to a swimming pool, then realised an invisible dog was already more than enough to be dealing with.

"Americano?" the young man behind the counter asked.

"Thanks." She took it and headed out into the streets, a small headache pulsing behind her eyes. She used to get migraines every time she encountered something Folk-ish, but that at least had improved. This was a *lot*, though. Every building seemed to wear a shadow, the human York that thronged with tourists and industry holding a second version which moved to its own heartbeat. She thought of Rory saying York wasn't just a human city, and wondered again just how much he knew about this world.

But she didn't have time to dwell on the secret aspects of the place, or to become a tourist herself, no matter how intriguing it was. Instead, she headed straight to Ash & Yew. The hanging wooden sign above the door was entwined with foliage, and the display window with its small, divided panes was surrounded by evergreen branches. It gave her the sense that the shop had grown from the earth rather than been built.

The door was unlocked, and a bell tinkled elegantly above Adams as she pushed it open, coffee still in hand. She stepped into a warm, pale interior, tranquil and gentle and deeply expensive. Soft light glittered on gold and silver and precious stones nestled in display cases, and a slim, broad-shouldered woman of oddly indeterminate age looked up from a stool at the small counter. She had a selection of earrings laid out in front of her, polishing them with a soft cloth, and she inclined her head slightly.

"Detective Inspector," she said. "Thank you for coming so quickly."

"Heather," Adams said. "It sounded urgent."

"*Hmm.*" Heather bundled up the earrings and put them back in a cabinet underneath the counter. "*Pressing,* shall we say. Something we need to get resolved to prevent any escalation."

Adams frowned slightly. That sounded unsettlingly ominous. "What exactly's happened?"

Heather gestured to a door at the back of the shop. It looked like it should open straight onto someone's sitting room, nothing about it suggesting the sort of security a place like this probably warranted. Despite that, Adams was certain the shop was better guarded than most bank vaults.

"We'd best talk to Charles," Heather said. She opened the door and led the way down a short corridor, its smooth white walls punctuated with framed photographs, scenes of the city in sepia tones. Adams could smell hot metal and a whiff of burning wood drifting toward them, and at the end of the hall they stepped into the brightly lit, cluttered interior of a workshop. It took up the full width of the back of the shop, the walls lined with workbenches and another running down the centre of the room. The ones at the sides were relatively tidy, the wood scarred with burns and gouges, and tools hung on the walls above them. The bench in the centre, though, held both a dog-sized hippo and an even larger cockerel, both wrought from metal, and piles of tin sheets and wire and pipes and mysterious offcuts, stacked with no sense of order Adams could see. Among them sprouted sleekly polished bunny rabbits, and spindly-legged bird sculptures, and more otherworldly things, all wrought with astonishing skill and looking like they could leap off the bench at any moment.

The only sign of life, though, was a man with thick grey hair and bushy eyebrows, perched on a stool and clutching a mug of coffee in both hands. His shoulders were slumped, and he stared at the hippo blankly.

"Charles," Heather said. "The detective inspector is here."

"Inspector," Charles said, trying for an easy smile, but it didn't seem to want to stay in place. "Lovely to see you again."

"Heather said there was a situation," Adams said.

Charles heaved a sigh. "You could call it that."

Heather clicked her tongue. "*Charles.* Stop sulking, for the Old Ones' sake."

"It's just so distressing. I don't know how this could have happened!"

"It's not going to get any less distressing if we don't do something about it," Heather said, with a certain sharpness in her voice.

Adams sighed inwardly, and watched Dandy hesitating on the threshold to the hall, his floppy ears back as he stared at the cockerel. She hadn't expected she'd have to *use her people skills*, as the horrifying phrase went. She wasn't even sure she had people skills, but she said, "Let's not worry about how it happened, or whose fault it is—"

"It's mine," Charles said gloomily.

"Evidently," Heather said.

Adams nodded. "Right, well. Glad we've cleared that up. But what's happened, exactly?"

"A theft," Heather said, when Charles didn't answer.

"A jewellery theft?" Adams frowned. "You should be talking to the York police."

"Not jewellery. And even if it was, we wouldn't be talking to them." Heather examined Adams. "Anyone who could break in here won't be found by regular police." The way she said it suggested she wasn't sure Adams was going to do much better.

"What was taken?" She was really hoping it wasn't going to be some sorcerer's necklace again.

"A charm," Heather said.

"What, like for a bracelet?"

"No." Heather sounded like she was trying very hard not to roll her eyes.

"A master charm," Charles said, his voice so quiet he seemed to be talking to his mug. "A very old thing, a very *precious* thing, power wrought in pure metal."

Well, that didn't sound ominous *at all*. "Right," Adams said aloud. "And when did this happen?"

Heather and Charles exchanged glances. "A week?" Charles offered.

"And you only just noticed?"

"We've been trying to find it ourselves," Heather said. "As I say, it's not police business. But we seem to have run up against a wall."

Adams nodded, tucking her free hand into her pocket and having a sip of her rapidly cooling coffee. "You don't say."

"It's become rather urgent now," Charles said.

"And a lot harder to find evidence a week after the fact," Adams pointed out.

Charles grimaced.

"Well, we've called you now," Heather said. "And we need it finding *quickly*."

"Why?" Adams asked, a horrible sense of misgiving rolling in her belly. "What does it do?"

"I build guardians," Charles said, nodding at the hippo.

Adams looked blankly at the thing's smooth round flanks. "Sculptures?"

"Sculptures with defensive capabilities."

She didn't much like the sound of that. "Alarm systems?" she asked hopefully.

"More like guard dogs," Heather said.

"So they're dangerous."

"Not much of a deterrent if they aren't."

Of course it wasn't. "And this missing charm does what, exactly?"

Charles sighed deeply. "There always has to be a master key, a way to take control of the guardians if the owner is incapacitated."

"So this master charm can deactivate them?"

"Exactly."

She frowned. "Well, that doesn't sound too bad—"

"Imagine someone getting the security code to unlock a

rather elite selection of bank vaults," Heather said. "As well as priceless collections of art, and stockpiles of weaponry, and the front door key to the homes of an awful lot of people of wealth and interest and importance."

Adams looked at the jumble of half-finished sculptures. Half-finished *guardians*. "Ah," she said, and thought this was a larger step up from frog trophies and hedgehogs than she'd been planning on.

3

COLD HARD EVIDENCE

"Are we really talking bank vaults and weapon stockpiles?" Adams asked, taking a large mouthful of coffee and wishing she'd asked for four shots. People got a bit weird about that, though, as if they were the ones drinking it.

"Any number of them," Charles said.

"And what are guardians, exactly?"

"Just what they sound like. They're set to protect properties or items, and can be as big or small as necessary." He smiled suddenly, looking past her at something unseen. "Do you know the Eiffel Tower?"

"Yes, obv— *What?*"

"Oh, no, it isn't one. Not anymore, anyway. Originally, though—"

"Charles," Heather said, a warning note in her voice.

"Oh. Yes. Anyway, I build them out of metal, and as I do so, I impress into them whatever's needed – who or what they're protecting, basically. Then the owner gets a simple charm which allows them to control the guardian without changing the basic programming. So they can't be sold on or used for any other purpose."

"One only makes that mistake once," Heather said.

Charles nodded. "But, just in case, the master charm is a failsafe, a security measure for if something goes wrong."

"So, given the Eiffel Tower, I'm guessing you don't sell these guardians just in Yorkshire," Adams said.

Heather made a small, scoffing noise, and Charles said, "We're somewhat of an international supplier."

"Of course you are," Adams muttered, looking around the workshop, with its constant scent of metal shavings and heat, its islands of chaos and order. "How many are we talking?"

"We've been doing this for a long time, Inspector," Heather said. "Let's just say *a lot*, for ease."

"That hardly helps me narrow things down. Do you have a list?"

"Did you not understand what I said?"

Adams looked at Heather, raising her eyebrows.

Heather shook her head. "Yes, I have a list."

"Good. I'll need it. What about security in here? Cameras?"

"They don't work."

"Right." She'd forgotten, but Heather had told her that when she'd been here before. Cameras and Folk had a fractious relationship at the best of times, the devices malfunctioning or bringing back unusable images. It was part of what kept Folk safe. "Other security measures?"

Charles got up off the stool with another heartfelt sigh and walked to the back door. He'd shown Adams outside here before, and she knew it opened into a little alley equipped with a couple of ubiquitous shop bins. Assuming he was going to show her some sort of Folk alarm system, she joined him as he opened the door, already starting to ask if there was a code or how it worked.

The words melted away before she could manage more than a questioning, "Is ..." She blinked at the view revealed beyond the door, then looked around the workshop, searching for another entrance. There was only the one she'd come through from the hallway, and she turned back to the door, taking a hesitant step up to the threshold and touching the frame, as if to check it was real and not some painted backdrop.

Instead of a plain and uninspired little alley, two steps led down into what she had to term a garden, for want of a better word. It was substantial, the size one might expect to find behind a decent-sized detached house on the outskirts of town, not the back of a narrow shop in the centre of a city. High red brick walls hemmed it in, concealing it from the outside world and giving it a secretive, hidden atmosphere that made Adams feel the whole place should've been full of green lawns curling between boisterously crowded flowerbeds and stands of old shrubs and small trees, with probably a fishpond and cosy, hidden benches, and a swing hanging invitingly in the shade.

But all that grew here was iron and steel. Paths trekked through twisted outcroppings and upthrusts of metal, filling every scrap of space with savage, rusting edges and blooming flowers of corrosion. Brutal shards of steel sprouted out of the ground, interspersed with twisted lengths of discarded tin, and paint still clung to the sides of old buses and the broken doors of cars. Lengths of twisted aluminium guttering and shiny copper pipe stitched their way around the bent corners of corroding containers that surfaced out of the earth like icebergs, and everywhere were bicycle wheels with broken spokes, old iron girders, mesh and drums and crates and metal fencing. The place contained an astonishing amount of debris, all blossoming into abstract sculptures and shedding filings like new shoots, and Adams stared from it to Charles.

"Wasn't there an alley out here?" she asked, because every

other question had *where* and *how* and *impossible* in it, and she didn't think she was ready for the answers.

"There is," Charles said, stepping back and waving Adams with him. He closed the door, then opened it again with a complete lack of fancy hand gestures or arcane muttering. The alley and its bins looked back at them blandly. He closed the door again and opened it once more into the metallic jungle.

"Right. I'm not even going to ask how that works," Adams said.

"Probably best," Charles said, sounding a little cheerier. "I don't really know myself, to be honest. And sometimes it refuses to change for a day or so, which is annoying, especially if I need something."

"So what happens if someone tries to get in through this door from the alley? Can they?"

"It's a three-way system. If you come from the alley, you might end up in the garden or in here."

Adams frowned. "How does that make it secure?"

"Unless you have a key or someone lets you in, it's always the garden."

Adams looked at it. "I mean, it looks a bit sharp, but …"

"Show her," Heather said.

"Is it a guardian?" Adams asked, peering into the garden apprehensively. There could be anything hidden in there. The whole thing could be one giant guardian, like a mat of metallic Venus flytraps, snapping up intruders.

"It's Wilfred," Charles said.

"Wilfred?"

"Come on." Charles led the way out into the metal wilderness. Everything shone with exposed, sharp edges, or slumbered under blooms of rust, and Adams couldn't see any wildflowers or weeds growing up among the shards of old industry. There were no scraps of wood or lingering threads of plastic or fabric either, no litter caught among the limbs of metal, just great flanks of steel and aluminium interspersed with strips of tin like shards of broken ice, and tumbled piles of copper and lead pipe growing like fungi.

A narrow path of old stone wound toward the high wall that encircled the garden, and beyond it Adams could see buildings formed from old, stained stone or mildewed plaster, sprouting crooked towers and dormer windows and exposed beams in a jumble that was *like* the Shambles, yet utterly alien. She had the sudden, unshakeable certainty she was deep within a very different version of York, and if she wasn't careful she could lose herself and never find her way out again. She pushed the thought down and reached out for Dandy with one hand. He didn't seem too keen on the garden either, and leaned against her leg with a low whine.

"This isn't regular dimensions, is it?" she asked. "This can't all fit back here."

"I don't know the technicalities of it," Charles said brightly. "But I suppose you're right." He looked around at the sunlight shining on his ferocious yard. "Wonderful though, isn't it?"

Behind Adams, Heather said, "They're the dimensions of this face of York. Things get a bit blurry other than that."

Adams glanced back at her. The other woman was following them down the path with her long skirts lifted in one hand and her nose faintly wrinkled in distaste, thick, darkly glossy brown hair spilling over her shoulders. Her feet were bare, and Adams wanted to tell her to be careful, but stopped herself. Heather no doubt knew better than Adams did what was safe and what wasn't.

Instead, she just said, "Great. I love blurry."

They followed Charles halfway to the wall at the bottom of the garden, which seemed to take longer than was reasonable (and which had Adams muttering, *"blurry,"* to herself), but finally he paused and looked up at a conglomerate of assorted panels of stained metal and hefty bits of rebar. Something about its proportions suggested a stag, with a broad chest and a narrow head, antlers of old plumbing protruding at startling angles from its head and neck. It was even larger than a stag should be, though, taller than Adams at the shoulder, and its barrel body was supported by thick legs that looked to be formed in large part from bundled lengths of railway tracks. It towered above them, head lifted and proud, and sunlight gleamed dully on tin plate eyes.

"There," Charles said, with a flourishing gesture.

"What the hell is that?" Adams asked.

"Wilfred."

"Right." She examined the great structure for a moment, her arms crossed over her chest and her feet planted wide. Finally she said, "It's not doing anything."

"You're watching."

"It's shy?"

"We've never seen him move," Heather said.

"So it – he – just stands there looking a bit freaky, and that's enough?"

"He moves when he needs to," Charles said comfortably, and patted Wilfred's flank, setting up an echoing clang that bounced around the garden, whispering through the metal forest like the sea. Adams shivered. She felt as if a fine metallic dust was settling on her from all angles, drifting deep into her lungs.

"What happens when he moves?"

"He gets rid of intruders," Heather said.

"How?"

"I couldn't say. We don't see what he does."

Adams rubbed the back of her neck. "He's sentient?"

"More like automated," Charles said. "The charms dictate that they act in the required manner, to protect. But there is a certain amount of interpretation, which is caused by the raw material. Everything has its own instincts, after all."

"Even oil drums?" she asked, nodding at the rusty yellow paint of one that formed part of Wilfred's hindquarters.

"Metal still came from the earth once. It remembers."

Adams considered asking for a little more explanation, but in the end she didn't need it. Not for the issue at hand, anyway, and anything else could wait. "So there's no way anyone could've got past him?"

Charles and Heather looked at each other. Her eyebrows were arched pointedly, and he gave a little shrug. "No."

"And does anyone else have access to the workshop?" Again that hesitation, and she waited, then said, "I can't help you if you don't tell me."

"No one *should* have," Heather said.

"But?"

Heather glared at Charles so fiercely Adams could almost see him wilting under it. Finally he said, "Sometimes I invite people back."

"Back?"

"After the pub. You know, if it's been a good night, and they're kicking everyone out, I might say 'oh, come by mine, I've got whisky,' or something."

Adams looked at Heather, who shrugged. "I came down one morning and found two dryads and a faun asleep on the workshop floor, plus a brownie trying to make eggy bread on the boiler. He's a *nightmare*."

"That was at least thirty years ago!"

"Doesn't change the facts, though, does it? And you had four humans in cloaks upstairs pretending they were taking one of my *personal* rings to Mordor only last week."

"They were harmless."

"They were so drunk one passed out with his head in the

washing machine, and when I woke him up he said he was listening for drums in the deep."

Adams wondered, not for the first time, how people put up with things like this. The idea of having one other person in her home, let alone four uninvited ones, made her skin itch. Or that might've been the metal dust again. Evidently it worked for some people, though. Aloud, she said, "So anyone you invited back might've had the chance to nab the charm?"

"They shouldn't have," he said. "That charm's kept safe, plus the shop has protections. People can't leave with something that doesn't belong to them."

"Evidently not that safe," Heather said. "I keep up the general protection charms, but *someone's* meant to maintain the ones for the master charm. The person who works with it." She arched her eyebrows at Charles, and he rubbed the back of his neck.

"I've said sorry," he said.

"Well, it sounds like the general ones didn't work, either," Adams pointed out, and Heather gave her a look so sharp she wondered if she was about to have Wilfred set on her. But she continued, "If it's missing, the thief got it out through both sets, didn't they?"

Heather huffed. "If they knew how to work the master charm, they could've used it to bypass the shop ones."

"That's true," Charles said. "And they must've known what it was to take it. They could've taken jewels, sculptures, anything. Things a lot easier to sell. But they only took the charm."

Adams blew air over her lower lip, tucking her hands into the pockets of her coat and turning in a slow circle, her fingers closing over her brass keyring. It was actually a torch in the shape of a rubber duck, and she hadn't been anywhere without it since London. It was oddly comforting to find something in here that might be metal but felt less likely to eat her. She looked at Dandy, who was still sticking as close to her as he could, although he was examining Wilfred with great interest and flattened ears.

"And the front door?" she asked.

"That's my department," Heather said. "No one comes in there without my knowing about it. And *I* don't go inviting my drinking buddies back."

"Have you had break-ins before?"

"No," Heather said, the word flat and brooking no argument.

"Attempted?"

"Not for a long time," Charles said. "Wilfred is an excellent deterrent." He gazed up at the monstrous sculpture affectionately.

"Sorry, what does he do, exactly?"

"Deals with things," Heather said. "The bodies usually turn up in the river."

"Excuse me?"

"Joking," she said, in a tone that suggested she wasn't joking at all. "He's a giant metal monster, Inspector. That's enough to send most people running."

Most people. Adams pinched the bridge of her nose. "Are you seriously telling me you've got a killing machine in your backyard? Is this why you didn't want to call the York police? Scared they'll trace a bunch of murders back to you?"

"We have been here a very long time," Heather said. "Folk learned long ago that Ash & Yew is not a viable target. And as far as the police, *if* there were any disappearances, historical or otherwise, there would be nothing to connect us to them. But your average police officer wouldn't see the garden. At all. Rather hard for them to investigate anything without your certain skill set."

Adams looked at the stark, rather jabby reality all around her and sighed deeply. "Lucky bloody me. Right. Our list of suspects now includes anyone Charles had a pint with, does it?"

"Pretty much," Heather said, and Charles grimaced, but didn't protest.

"What about the master charm itself?" Adams asked. "What were its protections?"

"I'll show you," Charles said.

They wound their way back up the path, Dandy still just about tripping on Adams' feet with every step, and Heather let them back into the workshop. Adams took a last, wary glance over her shoulder, both happy to escape the whispering wilderness of metal, and oddly uneasy about leaving it unsupervised. Wilfred seemed to have shifted his position a little, the sun hitting one of his huge eyes and turning it into a smeary pool of light that stared at her until she was inside and away from the door.

Adams expected Heather to continue into the shop itself, or maybe detour off to wherever they kept the jewellery that wasn't on display, but instead she just leaned against the big workbench in the centre of the room and looked expectantly at Charles. It felt even more cluttered in here after being out in the open air, and Adams found herself eyeing up the half-finished sculptures suspiciously, as if they might get up and stalk off at any moment.

"Are these all going to be guardians?" she asked.

"Sometimes," Charles said. "Sometimes they're just for decoration. Gardens and stuff, you know?"

Adams was never going to look at a display of garden centre art the same again. But, she had to admit a little glumly, that was the case for a lot of things.

Charles crossed to the bench where it ran underneath one of the windows, the surface mostly clear other than a fabric fish and a tennis ball. A metallic cat-type beast the size of a spaniel was curled up in the sunlight spilling over the windowsill, its tarnished body gleaming dully. A set of sharp-edged, filigreed wings were folded tightly to its back, and its paws were tucked neatly underneath it. Charles tapped the bench in front of it, and its eyes swirled open like a pinhole camera, exposing large, glossy black orbs. The creature looked at Charles without moving, bent wire whiskers trembling.

"Off you pop, Fergus," Charles said.

Fergus showed off some literal needle teeth in a yawn and shook his wings out, then stood, stretching as he did so. The movement was jerky and not quite coordinated, like a stop-motion film, but still unmistakably cat-like, unnatural and predictable all at once. He prowled a couple of steps down the bench, his paws all metal blades, then sat down, his unsettling gaze fixed on Adams.

Charles pressed the bench lightly, and a spring-loaded panel popped up to reveal a small cavity underneath. He removed a box made of battered tin and held it out to Adams.

She fished in her coat pockets, finding a set of blue plastic gloves and pulling them on before she took it carefully. The surface was covered in old etchings and tarnish, and she looked at Fergus warily. The creature's eyes hadn't shifted from her, and a mechanical rumble echoed from his chest. "He's not going to take my head off when I try and open this, is he?"

Fergus yawned again, and dug his claws into the old wood of the bench. They sank in effortlessly. His body wasn't fully enclosed, and Adams could see the pistons and gears, the springs and coils and cables of his inner workings.

"You've got full permission to open it," Charles said, and she lifted the lid carefully. There was nothing inside to say what should be there, no mould or support or even a little label saying *Master Charm Here*. Just an empty tin cavity, a little roughly finished and dented in places. She looked at Charles questioningly.

"That's it," he said.

"That's what?"

"Where it should be." He waved vaguely. "And now it's not."

Adams looked at the box again, then put it down on the workbench, keeping her distance from Fergus. "So it was in an unlocked box, in an unlocked cupboard—"

"Hidden compartment."

"—with no alarms, cameras, or any other method of security."

"There's Fergus."

Adams looked at Fergus, who had shifted his attention from her to Dandy, his head tipped a little awkwardly to one side. Dandy, for his part, was hiding behind Adams' legs, stealing glances at the metallic cat. Fergus put a paw out and knocked the tennis ball to the ground, bouncing it past Dandy. He took a step after it, then retreated again when Fergus jumped to the floor and trotted jerkily in pursuit.

"I see," she said.

"Dammit, Charles – you haven't updated the charms on Fergus, have you?" Heather asked. "I *told* you to."

"Is that like updating software?" Adams asked.

"What?" Charles asked.

"Near enough," Heather said, and looked at Charles. "Like your phone. Updates to stop security breaches. I thought you'd sorted this!"

"He's not a *phone*," Charles protested. "He's not some electronic *thing*. He's got a personality."

"He's not meant to. He's meant to be a guardian, and that means he does his job and nothing more," Heather said. "Personality only creates glitches. You were meant to fix it."

"I'm selling a lot more to humans, though," Charles

pointed out. "They like personality. It makes them more comfortable."

Adams watched Fergus bat the ball toward Dandy and wait. Dandy fled out into the hall, tail between his legs, and she sighed. She *did* like personality, but Heather was right about glitches. "So someone could've thrown a ball for Fergus, and he'd have just trotted off after it?"

"*No,*" Charles said, and Adams nudged the tennis ball with her foot, sending it tumbling across the room. Fergus shot after it in surprisingly silent pursuit. "Maybe," he amended.

Heather muttered something in a language Adams didn't recognise, but she was fairly sure it was swearing in any dialect. "How long's Fergus been like this?" she asked.

"Too long," Heather said. "Something was bound to happen."

"It wasn't," Charles said. "He's still a good guardian."

Fergus rolled over the ball and kicked it enthusiastically with his back paws, impaling it on one claw. He froze, staring at it with his whiskers drooping.

"Terrifying," Heather said, and Adams rubbed her face with one hand to cover a grin that surfaced despite herself.

"He was never meant to be a frontline guardian," Charles said. "No one should ever have got this far."

"And yet here we are."

"Right," Adams said. "Well, I need a list of everyone you've invited back here, and details on where these guardians are, so I can try to track down if any have been … activated, or deactivated, or whatever. I'd like to take that box to get it fingerprinted, too." She'd like to get the whole place finger-printed, really, but she already knew what the answer to that would be.

"I don't think fingerprints are going to get you very far," Heather said. "You're approaching this from the wrong angle with all these human things."

"I am human. Besides, you called me for help, and this is how I do it. So do you want me to look into it or not?"

Heather raised her hands. "As you want."

"Good." Maybe it *was* the wrong angle. Maybe she should be diving straight into some esoteric method of crime solving, but she didn't know what that entailed, and, to be honest, she didn't want to know. Fingerprints were concrete and real, and gave her something to get a grip on, until she could start to see the shape of the case. It was a *start*, and that was what every case needed, even if it was the wrong start. The right path would come from it eventually. In the end it didn't matter whether it was a Folk case or a human one, or how many limbs or tails or tentacles one had. Everything always came back to power, desire, and cold hard evidence. Someone wanted something, and they took it, and they *would* have left some trace behind.

So that was where she'd start. It was work just like any other, even if her cases usually didn't involve mechanical cats and Wilfreds. Or hadn't previously, at least.

4

FEWER FINGERPRINTS, MORE BLOODSHED

Adams discovered that Ash & Yew had such modern conveniences as Ziploc bags, and claimed one large enough to put the tin in. "I'll need to get your prints for elimination purposes," she said to Heather and Charles. "You can do it at the York station."

"I'd rather not," Charles said. "Makes me feel like a criminal."

"You don't have anything to worry about if you haven't done anything, do you?" Adams pointed out.

He sniffed. "It's the principle."

"Well, one of the principles with fingerprinting is eliminating known ones so I don't end up chasing around after some print just to find out it's one of you two."

"This isn't going to get you anywhere," Heather said.

"Maybe, maybe not." Adams put the bagged tin on the end of the workbench, Fergus watching from a perch on the windowsill. It was hard to tell exactly where he was looking with those round, glossy black eyes, but she had a feeling it was at her. She didn't like it, either the unblinking stare or the weird, disjointed movements of the sort-of cat, and

Dandy didn't seem to either. He was still in the hall, putting his head around the corner now and then and whining plaintively.

Now she opened the workshop door onto the metal garden, frowned at it, closed the door, tried again, then closed it a second time and looked at Heather. "Is there a trick to this?"

"Try again," Heather said. "It'll get there eventually."

Adams did, opening it again onto the garden, the sun gleaming dully on the metal shards and panels. She hissed through her teeth. "There's no secret knock or anything?"

"That would be ridiculous."

Adams didn't bother pointing out how ridiculous it was to have a door that didn't open to the same place every time, and in fact made its own mind up about where to let you out. Instead, she tried one more time, muttering dire threats under her breath as she did so. Either that worked, or the door was bored of being difficult, because she opened it onto the dull brick of the alley, the big industrial bins leaning against the walls and a couple of pigeons squabbling over a scrap of bread. She stepped out onto the doorstep and crouched to examine the frame, running her gloved hands over it lightly, and inspected the latch and lock carefully. No splintered wood, no scratching around the lock. No sign of it being forced at all.

She stood with a frown and said, "Do you lock this door?"

"Obviously," Heather said. "Just because we have a giant killing machine in the garden is no reason to be careless."

Charles gave her a confused look, and Adams looked back at the lock to hide her grin. She wasn't sure she trusted Heather, but it was hard not to like her, at least a little. "I don't see any sign of forced entry. Could someone use a charm to unlock it, perhaps?"

"No," Charles said. "It's protected."

Adams straightened up. "No key hidden outside?"

"No," they both said, a little too quickly, and she frowned at them.

"We did have one," Charles said.

"*You* had one," Heather said. "And you don't anymore. Who leaves the key to a *jewellery* shop stuck in a fake rock?"

"It wasn't a fake rock, it was a little metal ladybird, *and* it was charmed. Sometimes I misplace mine," he added to Adams, and Heather shook her head.

"Sometimes at the pub, you mean."

Adams was starting to feel the pub was a bigger problem than anyone was admitting to just yet. "Does that mean you lose it sometimes? What about recently?"

"No." No hesitation, and Charles didn't flinch from her gaze, so she nodded and came back inside, closing the door behind her.

"Is there another way into the garden?"

"There's a gate," Heather said. "It's locked too, before you ask."

"Can I take a look?"

"Be our guest. It's straight down the path." She gestured at the door, and Adams opened it again, expecting it to put her back out in the alley, just to be difficult.

Instead, it revealed the garden, and she headed down the path, the gravel creaking beneath her boots. Dandy scuttled out the door after her, and she looked down at him. "Garden not as scary as Fergus, huh?"

He huffed at her in a way that seemed faintly reproachful, and stayed close as she walked past Wilfred, giving him a nod. She thought he might've moved a bit, his head turned to look further down the garden, one vast leg a little closer to the path than it had been before.

"No eating me," she said, her voice low, and surveyed the garden. Part of her wanted to believe she'd simply blundered into a scrapyard, or the metal section of a tip, because it was impossible that this thicket of sharp edges and rust existed out the back of some shop in the middle of a city. Yet here it was, glowering with threat but oddly lifeless when one considered the name of the shop itself, and the flourishing greenery at the front door. A few windows in the neighbouring buildings were open onto the sharp spring air, but nothing moved beyond them. She had a feeling that even if they overlooked the garden, they wouldn't have seen anything. It was that sort of place. She shivered despite the sunshine.

The path curved around what appeared to be the shell of an old chest freezer, dented tin guttering emerging from its maw like the legs of a hermit crab, and she glimpsed a gate set into the wall that faced the house. She wasn't about to pick her way through the fields of metal corpses to reach it, though, so she kept following the path as it weaved its way through rusty outcroppings and sprouting stands of old pipes like bamboo. At the corners of her vision she thought she glimpsed creatures that recalled horses or wolves or delicate, long-legged birds, but when she looked directly at them they resolved into just more scrap. Nothing moved within the walls, not even birds venturing down off the rooftops, and any greenery had apparently been swallowed by the inhospitable ground.

A niggling thought insisted the gate would keep retreating, the path looping back on itself over and over, the garden expanding in strange ways to keep her trapped. But finally she rounded the dented frame of an old VW Beetle with a shard of container fixed to its roof like a shark fin, and found the heavy gate just where she'd seen it before. It was mostly solid, just a sliding viewing panel to break it up. The panel was eye-height for someone rather taller than her, but she slid it open with one gloved hand and stood on her tiptoes to peer out. An unfamiliar alley stretched out to either side beyond, its brick walls revealing no other gates, no windows or doors or people passing. She checked the lock, but it was as un-tampered-with as the one at the workshop, so she tried the handle just for the hell of it. It was locked, of course, so she trailed back to the house, saying to Dandy, "Should've taken the key in the first place, shouldn't I?"

He didn't offer any opinion on it, just hesitated on the path as she approached the door, apparently not sure if Fergus or the garden were the most terrifying. He'd shrunk again, almost terrier size, and Adams looked at him. "You might need to be bigger than that if anything jumps you."

He just whined and hustled after her, almost tripping her as she stepped back into the workshop. It was empty other than Fergus still perched on his windowsill, and he looked at her, giving a rusty, unpractised mewl.

"Hi," she said. "Any idea where the key for the gate is?"

He got up, stretched, and leaped from the bench in a shiver of metal. His wings unfurled crisply, turning the leap into a glide, and Adams jumped back before he could catch her with their sharp edges. He avoided her easily, though, and landed lightly on the bench on the other side of the room. His movement still had that awkward and slightly creepy juddering to it, but despite that he was all but soundless, with none of the creaking or grinding of metal she'd expected. He closed his wings with a businesslike snap and pointed his snout at a selection of keys hanging on the wall.

Adams joined him, reaching for the first one, and Fergus made a sound like a boiling kettle. She snatched her hand back. "Alright, sorry." She stared at him, and he stared back with those unsettling, glossy eyes. She pointed at the next key along, an old-fashioned, ornate thing with a chunky barrel, and he gave a raspy noise which, after a moment, she realised was a purr of sorts. Or a gear was caught in his innards, but he didn't move when she took the key down. "Thanks."

She trotted back down the garden, nodding at Wilfred again as she passed, the greeting feeling somehow both necessary and natural. The gate was still there (she hadn't been sure it would be, given the fickleness of the workshop door), and the lock rolled open on the first try, well-oiled and silent. She left the key in place as she pushed it wide, stepping out onto the cobbles of the alleyway, and Dandy joined her, shaking himself off as if to rid his heavy coat of the metallic dust of the garden. They stood there in silence, looking one way then the other, the alley extending long and featureless in both directions.

There were no windows, no doors, nothing except gently worn and stained brick walls going on and on, the cobbles underfoot muted with old dirt and a little mud but almost as featureless as the walls. As far as she could see, there were no turns or junctions, and there was something disorienting about the endless lane, as if it might be nothing more than a trick of perspective, a painted backdrop shielding the truth of the world. And it almost had to be, didn't it? It *couldn't* go on forever, the alley narrowing to shadows in the distance in both directions. Then again, dimensions didn't exactly seem to be in normal working order around here.

Adams shifted her stance slightly, securing her grip on the world as her hand drifted to the duck keyring and she thought of some very similar passageways in London, as empty as this other than some very hungry bins. But she hadn't had a duck then, or a dandy. At least not at first. She glanced down at him. He was back in golden retriever size, so evidently the alley was less worrying to him than Ash & Yew had been.

"Odd, isn't it?" she said, and scratched him behind the ears.

He tipped his head, which she took as both agreement and a comment regarding the general oddness of the world in which they both found themselves. For all she knew, car rides and ear scratches were more odd to him than this was, but he'd taken to them just as well as he had caffeine.

The alley was devoid of cameras or possible witnesses, and it was still making her uneasy, so she examined the outside of the gate, discovering with no great surprise that there was no sign of any tampering with the lock, then went back into the garden. No one had broken in, she was sure of it. Either they'd had a key, or they'd come in some other way. She regarded the walls thoughtfully, but she doubted their height was the only deterrent, and anyone clambering in would still have had to get into the building itself.

She locked the gate and headed back to the workshop, almost stumbling over Fergus as she walked in. He looked up at her from the worn doormat and gave his rusty mewl again.

"Hello," she said to him. "Any idea how this break-in happened, then?"

He blinked, the pinhole shutters on his eyes spiralling down to a dot then opening again. Dandy barked, and Adams shushed him, then looked back at Fergus.

"How about the master charm? They must've deactivated you somehow, to get it out from under you. Did they know you?"

He twitched his whiskers.

"You're even less helpful than most cats," she said. "But you do talk less. I appreciate that."

One more creaking mewl, and she nodded.

"My thoughts exactly." She picked up the bagged tin and headed down the hall into the jewellery shop. It was like emerging into a different world, crossing out of the sharp-edged metallic garden and cluttered, vaguely restless workshop into the soft pale tones and warmly lit curves of the front room. Plants bloomed in the corners, and the heavy, rough wooden beams of the ceiling overhead made the whole place feel deeply rooted to the earth, persistent and organic. Soft music drifted from unseen speakers, and Heather was back on her stool, polishing more earrings.

"Find anything?" she asked.

Adams crossed to the front door and opened it to check the lock and frame, not expecting to find anything. She didn't, and she closed it again, then stripped her gloves off and shoved them in her pocket. "Any other ways into the shop?"

"No."

"Sure? No one could've come in a window?"

"The back windows are over the garden," Heather said, inspecting an earring and laying it down on the counter before picking up the next. "The front are onto the street, and I rather doubt anyone could've climbed in a window in the middle of the Shambles without being noticed."

Adams nodded. She could check the street CCTV anyway. "No secret passageways or hidden tunnels or anything?"

She gave Adams an amused look. "Do you think they wouldn't be protected if there were?"

Adams tucked her hands into her pockets. "Well, I can't see any signs of a break-in, so are you sure no one has access to a key? One couldn't've been copied?"

Heather didn't answer straight away, then finally said, "Not to my knowledge."

"What about Charles?"

"He said no."

That wasn't an answer, not really, but Adams left it for now. "What about Fergus? How do you think someone got past him?"

"That I really don't understand. He has been getting a bit odd, though. I did tell Charles giving guardians personality was a bad idea. The best guardians are like Wilfred. You don't even realise he's there until you need him."

"What was the reason behind giving Fergus a personality, then?"

"*Marketing*," Heather said disdainfully. "Charles takes on apprentices from time to time, and one of them suggested personality would widen the market appeal. It did, but I'm not sure it was worth the trade off."

There was a scratchy *mrrraow* from the door to the hall, and they both looked around to see Fergus standing on the threshold, his segmented tail twitching.

"As I was saying," Heather said. "What're you doing in here?" Fergus didn't answer, just stared at Adams, and Heather shook her head. "I don't know. It shouldn't've been possible to override his protective programming, but one wonders, when they start wandering around on their own like this."

"So ... what? Someone could've bribed him with a metal sardine or something?"

Heather arched an eyebrow. "I doubt it. But it is possible they distracted him somehow."

Adams nodded. "And Wilfred?"

"He doesn't have the same personality issues."

Fergus gave an insulted creak.

"What about a countercharm?" Adams asked.

"In theory, no. You'll find most places have protections built into the stone to make sure hostile charms can't be cast, only protective ones, and obviously, this being a place of business, we're well defended."

Adams thought about it for a moment. "What about this apprentice? The one who suggested the personalities?"

Heather frowned. "Violet? She decided metalwork wasn't

for her. Last I heard, she was working as a herbalist in true York and telling fortunes for tourists in this one."

"She doesn't still have access to the shop?"

"No. Apprentices don't get keys. They work with Charles, not independently."

"Right," Adams said with a sigh, and looked at Fergus as he rolled the tennis ball to her feet. She nudged it away, and he trotted after it. "Well, I may as well have a word with Charles about these people he's had around. Is he about?"

Heather grimaced slightly. "He's gone out."

"Now? Really?"

"He's a little stressed."

"Even more reason to stay around, considering I'm apparently your best hope of finding the big scary charm."

Heather shrugged. "Of course. But Charles is artistically inclined in both temperament and ability. He has a touch of genius, but it rather comes with its downsides."

"Do you mean he's"—she almost balked at the word, but kept going—"magically gifted?"

"Genius is its own sort of power, separate from what you probably mean by *magic*." Heather wrinkled her nose slightly as she said the word, making Adams feel slightly better about her own distaste. "Charles has both, in his abilities with charms and metal. Plus he's been doing this for a very long time indeed, so he's refined his skill far beyond what the raw talent gave him. But he's also inclined to indulge in a deeply irritating degree of what he considers to be artistic behaviour and what I'd term self-indulgent and irresponsible. When he gets very stressed there's no reasoning with him. It's best just to let him get on and do what he does until it's out of his system."

"And he does what?"

"Get drunk, tell tales, probably eat a kebab from a shop

that's never even heard of hygiene ratings, and come home at about two in the morning, usually missing at least one sock."

"Doesn't seem healthy for a man his age," Adams said.

Heather snorted, a small, inelegant sound. "It's not healthy for anyone. And his age is a different question entirely."

Adams decided it was also a question she'd leave alone for now, since it didn't seem particularly relevant. "Do you know where he's gone?'

"Yes, but I wouldn't bother. You'll have trouble finding it, and he's told you as much as he can today. Run your fingerprints, do your policing, and come back tomorrow. By then you'll have realised all your little human tricks aren't going to get you anywhere, he'll be sober, and we can get started." There was a short, dismissive tone to Heather's words, and she kept her attention on her earrings, as if Adams was wasting her time.

Adams frowned. "*You* called *me*. I'm way off my patch here. This is a favour, not my job."

Heather looked up, smiling slightly. It wasn't a friendly expression. "Is that what you still think?" They watched each other for a moment, the shop creaking with its load of secrets and history, then Heather reached under the counter and lifted a hefty ledger book out with both hands, setting it next to the earrings. "There's your list of guardians."

Adams stared at it, as big as one of her mum's old photo albums and faded at the edges. "That's ..." She couldn't find any words except *utterly impossible,* which was unhelpful.

"I told you, we've been doing this for a very long time."

"And never computerised anything?"

Heather shrugged. "We take card. Does that help?"

"For guardians?"

"No. That's a whole different revenue stream."

"Of course it is," Adams said with a sigh, and wedged the

tin into her coat pocket so she could pick up the ledger. On the plus side, if anyone jumped her on the way back to the car, she wouldn't need to reach for her baton. She could just bludgeon them with the book. "I'll see what I can do."

"Quickly, Inspector. We need to know if you're going to get anywhere as soon as possible." Heather raised a hand, more as if she wanted to soften her own words than to silence Adams. "Forgive my bluntness, but this is urgent. And it's not that I don't respect you, it's just that I don't think you've quite grasped your role yet. I wouldn't have called you if Charles hadn't insisted, and we don't have time for you to learn on the job. But it's true that it would be better if you did sort this out. My next step might be a little … forceful."

"Oh? And what would that be?"

"Charles's guardians aren't our only method of protecting the shop. I have my own. If we can't find the charm, and quickly, I'll be forced to set them loose on the city until someone gives up the culprit."

"Define *set them loose*."

"Fewer fingerprints, more bloodshed."

"*I'm sorry?*"

Heather shrugged. "It's a better option than having someone out there with the ability to unlock the guardians. Many of them are guarding things that should not be left unattended, let alone allowed to fall into the wrong hands."

Adams looked at Fergus, who had brought her the ball again. "How many guardians are there?"

Heather gestured at the ledger. "More than enough to be a problem."

"And if no one gives up the thief?"

"They will, eventually," Heather said, her voice filled with the same sunlight-on-bluebells warmth. "No matter what I need to do. The master charm cannot be lost. Not just to protect our clients, but to protect ourselves. And it must be found quickly, before too many guardians are taken under its control."

Adams mouth was abruptly sticky. Nothing about Heather suggested idle threats, with her bare brown feet and her grey-streaked hair, and her ageless, deep-rooted connection to the worlds of both Folk and human. Adams had the sudden, unshakeable sense that the other woman – or whatever she was – would throw her to these *protections* just as easily as anyone else, if it suited her. If she stood in the way of what needed doing. "What are your methods, exactly?"

"If Charles is steel and iron, I am tree and root," Heather said, and the plants in the room trembled, leaning toward her. "And such things can take the world of man apart, brick and bone and stone."

Adams held Heather's gaze as steadily as she could, the other woman's eyes cool and green and unflinching. Finally she said, "I suppose I'd better hurry up then, hadn't I?"

"You had."

There was silence again for a moment, then Adams said, "Any other safeguards around here that would've needed to be bypassed? It's just a door key, and a way past Fergus, then the master charm would've taken care of the rest?"

"*Just* that," Heather said, and turned back to her earrings.

Adams gave one short, sharp nod, feeling dismissed and frustrated all at once, her stomach tight with a seesawing, nauseous tension. She turned to the door, the bell jangling as she opened it. "I'll see you tomorrow," she said, and stepped over Fergus, walking out onto the cobbled street with the bell tinkling irritatingly in her wake. *Fewer fingerprints, more bloodshed.*

"Bloody civilians," she muttered to Dandy, who looked up at her with the glint of LED red eyes just visible behind his dreadlocks. "Bloody *Folk.*"

She wondered how long she had. She had an idea it wasn't going to be as long as she needed.

5

LITTLE POLICE THINGS

MID-AFTERNOON WAS ALREADY BRINGING HEAVY SHADOWS TO the Shambles, deepening the lingering chill that rose from the cobbles. The shop windows were rendered as oases of light, the cafes and bars sending out a siren song of hot coffee and warmth. Adams tucked the ledger more firmly under her arm and turned right, away from the centre and toward where the regular alley, the one with the bins, should be. She half expected it'd be invisible, hidden by some enchantment or trickery, but she found it easily enough, just a couple of shops down the row. It doglegged behind the buildings, offering access to the backs of the other two premises as well as Ash & Yew before dead-ending where the big industrial bins sat a little sulkily, scuffed and dented. She gave them a suspicious look, but they seemed to be nothing more than plastic and metal, one with its lid partly open, hooked on an unflattened cardboard box as if it had been caught in the act of chewing it up.

"Any ideas?" she asked Dandy.

He tipped his head, then padded to the bins, rising up on

his hind legs and hooking his front paws into the top of the open one so he could snuffle it thoroughly.

"What is it? What've you got?"

Dandy jumped up and vanished into the bin, a smooth, easy movement that Adams felt she somehow hadn't quite seen properly. He should've had to wriggle through the gap, and probably would've knocked the box out of the way, but neither of those things happened. He was just standing outside one moment, and the next she was listening to cardboard crumpling and paper scrunching as he scrabbled around inside.

"Dandy?" She lifted the lid and stood on her tiptoes to stare in at him. His shaggy head surfaced out of the mess, a used coffee filter in his teeth. "Oh, for—" She let the lid go and turned to look at the alley instead. Bloody invisible dogs should be more useful, especially if one had to put up with them getting river water and mud all over the car.

There were no mysterious doors or strange archways in evidence, nothing that suggested this was anything other than an average alley, and Adams headed back around the dogleg, where she could see the steady foot traffic of the Shambles at the end. To her right, on the opposite side of the alley to the block holding Ash & Yew, a swinging wooden sign marked the door to a little bar, a couple of slightly dishevelled potted bay trees festooned with fairy lights framing it. Adams pulled open the old wooden door and found a stairwell heading down, the walls papered with cheaply printed posters for comedy nights and open mic events. She ventured down into a dimly lit, low-ceilinged basement bar, furnished in an astonishing array of mismatched furniture and smelling of wood polish and raspberry soap, on the off chance this was Charles's local.

Instead she found the entire clientele consisted of a bunch of students, their chairs gathered in a semicircle around a slightly precarious-looking stage. Their attention was fully captured by a young person in flowing trousers and a fluffy green hoodie who was standing on it, reciting poetry with one hand pressed to their chest and the other gripping a phone. Adams caught just enough to know that her affection for poetry remained non-existent (and possibly also outdated. She didn't understand half the words the poet was using), before the poet saw her and stopped. The entire group turned as one to stare at her, silent and hostile, and she stared back, unsure if they were some sort of underground-dwelling, possibly dangerous Folk, or simply too poetic for her comfort.

"Sorry," she said, and retreated. They watched her go without moving.

Dandy was waiting for her outside, coffee grounds on his snout, and she frowned at him. "I think you've got a problem, you know."

He huffed, and she nodded.

"I know. Me too."

She checked around the bar's door, but there didn't seem to be any cameras in evidence. At the end of the alley, though, she could see a council one pointing down the street, and she took a photo of it so she remembered the location, getting the name of the shop beneath in the frame. Maybe it'd be of no help whatsoever, but it was worth trying. Half of police work was elimination, after all. If not more. She shoved her phone back into her pocket, nodding at a small, dark-haired man in a heavy coat done up to his chin, who slowed as he passed, eyeing her curiously.

"Maintenance?" he asked.

"Keeping the streets safe," she said, and he grinned at her, but didn't say anything else.

Back among the shops, she wound her way through the leaning, uneven lanes, keeping Ash & Yew roughly in the centre of her search area, taking photos of more CCTV cameras in case they revealed anything helpful. The place was riddled with wonky lanes and unexpected snickets, some empty, others yielding tiny, weirdly specific shops, such as one that sold nothing but rare mushrooms in a variety of forms – captured in jars or in powders, in pickles, teas, and half a dozen other forms. Another was dedicated to hand-made vegan sweets, which wasn't weird, except that they were all shaped into uncomfortably accurate renditions of cuts of meat, and still another sold an extensive and extravagant range of pet clothes and accessories, all of which were sold with coordinated human versions. Dandy stole a chew bone from the display outside the shop and bolted back down the lane with it before Adams could catch him, meaning she had to go in and pay for it. It was one thing him stealing things when her back was turned, but she couldn't ignore it when he did it right in front of her.

But none of the alleys revealed the endless span of blank high walls she'd seen beyond Ash & Yew's garden. Not that she'd really expected them to. She had a feeling that was all part of Rory's *other* York, and she wasn't quite sure how to access it. The Folk-ish shops were right in front of her, though, and she walked into one, looking in fascination at tanks full of luminous fungi and large jars with labels like *Bats' Toenails* and *Newts' Scales.* It had the same incense-heavy scent of esoteric shops everywhere, and a similar reliance on crystals as the primary form of light, decor, and stock, and Adams wondered how many other shops she'd walked past over the years without realising she could've been stocking up on phoenix dust and desiccated siren tears. She also wondered how much of this was real and how much was a scam. She'd spotted a few gleaming drops in the corner of the luminous fungi tank that she suspected were from glow-in-the-dark paint.

The second Folk shop she investigated, hoping to find a back way out into some other dimension of York, was a hat shop staffed by one large, overenthusiastic woman with a suggestion of too many limbs folded under her poncho. Adams fled when the woman started trying to jam a succession of feathered, ribbon-bedecked hats on the inspector's head, as well as Dandy's, chattering excitedly about them enhancing one's natural sensuality.

That horrifying brush with sensuality aside, neither shop offered anything, and she felt far too obvious traipsing in and out of one after the other. She could always go back and access the alley through the garden, after all. Instead, she found a coffee shop and got herself another drink in a to-go mug, surreptitiously picking up Dandy's bone when he dropped it in his search for coffee grounds. She had to carry it out of the shop pinched in her fingers, pretending she didn't have invisible dog drool painting her hand, and he refused to take it back when they got outside.

"I should adopt you out," she muttered to him, and trekked back to the car with the ledger in one hand and both the bone and her coffee in the other.

SHE WAS STILL EARLY ENOUGH that, once she was out of York, the roads were fairly clear, but despite that, the drive back to Skipton seemed to take an unreasonably long time. Part of it was how much of the route was spent winding past working farms and through tangles of small villages, constantly on the lookout for stray sheep and dim-witted pheasants and unpredictable ramblers. But even when the roads quietened further, and she was back into the reluctantly familiar and more reassuring fields that climbed to distant fells, the air smelling of wild places, she could still feel a creeping, uneasy impatience. She was pretty sure she could attribute that directly to the idea of rogue guardians being let loose, and Heather with her *fewer fingerprints, more bloodshed.*

Finally, though, she pulled into the car park at the Skipton station, getting out with a shiver. She'd had the passenger window open the whole way because Dandy was still giving off a distinctly wet dog smell, and now she could barely feel her fingers as she took the ledger and the bagged tin from the boot and headed indoors. She went straight up to the office she shared with DI Colin Collins, nodding at PC McCleod as she went past the front desk. He nodded back at her jerkily, dropped his pen, and vanished under his computer, and she wasn't sure if that was deliberate or not. Apparently she was much scarier than any of the drunk and disorderlies that came through the door.

Upstairs, she found Collins hunched over his desk, a big man with big hands that seemed far too large for the speed at which he was clattering away on the keyboard. He looked up as she came in. "Ay-up, Adams. Isn't it your day off?"

"It is. I got distracted."

"You may need to look at your work/life balance."

"I don't know what you mean."

He grinned, leaning back and stretching. "What've you got, then?"

She dumped the ledger on the desk with a hefty thump, and set the tin on top of it. "I need to get this fingerprinted."

"But?"

"But it's not entirely my case."

"*Ooh.* Is this a bit Toot Hansell?"

A bit Toot Hansell having become the best way they'd found to refer to cases that weren't entirely human without using the dread word *magic.* Adams still favoured *other* in her head, but that had quickly become far too confusing in speech. "A lot. And it's also in York."

Collins nodded, and took a swig from a mug of tea sitting neatly on a coaster by his keyboard. "Tricky. What is it?"

She tapped the tin. "A master charm that can be used to control metallic sculptures that act as alarm systems and guard dogs, apparently all over the world. Stolen from this box, from under one of the said guardians, out of a locked jewellery store with no sign of forced entry."

Collins didn't answer for a moment, then he just said, "Suspects?"

"None. Apparently Charles, who creates the guardians, is prone to getting boozed up and inviting people back for after parties, but no one seems sure how anyone got past the tin's guardian, except that he's glitching, apparently."

"Charles?"

"Fergus. The guardian."

"Of course." Collins took another mouthful of tea. "What's your plan?"

"Pull the CCTV footage from around the shop and see if anyone looks dodgy. See if any fingerprints of interest come up. Check out the names in this book and cross-reference for any recent reports of thefts or suchlike. They're all people who've bought guardians, apparently often to guard fun things like banks and weapons stockpiles. So they may be targeted by whoever has the master charm, or they may be behind it, since they'd know how it works."

"*Huh,*" Collins said. "Big job."

They looked at each other for a moment, and eventually Adams sighed. "Will you ask Lucas if he'll check for fingerprints?"

"Why don't you do it?"

"Because you and Lucas are besties, so he's more likely to do it without asking awkward questions if it comes from you."

"Lucas likes you just fine."

"But you're better at getting people to do things than I am."

"It's called asking nicely, not *getting people to do things*," Collins said. "You should practice more."

"Sure, but like you say, big job to be getting on with. And I don't want to practice."

Collins finished his tea with a satisfied sigh and put the mug down. "Maud's not going to love both of us getting tied up in Toot Hansell stuff again. Let alone using Lucas's time."

Adams grimaced. "I know, but, on the other hand, last time we did prevent her arresting half the county over misplaced apostrophes."

Collins snorted. During an incident with charmed beer in Harrogate their DCI, Maud Taylor, had been one of the victims, seized by an overwhelming urge to react with disproportionate force to the smallest transgressions. She certainly hadn't complained about their handling of that. "Fair enough," he said. "And I don't think you'd be doing this for no good reason. Weapons stashes and bank vaults sound worrying."

"It's more than that. Apparently the guardians aren't the shop's only protections, and they're going to let the others loose on York if I don't find the charm in some very short time frame they haven't actually specified."

Collins frowned. "That is problematic." He got up, picking up the tin. "I'll talk to Lucas."

"Thanks." She dropped into her chair, pulling her phone out. Skipton station had an excellent computer tech called Jules, but Adams wasn't entirely sure she didn't bite. There had been a very near incident of just that during the beer issue, and Adams had a lingering suspicion it wasn't all the fault of the charmed booze. Plus she'd have to explain why she was after CCTV footage from York, and she didn't know how likely Jules was to go straight to Maud for authorisation.

She needed to put a bit of people skills into that relationship, but that was a long-term plan. For now she just hit dial on her mobile, chewing on the edge of one thumbnail as she did so.

The phone rang a few times before a woman answered, her tone neutral. "Adams. To what do I owe the pleasure?"

"Hi, Isha. How—"

"Nope. What d'you want?"

Adams grimaced. "I was hoping you could do me a favour." Isha was the computer tech in Leeds, where Adams had worked when she'd first arrived in Yorkshire from London. They'd had a few social outings together, and Adams supposed they were technically friends, or more than, or had been, but the whole thing had just been very personal and therefore *messy*, and she'd admittedly not been very good at keeping in touch since she moved the whole hour away to Skipton. She'd had other things to worry about, which had been a quiet sort of relief, for all that the *other things* had been distinctly alarming, on the whole.

"Of course you were," Isha was saying. "Yet you still haven't explained to me what sent you scampering off to Skipton, or what the whole deal with the beer in Harrogate was."

"I know."

"And you were going to buy me a drink, or dinner."

"I know that too."

"And yet still you're asking for favours."

"I would point out that you hacked me and sent all my personal details to a journalist," Adams said.

"I was under the influence of something that you haven't explained to me, so that's still your fault."

"Victim blaming. I'll complain to HR."

Isha chuckled, a warm throaty sound. "Alright. I suppose I owe you a *bit* for that. What do you need?"

"Can you pull some CCTV for me?"

"You have those in Skipton?"

Adams snorted. "We do, but no. York."

"Ah. So not your patch *or* mine."

"No," Adams said, and waited. She could almost see Isha, a tall woman with strong shoulders and a mess of thick dark hair, nose ring glinting in the light of her screens and her office bristling with a jungle of potted plants.

"Dinner?" Isha said finally.

"Deal."

"Alright. Don't make me come out to Skipton, though. I'm not settling for pie and chips."

"It's not so bad here," Adams said. "They've even got decent coffee."

"Careful, Adams. You'll have wellies and a dog before you know it. Send me the camera locations."

Isha hung up, and Adams looked at Dandy. "You don't count," she told him. "And my wellies are because every bloody thing around here seems to involve animal effluent."

Dandy didn't answer, and Adams flicked through her phone to the photos, trying to settle the gnawing feeling of guilt at involving Isha. But it was only cameras, and she'd be able to keep her out of it otherwise. The last thing she wanted to do was pull Isha into the middle of Folk business. She'd already dragged Collins in, before she'd realised there was no coming back from seeing the hidden world, and that it wasn't all dragon tea parties and swan-fixated sprites. But he'd proved to be both distinctly resilient and steadfastly openminded for someone who looked as if he should be holding forth in the local pub on topics such as 'the good old days of policing', and 'not to be racist, but'.

Unlike another Leeds colleague, DC James Hamilton, who had ended up accidentally stumbling into a few Folk things. Well, being mugged by some. Twice. And though he was young and smart and seemed as if he should be rather more adaptable than Collins, Adams knew James still had nightmares about his brush with *otherness*. Not that she didn't sometimes, but he didn't seem to deal with it too well.

So she tried wherever she could to keep the Folk part of her work separate from the human part. Just as she understood Folk needed protection from humans, so too humans needed protection from Folk. There was a division between the worlds, and as much as it went against her nature to accept it, she knew there was a reason for that divide. So she enforced it as much as possible, although technically the policing of that was mostly handled by cats. Or so a cat had told her. Heather had been right when she'd said Adams didn't really know what her role was, and she wasn't at all sure how she'd ended up with it in the first place, but here she was, and there was no point fighting it.

Although talking to the cat about guardians might be a good idea.

SHE WAS PAGING SLOWLY through the ledger when Collins came back into the room.

"Success," he said. "Lucas says you owe him a cheese plate, though."

"You two and your cheese. Have you had your cholesterol checked recently?"

Collins wrinkled his nose. "Low blow, Adams. I've seen what you eat."

"It's very balanced," she said, squinting at the tiny print in the book. The dates were … concerning.

"I didn't know instant noodles were such a complete meal."

"I eat more than that," she protested, although she had to

admit they might qualify as her major food group. Somehow her student eating habits hadn't been left behind quite as fully as she might have liked. There just never seemed to be time for actual cooking. She tapped the ledger. "This is ridiculous. It goes back to 1812, and those are only the ones I can read. There's even older stuff that looks like someone spilled a pint of brandy on the pages."

"Really?" he asked, leaning over the desk and peering at the book. "Is the shop multi-generational or something?"

"I don't think so."

"Right." He frowned. "And the newest ones?"

"Last month. But I think this is going to be a washout. We can't go through them all."

"No," Collins agreed, flipping a few pages over. "Bloody hell, there's hundreds in here."

"Thousands." She rubbed her face with both hands. "I'm going to have to hope the CCTV or the fingerprints turn something up."

Collins nodded. "Let's go the other way. I'll poke around for any reports of big thefts and cross-reference back to the book."

"That'll take you ages. It's not alphabetised."

"I can scan it and convert to text," he said. "Bit fiddly, but it should work."

She stared at him. "When did you get all techy?"

"One has to move with the times, Adams. I did a work-shop. Besides, I've always been a bit techy. You're the one who gets twitchy if you have to use an app."

"Why can't I just go to a website? Why does *everything* have to be an app?"

"I think you're very suited to a world where people still keep handwritten ledgers."

Adams scowled at him, and pushed the book across the desk. "Help yourself, then."

He picked it up. "What's your plan?"

"Enjoy the last"—she checked her watch—"ugh, *half an hour* of my day off, and hope we get some more info tomorrow. I'll head back up to York in the morning and do some legwork."

"Want some company?"

"No," she said, getting up. "Maud'll throw her toys out if we both go."

"Fair point. Are you telling her *you're* going?"

Adams grimaced. Tomorrow was Saturday, and she should be in. "I might throw a sickie," she said aloud, and Collins nodded.

"Probably for the best."

Adams gave him a quick nod and headed out the door, Dandy trailing behind her, and waited until she was in the car to unlock her phone. She was going to have company tomorrow, but it wasn't going to be Collins. She took a deep breath and hit dial.

It rang for so long that she was expecting voicemail to kick in when Rory answered. "Hello, Adams. How was York?" he asked.

"Interesting."

"I love how you share so much detail with me," he said, when she didn't say anything else. "Was that all?"

She sighed. "You said you knew about another side of York."

"I do," he said, the amusement fading from his voice.

"I need some help navigating it. Fancy a day trip tomorrow?"

There was a pause, and for a moment she thought he was going to refuse, then he said, "Alright."

"Are you sure?"

"Yes. I'd rather go with you." He didn't add the rest, but she heard it anyway. *You shouldn't go alone.* It irritated her, but at the same time, Rory had barely raised an eyebrow when confronted with werewolves. His unease with York was concerning.

She wondered if it was to do with his mum, or something else, but aloud she just said, "Thanks, Rory."

"Sure. Meet you there or pick me up?"

"Meet me there is easier." The last thing she needed was someone chatting at her for an hour in the car, especially when her caffeine levels might be low.

"Oh, *now* you have faith in my car." There was a smile sneaking back into his voice, but it was a shadow of his normal tone. He paused, as if he wanted to say something else but didn't know how, then just said, "See you then."

She hung up and looked at Dandy, sitting bolt upright in the passenger's seat with his floppy ears pricked. "It's a start," she said, hearing the uncertainty in her own voice.

He huffed and put a paw on her leg, so she scuffed him under the chin.

It wasn't much, but it was going to have to be enough. She started the car, ignoring PC McCleod, who was trying not to look at her, and hoped he hadn't seen her petting the invisible dog. It was only going to make him more nervous, and she didn't want to be responsible for him putting in for a transfer.

6

UN-MUGGED & IN ONE PIECE

Adams passed a restless night, her dreams peopled with metallic monsters demanding tin sardines (as opposed to *tinned* sardines), and turning everything they touched to a wilderness of rust and corrosion. Still, she was getting what passed as some form of sleep, until someone said in her ear, "Did you say something about sardines?"

She shot upright with a yelp, rolling away from the voice and off the bed, dislodging Dandy, who tumbled to the floor in the narrow gap between the wardrobe and the bed frame with her, both of them landing in a tangle of limbs and duvet. Adams hit her head on the wall, thrashing wildly to get to her feet, then finally made it to her knees, Dandy's red eyes bright as taillights in the dark.

"Well, I can tell neither of you have any cat in you," the same voice said, sounding like a BBC presenter who'd been smoking a pack a day for the last fifty years.

"Thompson?" Adams asked.

"Obviously," the cat said, and Adams got up, stumbling through the tangle of duvet and around to the other side of the bed to put the bedside light on.

She squinted against it at the large tabby tomcat sitting in the middle of the mattress, his eyes narrowed against the light and his ragged tail curled over his toes. "What the *hell* are you doing?" she asked him.

"Good morning to you, too."

She checked her watch. "It's five a.m."

"That's morning."

Adams took her hoody from the hook behind the door and pulled it on over her pyjamas, then headed out of the room and downstairs, the floorboards creaking under her feet. Dandy and Thompson trailed after her, Dandy keeping a wary distance from the cat. She knocked yesterday's coffee grounds into his bowl, set the machine up with her mug under the spout, then leaned on the tiny kitchen table and crossed her arms over her chest, frowning at Thompson.

"Tuna?" he suggested, and she sighed, but went to find a bowl and one of the packets of cat food she'd started stocking. She gave Dandy some steak she'd cooked up the night before, too, and Thompson gave her an affronted look.

"*He* gets steak?"

"He won't eat dog food."

"Then I won't eat cat food."

"Well, I don't have any tuna. And you don't live here, you realise?"

"Give me some of his steak, then."

Adams grabbed her coffee off the machine and took a hefty gulp, almost scalding her tongue, then chopped some of the steak into smaller pieces and swapped it for the bowl of cat food.

"Wait, I'll have that too."

"You said you didn't want it."

"I said I won't eat it, but, you know. I might change my mind."

Adams dropped the bowl back on the floor with a clatter,

and went to wash her hands. "I don't even eat meat," she complained. "Now I'm spending half my sodding wages on steak for an invisible dog, and cat food for a cat who doesn't live here and isn't sure he even wants it."

"Call it payment for information," Thompson said indistinctly, around a mouthful of steak. "Can you put this on the table? Unless you want to sit on the floor while we talk, of course."

Adams did some creative swearing, mostly under her breath, and put the cat's plates on the table. "Anything else? Linen napkins? Paw massage?"

"No, but I think you'd better have some more coffee. You're not a morning person, are you?"

"It's *five a.m.*," she repeated, but put another mug under the machine and set it up again anyway. She hadn't finished her first yet, but that hardly seemed relevant. "What're you doing here? Please tell me there's not some crisis in Toot Hansell. I can't be dealing with dragons right now. I've got other things to do."

"So the big man tells me," Thompson said, sniffing his steak carefully. "How fresh is this?"

"It was on sale."

"When?"

"Yesterday. You're a bloody stray, you know. You can't be *that* fussy."

"I've got half the Toot Hansell Women's Institute feeding me. I can be as fussy as I like."

"Go and eat there, then," Adams said, and tipped her new cup of coffee into her first one before she sat down at the table opposite the cat, frowning at him. Dandy put his head on her lap and she scratched his ears absently. "What's up?"

"Your mate Collins does a nice line in cheese and smoked salmon, so I swung by there last night. He said you had some issues in York with guardians."

"You know about them?"

"Yes. The Watch aren't big fans. Not much cats can do against armoured bloody caterpillars or whatever they're doing these days."

"I saw a winged cat, actually."

"*Sacrilege*," Thompson said, licking his chops. "But, yeah. They're expensive as elven toenails, so it's not like they're in every magic-worker's back garden, but for those who get more successful, they're sometimes used in conjunction with lock charms to make sure the Watch can't come sniffing around. And, I mean, shift locks might keep us out, but guardians can keep *everything* out."

Thompson was a member of the Watch, the cat council that held the line between humans and Folk, but Adams wasn't sure if his loose interpretation on how exactly to enforce that was his nature or a more general cat attitude. She hadn't met any other Watch cats to ask, and according to Thompson it wasn't recommended to draw attention to herself by talking to random cats about that or anything else. She was human, after all, and cats had their ways of making sure humans didn't remember their encounters with Folk. She had a suspicion that it could be a deeper and more final solution than the hypnosis-style approach she'd seen Thompson use, too.

"Are they sentient?" she asked now. "The people who make them said not, but the cat one was acting pretty oddly for an automaton."

Thompson sniffed. "Heather and Charles, you mean."

"Yes. You know them?"

"If it's York, it's them. There are others who make guardians, but not like Charles, and not in the north. There's another in Scotland, one in Wales, and one in London, but none of those are as good. But when someone's as skilled as Charles, they start seeing nothing but their ability in the creatures. They forget that if they give something a semblance of life, it's not going to rest there. Not easily, anyway. Life craves life."

Adams hesitated. "What *are* Charles and Heather?"

"Old," Thompson said around another piece of steak. "*Mnngnnn.*"

"What?"

He swallowed hard. "Magicians of sorts. Witches, if you prefer, but everyone went off that term after all the burnings at the stake and so on."

"Alright," Adams said, taking a mouthful of coffee. "So the issue is someone's gone and nicked the master charm for the guardians. They can use it to control any of them, anywhere, and Heather's about to launch a mass plant attack on York unless I get it back."

"Ouch. How in the name of spiky metal gods did that get stolen?"

"If I knew that, I'd be a lot closer to finding it. I'm heading up there again this morning. Can you help me out? I need a guide, and I've *sort* of got one, but you must know York. *Other* York, I mean."

Thompson wrinkled his snout, exposing yellowed fangs. "A bit. But I can't just go trekking about up there."

"Why not?"

"Other York isn't just a few spooky streets. It's not like a pocket."

"A pocket?"

"*A pocket,*" Thompson said impatiently. "When are you going to start learning all this? A pocket's a Folk town or village. They're all tucked out of human sight, and usually exist down empty roads in the countryside, or on the outskirts of places."

"Right," Adams said, deciding it was too early to be

offended by a cat. Instead she added, "But York's not like that?"

"No. It's a whole *city* which simply refused to move when the humans took over, and instead persists in parallel with it. There aren't a lot like it, and it's well guarded, which means I'll be noticed. It's well off my patch, and I'll have to explain myself to the Watch, which I don't fancy. The more I can keep a low profile, the better I can protect Toot Hansell."

Toot Hansell and its dragon tea parties, which were *very* much against the ethos of the Watch. The dragons were far too good at drawing attention to themselves. "Fair enough," she said aloud. "Can you find out about any guardians who might have gone rogue, then? See about that?"

"Sure. That I can do."

"Anything else I should know about them?"

"Not really. Just watch yourself in York. Rumours about you and your mutt are spreading, and not everyone's too keen on the idea of some magical police officer."

Adams looked down at Dandy, who stared up at her with his eyes hidden behind his dreadlocks, tail wagging gently, then lifted his head out of her lap and flopped to the floor, offering his belly for a scratch. "We are formidable," she said, rubbing his stomach with one bare foot.

"You're an unknown quantity," Thompson said. "Folk might be better at the unknown than humans, but that doesn't mean they like it."

"Awesome," Adams said.

"Exactly." He stretched, the movement recalling Fergus's arched back. "Tuna wouldn't go amiss next time, though."

"Neither would a more civilised hour," she said, but she was talking to an empty chair. Thompson had shifted, stepping sideways into some space that ran between the worlds, to reappear again somewhere else, a cat's secret method of travel. To Adams it sounded like teleportation, but

Thompson got unreasonably miffed any time she suggested that and insisted it was magic, not sci-fi. So she persisted in calling it teleportation whenever she could.

But he wasn't here to hear her malign his abilities, so she just got up and trekked upstairs with the remains of her coffee. If she was up early, she may as well get on the road. Catching Charles hungover and barely awake might just work in her favour.

THERE WAS no one in the shop at Ash & Yew when she got there at just after seven, and no one answered the doorbell. She went around to the alley instead, Dandy trailing her, and banged enthusiastically on the back door, which was bell-less.

"All deliveries to the front, do you think?" she asked Dandy, and he gave her nothing but a tipped head.

She knocked again, and stepped back to look up at the windows, but none of them were open. Also Heather had said they overlooked the metal garden, so she wasn't quite sure if she was actually seeing windows or an illusion of windows, and despite her three cups of coffee it felt too early in the morning to be wrestling with such things. She went to bang on the door again, and it opened before she could touch it, revealing Heather in a long grey cardigan, Fergus at her feet.

"Morning," Adams said.

"Bit early for house calls, isn't it? And on a Saturday."

"Crime never sleeps and all that."

Heather gave her a half smile and stepped back to let her in. Her hair was gathered into a plait that hung over one shoulder, and her feet were still bare, strong and brown.

Adams looked down at Fergus, who creaked at her,

blinking his glossy eyes in that weird, pinwheel motion. She managed to suppress a shudder, not sure if she could hurt the scary cat's feelings, but not wanting to risk it when said scary cat had really scary claws. "Hi," she said. "Mind if I come in?"

Fergus looked from her to Dandy, then turned and jumped onto one of the benches, moving with that same faintly unnerving, juddering motion.

"I really need to get Charles to fix his charms," Heather said, and led the way across the room. "Come on. I'll put the kettle on."

Adams followed her, pulling the door shut behind her and nodding at Fergus as she passed him. He lifted his chin in response, and she wondered if it was really just down to charms. It seemed a lot more like real personality to her.

Heather opened one of the doors in the short hall, revealing the coil of a spiral staircase, black metal and warm wood. More framed photos hung on the walls, and Adams wondered uneasily if Heather had been the one to take them, old, sepia-tinted things with dates handwritten in the corners, a record of York across the decades, interspersed with even older line drawings. The stairs delivered them straight into an open-plan living and dining area that took up the whole back of Ash & Yew, above the workshop. It wasn't huge, but the ceiling had been opened into the attic space, giving it an airy feel under the framework of old beams, and it held a couple of comfortable-looking sofas, a long breakfast bar, and a kitchen that was modern without being hard-edged. Plants were everywhere, framing the big windows and the glass doors that opened onto a narrow balcony, clambering along shelves in the walls, hanging from hooks in the exposed beams, and sprouting from stands. There was even a section of wall in the kitchen given over to what Adams assumed were herbs, as she could identify a few of them as basil and rosemary and mint.

Heather waved at the breakfast bar, and Adams sat at one of the stools, watching the other woman flick the kettle on. "Is Charles up?" she asked.

"I'll wake him," Heather said. "Tea or coffee?"

"Coffee, if you have it."

"And for the dog?"

Adams looked at Dandy. "You can see him?"

"I think you'll find most non-humans can."

"No one seems to notice him."

"He doesn't look quite as if it's safe to notice him," Heather said, taking a coffee press from a cupboard. "Does he want water or something?"

"He's fine," Adams said. "Just don't leave the coffee out or he'll have it."

Heather didn't reply to that, just finished setting up the mugs then headed into a hall that branched away toward the front of the building. It was silent in the wake of her departure, and Adams watched the brightening sky through the glass doors. It was colourless still, but clear of clouds. It was going to be one of those crisp spring days that whispered promises of summer, but still held space for winter in the shadows.

"*Mmmraow?*" a creaky voice said, half lost under the sound of the boiling kettle, and Adams turned to look at the top of the stairs, where Fergus stood with his multi-jointed tail twitching.

"Hi," she said, as Dandy vanished behind the kitchen island, peering at the cat warily.

Fergus tipped his head at her, then walked across the floor to join her, metal claws clicking loudly on the wood. He jumped to the island and stared at her from close quarters, and she barely managed not to recoil.

"Yes?"

He lowered his head and set something on the worktop,

watching her the whole time with those dark, unnerving eyes. She looked at his gift, raising her eyebrows slightly. It was a duck, smaller than her own, made of textured metal.

"What's that?"

Fergus nudged it toward her with one paw, and she wondered if he wanted her to throw it for him or something, but before she could decide she heard Heather coming back along the hall. Fergus leaped from the island and trotted back to the stairs, and she picked up the duck, rolling it in her fingers, the metal oddly warm and dense, heavy for its size.

Heather topped up the coffee press and the two mugs before looking at Adams. "He's coming," she said.

"Great." They didn't speak after that, only for Adams to turn down both sugar and milk, and take a sip of decent but not amazing coffee, while Dandy looked up at her longingly.

Finally a door opened in the hall, and careful footsteps approached. Charles emerged, his grey hair looking like something had been nesting in it, and he stumbled to the nearest stool, sinking onto it and pulling a packet of ibuprofen toward him when Heather set it on the worktop.

"No hangover charms?" Adams asked.

"If anyone figures that out, they'll make a fortune," Charles said, his voice rough with sleep and alcohol. He washed the tablets down with a gulp of tea, and attempted to smooth his hair. "Good morning, Inspector."

"Morning," she replied. "Rough night?"

"Somewhat."

"Every night's been rough for you since the master charm was stolen," Heather said, leaning against the cabinets in the kitchen. "Your liver's going to pack it in before you know it."

"Now *that* there's a charm for."

"Only if you remember to take it before you start drinking, and by the look of you, you didn't."

"Well, no," he admitted, and took another mouthful of tea. "Any chance of some toast, love?"

"You know where it is."

"Fair enough," he said with a sigh, and looked at Adams. "Do you have something for us?"

"Not yet. Do you tend to drink at the same place all the time?"

"Mostly. The Blighted Basilisk."

"Right. And where's that?"

He waved vaguely. "It's local."

Adams sighed slightly. "I'm not going to find it on Google maps, am I?"

To her surprise, Charles said, "It's on Tripadvisor. Or an aspect of it is."

"One-star rating," Heather said. "Keeps the tourists out."

"Alright. And do you tend to drink with the same people?"

"Mostly," he said again.

"And has there been anyone new recently? Someone who's worked their way into your group or anything like that?"

He thought about it, scratching his hand through his hair absently, then looking in astonishment at a piece of lettuce he fished out from behind his ear. "*Huh.*"

"The rest of it's in the bath," Heather said. "You told me you were a raccoon and wanted to wash your kebab."

"*Huh,*" Charles said again, and gave her a strained grin. "Sorry, love."

"Doesn't matter to me," she said, her tone short. "I've left it for you to clean up."

He nodded, and looked at Adams. "Do you want me to show you the pub?"

"I can find it. Anyone new, though?"

"Not that I can think of. Different people come and go, of course, and it's not like the pub's *all* regulars, but most are.

Like Heather says, they kind of take steps to keep newcomers out."

"Alright. Have you got your phone?"

He looked around vaguely, and Heather opened a cupboard, took down a box of chocolate cereal, and fished a phone out of it. She handed it to Charles.

"Oh," he said. "I haven't seen that since Wednesday."

"I know," she said. "I was waiting to see when you'd finally ask."

Charles blew cereal dust off it and unlocked it. "It's even still got some charge."

"Good," Adams said. "Text me the names of your drinking buddies."

He nodded, taking another gulp of tea, and found a pair of glasses in his pocket. He tapped away at the phone with surprisingly little hesitation.

Heather held the coffee press up, eyebrows raised, and Adams nodded. As the other woman topped up her mug she said, "You mentioned apprentices."

"Yes. Charles is in demand for that sort of thing, but he's picky about who he takes on."

"It's delicate work," he said, not looking up from the phone.

"Tell me about Violet. The one who gave Fergus a personality."

"Violet Brennan," Heather said. "She was a good silversmith."

"Very pretty stuff," Charles agreed. "I think she was more interested in your work, though, Heather."

"Her work was very organic," Heather agreed. "And she came for the jewellery, not the guardians. But she took a bit of an interest in them, and suggested that if we wanted to sell more we should add some personality. I didn't agree, but she and Charles messed about a bit with Fergus."

"When you say she was interested in your work," Adams said, "do you mean the … nature stuff?"

Heather shook her head. "There's no apprenticeship to be had in that. But I design a lot of Charles's jewellery."

"Show her your books," Charles said.

"The inspector doesn't need to see them," Heather said.

"Go on, they're beautiful."

Heather just shook her head, so Charles pushed the sleeve of his jumper up, revealing thin yet muscular forearms with a twining filigree of old tattoos, marred here and there with the scars of burns. "She did these."

Adams leaned forward, examining the design. It *was* beautiful, leaves and branches coiling around blooms and stars and galaxies, and everything seemed almost to shift under her gaze, subtly and gently alive. "Lovely," she said.

"Protective, too," Charles said. "Probably why no one's ever mugged me on the way home." He smiled at Heather, and she smiled back, something weary yet loving.

"It was meant so you didn't chop your own damn arm off," she said. "But sure, whatever works."

"Well, I'm un-mugged *and* still in one piece," he said, and poked his phone. "There you go, Inspector."

"Thanks," she said, as her mobile dinged.

Charles got up. "I need to clean out the bath and have a shower," he said, and wandered off.

Adams examined the list. "Byx? Snoops? Dartmoor? These aren't names."

"Close as I've got," Charles called back as he vanished into the hallway. "We don't go in for full names." A door closed in his wake, and Adams looked at Heather.

"Full names are dangerous," she said.

Adams searched her memory for one of Rory's books. "Fae? They can steal your souls or something?"

"More like your bank details," Heather said. "But with his

friends it's more because they've got about six different identities each and either arrest warrants or curses on half of them."

"So Fae can't really steal your soul if they have your name?"

"Depends on the Fae."

"Helpful," Adams said with a sigh. "Do you have contact details for Violet Brennan?"

"She was barely interested in the guardians when she was here, Inspector. Nothing but a young girl trying to figure out what she wanted to be."

"I'm just doing my little police things."

Heather smiled faintly at that, and picked up her own phone, swiping through it. A moment later Adams' mobile dinged. "That's her number. It's all I've got. Or you could try the herbalist's. *Woad in the Wold*, it's called." She took a sip of tea, looking at Adams over the rim of the mug. "If you can find it."

"The one that's not in this York?"

"You won't find it if you're looking from this side, put it that way."

Adams decided she was already thoroughly sick of alternate versions of York and wonky dimensions, and also that if Heather hadn't offered to show her a way through them, she wasn't going to ask. She could figure this out herself. "Great," she said aloud, then finished her coffee and got up. "I'll be in touch."

Heather nodded, and escorted Adams downstairs and through to the front door of the shop. The Shambles was still quiet, the cafes only just setting up, and Adams paused on the threshold, looking at Heather. "How many messes of Charles's have you sorted out?"

Heather looked at her for a long moment, and for the first time Adams saw her age painted in her eyes, bright but weary, full of long, old memories and strange passages of time. "A lot, Inspector."

"Is this the worst?"

She grimaced. "There was another that came close, a long time ago. Before York was so human."

"And?"

"And half the city fell to ash and oak and yew," she said, and Adams saw the doorframe shiver, dark wood surfacing under the smooth white paint then sinking away again, like a leviathan shifting. "But this will be worse if we don't stop it in time. There's so much more metal in the world, so much for the guardians to call on, if the user of the charm knows how."

"Do you think they do?"

"They knew enough to steal it."

Adams nodded. "Are you going to give me time to sort this out?"

"If you're quick," Heather replied, and pushed the door shut with a final click, vanishing behind the distorted glass and leaving Adams and Dandy on the cold, clean-swept cobbles as the day crept in, promising nothing but more questions.

7

TOO MUCH RED MEAT

VIOLET DIDN'T ANSWER WHEN ADAMS TRIED THE NUMBER Heather had given her. It was in service, but just went to a generic answering service, and Adams didn't leave a message. She preferred to talk to Violet face to face, anyway. She went searching for the pub instead, and found *an aspect* of it, as Charles had put it, after circling the same block three times and eventually noticing a window behind heavy iron bars that were deeply encrusted with old flyers for rug sales and no-questions-asked car purchases. She pulled a few of the flyers free, enough to be able to see a patch of glass, but it was too dirty to glimpse anything through. She checked the Tripadvisor listing on her phone, and the map attached to it. She was definitely in the right place.

There weren't a lot of reviews, but the main thread running through them was *drink here at your own risk, if the beer doesn't kill you the bathrooms will.* To make it more interesting, the proprietor had replied to a couple of them with things like, *you must be southern coz you don't know good beer when it bites your face off,* and she was wondering if they were being literal about the biting-faces-off bit. Either way, they were doing a good job at fending off even the most adventurous tourist who might be searching for an authentic York pub experience, and the fact that she couldn't see a single sign suggested they were keeping up the same effort in person.

She knocked on the door sharply, hearing it echoing inside, but no one came to open up. She hadn't really expected them to. It was after eight, but it didn't look like the sort of place that offered breakfast, or bothered with an early cleaning crew. Plus she suspected that Charles's version of the pub might exist only in some other level of York, and she wasn't sure how to access it. But there was a narrow alley right next to the shop, and she ventured down it, wishing she'd brought her wellies. An unpleasant sludge coated the crumbling tarmac, and a nasty scent of old beer, vomit, and other bodily fluids drifted around her.

A *whuff* came from behind her, and she looked back at Dandy. He'd stopped at the mouth of the alley, one front paw raised and his floppy ears as back as they were able to be.

"Good call," she said. "Stay there."

He whined, but did as she said for a change, and she discovered a side door with someone's half-used dinner decorating the threshold. She reached over it to knock, holding her breath, then stepped back while she waited for a response.

The building remained as bland and silent as it had been when she arrived, and after trying one more time she retreated to join Dandy, breathing a little easier once she was on the street. Tripadvisor reckoned the place was still operational, so she'd have to try again later.

Her phone rang, and she pulled it out, hoping for Collins. She'd texted him Violet Brennan's details, but hadn't heard anything back. She supposed he'd only just be getting into work, but he was often early. Instead, though, Rory's name flashed up, and she grimaced, considering. Yesterday it had seemed like the best option, roping him in as her guide. She'd had nothing else to go on. Now, with Violet's details handed to Collins and the pub right in front of her (even if she was fairly sure she wasn't going to be able to find *Woad in the Wold*, and the pub was a definite health hazard), she wasn't sure she needed him. It'd be helpful, sure, but she didn't know how risky the whole situation could turn out to be. She wasn't liking the signs so far.

She hit answer. "Morning."

"Egg barm or croissant?"

"Sorry?"

"Do you want a fried egg barm or a croissant? They've got almond ones. And muffins, but I thought you might be more a croissant person."

"Muffins are just cake for breakfast."

"Knew it," he said, and she could hear the grin in his voice.

"Rory, I don't think you need to come up," she said. "I've got it in hand."

"I thought you might say that," he said, and she could hear a coffee machine going behind him. "That's why I'm already here."

"Well, you can leave again."

"Look, if you won't tell me what you want, I'm going to get you a croissant. Everyone likes a croissant."

"No, they flake everywhere. And I'm hungry again five minutes later."

"Egg barm it is." His voice faded for a moment, and she heard him ordering.

"*Rory.*"

His voice came back clear again, and very calm. "Adams, I know you're thinking you shouldn't involve me, and I get it. I'm not trying to interfere in anything, and I know you can look after yourself. But York isn't as easy to get into as you might think, and figuring it out's going to slow you down. And I'm guessing you don't have a lot of time to spare if you asked me to help in the first place."

Adams didn't answer immediately, staring at the blinkered eye of the pub's window. Finally she said, "Can you get me some ketchup on the egg barm? And runny yolk."

"Damn. I had you down as a brown sauce person. Send me your location." He hung up, and Adams walked back to the nearest stretch of larger street with a sigh. He was right. She didn't have a lot of time. But what was he really going to show her she couldn't figure out herself?

"Look at it out of the corner of your eye," Rory said, around a bite of a bacon sandwich. It was on hefty-looking sourdough bread, and he was having trouble getting through it. Midge, Pinto, and Dandy were all watching carefully in case he needed help.

"I am," Adams protested, taking another bite of her own sandwich. The bun was soft and the egg perfectly cooked, but the whole thing was already almost cold so she was trying to eat it as fast as she could.

"You're not." He managed to wedge the oversized sandwich into the same hand as his coffee, and used his free hand to turn her side-on to the large glass window of a cobbler's. It was a big chain one, and there was already a bored-looking teenager behind the counter, watching them curiously. "Now try. Not the shop itself. Next to it."

Adams started to say she still couldn't see anything in the vacant building next to the cobblers, then stopped. It swam into view reluctantly, as sepia-toned as the photos in Heather's stairwell at first, then filling in with colour, a low display window bellying out from a narrow shop, a wooden door next to it. The name was innocuous enough, if a bit gruesome: *The Meatworks*, picked out in peeling gold paint on the window. Under that, though, in smaller print, was *Meats of Unusual Provenance*, which Adams found even less appealing than an average butcher's shop.

"Really?" she said. "A *butcher's?*"

"I know," Rory said, tearing the last of his sandwich into three and giving one piece each to Midge and Pinto, then waving the third vaguely in the air. Dandy took it delicately, and Rory gave a startled "*Oh*" as it vanished.

Adams looked at her own sandwich, and decided she didn't need to share. It wasn't that big.

"You can look at it properly now," Rory said. "I usually find that once I start seeing them it's like a switch flicks, and you can see everything properly."

Adams turned and stared at the shopfront, which didn't look any better now she was looking at it head-on. The glass was smeared and slightly grimy, and three fly strips dangled from the top of the frame, spaced unevenly. The sight made her fingers twitch. Underneath them, a display of dusty jars took up half the window, chutneys and rubs and sauces that looked like their use-by dates had come up some time around when the shop had sold its first Sunday roast. It looked uninviting, and rundown, and unpleasant, but no more *other* than the places she'd been into yesterday. There definitely wasn't any sign over the door reading, *Other York This Way!*

She frowned at Rory. "I saw non-usual shops yesterday."

"Sure," he said. "You're tuned in. But there seems to be levels. Some places everyone can see, some places people like us can see straight away but most can't, and then there's the places like this, which give access to the other York."

"Is there an actual name for it? *Other York* is just a bit clumsy."

"York," he said, grinning. "If you ask anyone there, they'll say *this* is the other York. It's newer, for sure."

Adams looked dubiously at the old cobbles and uneven walls of the buildings surrounding them, then had her last bite of sandwich and crumpled up the bag. Three matching canine whines greeted her, and she looked at the dogs.

"So mean," Rory said.

"It was only a little sandwich!"

Rory dug in his pockets and handed her three dog treats. "Don't you carry any?"

"I don't have a dog," she said, sharing them out.

"You do." He hesitated. "Wait, he's not actually some gruesome monster with horns and six eyes, is he?"

"No, he's mostly a very good boy," she said, scratching Dandy behind the ears. "Only periodically useful, but good nevertheless."

"Right. Then you need to carry biscuits. And poo bags."

She looked at Dandy. "I've never thought of that."

"What, you just let him go wherever? Is that invisible too?" Rory sounded horrified.

"I think he must be very private about his bathroom habits. And, I mean, things go invisible once he picks them up, so I suppose the reverse would also be true?" She looked at Dandy dubiously, and he panted at her. Rory was staring at roughly the same spot, as if expecting Dandy to give a demonstration.

Adams decided the question of invisible dog poo was one which, like many others, could wait, and nodded at the shop. "Do we have to go in there?"

"It's the only place I know that's open now. Folk can find their own way between the Yorks, but without a local we won't be able to get through unless we use a doorway." He said it matter-of-factly, someone describing the best route to the local supermarket, and she looked at him curiously, with his brown waxed jacket zipped up to meet a tartan scarf, and a grey woollen hat pulled down over his ears, scraps of hair sneaking out from under it. She'd have walked past him in the street and thought nothing of him, other than to expect him to sound a bit posher than he actually did. Except for those sharper edges, that more-in-the-world shine to him. It seemed brighter now, as if in coming here and exposing himself to other York he'd shown more of who he was, willingly or not.

Adams finished her coffee and held her hand out for Rory's rubbish. He gave it to her without comment, and she went to the bin outside the cobbler's and dropped it in, then turned to the butcher's, tucking her hands into the pockets of her own coat. She chose all her jackets for good storage, favouring small men's ones if the women's styles were stingy on space. Extendible baton in her right pocket. Duck and a small multitool, both on her keyring, in the left, along with a compact torch, her lock picks, and, she discovered, Fergus's duck as well. She must've picked it up without realising, and it was a good thing the pockets were roomy if she was going to be going about magpie-ing every duck she saw. She sighed. Things she hadn't realised she'd need to worry about. Anyway. Phone and notebook in her inside pockets, so the only thing she was missing was Yorkie bars, and she was going to have to remember to bring her backpack next time.

"Alright," she said to Rory. "Lead on."

Rory looked at Midge and Pinto, said, "Heel," then led the way to the shop door with the dogs padding silently next to him. A retractable leash protruded from one of his coat pockets, but he didn't seem to bother using it much.

Adams looked at Dandy and raised her eyebrows. He

panted at her and trotted after Rory. "You're solely motivated by your stomach," she said, and joined the procession.

There was no tinkly bell over the door to the butcher's shop, just a creaking hinge and a wall of meaty stink that hit her like a wet towel. She almost took a step back, out into the fresher air of the city, but instead pulled her scarf up over her nose and pushed. The shop was small and narrow, a display counter and a set of scales taking up most of the wall that ran back from the window. There was a door in the far wall, and shelving holding more chutneys and spices, as well as faded bags of dried pasta, took up the wall opposite the counter. A large man was at the workbench behind the display case, a hefty cleaver in one hand. He barely glanced at them, working methodically to dismember something Adams didn't look at too closely.

She looked at the display case instead, her gaze drawn there almost against her will. She expected it to be grey and stinking, as filthy as the window with its dust and flies, but the whole thing gleamed, the glass immaculate and the metal trays of meat shining. Chops and fillets and sausages were arranged in neat, visceral piles, divided by arrangements of lemons and bundled herbs, and it all looked as nice as dead animals could. But it didn't stop with the familiar cuts. A selection of jars sprouted different sizes of birds' feet, and bowls of various organs were lined up in a neat constellation around them. A platter held unidentified, skinned heads, and in a glass jug what looked like a small mozzarella ball bobbed gently around to reveal a staring iris and milky pupil. Adams looked away and at the butcher instead, swallowing hard.

"Morning," Rory said.

The butcher didn't look up, chopping a limb into serving sizes, the cleaver driving through flesh and bone without hesitation. He was a huge man, head giving to shoulders without bothering about a neck, and the seams of his immaculate white shirt were strained to ripping point in a few places.

"Can we use your door?" Rory asked.

The butcher looked up at them finally. He had a heavy, hanging face, and small tusks jutted out of his jaw. He looked at the display case, then back at Rory.

Rory nodded. "Got some dog bones?"

The butcher waited.

"Three dog bones."

Still nothing.

"Three dog bones and some lamb chops."

Silence.

"Three dog bones, some lamb chops, and some braising steak."

The butcher finally ground into movement, selecting the meats from the display case and bundling them up in waxed paper. The bundles went into a paper bag, and Adams looked at Rory. "Shopping for the week?"

"There's no charge for the doors, but, you know. People have to make money somewhere."

The butcher handed Rory the bag, then held a portable card reader out.

Rory looked at Adams. "Any chance you can get it on expenses? I just bought a load of roofing tiles and I'm a bit strapped."

"Of course you are," she said, but clicked the wallet on her phone open and held it over the reader until it beeped. "Thanks," she said to the butcher.

He put the card reader down and picked up a large, freshly cleaned bone from among the debris on his bench, holding it out to her. It looked like something's femur, but she didn't like to think what.

"Oh." She shoved her phone back into her inside pocket

and took the thing gingerly, meat still clinging to it and cartilage gleaming palely at the joint. "Right."

"Cheers," Rory said, and headed for the door at the back of the shop.

The dogs and Adams followed, and as they pushed through into a large commercial kitchen she brandished the bone and said, "Can I put this in the bag?"

"Probably not," Rory said. "He gave it to you for a reason."

"Should we ask what the reason is?"

"He didn't seem too chatty."

"Great." She inspected the kitchen as they crossed it. There was no cooking range, just large double sinks and long stainless steel workbenches, all entirely empty and polished to an almost painful shine. A bank of walk-in fridges or freezers lined one wall, and Adams eyed them suspiciously. She didn't want to know what was inside.

There was a door by the sinks, and Rory paused at it. "Ready?"

"For what?"

"No idea," he admitted.

"Wait – you've not been through here before?"

"I was usually later in the day. I heard about this place as one of the entry points, but never had to use it."

"What's behind the doors in other places?" Adams asked.

"Well, other York. But also safeguards for in case anyone comes through without permission. The doorkeeper gives you a token – you know, a coin for the ferryman type thing."

"You're comparing this to Charon and the River Styx?"

"It was the first thing that came to mind."

"Well, great," Adams said, and waved him back. "I'd better go first, then, if this is the token."

"I can take it if you want—"

She was already pushing the door open, stepping out onto the cobbles of a back alley that looked no different to any other, red brick walls rising up around them and a drain sunk into the ground not far from the door. A moped was parked against the far wall, and a distinctly whiffy bin squatted next to it. Adams moved away from the door so Rory could get through, already starting to say something, then a *whuff* that seemed to echo in her bones exploded across the alley. A black dog with the build of a pit bull but taller than a Great Dane charged out of a crate next to the bin, truly impressive teeth bared in a snarl that drained all the strength from Adams' legs.

"*Run!*" Rory shouted, and hurled the bag of meat at the massive dog. Dandy was barking, but it sounded puny next to the beast's baying, and the creature kept coming. Dandy surged in front of Adams, swelling up out of Labrador retriever size and growling furiously as he rose to meet the creature. She grabbed a handful of his dreadlocks, trying to haul him back, but he was already too heavy to move, so she threw herself around him instead, facing down the giant dog and pointing the bone at it imperiously.

"*Sit!*" she yelled.

The dog dropped its hindquarters to the ground, sliding to a stop so close to her she could feel its breath on her face. Its head was level with hers, teeth at alarmingly short range, and Dandy panted over her shoulder, just as huge and growling steadily. She felt like a toddler abandoned in a wolf den. Dandy snarled, and she snapped, "Stop that."

The huge alley dog regarded her with eyes even darker than its coat, endless voids she could see herself reflected in. She held up the bone, and its gaze shifted to it.

"Lie down," she said.

"*Adams,*" Rory hissed, and she ignored him.

"*Lie down,*" she insisted, pointing at the ground. The big dog tried to grab the bone, and she pulled it away. "*Bad dog.*"

It whined, and slowly sank to the ground.

"Good dog," she said, and held the bone out. It took it very delicately, then started to get up. "Stay."

The dog stayed, and she took a couple of steps back, pulling Dandy with her. He came reluctantly, red eyes still on the creature. It watched them go, and once she'd reached what felt like a safe distance she said, "Alright. Off you go."

The dog got up and trotted back to its crate. Adams watched it set the bone down, then pick up a ragged stuffed toy and look back at her, ears pricked.

"Good boy," she said again, and its tail waved eagerly before putting the toy down and turning its attention to the bone. She looked at Dandy, finding him back to his favoured size. He whined, and she scuffled his ears. "Silly," she said to him. "Don't go picking fights." She looked around, and found Rory staring at her, his hands gripping Midge's and Pinto's collars. "Alright?"

"Is he always that size?"

Adams looked back at the black dog. "I suppose? He looks pretty comfortable with it."

"No, Adams. Your invisible dog got very visible, and he's also very big."

"Oh." She looked at Dandy. "Yeah, he did that once before. Angry size, perhaps."

"What size is he now?"

"Bit bigger than your two. That seems to be his favourite, but if he gets nervous he shrinks."

Rory thought about it for a moment, then nodded. "Sure. Why would that be any weirder than being invisible?"

"Exactly." Adams looked down the alley, toward where it opened onto a busier street. She could see people passing, clutching shopping bags and coffees, everything outlined in that curious brightness that had nothing to do with the sun that was trying to creep its way between the walls. "Can we find the Blighted Basilisk from this side, do you think?"

"Probably easier than from our side," he said, and looked back at the dog. "I lost the meat."

"You didn't lose it, you panicked and threw it at the big dog."

"That could've been my dinner for the next week."

"Far too much red meat for one person," Adams said, heading toward the street.

"I hope he eats it," Rory said, falling into step with her, the dogs back to their customary spot at his heels. "I don't want it going to waste."

"You could go back and get it."

"No, that's alright."

She gave him a sideways look. "That just about ate up my food budget for the rest of the month, you know."

"Ah. Well, you'll just have to come to mine for dinner, then, won't you?" He grinned when she narrowed her eyes at him, and they stepped out into the surging streets of the other York, strange and familiar all at once.

8

TREE-LINED AVENUES

They emerged into the narrow streets of the Shambles, which were busier than they had been before their traverse of the butcher's shop, but not yet as overrun as they'd get later. There were more workers and fewer tourists, and the scents of coffee and frying bacon and woodsmoke snaked through the pedestrians, singing siren songs of cosy corners and slow mornings.

Adams looked at Rory, raising her eyebrows. "It looks the same. There's even a bloody Costa."

He lifted his chin at the street. "Look properly."

"I am." A young woman ducking furtively into a shop door. An elderly man leaning out of a window, a cigarette in one hand, and casually dropping something to the street below, not looking as it fell. Someone with their hood pulled well forward caught it without pausing their saunter down the street. A well-dressed woman cutting through the walkers with her eyes on bags rather than faces. A shop selling postcards and souvenir T-shirts, open too early to make sense. Nothing that required her to *do* anything right now, simply things she noted and filed, habitual and aware.

Rory looked from the shops to her, and said, "You can't be."

"I always do," she said, a little more sharply than she intended.

"You always do *as a copper*," he said. "That wasn't how you saw werewolves, was it?"

She scowled at him, but closed her eyes for a moment, aware of the chill air on her cheeks, the sun not reaching them between the buildings. The scents were stronger when she wasn't looking, carrying hints of burnt sugar and charred rosemary, and a faint whiff of ozone, like rain on hot tarmac, even with summer still lurking well out of reach. Someone laughed, quick and high, and someone else shouted in a language she didn't recognise, not even remotely. A dog barked, and somewhere there was the rhythmic sound of great bellows.

None of it was *exactly* out of place in the centre of a Yorkshire city. None of it was *exactly* inexplicable, or unfamiliar, or ominous.

But none of it was quite right, either.

She opened her eyes and looked *properly*.

The shop selling T-shirts and postcards was still there, still open, but one of the T-shirts had a werewolf on it, howling at York cathedral, and the slogan said *I went wild in York!* A sign above the T-shirts advertised that many designs were available in Winged, Troll, and Extra Limb sizes.

The elderly man leaning out of the window licked his eyes with a quick flick of his tongue, and took another drag on what was clearly a pipe almost as tall as he was.

The shop the young woman had crept into had a sign above the door which read, *Madame Melvin's Faun-Friendly Therapy. Fix your compulsion to eat the laundry today!*

The well-dressed woman whom Adams had thought was eyeing up bags for a little dipping was instead trying to keep

the many limbs of what appeared to be an octopus out of
them. She had the creature clutched to her chest in a gold-
fish bowl that was strapped into a harness, and Adams
could hear her saying, "Now, you're doing really well. Just—
No that is not your chicken put it back!" The chicken in question, a half-grown bird plucked from the pocket of a stout
man in a bobble hat, screeched in fright, and the man spun
around.

"Thieving sodding cephalopods!" he yelled. "Give me
back my chick!"

"Sorry, sorry," the woman said, trying to grab the chicken,
but the octopus was passing the startled bird from tentacle to
tentacle, keeping it out of her reach. "I'm trying to rehabili-
tate him. He's a rescue from Blackpool."

"Well it's going *bloody well,* isn't it?" the man demanded.

"It's only been a month! One has to have patience!"

"One has to give me my damn chicken back!"

Adams rubbed the back of her neck with one hand.
"Right," she said.

"Got it?" Rory asked.

"Yes. Why couldn't I see it straight away, though? We're
through the door, or whatever. Surely it should just be *there.*"

"Not *here,* though," Rory said, tapping his own forehead
lightly. "You've still got to make the same switch as with the
shop. Your brain gets all protective and tries to cover
things up."

Adams didn't answer straight away. Over and over she
was reminded of all the things she must've walked right past
in London, seeing them as something else entirely, or not
seeing them at all. And maybe plenty had been innocuous,
like octopuses undergoing rehabilitation from criminal
activities, but not all of them would have been.

She gave Rory a sideways look. "Do you see it all the
time?"

"No," he said. "Might've realised I was renting my buildings to werewolves if that had been the case."

"To be fair, they looked pretty human when they weren't furry."

He nodded, looking up and down the street. "Where d'you want to start?"

"The herbalist's. By the time we've done that there might be someone at the pub and we can see if anyone was hanging about asking the wrong sort of questions."

"Fair enough." Rory headed onto the street, and smiled at an elderly woman dragging a tartan shopping trolley behind her. "Morning. Could you—"

"No," she said, not slowing. "Don't want a new phone plan."

"It's not—"

"Or life insurance."

"I wasn't—"

"And I've got my own religion. Don't need yours." She toddled past.

"Yes, but—"

The woman didn't interrupt this time, but a large and very toothy lizard's head emerged from the tartan trolley and hissed at Rory. He jumped back, pulling Midge and Pinto with him, and the woman kept walking. The lizard stuck its tongue out, then vanished again.

"Good effort," Adams said. "I take it you don't know where the herbalist's is, then?"

"I don't," he admitted.

"You're a rubbish guide." She stepped into the street and looked up at the elderly man, still leaning in his window. "Hiya," she called.

The man blinked down at her, translucent eyelids gliding horizontally across his eyes then retreating. He blew a spiral of smoke into the warming sky and said, "Yah? You want?" He held the pipe up, with some difficulty.

"No thanks. Do you know where Woad in the Wold is? The herbalist's?"

He considered it, taking another long drag on the pipe. "Yah."

"Where?"

He pointed down the street. "Vun block dere. Two block right. Left to river."

The river. Adams swore to herself, but just gave the man a wave that was part salute. "Cheers."

"Yah." He settled back onto his windowsill, blinking contentedly at the sun.

"You can go back," Adams said to Rory. "I can take it from here."

"No," Rory said, tucking his hands into his pockets and almost dislodging the leash.

"Yes. Police." She waved at herself.

"I wouldn't say that too loud around here."

She glanced around. "They're not all going to be criminals."

"No, but Folk are pretty self-governing. You don't want them thinking you're coming in here telling them what to do."

"Fine, I won't." They looked at each other for a moment, Rory smiling faintly, and eventually she sighed. "Alright. Let's go." She turned and joined the flow of pedestrians, trying not to step on anyone's tail. That would be the last thing they needed, her starting a Folk/human war over a bruised extremity.

THE ROUTE TO Woad in the Wold took them out of the Shambles and down to the River Ouse, past cafes and bars and newsagents and clothes shops, stalls selling phone cases and cheap handbags, pharmacies and shoe shops. Taxis plastered with advertising and buses promising cheap fares and punctual service lumbered through the streets, and couriers darted past on bikes. White vans sprouting ladders and muddy wheels paused at traffic lights, and motorcycles grumbled moodily at the interruption. It was the same as any other high street in the country, and entirely different, too. Among the usual advertising for mobile phone companies and travel agencies were promises to shift-lock homes, or to build personalised altars for sacrifices. The fridges of energy drinks held bundles of trimmed grass and fish in jars alongside the caffeine-heavy cans, and the shoe shops offered hoof-fitting services.

And just as Adams had been able to glimpse Folk shops among the human ones, here she glimpsed human ones among the Folk, a WHSmith here, a Boots there, stitching the worlds together and catering to everyone. Humans walked through the crowds too, indifferent or oblivious, some carrying that slightly sharper edge she'd come to associate with those who were clinging to the cracks between the walls, and a pair of uniformed police officers turned down one of the streets, one eating a sausage roll with evident enjoyment, the other with his dark eyes on a multi-limbed, chitinous creature with its back to an electronic shop and its tail fishing surreptitiously in a bin of headphones. The dark-eyed police officer looked vaguely familiar, and Adams frowned at him, then dismissed it. It didn't matter right now. She couldn't even begin to make sense of how the whole place worked, and she set the question aside for later. She'd ask the cat about it and see if he'd be a bit more forthcoming. He owed her for the early morning wake-up call.

Sunlight glittered on the brown surface of the river as it came into view, sparkling brightly among the ducks and swans paddling purposefully along its edges. Adams closed her hand around her own duck, eyeing the nearest bridge distrustfully. Nothing moved in its shadows, though, and there was no fog about. The fog was when things got really dodgy.

"There it is," Rory said, pointing along the uneven street. The area seemed to be in the throes of urban renewal, the riverside buildings polished up, seating and green spaces filling what had likely once been derelict areas. A couple of restaurants were already open, metal tables and chairs set out with cushions and menus, as if they weren't in the midst of a North Yorkshire spring. But given she could also see the flood markers with the max well above the heights of the restaurants, she supposed they traded in optimism.

A blackboard was set up at the edge of an alley, an arrow pointing down it and *Woad in the Wold! Hexes, poisons, and curses!* printed on it in big white letters. *Also takeaway tea and cake!* was written in smaller print underneath, with a smiley face.

"Curse or cake?" Rory asked.

"Depends. I quite like the idea of a hex. One to keep people away."

"I'm going to choose to believe that wasn't aimed at me."

They headed down the alley, shadows cast to their sides before the buildings swallowed the sun, the three dogs trotting along with them. The shop was halfway down the block of unevenly connected houses, marked by another blackboard on the pavement outside next to a two-person, pink metal table and two matching chairs. A leaning cactus sprouted from a pot in the middle of the table, and a sign on the wall listed a dozen different herbal teas, all of which sounded to Adams suspiciously like varieties of less legal herbs. A shorter-than-regulation door separated the table from a cluttered, fat-bellied display window with more signs stuck to the glass, advertising massage and yoga and artificial gills.

The door was shut, but it pushed open under her hand, and she stepped inside, having to duck to get under the lintel. Three worn stone steps led to the shop floor, and there was a *thunk* behind her, followed by Rory muttering, "Ouch."

"Mind your head."

"Thanks so much."

She glanced back at him, spotting Midge and Pinto peering anxiously through the display window. Dandy had come in with her, though, and was sniffing a sack of dried lentils curiously.

"Morning!" someone called from the depths of the shop. "Be right with you."

It wasn't a big space, every scrap of wall covered with shelves sporting herbs and creams and tinctures, and a couple of free-standing shelving units in the centre were given over to organic seeds and pulses and ominous-looking dried mushrooms. At the back of the room was a counter, and a refrigerated display case a fraction the size of the one in the butcher's, sporting far fewer dead things, thankfully. Instead it held ready-made burping cures and insomnia treatments, none of which had prices on them. Adams patted her leg, coaxing Dandy to her. The last thing she needed was him eating something in here. She'd already spent far too much money on this little excursion.

A rounded, older woman in a flannel shirt with the sleeves rolled up emerged from a door which looked like it led to a kitchen, wiping her hands on a towel. She had an apron on over her shirt and jeans, with *Woad in the Wold* embroidered on the chest, and she smiled at them broadly, exposing a chipped canine.

"What can I get you? Oil for troubled waters? A piece of peace? De-selective hearing?" She winked at Rory on the last one, and he snorted, turning it into a cough.

"No," Adams said. "Thanks anyway. I'm looking for Violet Brennan – I heard she works here?"

"Ah," the woman said. "Perhaps a little pinch of rosy glasses? A splash of starry eyes?"

Rory examined a jar of beans, his mouth twitching.

"Just Violet Brennan."

"Not even some kindled feelings?"

"Definitely not," Adams said, and Rory took the beans to look at in the light from the window.

"No one has any sense of romance anymore," the woman said, and looked at Dandy. "Oh. You can't have him in here."

"No dogs?"

"No … him." She waved at Dandy. "Funny aura."

Adams found herself having to bite back the words, *you've got a funny aura*, and instead said, "Sorry. I'll take him outside. Violet, though?"

The woman sighed, turned to the back of the shop, and yelled, *"Violet!"* in a tone that made Adams immediately check she hadn't put a glass down without a coaster. The woman looked past Adams at Rory. "Do *you* want a heartfelt moment?"

"Never on a Saturday," he said, and the woman huffed, wandering back behind the counter as a younger woman popped through the kitchen door, her hands a luminous pink.

"Sorry!" she said cheerfully. "I was squeezing beetroot."

"No point," the older woman said, examining the display cabinet with a scowl. "No one wants heartfelt moments anymore. It's all get-rich-quick charms and skin smoothers."

Violet ignored her, smiling at Adams. She had a round, open face, with curly blonde hair and light blue eyes, and was in no need of skin smoothers. "Can I help you?" she asked, wiping her hands on a tea towel that was already covered in luminous stains. "You're not here about the faery circle, are you? Only there aren't many at this time of year, so the hunts are pretty booked up—"

"No," Adams said, and glanced at the older woman, who was showing no inclination to leave the counter. "Can I have a word outside?"

Violet's smile faded. "Of course. Is something wrong?"

"I just need to take my dog out."

Violet looked around, puzzled. "Dog?"

Dandy panted up at the young woman, investigating the tea towel still hanging from her hand. "Never mind," Adams said, and beckoned Violet after her, out into the chilly, unsettled day. The sky was still clear, but the wind had teeth and whispered threats of falling back into winter. Violet shivered, hugging her arms around her, and Adams looked at Rory, who'd followed them out as well. She raised her eyebrows at him, but he just leaned against the wall and grinned back, so she supposed she wasn't getting rid of him. She turned to Violet.

"Violet Brennan, yes?"

"I mean, obviously."

"My name's …" She hesitated, then swallowed the *DI*. "My name's Adams, and I'm looking into a little problem that's come up. You were apprenticed at Ash & Yew?"

Violet made a face. "Yes."

"You didn't like it?"

"I mean, it was okay? But I mostly went because of Heather, and then all the work was with metal. Which is cool, you know, but it's very *human*."

Adams looked at Dandy, who had rolled onto his back next to Violet, offering his belly up for a scratch. She still showed no sign of seeing him, so evidently she wasn't that *not*-human. "What were you hoping for?"

"Nature magic," Violet said. "I mean, she has her ceremonies here and there, but they're very erratic, and you never *learn* anything. I thought working with her would mean she'd actually teach me, but instead I was stuck sweeping the workshop and picking bits of stainless steel out of the garden for Charles."

"They weren't clear with you when you signed up?"

Violet shook her head. Her hair was a ragged, curly bob, and it bounced cheerfully with the movement. "I stuck with it for a while, but, ugh. You can only take so many metal splinters and watch them shout at each other so many times, you know?"

Adams nodded. "Did you work with Charles on the guardians?"

"A bit."

"He said it was your idea to give them personality."

Violet sighed, rubbing the back of her neck. She was only wearing a T-shirt, and her arms looked softly rounded and pale under a smattering of inexpert tattoos. "Yeah. I thought it'd make them more appealing to people, but I forgot they'd still treat them as machines. I feel kind of bad about it now, you know? Like I gave them a whole bunch of new puppies to kick. People suck."

"What people?"

"Well …" She hesitated, looking around, then said, "Charles was alright, but Heather *hated* it. I think she felt I was taking the mick out of her, or nature, or whatever. I had to leave after that. She made it unbearable, and I wasn't enjoying it anyway."

"How did you give the guardians personality?" Rory asked, and Violet gave him an odd, assessing glance that was far older than her wide-eyed enthusiasm of earlier.

"I just suggested a couple of changes to the charms," she said.

"How did you know how to do that?" Adams asked.

"I looked it up," Violet said, shivering and rubbing her arms. "What's this about?"

"Something's gone missing from the shop."

Violet took a step back, a scowl tightening her face. "And you're here talking to me?"

"No one's accusing you of anything," Adams said. "I'm just trying to find out who might've had access to the shop."

"It's Heather, isn't it? She sent you here."

"Did you have a key?"

"*No*," Violet snapped. "No one has a key, unless Charles got sozzled and gave one away, and even then there was Wilfred in the garden and Fergus in the workshop. If Heather says I did, it's because she's setting me up. I *knew* she didn't like me."

"Why didn't she?" Rory asked, and Violet gave him an almost disgusted look.

"*Of course* you wouldn't get it. *Men.*" She turned back to Adams. "Tell Heather to stuff it up her tree-lined avenues."

Adams started to answer, but Violet was already stomping back down the steps into the shop, slamming the door rather dramatically behind her. A couple of flyers flew off the inside and drifted to the floor, and through the glass Adams saw Violet gesticulating wildly. The older woman at the counter nodded a couple of times, then gave Adams the universal sign for *I'm watching you,* then a couple of other universal signs. She sighed.

Rory looked at Adams. "Well. That wasn't very useful."

"No," she agreed, tapping her fingers on her thighs. "She couldn't see Dandy."

"No?"

"No. She couldn't see Dandy, but she knew enough about

Heather and Charles to find an apprenticeship there, and to be able to mess about with charms."

Rory pushed himself off the wall, glancing into the shop. Adams couldn't see either woman, but she was sure they were still observed. "You think she's involved?" he asked. "Or do you think what she said about Heather setting her up is right?"

Adams adjusted her scarf to keep the breeze out. It was trying its best to get through to her bones. "I can't see Heather bothering to set anyone up. Or being threatened by a younger woman, assuming that's what Violet meant."

"So she's involved?"

"I don't know." *Unless Charles got sozzled and gave one away*. The pub was feeling more and more as if it might be the most likely culprit, and no wonder Charles had been trying to sort things without Heather knowing. It didn't answer how anyone had got past Fergus, but one question at a time. One clue led to the next, and the next. She turned toward the Shambles. "Come on. Let's see if the pub's open yet."

Rory fell into step with her without comment, and they headed away from the river and back into the heart of town, Adams happy to leave the spectre of bridges behind.

They walked in silence for a bit, before Rory said, "She seemed kind of familiar, didn't you think?"

"Violet?"

"Yeah. She looked like someone. An actor, maybe?"

Adams thought about it. There *had* been something familiar about her, but then she'd thought that about the police officer, too. She was seeing ghosts. But she said, "Maybe," and took her phone out to check it. It was after ten now, and there still hadn't been anything from Collins or Isha. It wasn't like they'd had a lot of time, but the silence was making her uneasy.

"I wish I could think what I knew her from," Rory said. "It's annoying me."

"The whole situation's annoying me," Adams said. "It's not adding up."

"You could tell me about it. Fresh eyes and all that."

"No, best not."

Rory shrugged. "Up to you. But I'm here, in the middle of it, so you may as well."

"You're not in the middle of it, you're my tour guide for the morning," she said. "You should be happy about that."

"Not so much."

She didn't bother answering. It was like he thought werewolves were the only things to be worried about. Werewolves were overgrown puppies. She glanced back at the river vanishing behind them, tasting copper and salt and old, thick mud at the back of her throat.

There were much worse things than werewolves.

9

NO PAY, NO PLAY

THE BLIGHTED BASILISK WAS IN THE SAME SPOT IN THIS version of York as in the other, one of those points of contact that bled through the worlds, or dimensions, or whatever the hell they were calling them. Adams still didn't know. The pub looked more appealing on this side, but it still wasn't exactly somewhere she imagined anyone popping in for a little mid-shopping refreshment. Hanging baskets were suspended above the front, sporting a collection of dandelions and dead plants, as well as what she suspected was the bleached skeleton of a rat, and a large wooden bench was installed below the window. A very old man with legs too short to reach the ground perched on it, clutching a pint glass with a handle precariously in both hands. He slurped it as they approached, his flat cap almost sliding into the mug, then stared at them with small, sharp eyes. A whippet lay under the bench, watching Dandy with its ears back and teeth bared.

"We don't do brunch," the man said. "Or sodding *buck's fizz.*"

"Good to know," Adams said, pushing the door open.

"Damn *tourists*," the man muttered, returning to his drink.

Inside, it took a moment for Adams' eyes to adjust to the low light shed by dusty wall sconces and table lamps with cracked shades. It was cleaner than she'd expected, just worn and tired, fraying at the edges, a working pub where things were replaced as they broke and not before. Old oil paintings faded almost beyond recognition decorated the walls, along with the ubiquitous vintage Guinness prints and mirrors with ancient gold paint proclaiming the names of unknown brewers. Nooks formed by wooden benches with red upholstery lined the walls, and plain, solid tables with matching chairs filled the floor between them and the bar, which was more heavy wood with a low overhang of shelves. A woman with mossy hair and a tangle of tattoos on her arms watched them approach as she dried a glass and set it out of sight on the overhang somewhere.

"Morning," Adams said, when they'd reached the bar without the woman saying anything.

"No coffee," the woman said.

"Okay. I understand Charles Worthington drinks here."

"And?"

"I'm trying to find out if there's been anyone new around lately. Someone a bit too interested in him, perhaps."

The woman leaned her forearms on the bar, eyeing Adams with oval pupils. "There has been," she said.

"Oh? Could you describe them?"

"Take a look in the mirror," she said, straightening up. "Charles's business is his own, just like anyone else. It's not for giving away to strangers."

"Sure," Adams said. "I'm just trying to help him out."

"Then get him to come in with you." She pointed at the door. "Off you go."

"What's happening, Kaz?" a deep voice asked, and Adams turned to see three people gathered at one of the furthest tables. The speaker was standing, a big man wearing a black suit coat which strained at the shoulders over a neon green T-shirt, his head as dark and bald and bare as his taloned feet.

"They're leaving," Kaz said.

"We're following up on something for Charles," Adams said, examining the group. One was in some sort of velour leisure suit, or seemed to be. She was pale and sleek and smoothly curved, with dark hair spilling over her shoulders, and it was hard to make out her exact shape, as if it shifted when Adams looked at her. The third man was skinny and tanned and angular, one knee pulled up to his chest as he rolled a cigarette with sharp fingers. "He said he drank here. Is one of you Byx?"

No one answered.

"Dartmoor?"

Still no response, but the skinny man twitched.

"Snoop?"

"What?" a reedy voice demanded from the door, and they turned to look at the old man and his whippet. "What d'you want?"

"You're Snoop?" Adams asked.

He pounded his frail chest, then coughed. "Oldest were in York, me."

"You've got to stop saying that, Snoop," the big man said. "You know what the packs are like about privacy—"

"Shut your mouth, Pip! I'm *old*. I can do what I want, and sod the packs!"

Adams nodded slightly. "Can we talk to you all?"

The skinny man licked his cigarette with a forked tongue. "What d'you want?"

"Dartmoor or Byx?"

"I'm Byx," the woman said, her voice a purr. She had big,

liquid, eyes and very sharp teeth. "*You* can call me whatever you want, though."

"Thanks. I just want to know if anyone's been unusually interested in Charles, or in Ash & Yew. Trying to join you for drinks or something."

"This about the robbery?" the skinny man asked. Dartmoor, Adams supposed.

"He told you?"

"Just about crying in his whisky every night since," Snoop said, tottering to the table with his beer still clutched in both hands. "Silly sod."

"Don't be mean," Pip said, turning back to the table. Tattered, leathery wings protruded from custom gaps in his coat, and were folded tight to his back. "He's worried about Heather being upset at him."

"Then he shouldn't spend all his time here, should he?" Kaz asked.

"So can you help us?" Adams asked.

"Play you for it," Dartmoor said, tapping a stack of cards in the centre of the table.

"No," Adams said.

"No play, no pay," Snoop said, and cackled.

"Look, it's just a question—" Adams stopped as the four turned to the table, dismissing her. She looked at Kaz, who shrugged.

"Can't help you."

"I'll play," Rory said, unzipping his jacket.

"What?" Adams asked.

"What's your stake?" Snoop asked.

"Companionship," Byx said, sharp teeth flashing in a grin. "Come and play with me in the waves."

"Byx, *no*," Pip said. "Behave."

"I've got some cash," Rory offered.

All four players sighed dramatically.

"*Boring,*" Snoop said. "How 'bout one of your dogs?"

"Absolutely not."

"Leave it," Adams said to Rory. "I'll come back with Charles."

"But maybe they'll say something different without him here to guide things," he said in a low voice, then added to the players, "Land Rover?"

The group looked at each other. "Coat," Dartmoor said, looking Rory up and down lazily. "I like your coat."

"Deal," Rory said, and pulled up a chair.

"Rory," Adams started, and Snoop flapped a shrivelled hand at her.

"Back to the bar with you. No peeking!"

Rory looked at her. "It's okay. I've got this."

And she didn't know if he did or not, but he had a point about getting answers without Charles being here, and she couldn't play cards. Not and win, anyway. Family card games had been a foregone conclusion when she was a kid, her brothers mostly betting on how much she'd lose by. So she went back to the bar, sat down, and hoped.

ADAMS LEANED ON THE BAR, fingers drumming nervously on the rich-hued, varnished surface, ignoring the old beer mats and dents from ancient fights. She couldn't hear what was being said at the table, the players talking in low voices. Rory was sitting with his back to her, presumably so she couldn't peek at the other players' cards and tip him off, but when he turned his head to say something to Pip, who was sitting next to him, she could see the easy curve of his smile, the corners of his eyes crinkling. Pip laughed, and Rory leaned back in his chair, relaxed and assured all at once. Midge and Pinto were lying on the floor next to him, the whippet peering at them with nervous, white-rimmed eyes. She wished she hadn't brought him with her. What was he *doing*, playing poker with a pack of Folk who were absolutely going to fleece him? He'd lose his coat, his Land Rover, *and* his dogs, and have to go and be a companion to Byx in the waves, whatever that meant.

"Here," Kaz said, and slid a mug across the bar to Adams.

She looked at it. "What's this?"

"Coffee."

"I thought you didn't do coffee?"

"I don't, but you're going to wear dents in my bar if you keep that up." She took a sip from her own mug, watching Adams with dark brown eyes. Adams had thought her arms were tattooed, but now she looked more closely she could see it was the skin itself, warmly textured with whorls and birds' eyes and dappled grain.

Adams took the mug and sniffed it. It wasn't coffee shop standard, but it wasn't instant, either. She took a sip, and nodded at Kaz. "Thanks."

"Sure." She set her mug down, and Adams caught a whiff of something earthy and herbal. "Your man there seems to be settling in well."

"Not my man. But yes, a little too well."

Kaz gave her an amused, sideways look. "He was quick enough to play, to help you out."

"I know, but ..."

"He not your thing?"

Adams shrugged, meeting the bartender's eyes. "Some-times. Sometimes not."

Kaz grinned at that. "Variety's the sprite of life and all that."

"Spice."

She looked thoughtful. "That makes more sense. Sprites

are a bloody pain, so I thought it was to do with them being a nuisance. Never understood why that was a desirable thing."

Adams snorted, and glanced back at the table. Everyone was intent on their cards. "A young woman called Violet come in here much?"

"Here and there," Kaz said.

"Did she and Charles get on?"

"They didn't *not* get on."

"How do you mean?"

Kaz sipped her tea, or infusion, or compost water, whatever it was. "You ask a lot of questions."

"I told you, I'm trying to help Charles out."

The bartender got up, took a jar of dog treats from the overhead shelves, and fished one out, leaning over the bar with it. Dandy looked up from his spot next to Adams, and took the biscuit delicately. "Distinctive sort of pup."

"I suppose."

"I heard you were very *police*-y."

Adams looked at her. "You heard?"

"Rumours spread. People talk. You made a bit of an impression at that auction a while back. Plus not many people are willing to tackle a were pack."

"To be fair, I wasn't aware they were werewolves to start."

"*Weres*, not werewolves, or old Snoop there'll bite your ankles."

"Like only say *faeries* with an A-E?"

Pip looked around at them, eyebrows raised, and Kaz lifted her mug to him. He nodded and went back to the game. She looked back at Adams as she took down a couple of pint glasses. "It's advisable, yes." She started one glass on the Guinness before slowly pulling an ale into the other. *Wand Wobbler* was the name on the tap label, and Adams was sure she wouldn't come across it in an average pub.

"Well, if you *heard*," she said aloud, "then you know police-y comes with the territory."

Kaz nodded, turning off the Guinness to let the beer settle, and running a lager called *Toadspittle* into a pint mug. "Yet you're letting your mate there play a game for info instead of shouting it out of us."

"Sometimes different techniques are called for."

The two beers went onto a tray, and Kaz busied herself making a cranberry and vodka, sticking a slice of orange on the side of the glass. "Good call," she said. "Me? I'm not bothered what you do. Some people are going to be, though. Work out a way to keep out of the way of cats, and along comes a detective and a not-dog. It's annoying."

"Well, I suppose I'll just have to deal with people being bothered when it comes to it."

"Yes," Kaz said, topping off the Guinness. "You will." She ferried the drinks to the table, handing Pip the vodka, Snoop the lager, Dartmoor the ale, and Byx the Guinness. "Anything for you, love?" she asked Rory.

"No, thanks."

"Right you are." She patted his shoulder, collected the empties and came back to the bar, looking at Adams. "Violet was in here a bit when she was apprenticed with Charles, mostly to ask him if he was going to work on whatever project they had going. She was quite keen. He'd say he'd do it when he was ready, and she'd storm off."

"So they did argue."

"Violet argued. Charles was as oblivious to her as he is to everyone else telling him to go home. Heather's the only one who can move him, but mostly she doesn't bother. You don't live intertwined lives for that long without making allowances for each other."

Adams sipped her coffee. "What allowances does he make for her, then?"

Kaz smiled slightly. "You do like your questions, don't you?"

She shrugged.

"Heather is old, and deeply connected to the woods and the earth. Lots of young women – and older women – see her as something like a goddess. She doesn't disabuse them of that notion."

Adams wrinkled her nose. "She takes advantage of them?"

"They're more than willing." Kaz swirled her drink, releasing more of that earthy odour. "But, yes. The power dynamic isn't great."

"Would she ever want to be rid of Charles, do you think?"

"Who knows what a relationship looks like from the inside? But I doubt it. They're two halves of a whole. Earth and wood, steel and fire. I'm not sure one could exist without the other."

"Did Heather and Violet get along?"

"No idea. Violet was only in here to find Charles, and Heather only ever comes by if it's been a few days and he hasn't made it home."

Adams grimaced. "Right. And the card games. He lose a lot?"

Kaz shrugged. "I don't play. You'd be better asking them." She nodded at the table as a cheer went up, and Rory raised both fists in triumph.

"Misspent youth for the win!" he shouted, and the other four booed him.

"You're about as misspent as an Eton old boy," Dartmoor said, pushing his cards away.

"Exactly my point. See how many of them become politicians? And they're *excellent* at hustling." Rory twisted in his chair. "Adams, I won."

"Got that," she said, as Kaz snickered.

He waved Adams to join them. "Come and ask your questions."

"Is this what they teach you in posh schools, then?" Snoop demanded. "I thought it were like what fork to use and stuff."

"No, I never figured that out," Rory said. "And my aunt stole most of my silver, so ..."

Byx stroked his arm. "I can show you where to find more."

"No thanks, it's a pain. Always needs polishing." He shuffled his seat around to make room for Adams as she drew a chair up from a nearby table.

"Charles, then," she said. "Anyone new hanging around? Asking questions?"

"There were that lad," Snoop said. "Pretty boy. All a bit lost."

"He *was* pretty," Byx said. "I liked his skin." She looked speculatively at Adams. "I like your skin, too. Can I touch it?"

"You'd need to buy me dinner first, at least. Who's this lad?"

"Frank. Percy. Martin. Something like that," Dartmoor said, and drummed long, thin fingers on the table, staring at Rory. "I really liked that jacket."

Rory looked down at it. "I got it in Oxfam, to be fair."

"Frank?" Adams asked. "Percy? Which?"

"Joe," Pip said.

"Yes, Joe," Byx said. "Such soft skin, and all a bit lost. He had metal he wanted to sell Charles, I think."

"Charles didn't recognise him, though," Kaz said. She was leaning on the front of the bar, brown arms folded. "So he hadn't bought from him before."

"Charles doesn't always recognise people, though," Pip said. "He can be a bit absentminded."

"Does Joe have a last name?" Adams asked.

The group looked at each other. "Not that I heard," Pip

said, straightening his luminous T-shirt over the swell of his belly. It had a koala drinking a beer on it.

"And that was all Joe wanted? To sell him metal? Why come here and not the shop?"

Snoop slurped his pint. "He reckoned he'd already sold him the metal. He wanted into the game."

"He wanted *companionship*," Byx said, stretching.

"Put it away," Dartmoor said to her. "Snoop's right. He wanted to play."

"Popular, is it?" Rory asked. "At the risk of being rude, it doesn't seem too high stakes if you were willing to play for my charity shop jacket."

"It was because Charles was playing," Kaz said, when the others just looked at each other. "Honestly, all you lot can see is the bloody cards. I thought the kid was maybe hoping to get himself an apprenticeship, but I didn't see how. He was even more human than you, posh boy."

"Rory," Rory said.

"*Rory*," Byx repeated, rolling the Rs slowly. Her skin was very pale, the contrast stark with her dark hair and eyes. "I like it."

"I had a dog called Rory," Snoop said. "Right mutt, it were."

"I've been called that before," Rory said affably, and the others laughed.

Adams managed not to roll her eyes. "How did Joe find this place if he was so human, then?"

"He came in the back way," Kaz said. "Someone must've put him in the door, but no knowing who. They weren't with him when he turned up, and once he knew the way he could just keep using it. That's how it usually works."

Adams leaned back in her chair, looking around the bar. "Where's the back way?"

"I'll show you. It's a quick route back to your York anyway."

It wasn't a dismissal, not quite, but Adams nodded. They weren't getting anything more here. She could ask Charles if Joe had been to Ash & Yew, and find out if Heather and Violet had had a falling out at the same time, when Heather herself wasn't hanging over Charles's shoulder. She got up, looking at the table. "Thanks."

They nodded back at her, friendly enough.

"Come back any time, Rory," Dartmoor said, fiddling with his cigarette. "I still fancy that jacket."

"I'll keep it in mind."

"And it's not always low stakes," Byx said, her voice low and smooth. "We'll play for your very soul if it suits us."

Silence followed that, and Adams waited for Pip to contradict her, or Kaz to tell them to behave, but no one said anything at all.

"Right," Rory said finally. "I might pass on that one." He got up, the dogs scrambling to their feet as well, and passed them a biscuit each, then handed Snoop one when he held his hand out. The old man promptly started gumming it.

"Oh. I thought…" Rory stopped, looked at the whippet, gave it another biscuit, then held one out vaguely until Dandy took it.

"Eighteen quid," Kaz said to Adams.

"What?"

"Three pints and the vodka. Happy hour prices." She held her hand out.

"Bloody *hell*." Adams dug her phone out of her pocket. "Card?" She wasn't going to argue. It'd only put the price up.

"Obviously." Kaz went to the bar, found a card reader, and tapped the amount in, then turned it to Adams, who held her phone over it, muttering. It beeped, and Kaz grinned. "I'll show you the way through."

"Thanks." Adams tucked her phone back into her pocket, trying not to think of her bank account, and looked at Rory. "Ready?"

"Whenever you are," he said, and they followed Kaz as she led them to a set of creaking stairs at the back corner of the pub. An arrow pointed down, with *Toiletes* painted on it, as if someone hadn't been sure if they were writing in French or English and had chosen something in between, just to cover all bases.

"Down to the bottom, into the loos – don't mind any splashing, you'll be fine on the way out – and into the door marked *Boiler*. Straight ahead three junctions, left at the fourth."

"Got it," Rory said, and headed down the stairs. Midge and Pinto whined, but followed with their tails down and their ears back.

Adams took a step down, then stopped and looked at Kaz. "What stakes do they play for?"

"You heard them. Whatever suits."

"Did Joe play, in the end?"

Kaz shrugged. "Maybe, maybe not. Believe it or not, detective, it gets busy in here. I can't watch everyone."

Adams nodded. "Sure. Do you know what sort of stakes Charles plays with, then? I get the feeling it's not so much money in here. Guardians? Charms?"

Kaz crossed her arms over her chest, strong and brown. "I run a bar, not a day care. You'd have to play them to find out, and I don't recommend it. Not for either of you. I'm not sure your mate there will have quite such an easy time of it now they have his measure. They're not as daft as they seem." She lifted her chin at the stairs. "Ask Charles if you want more info."

Adams watched her for a moment, as solid and deep-rooted as the building itself, then took a card from her pocket and held it out. "Call me if Joe comes in?"

Kaz took the card without looking at it. "Won't do a lot for my reputation, calling the filth in on the customers."

"Might do if it's protecting your regulars."

Kaz smiled suddenly, easy and amused. "Maybe. Or maybe I'll just call you anyway." She dropped her a wink and turned away. "Mind how you go."

"Um … right. Thanks." Adams loosened her scarf, suddenly far too warm, and trotted down the stairs into a murky dimness, the light yellow and flickering and the floor unpleasantly damp. She could smell toilet cleaner and old beer and a faint, swampy scent that was very unlike any bathroom she'd ever been in before.

"Alright?" Rory asked.

"Sure," she said. The door to the toilets was ahead of them, spelled right this time, and she headed for it, grabbing a handful of Dandy's dreadlocks to hold him back as he tried to push past. She didn't like the mention of splashing, and as soon as the door was open she heard it, a slow, lazy sound, as of something large and curious turning toward them. A row of three cubicles faced an ornate, oval mirror with two sinks under it, and beyond them the *Boiler* door waited innocuously, bland and distant. Something splashed again, and water spilled out from under the middle cubicle door.

"Don't like that," Rory said, and she looked back at him. He had his dogs' collars in his hands, but was stopping them fleeing rather than having her problem of holding Dandy back.

"Me neither," she said, but stepped forward onto the tiled floor anyway, still with one hand on Dandy. There would be other ways back to their York, but this was the route Joe took, and she wanted to see it.

He'd managed it, after all.

10

BETTER DOOR THAN A WINDOW

In the unsteady lighting, the bathroom's tiles were rendered dull and faintly grimy, as if the damp down here was sprouting new varieties of life in the grout. A heavy, pointed splash came from behind a cubicle door, as if something had sat up suddenly, and Adams abruptly wondered if it was really necessary to follow Joe's route. Perhaps heading back a different way was more prudent. Behind her, Rory swore, and she looked around to see him with one knee jammed behind Midge as the collie tried to back away.

"Midge, *walk on*," he said, his voice firm, and she rolled her eyes at him in horror. Pinto was standing her ground at his side, but that was possibly because she was shaking so much she couldn't move, her legs threatening to give way. Dandy gave an encouraging little yap, and the splashing sped up into the regular, rapid rhythm of something paddling eagerly toward them. "*Bollocks,*" Rory said, and tightened his grip on Pinto as she tried to turn and flee.

Adams dragged Dandy back a step and caught hold of Midge's collar. "I've got her."

Rory let go and picked Pinto up, leaving Adams with a hand on both dogs. "Um," he said.

Adams eyed Dandy. "No detours," she said. "Back to York." She nodded at the *Boiler* door. He looked back at her, red eyes gleaming under his dreadlocks, and she let go reluctantly, stooping to pick up Midge. She was shaking piteously, but not heavy, and Adams hefted her up. "Door," she said to Dandy, and he trotted toward the *Boiler* door, tail waving gently. "Ready?" she said to Rory.

"Lead on."

She hurried after Dandy, trying to ignore the way the splashing moved from one cubicle to another in pursuit – how did anyone use them? Were there other toilets somewhere? Did the creature know if you were only going to the loo? Or did everyone just hold it? – and the water running across the floor, alight with rainbow colours, less like an oil slick and more like someone had been getting happy with glitter about the place. At one point something banged on one of the doors, and she, Rory, and both border collies yelped, Midge following it up with a howl that was far too close to Adams' ears. Dandy barked three times, sharp and imperious, the sound echoing off the mirrors, and the splashing subsided, leaving Adams with the impression of a certain sulky acquiescence.

Then they were at the door, and Rory shifted his grip on Pinto enough to grab the handle. For one horrible moment Adams imagined it wouldn't turn, that Kaz had sent them down here to get munched up by a toilet monster for their impertinence at asking questions in her pub, then Rory swung the door wide. Adams hustled through into a dark hall, and the splashing surged into the sound of rising surf behind them. Dandy started barking again, a steady cacophony of fury, and Adams dumped Midge, squeezed back past Rory, and grabbed a handful of Dandy's dreadlocks just as a tidal wave of water burst the doors of all three cubicles open and washed toward them, dark and smooth and glimmering with unknown galaxies.

"*Move!*" Rory shouted, catching the back of her jacket and hauling her into the hall.

She kept hold of Dandy, staggering backward, and Rory reached past her for the door, slamming it in the face of the oncoming flood. Adams braced herself for the door to shatter under its impact, but all was silent and still and utterly, utterly dark, just the panting of the dogs to anchor her, Dandy's heavy coat under her fingers and Rory's hand still clutching her jacket. Or she hoped it was Rory's hand.

The thought sent her scrambling away, digging in her coat pocket for the duck. She pawed it out and squeezed its wings, flooding the hall with light from its tiny LED bulb. She shone it each way, but there was no one else around with hands, so she assumed it had been Rory, still tangled up with her after their rush through the door. He raised one hand to shield his eyes, and said, "That's the most eventful toilet break I've ever had, and I once walked in on an orgy in a club in London."

"I think I preferred the giant dog," she said.

"Me too," he said, and looked at Midge and Pinto. They were wagging their tails eagerly, crowding around Dandy and licking his snout while he bore it with his chest puffed out and his head lifted, his own tail wagging gently. "Oh, nice. And who carried you through, you little wusses?"

Adams found her other torch in her pocket, handing it to Rory, then shone the duck light down the hall. "Come on."

"Cheers," he said. "Straight ahead four junctions, right?"

"No. Three, then left on the fourth."

"Just checking."

"Ha." She headed off, Dandy trotting up to join her and giving her an expectant look. "Rory?" she asked.

"Yeah?"

"Got any more biscuits?"

"Told you you'd need them."

The hall was empty, silent and scentless, a nothingness of a space that existed only in the circle of light cast by their torches. Adams wasn't entirely sure if it was straight, or how long it was, or if they were heading uphill or down, but she also wasn't entirely sure what dimension it inhabited, so the other details hardly seemed important. What was important was that they passed three junctions without anything leaping out to try and eat them, and when they turned left at the fourth they arrived almost immediately at a plain, cheaply made door with a handle that wasn't fully attached to it. Adams took her baton out and snapped it to full length, and Rory gave her a startled look.

"Easy. Give a man a warning before you do that."

She ignored him and put one hand on the door, tipping her head toward it. She couldn't hear anything beyond, but the sound of the glittery toilet sea had been cut off as soon as they were through the last one, so it didn't mean much. She looked at Rory and said in a low voice, "Stay behind me."

The handle turned easily, the latch still working despite the precarious attachment, and she took a breath then threw it wide onto the room beyond, going through fast with her baton at the ready. She emerged into flat, unfriendly fluorescent light, a world of chipped white tiles and sticky floors, and a man at the urinal screamed and tried to run, tripped over his slipping trousers, and pitched to the floor, both hands still occupied.

"*Noooo!*" he wailed. "No, not like this!"

"Sorry, sir," Adams said. "Are you alright?"

"You can't *do* this! At least let me do my trousers up!"

"Didn't think anyone was going to be in here," she said,

closing the baton hurriedly and offering him a hand to get up. "I'm really sorry."

He looked at her hand, his own still tucked underneath him, and said, "I'd rather not."

"Right. Yes. I'm … We'll just let you get on, then."

"Cheers," he said, mostly to the tiles, and she, Rory, the two visible and one invisible dog walked around him and headed for the door.

Beyond it they found a pub at least as old as Kaz's, but not nearly as well-kept. It was less dirty than simply *faded*, even the crisp packets displayed on the shelves wearing packet designs Adams hadn't seen for years. Half the tables seemed to be missing, and the ones that were left leaned sadly on uneven legs, mismatched chairs clustered around them. The few bottles of spirits behind the bar were mostly empty, and there was no one in sight.

Adams looked around, frowning, and the bathroom door swung open behind them.

"Get out," the man said, pointing at the main entrance, an emergency sign glowing weakly above it.

"I'm sorry about that," Adams started.

"No! This pub is *shut*, and a man deserves some privacy, so you can bloody well get out!" He jabbed a finger wildly at the door, a slightly plump man with thinning pale hair and a red face. "Go on!"

"I'd just like to ask you—"

"*Out!*" he screamed. "Or I'll call the police on you! We're not open, and I'm *sick* of people coming through out of hours! Take your dogs and your filthy degenerate selves and *get out!*"

Adams considered saying she was police, and decided against it. He'd probably still call the York police, and that was just going to get complicated. "Alright," she said. "We're going."

"I should *think so!*" He watched them go, panting with fury, and they trailed out the door and onto the street, back into a slightly less sharp-edged world. Adams looked around with an unexpected feeling of loss. Not that she *wanted* giant dogs and toilet monsters, but the world felt a little bereft without them.

THERE WAS a CCTV camera at the end of the street, and Adams took a photo of the location. Not that Isha had given her anything on the others yet, but maybe the mysterious Joe would show up in both and gift her a decent suspect. She doubted it, though. Things were never that easy. She sent the photo to Isha anyway, while Rory watched curiously.

"Getting your hacker to help out?"

"She does owe me."

He nodded. "Now what?"

"Now you head off," Adams said, tucking the phone back into her pocket and watching the passing crowds. She felt like there were more Folk, or more questionable shops, or more angles to the world, or more *something,* as if in plunging into York's other dimension she'd woken some new way of seeing that she couldn't seem to shake. She wasn't sure she liked it. She was barely used to the fact that she saw the wings and tails and frankly excessive amounts of extra limbs now. She didn't need to be seeing whole extra cities as well.

"That's it?" Rory said. "Just *run along, you've done your bit?*" His tone was mild, but the words were pointed, and she looked at him, his hands in the pockets of his Oxfam coat and his hair mussed by the chill wind. He'd lost his hat somewhere along the way.

"No. Thank you for showing me the creepy butcher's, and

for playing for info, but it's back to police work now, and you can't help with that."

"It's not actually police work though, is it?"

"It's close enough."

He didn't reply straight away, just examined her with a thoughtful look she didn't much like. It was *evaluating,* and she found herself wanting to blurt out another thank you, for the card game or the toilet monster or *something,* but she didn't. Not that she didn't appreciate his help, but she'd already said thanks once. And what she needed was not to be worried about anyone else in the middle of things. She'd managed London alone, with its bridges and bins and toasties, and she hadn't even known about Yorkie bars then. It had only been since she'd got to Yorkshire that more people had seemed to stumble into the orbit of her cases, and it had to stop. It *had* to, because she couldn't be responsible for what happened to them if things went wrong. She'd never forgive herself.

"Well," Rory said finally, when she didn't say anything else. "I suppose I'll hear from you next time you need something." He turned and walked off, Midge and Pinto looking back at Dandy questioningly as they trailed after him.

Adams grimaced, and Dandy nudged her hand. "I know," she said, scratching the top of his head. "People are complicated."

He *whuffed,* sounding somehow reproachful, and she took her phone out again, scrolling through to Collins' number. There was no point dwelling on the bruised feelings of the landed gentry. She needed to get on.

She walked toward Ash & Yew as the phone rang, and eventually there was the click of connection and Collins said, "Ay-up, Adams."

"Morning. Lucas get back to you with anything yet?"

"Not so far."

"Dammit."

"*Hmm.* He said he ran into some technical difficulties, but no further explanation yet."

Technical difficulties. Adams didn't much like the sound of that. Self-destructing evidence? Prints with webbed toes and claws? Impossible to tell, and she hated that these were actual possibilities in her head. "What about Violet Brennan? Have you had a chance to see what her name throws up?"

"Nothing at all," Collins said. "And, according to my limited skills, there are many Violet Brennans in existence, but none seem to be York silversmiths."

"She's a herbalist now. Seemed not that keen on silver-smithing after all." She gave him a quick rundown of the morning's adventures into other York.

"A glittery toilet monster?" Collins asked, once she'd finished.

"I would like to say I'm making this up," Adams said, pausing in the overhang of one of the old buildings, the bulging walls feeling both eternal and precarious overhead. Ash & Yew was just a little further down the street, the windows glowing with warmth and fairy lights glittering in the foliage that framed them. There was a police officer at the door, holding it partly open as they leaned inside, and Adams drew back instinctively, finding the shadow of a shop door. In their heavy high-vis coat, it was impossible to tell at this angle if the officer was male or female, familiar or not.

"Adams?" Collins said.

"Yes, sorry. Do you know anyone at the York station?"

"Well, there's Farzana, and—"

"Of course you do, silly question. Any chance you can find out why they might be interested in Ash & Yew?"

"What, now?"

"No, not *now,* but can you get in touch, maybe have a word?"

"Sure. What's going on?"

Adams thought about it. She didn't know, not really, but something about the officer's presence was unsettling her. They weren't shopping, not with one foot still on the pavement outside, and there was something proprietary about the way they leaned into the shop. It wasn't a *friendly chat* posture, that way of standing which communicated a certain *presence* without threat. Maybe it was a literal friendly chat, though, a friend of Heather's stopping by. It wasn't as if she was the only copper with knowledge that the world was for more than just humans. She'd seen that in London.

But she'd also seen in London that not everyone was working in the same direction. Knowing about Folk didn't automatically make you the member of some exclusive club, pulling together toward a common good, no more than anything else. And she had strong suspicions that all was not well in the state of Yorkshire policing. The werewolves – sorry, *weres* – had vanished from custody without charge. The sorcerer's necklace had been removed from circulation, but questions still lingered about how deep its influence had crept in the Leeds station. Or the questions lingered with Adams, anyway.

"*Adams.*"

"Yes?" She'd been so busy watching the police officer, trying to get a better look without getting closer, that she'd forgotten to answer.

"What's happening?"

"There's a copper at the shop. Uniformed, can't tell anything else at the moment."

"You think they reported the theft properly?"

"I highly doubt it."

"Alright," Collins said, the last of the amusement vanishing from his voice. He'd been there to see the carnage caused by the beer, after all. "I'll get hold of Farzana and see what she can tell me."

"Cheers." She hit disconnect and popped the phone back in her pocket, seeing the officer straightening, as if about to step away.

"Better door than a window," a sharp voice said.

"What?" She looked around to see a very small, very pointy-featured, and spectacularly old woman glaring up at her.

"*You*," the woman said, jabbing a finger at her. "Are a better *door*"—she paused to wave in a way that encompassed Adams' entire existence, then continued—"than a *window*."

"I don't—"

"You're standing in the damn door and no one can get in! I want my voddy!" The woman poked her with one bony finger.

"*Ow!* And if I'm standing in the door, then of course I'm a better door than a window! You say that when you can't *see* past someone, not when you can't *walk* past them!"

"Don't be a clever clogs! *Move!*"

"I *am!*" Adams stepped aside to let the woman push past her into the shop, which she now saw was a grimy sort of off-licence. She couldn't tell if it was Folk or not, and was slightly worried that might mean things were getting, as Heather had said, a little blurry. But the woman hadn't seemed to notice Dandy, so that indicated maybe it was just an ordinary dodgy offy, somehow clinging on in the tourist streets despite the rising rents and rates and everything else.

She turned back to Ash & Yew. The officer had shut the door, but was lingering outside, a small, compact man with tan skin and his hat pulled low over sharp, dark eyes. She'd seen him before, in other York, with his mate enjoying a sausage roll. He seemed to be on his own now, though, checking each way along the street, and Adams *could* have just talked to him, and it *could* have been fine, and maybe she was being paranoid for no reason at all, but Dandy growled softly next to her, and that made her mind up. She ducked into the off-licence, almost knocking over the old woman, who swung her bag at Adams, a bottle (presumably the voddy) smacking into her shin.

"*Ow!*"

"*Assault!*" the woman screeched.

"*You* hit *me!*"

"I'm just an old lady trying to do her shopping in peace, and getting attacked by hooligans on every corner!"

"Pam, leave the lady alone," a young man said from behind the counter, barely looking up from his phone. "Don't make me call the cops again."

"Call them on *her!*"

"No," he said, still not looking up, and Pam glared at Adams, who stepped aside to let her out. She marched to the door, turned to look at Adams, and stuck her tongue out, accompanying that with a very heartfelt hand gesture.

"Right," Adams said, and peered out of the small bit of glass door that wasn't covered by flyers. The cop hadn't moved from outside Ash & Yew, and he struck her again as familiar, but she still couldn't place him. "Have you got a back door?" she asked the assistant, and he finally looked at her properly.

"*Are* you a hooligan?"

"No."

"Yeah, you don't look like it." He pointed to a door beside the counter, his attention already back on his phone. "Help yourself. Don't steal anything. Or do. Whatever. It's not my shop."

Adams let herself through the little door into a back room with a second door lying open onto a toilet off to one side that didn't smell too fresh, and the rest of the space taken up with a large, cluttered desk and even more cluttered shelves, stock spilling onto the flooring in a rush to escape. There was another door directly ahead of her, and she opened it onto a narrow ginnel, cobbled and strewn with weeds. It led off at an angle to the lane Ash & Yew was on, so she followed it, Dandy padding after her. At the end she peered into the street, hating the uneasiness in her belly. She shouldn't be feeling this way about people who were essentially her colleagues, even if it was a different area. But there was something about seeing the man twice over, once in this York and once in the other, that didn't sit right.

She glanced down at Dandy in time to see him trying to gnaw a packet of jerky open.

"Oh, *come on* – stop that!" She grabbed for him, but he shot past her into the streets, trotting off with his tail waving, shooting her glances over his shoulder. "You weren't meant to take him at his word," she hissed, hurrying after him, then took her phone out and pretended it was on speaker as a passing man gave her a distrustful look. Which was likely unconvincing even before it rang in her hand and she almost dropped it.

"For—" She jabbed answer, barely registering Collins' name. "*What?*"

"You alright?" he asked.

"Yes, fine, Dandy's just shoplifting."

"Who's Dandy?" another voice asked, a little more distantly than Collins.

"Lucas?" she asked.

"None other. Adams, what have you given me?"

"I don't know?" she said cautiously, wondering if she'd been right about the claws and webbed prints. Dandy had stopped in front of her, looking past her down the street, and she looked that way as well. She couldn't see anything, but when Dandy turned and headed off again, moving faster, she followed. "Is this about the prints? Collins said you were having some problems."

"It is," Lucas said. "Good news, bad news, or weird news first?"

Adams checked over her shoulder. Dandy was still keeping up a swift pace, heading back toward where she'd parked the car. "Ah— Bad news?"

"How predictable. The bad news is that the file I pulled was flagged."

"Flagged." Dandy was getting ahead of her, and she picked up the pace.

"Yes, flagged. I'd just got it up on the screen, and *bam.* Access revoked."

"Why? Was it a restricted file?"

"Nope. One Lister, Joe—"

"Joe?" She slowed. "You got a hit on a Joe?"

"Yes, but listen—"

"And his file was restricted?"

"You really don't know how to listen to a story, do you?"

Dandy barked ahead of her, flat and warning, and she broke into a jog, weaving through the foot traffic. "Sorry."

"I should think so. Anyhow. I was just scanning the file – nothing interesting, just some cautions and penalty notices, and a couple of community sentences. Nothing big, nothing escalating. One of those kids that'll probably be doing just the same thing in twenty years' time."

Dandy barked again. She had him in sight now, waiting at a junction, and as soon as she spotted him he veered away, loping down a side street. Adams glanced behind her, but she still couldn't see any pursuit. She shifted her jog up a notch, though. "It was just a regular file?" she said to Lucas.

"Deeply boring, but next thing I've been shut out and Maud's calling me wanting to know why I'd been accessing York files without proper paperwork."

Adams frowned. "But you weren't. It was just *his* file. That's not specific to York."

"Yes— Adams, what're you doing?"

"Running," she said, between breaths.

"Why?" Both Lucas and Collins spoke at the same time, their voices layered over each other.

She glanced back again, and this time she saw a commotion in the crowd, people moving to make room for someone coming through fast. *"Dammit."*

"Adams?" Collins said, his voice sharp.

"Call you back," she said, and broke into a sprint, chasing Dandy into the depths of the Shambles, her breath tight in her chest and the day clear and sharp at the edges.

SO MUCH POTENTIAL

ADAMS RAN HARD, DANDY SLIDING THROUGH THE CROWD effortlessly ahead of her. At least his passage cleared the way a little for her. People might not be able to see him, but they evidently felt *something*, because they moved apart slightly, leaving a passage she plunged down. Unfortunately it was also helping her pursuer, and he was evidently as dedicated to his own running habit as she was to hers, which was annoying. She didn't know the city, couldn't trace a route in her mind that would give her some cover, couldn't think of any back ways to escape, and she was already so turned around she wasn't sure which direction her car lay in, or any other landmark.

"*Stop! Police!*" the officer shouted behind her, and a man with a suit took a half-hearted step into her path. Dandy whipped past him, or maybe *through* him, and the man stumbled out of the way, looking around in bewilderment, before Adams could reach him. Her phone was still connected, and she could dimly hear Collins shouting something, but she ignored it, slipping on the cobbles and almost falling as she followed Dandy around a tight corner and into a mostly empty and suddenly familiar alley.

The butcher's lay ahead of her, and Dandy vanished through the door. Adams slowed, not wanting to be trapped in there, but the officer shouted again behind her. She might outrun him, but for all she knew he was on his radio, calling backup in to corner her. And without Dandy to guide her, she wasn't going to avoid them.

She ran for the shop door, shoving it open and unleashing a wave of meaty stench. She hurried to the counter, trying to breathe shallowly, and said, "I need to get through. Please."

The butcher didn't look up.

"I'll take—" She was cut off by someone hitting the door, trying to force it open, and she looked back to see Dandy sitting with his back to it, panting heavily. "Bollocks." The last thing she needed was him getting biting-size in here, or, worse, actually biting a police officer. She was going to have to just risk it. "Come on!" She ran for the back door, pushing through into the kitchen with Dandy plunging after her. The door to the street slammed open behind her, and through it she could hear the officer shouting.

She didn't wait to see if he was going to pay the toll or not, just bolted across the kitchen and straight out into the alley, spinning to face the huge dog as it surged to its feet, a snarl shaking the air around her.

"*Good dog!*" she yelled as it charged toward her, and Dandy shoved something into her leg. She snatched it without looking, coming up with the bag of jerky. She held it up just in time for the big dog to slide to a stop at her feet, tail wagging enthusiastically as it panted in her face. "Good dog," she managed again, and offered it the jerky. It just flopped to its belly and shoved a tattered stuffed toy at her. "Oh. Thanks." She took it and the dog rolled onto its back, offering its stomach for a rub. "Yeah. Nice pup." She rubbed its vast belly with one foot, looking back at the door to the shop. No one yet.

"Here you go," she said, setting the toy down and tearing the packet of jerky open. She shook the contents out, backing down the alley as she did so. "Yum!"

The dog rolled to its stomach, looking at the jerky then at her, and whined.

"Sorry. It's all I have."

The dog got up, picked up its toy, and trotted toward her.

"Oh, no. No, *stay.*"

It stopped, whining again, its ears drooping. It looked to be cut out of the night and placed here in the alley, abandoned and endlessly hungry for the dark, clutching its tattered teddy in an attempt to hold back a loneliness beyond all comprehension. But for all that, she couldn't let it follow her. She already had an invisible dog, who was looking mournfully at the lost jerky, and she certainly wasn't taking on feeding anything the size of this beast.

"Stay," she said again, just as the door to the kitchen flew open.

"Stay *right* there," the officer started, pointing at Adams, and the dog spun toward him, dropping its toy as it snarled. "Oh *sh—*" He vanished back inside, slamming the door again, and Adams took the opportunity to run for the street at the end of the alley. The big dog didn't follow, apparently intent on chewing its way into the kitchen, from the noises she could hear behind her, and she looked at Dandy as they turned onto the street.

"Nice work," she said, and he huffed, looking at a nearby coffeeshop hopefully. "Yeah, fair."

"*Adams!*" her phone yelled, and she blinked at it, startled. It was still in one hand, and she'd evidently turned the video on at some point.

"Hi," she said, holding it up. "How much of that did you see?"

"Enough to know that someone needs to get animal control out there," Lucas said, and she sighed. As long as he thought it was just a big dog. Otherwise she'd have to get the cat to pay him a visit.

"Give me a second," she said. "Dandy needs a coffee."

SHE CALLED Collins back once she'd bought a coffee for herself and a takeaway mug full of coffee grounds for Dandy. The young woman with pointy ears (Adams wasn't sure if she was Folk or if it was body modification) had barely blinked at the request, just handed it over to Adams, and Dandy had taken it delicately from her then swallowed it in one gulp. Now they were back out on the street, heading for the Blighted Basilisk once more. She didn't really want to brave the toilet monster again, but she wasn't sure how else to get back to her own version of York. There were hardly signs for it about the place.

"So. Fingerprints," she said, when Collins answered.

"What the hell happened?" he demanded.

"Lucas still there?"

"Yes."

"So let's talk fingerprints. Did you get any details on Joe Lister?"

"Hang on, I'm putting you on speaker," Collins said. "She wants to know about the fingerprints."

"What about the dog?" Lucas asked. "That thing was huge! And who were you running from?"

"I'll explain later," Adams said. "Joe Lister?"

Lucas made a puffing noise. "I really want to know what

you two get up to. Maud lets you go traipsing off to other counties—"

"Her, not me," Collins said. "I just go along for the fun of it here and there."

"Yeah, but still. And two DIs? Here? Really? We're hardly crime central."

"That's why I get to traipse off sometimes," Adams said. "Did you get any details on Lister before the file was yanked?"

Lucas grumbled, then said, "Well. His were the only set of fingerprints that made sense."

Adams didn't say anything, and after a moment he sighed.

"This is when one of you says, *what do you mean, Lucas?*"

"Sorry," Collins said. "I thought it was a dramatic pause."

"Git. Fine. The other fingerprints, the ones that didn't make sense, which you two are obviously *dying* to know about, had one hit from a civilian database that I use now and then. Armchair detectives digitising historical cases." He stopped again, waiting.

Adams checked the streets around her. She couldn't see any sign of pursuit, but she wished there was another way back. Or rather, that she knew where it was, because there had to be— "*Idiot,*" she said aloud.

"*What?*"

"Not you, Lucas. Me."

"You're not paying attention."

"I am." She paused, stepping into a small alley for cover. Ash & Yew. Ash & Yew would be in *every* level of York, but she also couldn't just walk straight back there. Someone was likely watching it. But she could call as soon as she was off the phone. "Carry on."

"You've taken all the fun out of it, but fine. The historical case was a bank robbery eighty-three years ago. The prints were fresh."

"*Huh,*" Collins said.

"*Huh?* Really? That's all you can say?"

"Interesting," Adams said. "Did you see an address in Lister's file before you got kicked off?"

Lucas huffed. "You are both *deeply* annoying. This is really fascinating, you know? Not Joe, who's pretty average, but what I'm assuming is our centenarian bank robber. Who remains unidentified, by the way, but imagine picking that up!"

Adams had an idea Charles was a lot older than a centenarian, and hoped this database didn't go back too far. "Lister?" she said again, and Lucas didn't answer.

"He's throwing his hands in the air," Collins said. "And not in a good way. Sorry, mate. We're not so worried about potential centenarian crime sprees."

"It's an overlooked demographic," Lucas said.

"We can look into it later," Adams promised. "But I need to know—"

"Yes, yes, Lister. Luckily I have a strange compulsion to screenshot things. I've just sent it to you."

"Lucas, you are a *star*," Adams said, as her phone dinged, and she examined the message attachment, at the top of which was a delightfully clear and very normal address.

"I know. So what is this? Lister's only twenty-three, so is it a cross-generational thing? Is he doing the heavy lifting for some one-foot-in-the-grave crime syndicate? Please say yes."

"I'll leave you to figure it out," Adams said, and hung up before either of them could protest, looking at Dandy. "Can you find Ash & Yew?"

He tipped his head, and she nodded.

"I'll take that as a yes."

ADAMS KEPT a wary eye both on the passersby and Dandy, but he seemed unconcerned now, so she assumed her new canine bestie had kept the copper in the shop. That, or given the fact he hadn't purchased anything on the way through, the butcher was restocking his fridges. She shuddered, and scrolled through the last-called on her phone, pausing on Heather's number before going to search her contacts instead. She'd had Charles's number in here since the sorcerer's necklace incident, and though Heather had been the one to call her, it had also been her shop the officer had been leaning into, not the workshop out the back. That set little, instinctual warning signals scuttling around her brain, and she'd been doing this too long to ignore them. She might not have Collins' *people skills*, but she had her own.

Charles answered just as she was about to give up, his voice low. "Detective Inspector?"

"I've just been chased into *other* York by some copper who was in the shop," Adams said. "I need to get back. Is your place clear now?"

"Um … no. Meet me at the museum."

"Which one?"

"York Castle," he said, and hung up.

Adams stared at the phone, then looked at Dandy. "York Castle Museum?" she asked him, and he tipped his head to the side again, the canine equivalent of a shrug. "Great." She poked her phone, half expecting it wouldn't give her any sort of directions in this other version of the world, but it popped up immediately, not even ten minutes' walk away. She turned to follow it, walking fast and keeping her attention on the crowd, not because of the people sporting tusks and tails, but in case any of them were sporting police jackets.

Instead of the route to the river they'd taken earlier, she headed more at an angle, following a wider road for a bit before taking a footpath squeezed between the steep wall of a sprawling shopping centre and a small, tree-lined river. Lush greenery pressed around her, a dislocating moment of wilderness in the middle of the city, then she was out into a car park, the green mound capped with Clifford's Tower visible across it. She gave a little huff of surprise. She'd parked here, and she looked around dubiously, not sure if her car would be present in this York or not.

It was. She detoured toward it before heading for the museum, putting one hand on the roof hesitantly. She almost expected it to pass right through. But, no, her car *was* there, and she wondered if she could just get in and drive back home, or if there'd be an entirely other version of it there. Trying to understand the different layers of the world was bringing her headache back, and she looked at Dandy.

"None of this makes sense," she told him, and he wagged his tail at her happily. "You don't, either," she added, and headed for the museum, old stone hulking up just beyond the car park. With any luck Charles could give her a simple explanation for the police presence. It'd be nice for *something* to be simple.

Charles was already waiting, and he hurried to meet her as she left the car park. He had a woolly hat pulled down over his messy hair, and a large puffer jacket swamping his stoop-shouldered frame.

"Come on, come on," he hissed, beckoning her into the shelter of the colonnaded main doors. They were locked and unused, the official entrance further on in a low-slung, modern addition, and Adams followed him, looking around curiously. From here they had a perfect view across a circle of green to another imposing building, but it was the tower which pulled her attention, the perfectly symmetrical keep perched atop its green hill, sprouting out of the flat land in a manner that made her think of a fully loaded pimple, even when she tried not to.

"Why's my car here?" she asked him, pointing at the car park, and he looked at her blankly.

"You didn't park it there?"

"No, I did, but in *other* York. I mean, my York. Other, other York."

"Oh, right. No, it's the same."

"*How?* I just went through a butcher's shop to get here, and a bloody toilet to get back before."

Charles nodded. "Yes, but that was there. This is here."

"That doesn't help *at all*," Adams said.

"No, of course." He took a deep breath, checking they weren't being overheard, but there was no one nearby. "The whole city isn't multi-layered, only parts of it, places that are deeply rooted. If you want to go between the versions of those parts, you need to use the doors. Otherwise, you can just walk out, as you did, because it's not like there are walls. But it's one way. Even if you turned around immediately and tried to walk back in, you'd just find yourself on the surface streets. It's like … snakes and ladders. You need a ladder to get in, but the snakes pop you straight back out again, and you can't go back up them."

"Except some ladders you can climb both ways on?"

"Exactly," he said, smiling as if he'd presented her with a perfectly plausible theory rather than something that was setting off floaties in her eyes, the sparking, twisting blotches that normally preceded her migraines. And which had also surfaced when she first started seeing *other* things. Which made her wonder if she'd ever had migraines at all, or if the whole time it had simply been her brain fighting it out with her vision over what was real and what wasn't. Fun thought, that, especially considering she'd had them since she was in her teens.

She pushed her fingertips into her forehead and said, "Right. So why are we here?"

"I wanted to speak to you. Privately." He took a packet of cigarettes from his pocket, plucking one out with scarred, hardened fingers.

"About the police at the shop?"

He grimaced. "I don't know why they were there. Maybe just shopping?"

"He chased me across half of town."

"Right." He didn't say anything else, busying himself with lighting the cigarette.

Adams waited for a moment, then said, "Do you want to tell me about Joe, then?"

He shot her a sideways look. "Joe?"

"Joe Lister. His fingerprints were on the tin, and someone called Joe was hanging around the Blighted Basilisk, trying to get in on your games. Did you lose a key to him, Charles? Is that what happened?"

Charles rubbed the top of his head, dislodging his hat. "I remember him. Skinny lad. But no. No, I wouldn't bet that."

"Really? I heard the stakes get pretty high."

He shook his head, hard. "Not a key. Not that."

"Not that? What, then? Charms?"

"Sometimes? But nothing that could get him into the shop. Nothing dangerous. I wouldn't."

Adams examined him, the cigarette half-crushed between his fingers. He'd taken his hat off, kneading it in his free hand, but he met her gaze, his own eyes steady.

"Not that," he repeated.

"Alright. Did you invite him back for an after-hours thing, then? He could've stolen a key, or made a copy."

"I'm not sure," he admitted. "I don't do that a lot, no matter what Heather says. But maybe? I'm usually a bit past remembering exactly who I invite back when it comes to those sorts of nights."

"Great," Adams said. "Very high security, for the stuff you do."

"There are safeguards, Inspector. I never imagined anyone could get past them, even if they had a key."

Adams sighed. "This is going well. No idea why the police were there, and no idea who you might've let into the shop."

"Sorry," Charles said, looking at the ground. "It's a mess."

"It is. But what did you want to talk to me about? And why here?"

He looked around. "It's quite … stony."

Adams looked at the green, then back at him.

"Sure, but *here*," he said, tapping one foot on the ground. "This building isn't *that* old, but it's built on the bones of others, and they're all full of human dreams and woes. It's not a place of wilderness. It's a place of *constraint* – castle, then prison, then holding place for artefacts."

"And?"

"And not a place my Heather frequents," he said, smiling slightly. "Not a place she can eavesdrop."

"Oh?"

Charles examined his cigarette, which had gone out, and relit it, the flame flushing his face and momentarily distracting Adams. She hadn't seen a lighter. Charles took a deep drag on it, then said, "Heather might have been the one to call you, but it took all my persuasion to get her to do so. I tried to hide the fact of the missing charm from her, and for a few days I was successful, but I had to confess in the end, when I wasn't getting anywhere in the search. I was lucky to persuade her to call you, after that."

"She wanted to go straight to her solution?" Adams asked.

"Yes. And she won't wait for too long before she implements it anyway. My love has clear ideas on how things should be handled."

"Why's it so urgent?" Adams asked. "I mean, I see that it's bad for your reputation, but surely you just tell people who have the guardians, and they put extra security measures in place."

Charles sighed, looking across the green to the tower. "One of the reasons for the master charm is to ensure that there is a deeper enchantment on the guardians, one their new owners can't breach. Because without that, a guardian can be turned into a weapon."

Adams didn't answer straight away, thinking of the vastness of Wilfred, towering above the garden and *dealing with* intruders. Finally she said, "They're that dangerous."

"With the master charm, yes. They can be turned into an army. And Heather will not stand for it. The clash of the two will tear every version of York to the ground, and half the country besides."

"You can't just ask her not to?"

"I can ask her many things, and she will tell me that if she has to clean up my mess yet again, she'll do it her own way." He smiled, something distant and wistful. "She's justified, of course. I am not the best of partners, in many ways."

"Pretty sure you're not bad enough to justify tearing down a city."

His smile widened. "True. And I suppose it's a *little* romantic."

"Not in the slightest." Adams tucked her hands into her pockets, rocking on her heels. "You must be keeping track of them. Any sign someone's actually taking them over?"

"Wilfred's restless. He's moving around the garden constantly. Usually it can be weeks, or months, where he doesn't move."

"Maybe he's upset someone stole the charm out from under him?"

Charles frowned. "That's not possible. He's born of metal, Inspector. He doesn't have feelings."

"Like Fergus?"

"Fergus was an experiment, and I'm going to fix it."

Adams nodded. "I spoke to Violet. She seems to think Heather didn't like her much."

"Heather neither wants nor needs apprentices, and I think she rather felt Violet had misrepresented herself when it turned out she wasn't all that interested in metal."

That seemed to roughly fit with what Violet had said, and got them no further forward. Aloud, Adams said, "Any other guardians acting up that you know of?"

"I checked on the one at the Minster this morning. It's still there, but it's moving about the place. It's a wonder no one's noticed." He hesitated, then added, "I have had a couple of calls from clients, too. One was a gentleman in Harrogate who had a bird of paradise guardian in his foyer – the bird, not the plant – and it's gone."

"That doesn't sound good," Adams said. "And you're sure it just walked off, or flew, or whatever? It couldn't have been stolen, or someone just been after what it was guarding?"

He made a small, amused noise. "That bird of paradise was guarding the entry to a collection of truly exceptional art. Old masters for the most part, but some new talent too. I saw it when I delivered the bird. Truly impressive. Do you know, there was a—"

"Charles, the point? Was it all stolen?"

He sniffed. "You're obviously not an art aficionado."

"I am not."

"It's all still there, anyway."

"*Bollocks,*" Adams said, then added something stronger.

"My thoughts exactly," Charles said.

"How long do we have?"

"I don't know. If Heather finds out, no time at all."

"Alright. I'm going to run down my human-side stuff this afternoon. See if I can speak to Joe."

"I don't see that it can be him. He didn't have a scrap of magic in him."

"He could be working with someone else," she replied. "And he's our best lead right now. You check if any other guardians are on the move, and also go back to the pub and see if you and your mates can put together a list of everyone you've had back after hours, alright?"

"That may not help. Even if we can come up with names, they probably won't be real ones."

"It's a start. Just doing it might jog your memory for if someone was acting particularly interested in the guardians or something."

He nodded. "Alright. I'll text you as soon as I have something."

"Good." She tapped her fingers against her thighs, thinking. "And keep me updated on Wilfred, too. Is he trying to escape, do you think? Being called by someone?"

"No," Charles said. "He could be over the wall anytime he wanted. But I went out earlier to get some tin, and everything's *off*, in the whole garden."

Adams frowned. "But he's the only guardian out there, right?"

"For now. But every scrap of old can or broken pipe out there has *potential*, DI Adams. That's what a sculptor does. Releases the potential in their material."

"Great," Adams said. "Don't do any of that just now, alright?"

"I promise," Charles said, pressing one hand to his heart.

Adams nodded. "Call me later."

"Will do," Charles said, and she left him huddled on the concrete step as she walked back to the car, the wind snatching at her coat and her hands in her pockets, closed over a duck in each, oddly reassuring in the face of the uncertain day.

1 2

EMOTIONAL SUPPORT ANIMALS

Back in the car, Adams started the engine to get the heating going, her hands cold and pinched. She was tired, and not just from her five a.m. cat-centric wake-up call. Her head was aching, both from the dislocating strain of seeing the world at different levels, sliding in and out of focus, and from the effort of understanding it. She leaned back against the seat, closing her eyes, and Dandy put his chin on her shoulder, panting in her face.

"You stink," she said to him, without much heat, and he tried to lick her cheek. "*Ew.* Get off." She scruffed his ears, then took her phone out. There was no point sitting here, not least because her new mate the copper might be checking car parks around the centre. She pulled up the message from Lucas and scanned the attachment quickly. There wasn't a lot that fit onto the screenshot, just date of birth, a photo, and an initial couple of cautions before the image cut off. Joe had a tight, wary face, a tattoo above one eyebrow and another curling up his neck, his cheeks still a little soft with youth and his short hair bleached blond. The cautions she could see were, as Lucas had said, all pretty minor, the sort of thing that was barely worth the officers' time in booking him, but also which couldn't be overlooked all the time. And the sort of thing that made it hard to ever find a job that would break the cycle.

Nothing about Joe suggested he might have the kind of knowledge that stealing guardians required, and she was still leaning toward the idea that someone else was behind it. From the look of his file, he wouldn't be too fussy about what jobs he took.

The screenshot did have an address, at least, and Adams popped it into her phone, then looked at Dandy. "Ready?" she asked him, and he tipped his head. "As you say." She backed out of her space and headed for the exit, thinking she probably did need a better social life. Saturday afternoon and she was talking to an invisible dog, on her way to hunt down someone who'd committed an impossible crime. It was better than sitting at home watching telly, at least. She supposed.

It didn't take long to drive to Joe's address, a flat in a low-rise block of council housing, three storeys of red brick and white paint and patchy flowerbeds. Matching buildings faced each other over a quiet street, cars parked along the kerb, and most of the flats had small balconies crammed with rickety barbecues, bikes, and folded clothes horses. Adams slowed, looking for somewhere to park, and eventually found a spot a little further down the road where an old Volvo Estate and a Smart car had left just enough room for her to squeeze between them. It wasn't as inconspicuous as she might've liked, but there were no skips to hide behind, or any handy side roads from where she could see the entrance to Joe's building, and she had no intention of walking straight up to it, given the way access to the file had been shut down.

She turned off the engine, settling herself further into her seat, and waited, wishing she knew exactly which apartment was Joe's. But there was no point wondering. She just had to be patient, and think.

She was doodling in her notepad, names and arrows spidering across the page as she tried to figure out connections and links, when the phone rang. She almost dropped the pad, jumping, and hit answer hurriedly.

"Hello?"

"Ay-up, Adams," Collins said. "You on the way back yet?"

"No," she said, yawning. "I'm keeping an eye on Joe's place. See if he turns up."

There was silence on the other end of the phone, then Collins said, "You shouldn't be doing this without backup."

"I've got Dandy. Besides, I don't fancy explaining to Maud if we're both rumbled up here."

"You can't keep running about on your own, either."

She made a non-committal sound and said, "I've got a bit more news on the guardians."

"Alright. Hang on, I've got Thompson here. I'm putting video on." There was some scuffling on Collins' side, then the camera came on, revealing a pink cat nose almost touching the screen.

"Really?" Adams said. "What about your teleportation gig?"

"*Shifting*," the cat said, as Collins adjusted the camera, evidently finding somewhere else to set it where it could take in both him and Thompson. "And it's York. Told you I don't want to head up there."

"Fair enough. What's up?"

Thompson looked at Collins. "Poor level of service in this place."

Collins sighed audibly, and dug in his desk drawer, pulling out a packet of cat treats. He tipped some onto the desk.

"Quality," Thompson said, and crunched into them while Dandy whined, looking at Adams.

"I'll get you some later," Adams told him.

"You don't have any dog biscuits on you?"

"No. Why do you have cat treats?"

"It stops him whinging."

"Fair point," she said, and Thompson stopped eating to bare his teeth at her. "Well?" she said to him.

He sat back, licking his chops. "No whispers from the Watch, but it's not like we have a community noticeboard, you know? There's definitely been some mutterings about the guardians, though. Apparently some giant crab's taken off from Scarborough, and a boar from Kendal."

"A giant crab?"

"Sounds fun, right?"

"Taken off how?" Collins asked. "Stolen?"

"Don't know," Thompson said, having another biscuit.

Adams sighed. "I had a word with Charles, and it seems the target might not be what they're guarding. It might be the guardians themselves."

"I suppose they'd be pretty valuable," Collins said.

"It's more what they can do. Apparently the master charm can be used to control them. Turn them from guarding to attacking."

"Oh, awesome," Thompson said around a biscuit. "Loving the sound of the crab even more."

Collins nodded, and turned to his computer. Adams could hear the mouse clicking quietly, just out of sight. "That tracks, actually," he said after a moment. "I've been having a bit of a nosy into theft reports. I only found a handful, but the places they're going missing from seem to have a lot of other things you'd imagine people being more interested in taking. There's a giant bat vanished from near Leeds that was right outside a room full of genuine movie props. Things like an original star trooper's suit, and the bike from Jurassic World, stuff like that. They'd have fetched a whole lot more than some tin bat."

Adams frowned. "How many have you got?"

"Just half a dozen that seem to fit. But from what you said, they're not all going to be guarding legitimate collections, so they're not all going to be being reported." He looked back at the camera. "When you say they can be used aggressively, how does that work?"

"Not sure on the specifics. The only one I've come across that's functioning right only moves when no one's looking at it, so …" She shrugged.

"I'm taking it we're not talking robotics," Collins said.

"No."

"And any idea of what they're going to be used for?"

"I don't even have a proper suspect. Just Violet, who seems to have not even been interested in them, and Joe, who doesn't sound to have had any ability."

"You're really acing this one," Thompson observed.

"Coming from the cat who can't even pop over to deliver news in person."

"Hey, I have dragons to keep in line."

"Good luck on that," Collins said.

"Did your mate in York call you back?" Adams asked him.

"Not yet, and I don't want to go poking too much into Ash & Yew in case that sets something else off," Collins said.

"Good call." Adams tapped her fingers on the wheel. "Maybe I should visit Violet again, see if I can shake anything else loose."

"Who's this?" Thompson asked.

"Charles's apprentice who suggested giving the guardians personalities. The personality may have been what let someone get past the one on the master charm."

"Great. Giving things a semblance of life wasn't enough, now they've got *quirks*," Thompson said. "Bloody humans."

"It all sounds a bit improbable, though. Violet's not some … sorcerer, or whatever. She's just a kid, and it seems she was more interested in Heather's plant magic."

"Plant magic?" Collins asked.

"Apparently she's seen as a bit of a goddess around here," Adams said.

Thompson huffed. "*Goddess.* Bloody humans. Anyone vaguely female gets a bit of power and suddenly they're witch or goddess, evil or divine, not just *someone with power.*" He yawned and looked at Collins. "Any more of those biscuits?"

Both Adams and Collins stared at him.

"What?"

Collins shook his head, and took the packet from the drawer, tipping some more onto the table. "Have you heard from Isha?" he asked Adams.

"No," she said, frowning. "I'll try calling her. I've got time."

Collins started to say something, then looked up abruptly, toward the door.

"Why is there a cat on your desk?" the crisp voice of DCI Maud Taylor said.

"Emotional support animal," Collins said. "You know, since Adams isn't here."

Maud snorted, and the camera angle suddenly changed as it was picked up and turned around. Adams raised a hand in a weak wave. "You don't look very sick," Maud said, examining Adams with her blue eyes narrowed. She was a small, solid woman with softly curling blonde hair, a ready smile, and a penchant for pretty blouses, all of which gave a very erroneous first impression. Calculatedly so, Adams was sure.

"Migraine," she said.

"Oh dear. Been to the doctor?"

"It's feeling a bit better. Floaties are around a bit, is all."
She waved vaguely in front of her eyes.

Maud adjusted her hair with one hand, the nails cropped
short and painted a vibrant shade of pink. "You'd better take
a few days off," she said.

"Well—"

Maud raised her eyebrows, and Adams stopped talking.
"As I was saying," the DCI said, "take a few days off. Someone
mentioned seeing you in York, and *obviously* it wasn't on
police work, was it?"

"Ah—"

"Acupuncturist," Collins said, from somewhere off-
screen. "I sent her to my mate up there. Did wonders when I
put my back out that time."

"That was it," Adams said, nodding. "Lots of tiny
needles."

"That makes sense," Maud said. "Because otherwise it'd be
sniffing around off your patch with no approval from me,
which makes me think this is Toot Hansell stuff, and I don't
want to know if that's spreading. I *don't*."

"Acupuncture," Adams said. "My aunt swears by it."

"Definitely want to take it easy, though, Adams," Collins
said. "It can have quite an aftereffect."

"Yes. That's why I'm sitting in the car. I didn't want to
drive yet. In case of the after-effects."

Maud looked away, presumably at Collins, then back at
Adams, and nodded. "You're a disappointment, the both of
you. Not a DCI between you unless you can get better at
lying." She handed the phone to Collins, giving Adams a
swooping view of the ceiling. "And get rid of the bloody cat.
Emotional support animal, you muppet." Her voice trailed off,
and Adams faintly heard the door click shut.

"I'm great for emotional support," Thompson said. "Or I
could be, if I wanted."

Collins put the phone back where it had been. *"Lots of tiny needles?"*

"Well, that's what it is, isn't it?"

"You may be missing the entire concept, but in strictly technical terms, yes, I suppose." He gave the keyboard a final tap and got up, taking his coat from the back of the chair. "I'm coming up."

"There's nothing to do. I'm just watching for Joe."

"Sure, until you end up dealing with glittery toilet monsters again." He picked the phone up. "I'll call you when I get there." He hit disconnect before Adams could argue, and she scowled at her phone, then looked at Dandy.

"Well, that's just bloody brilliant, isn't it?"

Dandy huffed in agreement, and she scrolled through her phone quickly, finding Isha's number. She hit call, fingers drumming on the wheel anxiously, so convinced no one was going to reply that she jumped when Isha answered.

"Adams."

"Isha. What've you got?"

"Afternoon to you too, pet."

"Sorry." She leaned forward, checking the road, but there was still no one of interest that she could see.

"Luckily I'm used to your peculiar charm," Isha said. "If you started going in for small talk I'd assume you'd been possessed by evil spirits."

"Always a possibility."

"I rule nothing out with you."

"So … what've you got?" Adams asked again.

"Nothing," Isha said.

"Nothing?"

"Not a blip. The night you requested? No one goes near the shop in any of the footage."

"Not out the back, either?"

"Nope. But here's the fun part. There are no files from

about one in the morning until five. I haven't had a chance to check the camera you sent me this morning yet, but I'm going to guess it'll be missing some chunks too."

"They've been deleted?"

"More the recordings just failed. I poked around a bit, of course, but when I couldn't find *anything*, no backups or even a sign the damn things ever existed, I called up to York and asked if the cameras had been offline. Said my maiden aunt was a bit dotty and had left her bag somewhere, so I was trying to retrace her steps."

"And they couldn't find them either," Adams said, less a question than a statement.

"Officer up there couldn't understand why there hadn't been so much as an error message about it."

"Both cameras?"

"You already knew that," Isha said. "In fact, I think this isn't surprising to you at all."

"Not *entirely*," Adams admitted. "But I thought there'd be more … *glitches*, rather than missing files."

"Like when the necklace went missing."

"Like then."

There was a pause, then Isha said, "What is this, Adams? Are you ever going to tell me?"

"Would it help if I said it's really safer if you don't know?"

"If I don't know but still go poking into things that are out of my department for you, you mean?"

"Yes. Sorry. I'll stop asking."

"That's not what I'm saying," Isha said, her voice uncharacteristically soft. "But you need to watch yourself. If someone's cleaning up camera footage so well I can't find a trace of it, and their own tech doesn't even know about it, we're not talking some small fudging of evidence. This stinks of something major."

All the more reason to stop involving you, Adams thought, but aloud she just said, "I'm being careful. Thanks, Isha."

"Sure." The phone disconnected without Isha saying anything more, and Adams rubbed her forehead slowly, eyes on Joe's apartment building. She had to go and check. *Had* to, but … the irritatingly familiar copper at Ash & Yew, chasing her through shops that opened onto other levels of York. Joe's shut down file. Even Collins' mate Farzana, not getting back to him. The apartment would be being watched, it *had* to be.

"Bollocks," she said quietly, and sat there, chewing on one thumbnail and trying to figure out what to do next.

SHE WAS STILL TRYING to figure it out when a car pulled into a delivery bay at the front of Joe's building. It was a nondescript Nissan, nothing she'd seen used as an unmarked car, and from here she couldn't see any of the telltale signs, no extra lights or antennae, but there was something about the lack of hesitation as it took the space that made her slide a little lower in the seat. A man swung out in plain clothes, looking up and down the street, and she made a little *ah-ha* sound, her stomach tightening in a mix of anticipation and misgiving. It was her pursuer from earlier. Her pursuer – and not only that, she recognised him now, with a big coat zipped to his chin. It was the man who'd spoken to her when she'd been taking photos of the cameras. How long had he been following her? *Watching* her? And in what capacity? Police or *other?*

"Now we're getting somewhere," she said to Dandy, and he whined softly.

The man took his phone out, but even as he did so a woman appeared from around the corner of the building, holding one hand up in greeting. They conferred briefly, then went inside, and Adams leaned over the wheel, waiting. She couldn't go in there and confront them. She just had to wait and see what happened.

For a little while nothing did, then a door slid violently open on a first-floor balcony, and a slim figure in a grey hoody and matching, too-short joggers hurried to the railing. They peered over the edge, glanced back into the flat, then swung themself over, stomach hooked on the top rail. Adams started the engine, and by the time she was working her way out of the space the figure was hanging from the bottom of the railing. It wasn't that big a drop, but she still winced as they let go, collapsing to the ground below. Above them, the police officer ran to the railing, followed by a woman not much older than Adams, her hair in a lopsided ponytail and her phone in one hand. Adams had her window down as she accelerated toward the building, and she could hear the woman shouting, although not the words.

The fleeing figure – and it had to be Joe, it was too much of a coincidence if not – sprinted across the road ahead of her and between the buildings on the other side. The door of his apartment block flew open, the female officer racing after him. Adams kept going, swerving into a side road that opened up ahead of her, cutting across the nose of a bus coming from the other direction and ignoring both its horn and the squeal of its brakes.

"Dandy, we need to find him," she said. "Help me, okay?"

She had one strange moment of dislocation where she was sure she could still see Dandy on the passenger seat out of the corner of her eye, while he was clearly on the pavement ahead and to the right, his nose pointed at an access lane that ran between two buildings. There wasn't time to think about the how of things, though, and she simply swung the wheel over, braking hard as she did so and barely stopping before she drove into a chain strung across the lane. Ahead of her, Dandy barked, then spun away and loped off down a path and out of sight.

"Helpful," she muttered, cutting the engine and scrambling out, hitting the lock as she peered after Dandy. Joe's building was out of sight from here, and she couldn't see anyone about, just a woman in a heavy hoody and hoop earrings staring down at her from a balcony, her arms folded and her face expressionless. When she met Adams' gaze she turned away abruptly, vanishing back inside.

Adams whistled for Dandy, but he didn't reappear, and she jogged to where he'd vanished, scanning the buildings for signs of motion. Nothing. All was still and oddly silent, no traffic passing on the street, no TVs blaring or music playing. Not even any wind. Just silent brick walls and windows blinded by curtains. She turned in a slow circle, hearing the scrape of concrete beneath her heel, as aware of her breath as if she could see it spooling in front of her in frosty air. She closed her eyes, searching for the edge of things, took a deep breath and opened them again, braced for what she'd see.

Nothing. It was just the same. She swore softly, then heard a sharp bark, accompanied by a very human yelp. She launched herself toward it, breaking into a run, and rounded the next corner directly into the path of someone sprinting from the other direction.

Both of them cried out, and Adams grabbed the other, both hands in the front of their coat.

"Let *go!*" they shouted, slamming their forearms into Adams', but she just let go with one hand, letting the other person swing away before bringing them to a halt again.

"Joe?" she asked, and the young man looked back at her, eyes wide.

"Who're you?"

"Someone who can help you," she said. "Unless you want to get nabbed by those two?"

"You're a pig," he said, his voice shaky.

"Yep. But I *will* help, if you come with me now."

"Why?" he demanded. He had a backpack clutched to him, one hand inside it, and she wondered what he had on him.

"I tried to get a look at your file, and suddenly I'm getting chased down by one of those two back there. I don't know why, but I'm going to find out, and I suggest you come along."

Dandy reappeared down the path, looking toward the corner of one of the buildings, and he barked once, a sharp warning. Adams released Joe, taking a step back. "We need to go if we're going."

Joe looked over his shoulder as the female officer rounded the corner. She was limping, and the knee of her jeans was torn. "*Oi!*" she shouted. "Get yourself back here!"

Adams ducked her head so the woman couldn't see her face. "Up to you," she said to Joe, and let him go, turning to run back to the car. She clicked her fingers at Dandy, but he was already veering into the officer's path, and as she darted back around the corner she heard a yelp and a thud.

Joe appeared as Adams started the car, scrambling around it to the passenger side and throwing himself in. Adams shifted into reverse, and as soon as the young man was fully in she accelerated, taking only the barest glance at the road before swinging out into it, jamming the brakes on as she turned. Dandy sprinted after them, and she said to Joe, "Watch out."

"What?" Joe asked. He'd taken something out of his bag, and was winding down the window. The female officer hadn't reappeared, but the male one from the Shambles had, running hard after them. Joe leaned out and hurled something into his path, staying hanging out of the window as he did so.

"What was that?" Adams demanded, expecting a crash or an explosion, but she had no time to look. She slammed the car into gear and accelerated away down the road even as Dandy appeared on Joe's lap, panting and delighted. Joe shrieked, shoving Dandy wildly until he slid into the footwell.

"What the hell is that?"

"I did tell you to watch out," Adams said, taking a turn at random and checking her rear-view mirror. The officer was still running, but not after them. He was trying to shake off something else, something small and determined, flashing metallic in the pale day.

She might've been wrong about Joe being clueless, after all.

13

OFF TO THE SHOP

Joe reached out a hesitant hand, and Dandy licked it. The young man gasped, pulled his hand back, then tried again, finding the dandy's dreadlocked back. "What … is it a *sheep?*"

Dandy snapped his mouth closed and gave Joe an affronted look.

"Dog," Adams said, taking another turn. She'd get the map up soon, but she wanted to get well away before the officers were in the car and after them. They'd have her number plate, which was going to be a problem, and though she'd kept her head down, she'd be struggling to pretend the car had been stolen. Still, she had an idea that whatever was going on, they wouldn't be filing any official complaints.

"An invisible, woolly dog?" Joe asked, petting Dandy, who licked his hand again. This time he laughed. "Oh, that is *weird.*"

"You're not Folk, then," Adams said.

"Uh, no." He gave Adams a wary look. "You?"

"No. Just have a sporadically invisible dog for some reason." She snaked through a one-way street and out the other side, keeping to the speed limit but not hanging around. So far there was no pursuit behind her, and she started to relax, wondering where to go.

"So what do you want?" Joe asked. "I mean, not that I don't appreciate the lift, but …"

Adams glanced at him. "What did you throw back there?"

"Just a thing."

"A thing?'

"Yeah. You know. A distraction." He looked at his hand, petting Dandy restlessly. *So weird.*

"Was it a guardian?"

"A what?" He looked at her properly, frowning. "What's that when it's at home?"

She gave him a sideways look. "Animated metal creatures?"

"Ah, I guess? But, I mean, they're just like little clockwork guys." He craned to look through the rear window, frowning. "I don't like losing them. They were cool."

"Clockwork?"

"Yeah, what did you think they were?"

She decided to change tack. "Where did you get them from?"

"A mate of mine."

"Right. You didn't pick them up at the Blighted Basilisk, by any chance?"

The flinch was so small Adams would've missed it if she hadn't been at a stop sign, looking straight at Joe.

"The … the what?" he asked.

"Win them in a card game, did you?"

"No?" he offered, his hand creeping toward his seatbelt buckle.

"*Stop.* Sit tight, unless you *want* to be picked up by the York cops."

Joe groaned, dropping his forehead to the pack on his lap. "No, I don't want. But what're *you* going to do?"

"Depends how much you can help me," she said. "Tell me about Ash & Yew."

"Oh, sodding hell," Joe said to the bag.

"Or I can drop you straight to the station."

The car was silent for a moment, then he said, "What d'you want to know?"

JOE HAD ROLLED OVER SO EASILY Adams almost didn't know where to start. "Where did you get the guardians?" she asked.

"They were a gift."

"From who?"

He hesitated, looking out the window. "I've been trying to find a better way to do things, you know? All the nicking cars and stuff's not getting me anywhere new, but no one's going to give me a job in a bloody office, are they? Can barely get one making butties in a greasy spoon, and that's not going to make rent for me and Mum."

"Seems unfair," Adams said.

He gave her a sideways look. "I'm not daft. I know I got myself into it, but I should get some credit for trying to get myself *out* of it."

"You should," she said, and maybe he realised she was being honest, because he leaned back in the seat with a sigh, still petting Dandy.

"Why d'you have an invisible dog?"

"No idea. What was your better way to do things, then?"

He didn't answer right away, looking through the rear window again. "You're not York police."

"No."

"That bloke back there was. He's a right nasty piece of

work. Jasper, he calls himself. Dunno if it's his real name or not." He looked at Adams. "Can you keep him off me?"

"I can try. You need to help me out, though."

He ran a hand back over his hair. It was darker than in his mug shot, and he had an earring in each ear. "Mum's not well. And the flat's damp. It's not helping. I was trying to figure out a way to level up, you know? And I met someone down the pub one night who needed a job doing. I did it, and he gave me another one, and I did that too, and then I started to get other jobs, you know, because I've got some skills."

"You're going to have to be a bit more specific." She was still driving, not sure where they were heading, just taking turns at random, and keeping an eye on the rear-view mirror at the same time.

"*Ugh.* Are you going to arrest me?"

She glanced at him. "Depends how helpful you are." She hated it, *hated* the fact that was always the game, but at the same time she played it, just like anyone else. And she did think it wasn't right that people like Joe, who had got them-selves stuck in a cycle that had been going long before they fell into it, who were just trying to make a living without anyone ever showing them the best way to do it, would get chucked in a cell while people who did a lot more harm but played the game a whole lot better got away with literal murder. She still hated the bartering, though.

Joe exhaled. "Ash & Yew. The jewellers."

"That's the one."

"Yeah," he said, and didn't offer anything else.

"I pulled your fingerprints off a tin box there. A box that something valuable was stolen out of."

He groaned, hugging his bag. "I didn't do anything. I've been set up."

"Why were your fingerprints there, then?"

"I guess I touched it? Look, a bunch of us went back one

night with Charles after the pub, and he was showing us stuff. It must've happened then."

Adams sighed. "Who else was there?"

He rubbed his head. "I was a bit tipsy myself. It was just a bunch of people from the pub."

"Violet Brennan?"

"Oh, Violet," he said, brightening. "No, she wasn't there. She worked with Charles for a bit, though. She gave me the little clockwork guys, actually. I think she made them while she was there."

"You're friends, then?"

"She's like my sister. We've known each other forever. She showed me—" He stopped, staring at his bag fixedly.

"Showed you the other York."

"*Yes.*" He looked at her, wide-eyed, then at the space where Dandy had been, passing his hand through it. "You know about it?"

"He's in the back now."

"Oh, right. Anyway, of course you know about it. You've got an invisible dog."

"How long has Violet known about it?"

He scratched the side of his head. "A while? She's always finding cool things, though. Tries anything, her."

"And is she your contact? The one you've been working with?"

"No. But she introduced us. Helping, you know."

Adams wasn't sure how helpful it was, dragging Joe into a world he had no understanding of, but she said, "This contact, did he know about Ash & Yew?"

"About me checking it out? No. He bollocked me when I mentioned it, actually. Got really worried the woman there would come after him for sneaking peeks."

"Heather?"

"That's her. Apparently she's pretty hardcore."

"I'm getting that impression." Adams tapped her fingers on the steering wheel. "Do you know where Violet is?"

"She might be at The Shop."

"The herbalist's?"

"No, *The Shop*, with, like, capitals. My contact runs it. He has the *coolest* stuff. That's why— Um. Never mind."

Adams was finding herself inclined to believe Joe's claim that he'd been set up. He was so keen to talk about all the cool things that she doubted he'd have been able to keep quiet about a master charm that could wake metal.

"Let's go to The Shop, then," she said.

"You want me to text her and ask her to meet us there?"

She eyed him. "Can you do it without letting on I'm here too? I have an idea she won't turn up otherwise. But I *am* trying to help you both out."

"Sure." He pulled his phone out, tapping a message out rapidly, then held it up to her. "Okay?"

Adams glanced at it. It just said, *Shop in 10*. "Perfect."

Joe tapped the phone, and Adams heard the swoop of the message sending. He looked around. "We need to head back toward the centre. Left up here."

"Alright." She indicated. "You don't suppose Violet might've taken the charm, do you? Since she had access to the shop?"

"No. Heather would *destroy* her."

"Only if she knew Violet took it, or could find her."

Joe snorted. "Oh, apparently she can find *anyone*, and apprentices have to sign in blood."

Adams stared at him. "In *blood?* Are you serious?"

"Yeah, not entirely up to health and safety," he said. "But Violet says it's so Heather can use it to track them if she wants. It's insurance, and when they leave they get the contract back, but Violet never believed she didn't have a backup of some sort. She almost walked when she had to sign, but she really wanted to learn from Heather, so she went through with it." He shrugged. "And then, of course, the job wasn't what she thought it was."

"*Huh.* So you don't think Violet might've been tempted to take something? Especially since the job was misrepresented?"

"You mean my clockwork guys? I think she was allowed to do those."

"I was thinking more … tools, say," Adams said. "To help her make them on her own."

"No, she didn't like the metal much, even though she was good at it. She's good at everything."

"Alright. Tell me about your side of things, then. Who's this person you're working with?"

Joe sighed deeply. "He's going to *kill* me for bringing you around."

"I'm not going to arrest anyone. I don't even want any details about what you've been up to, if it's just a bit of thieving."

"It was," Joe said firmly. "That's my field. Nothing else. I barely even drink, you know? Violet does … other stuff. That's how she started seeing the other York— *Wait.* She doesn't do it anymore."

"It's fine," Adams said, wondering how many things she was going to have to pretend she hadn't heard. This was worse that the bloody Toot Hansell Women's Institute and their *oops I fell into a murder investigation* tendencies. "Look, something was stolen from Ash & Yew. And it's a big thing. A *really* big thing. If Heather's as dangerous as she sounds, then you and Violet are going to need some protection. If I've found out you were there that night, she will too."

Joe stared at her, clutching his bag closer. "You think Violet's in danger?"

"Both of you."

"What about my mum?" he all but whispered. "Those bloody coppers were there. What if they hurt her?"

"They're connected, aren't they?"

He spread his fingers. "Jasper knows all about other York. And he turns up at my place right when you're hunting for this thing that's been stolen? He must be after it too."

Adams nodded. "It's alright. Let's get to this shop. Tell me what you can on the way."

WHAT HE COULD DIDN'T TURN out to be an awful lot. Violet had introduced him to someone called Eddie, who was basically using Joe to steal to order. Eddie provided some sort of spyglass that, Joe said, let him see the passageways between the layers. It meant he could make quick, clean getaways from surface York, which was how Joe referred to the non-Folk version of the city. It was nothing particularly nefarious, and nothing he'd stolen sounded that worrying. Eddie seemed to have an appetite for antique knickknacks and dinner sets, for the most part. Joe's own knowledge of the Folk world didn't even extend as far as the existence of the Watch, and Adams had to stop herself channelling her mum and clipping him around the ear for his foolishness. An entire *other layer of reality*, inhabited by kinds most humans thought were myth, and he found the most interesting thing to be the fact he'd met someone at the pub who had taught him how to pull pigeons out of a hat.

"Any hat, too," he was saying, as they reached the area where The Shop was. "It's not, like, a trick. It's *actual magic*. Everyone was getting a bit upset about the pigeons being in the pub, though, so now we mostly do card tricks."

"Great," she said, swinging into a side street that was separated from the river by a low red brick wall and some bollards. There was a parking space near the end, and Adams pulled into it, looking distrustfully at the water as they climbed out. The afternoon was dull, clouds banishing the sun as they gathered over the city, rendering the slice of river she could see matte and dark. A couple of swans drifted gracefully near the far bank, and she put her parking permit in the window, somewhat reluctantly. They were in a residents' zone, so it was that or risk getting towed. Hopefully no one would stumble across them.

"It's just up here." Joe turned away from the river, leading the way down the narrow street. The buildings peered across the road at each other from white-framed windows, their tiny front gardens crowded with pots planted up with flourishes of spring bulbs. Some of the doors had large, dignified white frames too, and the glimpses of the rooms beyond the windows were all cream walls and self-conscious bookshelves. A jogger went past, puffing steadily as he headed toward the river, as well as a couple of women pushing high-tech prams, and as Adams and Joe turned onto the main street at the end of the lane, she was startled to see the sheer stone sides of Clifford's Tower sprouting from its green mound, unexpected as a mirage. They'd come at it from the other side of town, and she hadn't realised they were so close to the centre again.

Joe turned away from it, heading between a muddle of old and new red brick buildings that lined the street, sporting a mix of graceful, irregularly shaped windows and extravagant towers, and boxy, efficient versions of the same, a marrying of two worlds. It was busy, buses and cars panting along the road, cyclists sweeping past with scarves pulled up over their noses, and pedestrians ploughing up and down the pavements.

They didn't walk far before Joe stopped at a black door in one of the old buildings, a small-paned window next to it holding nothing but a single daffodil in a white vase. A discreet, hand-lettered sign read, *May Be Open.*

"This is it?" Adams asked.

"Yep," Joe said, trying the door. It had an old-fashioned latch, the sort with a paddle to push down with a thumb, and it opened with a polite creak. A whiff of wood smoke and dust drifted out to greet them, and he looked at Adams.

"Go on," Adams said. "I need to make a quick call."

"Alright." Joe vanished inside, leaving the door open in his wake.

Dandy looked at Adams questioningly, and she nodded after Joe. "Stick with him," she said in a low voice. Dandy huffed, but slipped through the door, tail waving softly.

Adams looked at the street, at its plain, normal angles and familiar cars and posters and shops, then pulled her phone out and hit dial.

Collins answered almost at once, the sound of the car rumbling behind him. "Adams, good, I'm not far off—"

"More pressing issues," she said. "Have you got hold of Farzana yet?"

"No. I've tried her a couple of times and she's still not answering."

"Right. She might not. That copper who chased me earlier turned up at Lister's place. I got hold of Joe and have him with me, but I don't think he's our guy. He says he's been set up."

"And this is relevant to Farzana because?"

"He's had some run-ins with that cop before, by the sound of things. There's definitely something going on up here, so keep out of the way of any York police."

"Alright. Where should I meet—"

"I'll call you." She hung up before he could say anything else, ducking through the door. She didn't *think* Joe would run off on her, but it was impossible to say for sure. She certainly didn't want to give him too much opportunity to do so, just in case.

She wasn't quite sure what to expect inside, and was mostly just hoping it wasn't another pub. She'd had enough of them. But that wasn't what she found. Instead, a wide, tall corridor with a bare wooden floor dived toward the back of the building, which seemed to extend for an improbable distance. To either side, where there might've been rooms in an actual house, were open-fronted chambers. One was crammed with bookshelves, lining the walls all the way to the high ceilings, as well as free-standing shelves in the middle of the room packed so closely that the skinny aisles between allowed barely enough room for anyone to walk through. Another was brightly lit, the walls full of alcoves that were sparsely stocked with dark glass bottles and jars with minimalist labels. Herbs and flowers were arranged in heavy vases, and *apothecary* was the first word that sprang to Adams' mind. Another room was closed off with sliding lattice doors, and the scent of essential oils drifted past them; yet another held nothing but three deeply elegant pianos and an enormous harp. A very large woman with flowers woven into her hair was polishing the wood carefully, and she waved cheerily at Adams as she passed.

Adams nodded back, and kept going, already regretting letting Joe go ahead of her. How was she meant to find the right place in here?

She'd almost resigned herself to the young man having slipped away when she reached the back of the corridor, where a metal spiral staircase led upward. *To The Shop*, a sign on the wall said, the arrow marking the stairs, and Adams relaxed slightly. Maybe Joe hadn't vanished on her after all. She started up, the treads clanging underfoot, and emerged into a wilderness of old furniture and patchy mannequins, tarnished mirrors and leaning coat racks and bikes missing seats or wheels or handlebars. Chests of drawers were stacked with shade-less lamps, tatty bed frames loaded with rolled rugs and giant stuffed toys and fraying straw hats, and old road signs and shop signs and, for some reason, net-wrapped fishing buoys, lined the walls. She froze where she was, sure that if she put a foot wrong she'd be buried under an avalanche of junk. She whistled softly, half afraid even the noise might set off the landslide, but nothing moved. She tried again, a little louder, then spotted a path leading through the mess. It looked risky, but hopefully not catastrophic.

The place was a maze, a tangle of junk and antiques, the worthless and the priceless all jumbled up together. Other paths wandered off at intervals, and Adams started to spot hand-painted signs with things like *Music* or *Clothing* written on them, although there were also *Armaments* and *Deceptions* signs, neither of which filled her with great confidence. The path she was on seemed to be a main thoroughfare of sorts, though, and she kept going, whistling occasionally for Dandy, but he seemed to have taken himself off on his own business. She may as well be dealing with a cat for all the good he was doing.

She was just wondering if bribery via dog biscuits was the secret to invisible dog training when the path finished at an open area, washed with natural light. She'd walked all the way back to the front of the building, and a collection of windows let the slowly clouding day in, the lower ones tall, slim, and arched, while above them were smaller, petalled openings. Pigeons perched inside, helping themselves to seeds and water, squirrels scuttled along the heavy, exposed beams above, and below the windows was a collection of soft-looking sofas and chairs, some low tables, and any number of easels. Some had half-finished watercolours on them, others were mere sketches or blank, and almost all of them were studies of pigeons or squirrels. Or pigeons *and* squirrels.

"You found us!" Joe said, waving at her from a lime-green beanbag. He had a mug of tea in his other hand.

"I did," Adams said, frowning at Dandy. He was chewing on a bone, and gave her what she chose to believe was a guilty look.

"You don't mind, do you?" a deep voice asked. "He looked a bit peckish."

Adams turned to the speaker, finding a large and somewhat lumpen individual looking back at her. They had big, heavy hands, huge, grey-skinned shoulders under a paint-smeared singlet and overalls, and either armoured plates on their forehead or some pretty hefty body modification.

"He lies," she said. "But no, it's fine."

"Morris," the painter said, holding a giant hand out to her.

"Adams," she said, managing to swallow the *DI*. They shook, Morris's grip gentle. "Are you Joe's … colleague, then?"

Morris made a face. "Not at all."

"That'd be me," someone else said, and a man who was as slight and insubstantial as Morris was hefty emerged from behind a wall of old TVs. He gave her a mock salute, his features sharp and pointed. "Eddie."

"Adams," she said again.

"Adams what?"

"Eddie, behave," Morris said, and went back to his canvas. "She doesn't owe you her name."

"But she might give it to me. If I ask nicely, like."

"It's Adams," she said, looking around. "Violet not here, then?"

"Haven't seen her for a day or so," Morris said.

Adams looked at Joe, and he waved his phone at her. "She hasn't read the text."

"Try calling her." She looked at Eddie while Joe poked the mobile. "He's getting chased by some copper called Jasper. Know anything about him?"

"Information isn't free, Adams."

"*Eddie*," Morris said. "She's trying to help out."

"She's being nosy," Eddie said.

Morris fixed him with a steady gaze. Eddie withstood it for a moment, then flapped his hands.

"Alright, alright. I shall hold it for future favours, though." He pointed at Adams. "Why d'you want to know?"

"For his own safety," she said. "Maybe yours, too."

Eddie made a *hmm* noise, and Morris said, "About time. That man's been a blight on the streets for far too long."

"I can handle him," Joe said. "I'm just worried about Mum, you know?"

"Of course you are," Morris said. "You're a good lad."

Eddie shook his head. "We're a business, not a halfway house for lost humans." He nodded at Dandy. "Or hellhounds."

"He's not a hellhound," Adams said, as Dandy gave Eddie an offended look.

"Don't mind Eddie," Morris said. "He barks a lot, but never bites."

"Only when invited, my love," Eddie said, blowing Morris a kiss, and he rolled his eyes, but gave a giant, craggy grin at the same time. Eddie looked at Adams. "Violet introduced Joe to York's … idiosyncrasies. She and I had a couple of business arrangements, but she felt for my more day-to-day needs, Joe might be a better fit. He's reliable, true to his word, so I gave him some gear and got him started."

"Right. You have a lot of business arrangements with people?"

Eddie gestured, taking in the chaotic order of the junk around them. "One doesn't get this at the local car boot sale."

"I suppose not. Any of these arrangements concern Ash & Yew?"

Eddie took a step back from her. "Ash & Yew? Oh, no, you—"

He never got to finish his sentence, because in that moment the room exploded, every item surging up and toward them like a tidal wave, roaring with the sound of breaking plates and snapping wood, sending the pigeons scattering and the easels flying. Adams threw herself forward, running to grab Joe.

She didn't make it in time.

The beanbag opened like a maw and swallowed the young man, and Adams covered her head as the debris smashed into her, carrying her toward the windows and the street waiting below.

14

THE DANGER OF OFF-BRAND BEANBAGS

Dandy was barking, muffled and rhythmic, the only sound that broke through the cacophony of falling furniture and smashing glass, then even that was lost. The noise of the surging junk was an assault on the hearing, and Adams would've covered her ears if she hadn't been so intent on trying to protect her entire head from the monsoon of debris. It was moving in ways that made no sense, as if someone had picked up the room and shaken it furiously, turning it into a snow globe full of pointy edges. She couldn't keep her feet, and would've stumbled to her knees if the floor hadn't been lost in the mess. Something gouged her hip painfully, and something else smacked her shin, and she cracked her spine so agonisingly on an ungiving corner that tears jumped to her eyes, and she gasped. And still the endless shifting continued, the room in furious motion, defiant of physics or logic.

The windows hadn't been far from her, and she'd been carried toward them by the flood of junk, so she braced herself to wind up against the glass, to be either smashed through and hurled to the street below, or simply crushed in place. But that didn't seem to be happening, and instead she just kept getting tumbled by the attack. She fetched up against something unmoving, and risked lowering one arm away from her face to snag it. It was solid but free-standing, and she was able to hook her arm over it, a swimmer grabbing a life ring in a storm. She wrestled herself toward it, her head clearing the flood so she could use her other arm to help.

The debris seemed reluctant to let her go, snagging her trousers and clawing at her jacket, but finally she was seated on a wide wooden beam, resting above the carnage like a floating dock on floodwater. High, small windows still let the light in ahead of her, and the pigeons were swooping around the space, cooing in alarm. Adams looked around, frowning, and realised she was sitting on one of the massive old rafters that had swept so gracefully overhead earlier, sharing space with a dozen squirrels, one of which was clutching a thimble and screaming at her, apparently convinced she had designs on its stash. The wood under her was old and weathered, but she could still feel the life in it, warm and resilient.

"Bloody hell," she muttered to herself, then yelled, "*Dandy!*"

There was no response, no answering bark, and her heart squeezed painfully in her chest, fright and horror all at once. But he was an invisible dog who was unbothered by such limitations as walls. He'd be alright. Wouldn't he?

She shouted for him again, and tried a couple of whistles, but that only set the pigeons off, fluttering about the place in panic and leaving deposits everywhere.

"Joe!" she tried. "Morris! Anyone?"

The debris, which had still been rumbling and settling underneath her, was stilling, and she stared around. From here she could see the full expanse of the vast upstairs space, and it wasn't all full of junk. Everything had been scooped up and flung toward them, pouring into the art studio area below the windows like a lava flow. It tapered off further into the building, until clear floor reasserted itself toward the stairs. The woman from the music shop was slowly emerging from them, her eyes wide.

"Morris?" she called. "Eddie? What's happened?"

"Go back down!" Adams shouted. "It's not safe!"

The woman stared at her. "What're you doing up there?"

"Ah … sorting things. Is everyone alright there?"

The woman gave her a dubious look, then peered back down the stairs. "There's some woman up here says she's sorting it, but I think she's stuck on a rafter." Someone said something below her, and the woman looked back at Adams. "Ibrahim wants to know if the squirrels are okay."

"They seem to be."

The woman relayed this, and Adams clearly heard a "Dammit," from downstairs. The woman looked back at her. "Ibrahim's a barber, and the squirrels keep coming in and stealing the hair off the floor. Really freaks people out. They think someone's after it for voodoo reasons, see."

"Right," Adams said. "More worried about Morris and Eddie, to be honest."

"Of course," the woman said, and looked around in a distracted manner, as if expecting to see them perched up in the rafters somewhere as well.

Adams took a breath, then shouted their names again. There was nothing at first, then a very small shout came back from somewhere in the mess, away from the windows. Adams got to her knees on the beam, steadying herself with her hands, then very carefully straightened up to standing.

"*Ooh*, mind how you go," the woman said, stepping cautiously onto the empty floor of the shop. "Here, look how big it is when Eddie doesn't have his rubbish everywhere!"

That earned another muffled shout, this one sounding at least a little aggrieved.

"Stay back," Adams said to the woman, as a faun with a dark, well-kept beard emerged after her. "This whole lot could all go tumbling again."

"Well, see you don't knock it over," the faun said. "That's on you, that is."

Adams had a nasty feeling the whole situation was on her, as she doubted the shop going on the attack was a regular occurrence. But she just concentrated on making her way along the uneven beam without falling, heading toward where the shout had come from. She spotted one of the fishing buoys, a coil of stiff, barnacle-encrusted rope still attached to it, and sat down on the beam again, taking her baton out and using it to snag the rope and pull it toward her. It would barely unbend from its lashed position, but she unfolded it as well as she could, and towed it with her until she was at the closest point to where the shouts had come from. There she forced it around the beam and into a knot that was inelegant but hopefully effective.

"What're you doing?" the faun shouted.

"*Shh,*" she said, straightening up. "You might set it off again." The woman and the faun had been joined by a handful of others, human and not, all looking around with interest.

"Look," a very small, skinny person with soft blonde hair and a matching, elegantly groomed beard said, pointing at the wall of junk with pale pink fingernails. "That's your accordion, isn't it, Stef?"

"*Ugh,*" the first woman said. "And I thought it had been stolen! Bloody squirrels!"

She started across the room, presumably to retrieve her accordion, and Adams hissed, "*Don't!* You'll bring the whole bloody lot down."

The woman frowned, looking as if she were inclined to argue, but the faun pulled her back.

"Can you all go back down?" Adams asked. She didn't fancy setting off another avalanche and them being caught in it.

"No," the blonde person said. Adams assumed they must be from the spa-scented place, as they were wearing a white, medical-style tunic that reached the floor. They had immaculate make-up, and a pair of horns painted the same delicate shade as their nails.

"We want to make sure they're alright," Ibrahim said.

"And I want my accordion back," Stef said.

Adams sighed. "I'm working on it. Just stay back, okay?" She sat down on the beam and rested her feet gently in the mess of broken furniture and old trunks and faded stuffed toys, ignoring a fallen cuckoo clock that dinged in alarm and tried to fire its cuckoo out at her. Gravity worked against it, the bird just juddering inside with a grinding of gears.

Nothing collapsed underneath her instantly, and she slowly shifted her weight off the beam, one foot on an excessively fluffy ottoman and the other on a rolled rug. They held, so she leaned forward, using her hands to distribute her weight a bit more evenly, creeping over the flood with her muscles singing with tension and her breath tight in her chest. The squirrels chittered at her from the beam, then scampered in pursuit, passing her and investigating the clutter with squeals of alarm, while the pigeons still fluttered overhead, anxious and unsettled. She ignored them all, looking for solid foot- and handholds as she moved steadily forward. Once, her foot slipped and she lurched sideways with a curse, her leg vanishing into the depths, but she belly-flopped across the surface, stopping her fall, and managed to recover herself. Just after that, a leering face reared up at her and she had to force herself not to go scrambling backward.

It surged closer, then a squirrel bounded past, wearing a doll's head for some unknown reason, and she stayed where she was for a moment, panting and wishing Dandy were there. He'd have made short work of the bloody squirrels.

But finally she was as close as she thought she could be to where the shouts had come from.

"Morris?" she called. "Eddie?"

The answering call came from slightly ahead of her, against the side wall. "Are you still here? Haven't you done enough?"

A second voice said, "Stop it, Eds. She's helping."

"*She destroyed my shop!*"

"I'm sure it wasn't deliberate."

"It wasn't," Adams agreed. "Are you hurt?"

"No, but Eddie won't leave his glassware."

"*It's crystal.*"

Adams poked some of the surrounding furniture. She wasn't sure how she was going to fish the pair out without crushing them. "Okay, I have a rope, but this is really precarious—" she was cut off by an eruption ahead of her. She yelped, throwing herself backward and ignoring a chorus of shouts from near the stairs, all wanting to know what was going on. The debris shifted and shuddered, sending her clawing her way to steadier ground, and Eddie emerged, curled into foetal position and wrapped tightly around a crystal decanter in a velvet-lined box. Two huge hands clutched his waist, holding him aloft like a trophy.

"*Morris!*" he yelled. "You can't just throw me up here! What about my *stuff?!*"

The hands were wobbling a bit, and Adams reached out a hand to Eddie. He promptly thrust the box at her. "Save it!"

"Right." She set the box in a relatively secure spot and reached out to Eddie again. "Come on."

He reluctantly allowed himself to be hauled away from

the sinkhole in the mess, and she took the rope from around her own waist, tying it to him instead.

"Everyone just stay still, alright?" she called, and the big hands, now free of their burden, gave her two thumbs up. She scrambled back to the safety of the beam, the route seeming a lot shorter now, then called to Eddie, "Come on."

He did, lighter and more agile than she was, but also with the box back under one arm, which hampered him somewhat. She kept the rope taut as he clambered toward her, reeling it in bit by bit, and once he was sitting on the beam she called, "Morris, I'm coming back." How the hell she was going to get him across the treacherous surface she didn't know, since he probably weighed twice as much as her and Eddie combined, if not more, but she'd figure it out.

"Moz, get the glasses!" Eddie yelled. "The jug's not worth anything without the glasses!"

"Everyone clear?" Morris shouted, his voice muffled.

"*The glasses!*"

Adams was untying the rope from Eddie when the corner of the room *surged.*

"*Morris!*" Eddie bellowed.

Chairs and coffee tables and cast-iron pots and mysterious sculptures bounced and juddered, tumbling over each other, and Adams thought for a moment there had been a cave-in, her head already racing for ways to get Morris out. Then she realised that the cave-in was moving. It formed a steady trail, like the upheaval left behind by a rabbit in a cartoon, progressing slowly but inexorably across the room toward the stairs.

"Everyone out!" she shouted, almost falling off the beam as she stepped over Eddie. "Everyone back down the stairs, *now!*" She hurried along the beam as well as she could, to where she could see the stairs and the clear area around it. The wall of debris was crumbling, lights and croquet mallets and cushions bouncing across the floor. The shopkeepers stared at it, and Ibrahim bent to pick up a Rubik's cube that spun to his feet.

"*Out!*" Adams yelled again. "Or do you *want* to get squashed?"

Even as she spoke, a sofa fell from the wall, toppling end over end and almost reaching the group at the head of the stairs. They turned, pushing and scrabbling to be the first back down, the metal treads ringing under their feet.

Stef was the last to go, and she barely made it before the wall gave entirely. A tidal surge of junk roared across the floor, flooding every gap, sending smaller items tumbling down the stairs, the sound of cracking wood and smashing glass filling the air once more. Adams sat down abruptly as the floor of debris fell away beneath the beam, giving her a moment of sweeping vertigo as her brain tried to convince her she was flying up into the air, then everything slowly juddered to a stop.

Morris looked up at Adams from where he'd burst out of the junk and into clear air, his overalls torn and a small cut bleeding on the grey skin above his left ear.

"Well," he said. "That was a bit of a to-do, wasn't it?"

"But what about my collection?" Eddie almost wailed. "It was *precious,* and now it's probably all smashed to bits!"

Morris waded through the mess, casually breaking a few smaller items under his massive feet, then raised both hands to Eddie. "I saved *my* most precious thing," he said, giving a great, craggy smile. "Jump. I'll catch you."

Eddie huffed. "They were valuable!"

"I know," Morris said, beckoning Eddie down. "You'll find more, though, my clever little criminal."

Eddie scowled, but he jumped, and Morris caught him easily. Adams looked away, searching the room. There was no Joe in it, and no Dandy, and she swallowed hard, feeling abruptly and horribly alone.

MORRIS HANDED ADAMS A MINT PENGUIN. "Sorry, Eddie ate all the orange ones," he said.

"You make it sound as if that's not what they're for," Eddie said. He was prowling the room. The debris had settled in a blanket of broken and splintered and undamaged stock, piled up in great banks in some places, in others just a shallow covering. The pigeons had mostly settled back down, helped by a generous serving of seeds that Morris sprinkled on the window frames, while the squirrels bounced and chattered through the mess, uncovering forgotten nut stashes with great glee. "*Morris*," Eddie called. "They've got a damn nest in the back of a Louis XIV! Do you know how much I could've got for that?"

"No," Morris said comfortably, unwrapping his own Penguin. It was barely a bite for him.

"What happened?" Adams asked, looking at the patches of exposed floor around them. The wooden boards were glossy rather than worn, as richly toned as fresh-hewn trunks. "Earthquake?"

Morris shook his heavy head. "You don't really think that."

"No," she admitted. "I was just hoping."

Eddie snorted. "And I suppose you think it was *entirely* unconnected to you and your hellhound, too. Where did that thing go?"

"His name's Dandy. And I don't know. After Joe, I hope."

"Any idea where the lad could've gone?" Morris asked. "Our beanbags aren't usually in the habit of eating people."

"I was hoping you'd know," Adams said, taking a bite of

her Penguin. She needed to pick up some more Yorkies. It looked like it was going to be a day for it.

"It'll be his own damn fault," Eddie said, joining them with an ornate, gold-trimmed music box in one hand. It was dinging sadly. "He'll have gone and stuck his nose into something he shouldn't."

"Something *you* told him to," Morris said. "For what? Another crystal decanter?"

"That'll pay for our next holiday," Eddie protested. "Moorea isn't cheap, you know!"

"How's he been getting through the doors?" Adams asked. "He said you were helping him."

Eddie grimaced. "Yeah. Might have made a small misjudgement there, to be honest. Violet had already showed him into the pub, so it wasn't like he *didn't* know there were doorways. But I gave him a little spyglass that would let him find them, and next thing I know he's popping in and out all over the place, like he's Folk. I told him to stop it, that it was only going to draw attention, but he's a silly lad."

"He's a *lad*," Morris said. "Just a child. He thought he'd stumbled on this amazing way to make good money, and kept talking about how he was going to take care of his mum, and Violet. That's on you, that is, Eddie."

"He's an *adult*. It was a business arrangement," Eddie insisted. Morris just gave him a disappointed look, and Eddie stared at the music box, stroking its lid. "Ruined, it is."

"Right," Adams said, and looked around the shop again. "Is there a door in here Joe might've gone through?"

"It's downstairs, not up here." Morris said.

"Well, he must've gone *somewhere*," Adams said, looking at the jumble of junk and treasure. "He didn't just get swallowed by the bloody beanbags."

"I doubt it," Morris said, and looked at Eddie. "Where did you get those beanbags from?"

"Around," he said, giving Adams a sharp look.

Morris made a thoughtful noise. "Have you ever heard of beanbags eating anyone?"

"No," Eddie said. "But they were very off-brand, so anything's possible."

They both seemed to give this due consideration while Adams finished her Penguin and wondered at what point she'd stopped thinking a conversation about the eating habits of off-brand beanbags was unusual. "Alright," she said aloud, looking at the rich tones of the flooring, and the heavy beams overhead. They'd sprouted shoots in the joints. "I have an idea what might've happened." She fished a card from her pocket and offered it to the pair. "Give me a call if Violet turns up or Joe comes back, alright?"

Morris reached for the card, and Eddie snatched it first, sharp eyes flicking over it. "*Detective Inspector?* I thought you were going to *help* us with that bloody copper Jasper, not just be another—" He stopped short, shooting her a wary look.

"Another what?" Adams asked.

"Nothing."

She rocked on her heels. "I'm not on the take. And if I can help you, I will."

Eddie looked at the card, then at Morris. "A bloody hellhound. We should've known!"

"I did," Morris said mildly, handing Adams another Penguin.

"Why didn't you say anything? *She can't be here.*" He gestured at the devastated shop. "This was all about her! It has to be!"

"You're overreacting, my love."

"*I'm not.*" Eddie jabbed a finger at Adams. "It's *her.* The bloody detective and her sodding *dog!* We do *not* want to be in the middle of that, drawing attention to ourselves. And she's sniffing around Ash & Yew!"

Adams looked from one of them to the other, and deliberately unwrapped her Penguin. Eddie glared at her. "Oh, carry on," she said, seating herself on an upturned chest of drawers. "I'm not going anywhere."

"You bloody are. You're getting out of here, *now*."

"Tell me what you think you're in the middle of."

Eddie waved his arms violently, encompassing the chaos that had just descended on them. "This! *This!* Why do you think this *happened?*"

"Who did it?" she asked, having a bite of chocolate.

"*I don't know!*" Eddie looked like he was about to collapse from sheer exasperation, and Morris put a heavy hand on his shoulder.

"Eddie, love," he said, "Why don't you see if the kitchen's still in one piece and put the kettle on?"

"But ... but she's ... I ..." He threw his arms up again, then turned and stalked away. "*And stop your sodding squirrels eating my stock!*"

Morris watched him go, then looked at Adams. "He's a little excitable."

"I got that impression."

They examined each other for a moment, Morris's eyes small but sharp under the heavy, armoured plates of his forehead. Finally he said, "You're making people nervous. Word is you brought down the bridges in London."

Adams frowned. "I haven't brought down anything. They were standing just fine when I left."

Morris gave her a smile that was far too like the reassuring one he'd been using on Eddie. "Not the bridges themselves. Their essence. The creatures."

"Oh." She was quiet for a moment, thinking of that last glimpse of them, dragging themselves ashore, looking back at her as if *she* were the monster, not them with their fog and hunger and stolen children. "It wasn't intentional. I just had to get the kids back."

"I think that's what's making people nervous. You just *do* things."

She gave him a bewildered look. "Doesn't everyone?"

"No. Most people negotiate. Strategise. They're *politic*, if you will."

"They scheme, you mean?"

"Maybe. Either way, associating with you is risky. Certain people with influence don't like it."

"Meaning who?"

He smiled, revealing an array of broken teeth. "Meaning I could be here forever listing my ideas, but instead I think you'd best find Joe and Violet. There's more at play here than a couple of missing kids, but they're your way in."

"I know," she said.

"Then off you go, Detective Inspector. Go and *do*. I personally think we need more of it. We're businesspeople, not politicians."

Adams looked at him, wanting to ask any one of the dozen questions rolling around in her head, not least of which was *what are you,* which would be rude in any context. And the answers to the others, she had an idea, lay back in Ash & Yew. So she just said, "Alright. Contact me if you see Violet or Joe?"

"I will do. And next time you'll have to stop for tea. Eddie does an excellent Victoria Sponge."

"Good to know," she said, and headed for the stairs, wondering why everyone in Yorkshire was so fixated on baked goods. It seemed to be a cross-species thing, too.

15

FEED THE BEASTS

Adams slipped out of the building without being accosted by any of the other shopkeepers, although she noticed the bamboo plants outside the spa-type place had blossomed into a thicket that punched through to the floor above and blocked the door entirely. Someone was sawing away at them enthusiastically from the inside, swearing in a long and repetitive monologue, punctuated only by someone else saying, "I have to get to work! I'm going to be *late*, and this stress is *entirely* undoing the whole point of a massage."

She considered stopping to help, but judging by the short, small-featured person with big ears standing across the corridor from the spa, collecting money from onlookers and making notes on a tablet, there was some sort of bet running on how long it was going to take for the bamboo wall to fall. She didn't want to get in the middle of that.

Outside, she started toward the car, then hesitated. She was going to need Yorkies, she was sure of it. She still wasn't certain what the chocolate did, if it was simply the sugar hit to chase away shock, or if there really were some particular properties to the Yorkies themselves. She had noticed people using different types of chocolate, but Yorkies had stood her in good stead on the bridge, and she hated to change something that was working.

She turned on her heel and hurried down the road, spotting a newsagent's on the corner. It was a touristy sort of place, selling Viking mugs and tea towels with cityscapes on them, but it also had a generous chocolate selection. She cleared the display of plain Yorkies (again, the raisin and biscuit ones would *probably* be fine, but why risk it?) and set them on the counter, where the bored-looking assistant totted up the total without a flicker of interest. She left shortly after with a dozen chocolate bars in a souvenir bag with *I* 🤍 *York* printed on the flimsy plastic and a paper cup of vending machine coffee in one hand, and headed for the car.

She was already seeing things at that double level, places given extra dimensions and doors blooming in one layer of reality but not another. It made her eye twitch, and a headache start behind it, and she decided the Penguin bars were insufficient for such things. She juggled her cup, tearing one of the Yorkie bars open with her teeth while some wit called, "Easy, love, it's not running away from you!" She ignored him, taking a bite of the chocolate bar and turning onto the side street where they'd left the car, searching for Dandy even though she knew in her gut he wasn't going to be there.

And she was right. Dandy wasn't waiting at the car.

Someone else was, though.

The nondescript Nissan was parked at the top of the street, no one immediately visible in it, but she recognised the plates immediately. She turned on her heel, crossing the main road, her back tense and braced for a shout or pursuit as she dodged around a taxi and ran to avoid a white van bombing toward her with no sign of slowing. She glanced back as she reached the far side of the road and spotted the man from Joe's apartment – the man from other York, the man from Ash & Yew, the officer who'd chased her right through the butcher's, the one Joe had called Jasper – jogging across the road after her, his eyes on the traffic. The car was just pulling out of its space, and she dropped her coffee, breaking into a sprint with the bag of chocolate bars still clutched in one hand.

Had someone from the shops called them? Had they tracked her somehow? It hardly mattered. She weaved her way down the pavement, running hard, not wasting breath on declaring herself, while behind her Jasper yelled, *"Police! Stop that woman!"*

A large young man started to step into her path, hulking his shoulders as if he could stop her through intimidation alone, and a very elderly woman walloped him behind the knees with an umbrella, making him stagger away with a yelp.

"Run, woman, run!" she shrieked. *"Down with the pigs!"* She then proceeded to lay into the young man with her umbrella furiously, while he tried to fend her off, eyes wide with alarm.

Adams couldn't wholeheartedly support the sentiment, but she appreciated the help. She swerved down a side street, hoping wildly it didn't lead to a dead end, and spotted a metal door resting ajar, held open by a crate. She dived through it, discovering a set of old stone stairs beyond, dimly lit and uneven. She clattered down them, squinting as her eyes adjusted to the dimness, and found herself in a narrow, slightly dingy but better lit corridor, doors marked *Costume*, and *Staffroom*, and *Lockers* facing onto it, as well as some unmarked ones, and another door waiting at the far end. She sprinted for it, hoping she was guessing right and it wasn't going to lead to a cleaning cupboard or a coat closet as she heard the clang of the street door slamming at the top of the stairs behind her.

The new door opened easily, plunging her into darkness once again. Screams echoed from somewhere, and straw crunched underfoot. Red lights flickered in gaps in what looked like stone walls, and she tripped over heavy, rusting chains, banging her knee painfully on a heavy metal and wood contraption. A man was stretched out on it, and he moaned pitifully. Her breath caught in her throat as she glimpsed his ribs straining against his filthy skin, and the milky cast of his eyes, then someone said, "Hey, you can't be in there! Get out!"

Adams spun, startled, and spotted an equally filthy woman waving at her. She was wearing a long dress embellished with lace, but it was torn and discoloured, and the woman looked like she only had about five teeth left.

"What—" she started.

"Come *on*," the woman said, in a surprisingly posh accent. "If you want to audition, you have to speak to the manager. You can't just drop in here like this."

Adams looked back at the man on the rack, realising he wasn't breathing, despite the moans, which were recurring at a mechanical interval.

"Do hurry up," the woman said. "There's a group on the way, and it's hardly bloody atmospheric if you're blundering about in your street clothes." She adjusted her teeth, settling them in place more securely, and Adams scrambled over a low rope barrier that separated the agonised waxwork from the rest of the room. York Dungeons. She had to be in York Dungeons.

"Where's the way out?" she demanded, and the woman pointed across the room to a stone arch, where an emergency exit sign glimmered at the lowest possible level of brightness. Adams bolted for it even as the door opened again in the wall behind her.

"For heaven's *sake*," the woman complained. "What on *earth* are you all up to?"

Adams ran harder, gratified by a grunt of pain and a clatter behind her, as well as the woman berating Jasper for disturbing the display and ruining her work. The arch led to a tunnel pocked with barred alcoves containing skeletons and more lamps, a steady soundtrack of groans and wails following her. The next room was profoundly dark, and she could just make out a group clumped together in the centre of it. Lights flashed, revealing actors looming over the huddled tourists or crouching before them, eliciting screams and some swearing, then it went dark again. Adams stumbled toward where she thought the next arch lay, bumping into someone as the players changed position, then the lights flashed back on and another chorus of screams went up

She shoved her way past the actor she'd collided with, who muttered, "Easy, mate," as they were plunged into darkness again and she lost sight of the exit, walking straight into a wall. She swore, trying to orient herself in the glimpses of the room the lights granted her, but with the group in the middle and the actors moving about constantly it was all but impossible. She fished the duck out of her pocket and squeezed its wings, keeping her free hand slightly over the bulb as it washed pale light through her fingers.

"Hey, that's not allowed," one of the actors said, and she ignored them. She'd already found the next archway and she ran for it, dodging past someone who jumped out at her, hands hooked into claws and pustulant boils dotted all over their face.

Into another tunnel, and she almost ran past a door set into the stone. The light from the duck outlined it in shadows, and she came to a stumbling halt, backing up hurriedly and searching for the handle. She couldn't see it, couldn't even feel anything as she ran one hand over the stone, rough edges smoothed by centuries of passage. This was real, this wall, even if everything else in here was made in some props department, chicken wire and papier mâché. These were the bones of the city, sunk deep below the floodwaters of the Ouse, worn down and diminished, but full of power nonetheless.

"Please," she whispered. There was commotion in the room behind her, Jasper close on her trail, and she could keep stumbling from room to room, but she needed *out*, away from the possibility of the public getting tangled up in this, whatever *this* was, but she was sure it wasn't going to be just a slap on the wrist or a caution. *This* wasn't even going to be official. Whoever Jasper was, he was deep into things she was only just beginning to understand, and she wasn't about to face that in the bowels of some tourist attraction. The Watch would do her in, if Maud didn't first.

She eased her grip on the duck, not wanting to give herself away too readily. Its light vanished, replaced by the low red glow of the fake sconces, and the door went with it. She frowned, and squeezed the duck's wings again. White light outlined the door, and she hesitated, then put one hand flat on the stone, and pushed.

The wall stayed where it was, but a door-shaped section sank under her hand, receding as she forced it back. She glanced down the tunnel, where a scuffle of feet said she'd have company any moment, then stepped forward, almost expecting to bump her nose on the stone, the wall sealing over again and refusing her access. Instead, she followed the door as it retreated just enough to allow her to step onto dusty, uneven stone. She stepped to the side, releasing the panel, and it snapped back into place so swiftly she almost missed the movement, cutting off the noise of the tour group outside with a dull *thunk*.

Adams stayed where she was for a moment, trying to calm her breathing and listening for anyone else to try the hidden door. Jasper was evidently more than aware of other York, but, as she'd realised, that didn't mean he could find his way through wherever he wanted. She shone the light of the duck around warily as she waited, but there were no glittery toilet monsters or giant dogs stalking toward her. Just a tunnel of more old stone, and the undisturbed ground underfoot. No one knocked on the door behind her, and when she turned the light on it, it looked like an average, old wooden door, painted in a flaking dark green that reminded her of garden sheds. She wondered how much of that was real and how much was the duck, or if she was thinking of that all wrong, and the duck simply showed her what was real when her human eyes couldn't manage it on their own. Her head gave a little throb of warning, and she decided she needed to do more than just read Rory's books once this was over. She needed to talk to someone who actually knew about ducks and hidden towns. Probably not the cat though. That was only going to give her more headaches.

There was still no sign of pursuit, and Adams considered her options. She had no idea where this tunnel would lead, but she could be sure the police would be watching the Dungeons. Whatever regular, human exit she tried, they'd be there to nab her. And if her car wasn't clamped, they'd be watching that too. She sighed slightly. Being on the run from her colleagues had never figured into her career plan.

It made the decision for her, though, and she started down the tunnel, casting the pale beam of the duck's light ahead of her. Rory still had her torch, but she felt better with the duck, anyway. She didn't fancy missing the exit because her Maglite couldn't see it.

She hadn't gone far before she became aware of the noises. Little rustling movements, scuttling and creeping, washing around the edges of the light. She stopped, and the noises did too. She turned in a slow circle, but whatever it was stayed well clear. Some part of the darkness might've retreated just before the torch beam touched it, shadows within shadows, but she could just as well have been imagining things, creating shiftings in the murk that were nothing more than her own fright. She started walking again, and the movements immediately accompanied her, the soft scuffle of small claws on hard surfaces, the whisper of sleek bodies and smooth limbs, and a shudder ran over her shoulders. She was trying very hard not to imagine what might be out there, but it wasn't working. Her mind was creating horrors. She stopped again, and the response was instant. Utter silence.

"Alright," she said into it. "I have to pay a toll, right?"

The darkness was expectant, although she couldn't have said how she knew that. She patted her pockets hopefully, the bag of Yorkies swinging from her free hand and banging against her leg, and she looked down at it. She'd clung to the chocolate the whole way, and now she peered into the void.

"Do you like chocolate?" she asked it.

There was no response, so she answered herself. "Everyone does, right? Unless you're lactose intolerant. Or cats. Or dogs. Or vegan." She frowned. "Are you vegan?"

This time there was a single titter, and an immediate hiss from half a dozen different directions. Hopefully directed at the titterer and not her. Everything slid to silence once more.

Well, it wasn't like she had anything else to offer. She wrestled with the bag, trying to figure out how to get the chocolate out and unwrapped without releasing her painfully tight grip on the duck. She didn't fancy the light going out when things were *tittering* at her. For a moment it looked like she was going to have to, then she muttered to herself,

"*Phone*, Adams, you're not actually in the Middle Ages," and abandoned the chocolate to pull it out of her pocket. She flicked the torch on, setting the phone on the ground while she fished a Yorkie out and peeled the wrapper off, shoving it in her pocket, then broke the bar into pieces.

"There you go," she said, throwing them into the dark behind her. "Have at it." She added another couple for good measure, then picked up her phone and hurried down the tunnel. Behind her, she heard some violent scuffling, a few outraged squeaks, and then the sort of chewing and slobbering that did nothing to calm her imagination. She picked up the pace, wishing again that Dandy was with her, and before it felt like she'd gone more than a few metres the scuffling turned into pursuit.

"No no no *no*," she breathed, breaking into a run, the light from the phone's torch bouncing on the walls. A wave of scuttling, scratching movement pursued her, and she stopped again, swallowing hard. She couldn't just run headlong into the dark. She'd miss the exit, or run into a wall and knock herself out, and probably get eaten by whatever was back there. Behind her, there was a sound like something licking its chops, and she took another Yorkie from the bag, juggling her phone.

"Alright," she said. "Not enough, then?" She started walking as she unwrapped the chocolate, trying to ignore the way the movement seemed to be pressing closer to her. She broke a piece off and flung it over her shoulder, setting off a scuffle and some snarls, then enthusiastic chewing. She didn't stop, walking steadily as she looked for ways out and hoped they'd show up even without the duck. Every few paces she threw another piece of chocolate over her shoulder, setting off another tussle, and the noises grew closer, until she was sure she could feel breath on her heels, the brush of long fur against her trousers.

She was down to her last two Yorkies, swapping between using her phone to light her way and the duck to check for exits, when she saw a door ahead of her. It was arched rather than square, painted a pale colour that revealed itself as milky blue when she got closer. She wondered briefly if it was going to let her out in France somewhere, given that hue, but she was just going to have to deal with it if it did. She couldn't retrace her steps.

One more piece of chocolate over her shoulder, and she was at the door, finding a black-painted metal hasp for a handle. She reached for it, and a titter stopped her. It was ahead of her, not behind, and everything stilled. She looked down, the movement feeling jerky and uncontrolled, and met a pair of glittering, dark eyes, staring up at her from a pointy face within an equally dark, sleek coat.

"*That's* what you are?" she demanded. The thing was the size of a rat, and not even a large one. Its shaggy coat reminded her more of a cat, and she wondered just how tiny it was under all that fur. "I thought you were ravenous monsters!"

A chorus of titters went up from the floor directly behind her, but not just there. It washed down the tunnel, falling from the walls and the ceiling, a multi-layered wash of sound, and Adams' imagination immediately served her an image of the tunnel choked with the things, like a plug of hair in a drain. In front of her, the little creature licked its chops and leered up at her, exposing row upon row of tiny, viciously sharp teeth.

"*Absolutely not,*" she said, whether to the creature or to that awful image of them massing behind her, and hurled the bag with the last two Yorkies over her shoulder into the tunnel. The creature in front of her vanished, shooting after it, and she grabbed the door, hauling it open and charging out into the grey, cold, and utterly beautiful day. She slammed the door behind her, jiggling the latch to make sure it had shut properly, and stepped back, shoving her phone into her coat pocket and clawing out her extendible baton instead, waiting for a flood of furry backs to pour after her, their appetite only whetted by the chocolate.

Nothing happened. The door stood there, stolid and uninteresting, grey and peeling on this side, set into red brick. It didn't rattle. Nothing tried the handle. She swallowed hard and stepped back to the door, holding her baton at the ready and touching the wood gingerly with her other hand as if to make sure it was real. It didn't move, sagging and tired, and she rested her ear against it, the wood damp and slick in the rain. Nothing. And then, very faintly, a titter. She jerked away, shuddering, and wiped her mouth, taking a couple of deep breaths. She was out. Whatever those things had been, she was out, and she'd walked far enough that she must be away from the Dungeons by now.

She automatically checked her pockets as she waited for her breathing to return to something like normal, still with a wary eye on the door. Phone. Lock picks. Duck, with car keys for all the good that did her. The other duck charm Fergus had given her. No Yorkie bars left, which was unfortunate, but with any luck she wouldn't meet any more creepy tunnel monsters. Now she just had to figure out where she was. She looked around finally, at the long expanse of red brick and dull cobbles, their seams caked with mud and the edges where they met the walls marked with dandelions and weeds.

"Oh, *come on*," she muttered, turning slowly on her heel, but the other direction was just the same. Long red brick walls, the grey sky pinched between them, the clouds embracing the city. Endless stretches of cobbles, unmarked by bins or signs or people. Not even a cat or a rat in sight.

She was in the alley she'd glimpsed behind the garden at

Ash & Yew, or it looked like she was. But there were no gates opening onto it, no windows overlooking it, no doors, *nothing*. She looked back at the door she'd arrived by, not that she had any intention of opening it without a bulk lot of Yorkies to hand. It was gone, simply winked out of existence while her back was turned. She tried squinting at the patch of wall where it had been, but it made no difference. It was just more plain red brick.

"Okay," she said to the empty alley, and took the duck out. Its light was weak even in the grey day, but she could hold it close enough to the wall to create a pool of brighter colour. It revealed nothing. The door had been here, hadn't it? She straightened up with a sigh. It didn't matter. She couldn't search every square centimetre of wall in the hope it revealed something. She'd be in here forever, and maybe that was the point. Just another bloody trick to keep the secret byways of the city hidden.

She swapped her duck for her phone, not expecting it'd have any signal. To her surprise, it had three bars, and she called Collins.

No answer.

She frowned, and checked her calls. Five missed ones, three from Rory, two from Collins.

"Bollocks," she muttered, and tried Rory.

No answer.

"Not liking that." The words hung in the air around her, breathless and uncertain. She looked one way then the other down the alley, and decided it made no difference. She started walking.

16

IN THE BELLY OF WILFRED

ADAMS DIDN'T KNOW HOW LONG SHE'D BEEN WALKING WHEN she became aware she was being followed. The alley went on and on, just as she'd seen it from the back of Ash & Yew, and even though she stopped and examined the wall with the duck every couple of minutes, it revealed nothing. Not that she'd really expected it to, after the door from the Dungeons had vanished so completely, but she'd still been harbouring some small hope that something might reappear. A steady drizzle had started, bringing even heavier cloud with it, and she had no sense of where the sun was, no way to orient herself as to what direction she was travelling in, if there even *was* direction in here. She had the sneaking feeling she was in some liminal space, set as a safeguard to protect the borders of true York, and she may have made it this far, but she didn't have the right password to go further.

She was just fishing her phone out to try calling Collins again (although her three previous calls had gone unanswered, so she wasn't expecting the fourth would be any better, which was worrying her), when she realised her footsteps had an echo. Or not an echo, but a *companion*, not quite in time with her steps, a little quicker and lighter. She slowed, and they kept up their pace for a moment, then picked up her new rhythm. She sped up. Same thing.

The skin prickled on the back of her neck. It was coming from behind her, she was fairly sure. Not least because she couldn't see anyone (or *anything*) ahead of her, and an invisible pursuer felt like a push even for *other* situations. She'd put her baton back in her pocket, and now she folded her fingers over it again, easing it out gently without extending it, keeping it close to her leg. Her pursuer either didn't see or wasn't bothered, as they kept pattering after her.

She took a slow breath, bracing herself, then spun around, snapping the baton out at the same time, looking for some sort of stalking monster or creeping attacker. Empty cobbles greeted her, and she stared down the long stretch of featureless brick. No one.

"Oh, *come on,*" she said. "I had enough of this with the hairy sodding hamsters. Just show yourself, can't you?"

The alley gave her back a blank sort of incomprehension, and she scowled at it, trying not to think of brick-coloured giant spiders, or perhaps some sort of chameleon-type beast that would definitely have far too many teeth. She tapped the baton against her leg.

"Don't try me," she said. "I have at least two missing people, possibly four, since I can't get hold of Rory *or* Collins, and who knows what those two have gone blundering into. Dandy's taken himself off to who knows where. I've been chased by coppers, *three times,* plus by an entire shop's worth of junk and a pack of photophobic gerbils, and that's just today. Also I need a coffee. So I'd get out here if you know what's good for you."

There was an uneasy silence, in which she was sure she was going to have to keep walking, possibly forever, with that irritating patter of pursuit just behind her, then a small bump bloomed out of the wall. It resolved itself into a head with a round metallic gleam, and flat black eyes stared at her.

"*Fergus?*"

Fergus emerged out of the brick fully, trotting jerkily across the cobbles with his tail held stiffly behind him.

Adams crouched to meet him, barely resisting the urge to grab him into a hug. He might be metal, but he felt like the first living – sort of – thing she'd seen in a month, and she hoped this weird space hadn't done equally strange things to the passage of time. He paused an arm's length from her, the hard blades of his claws scratching the cobbles and his bent whiskers trembling. He blinked, his eyes pinwheeling down to a single tiny dot, then opening again. Adams blinked back, in case it was some sort of metal cat greeting.

"Hi," she said, for good measure. "What're you doing here?"

He took half a step toward her, rumbling somewhere deep in his belly, and she saw something dangling from his mouth.

"What've you got?" She held a hand out hesitantly, the memory of the needle teeth still strong, but he took another step and dropped his prize into her palm.

A key.

It was *a key,* and one Adams recognised. It was for the garden gate at Ash & Yew.

"Oh, you little star," she said, and Fergus mewled. She petted him awkwardly, not quite sure if he could feel it or not, his back cold under her fingers. As soon as she stopped he rammed his head into her hand, hard enough that she almost toppled out of her crouch. "Easy," she said, but stroked him again. He was vibrating with whatever passed as a purr, and she said, "Can you get me back?"

Another creaking mewl, and she nodded. "Let's call that a

yes." She got up, her eyes still on him, and said, "Lead on, then."

Fergus turned around and started back the way he'd come, and Adams looked down the alley, wondering if he was going to head-butt a route through the brick. He certainly had a hard enough skull. She was about to ask him, the simple act of having someone to talk to easing the sick tension in her belly, but as she gazed back along her route she forgot about that question entirely, because she suddenly had a *lot* more.

The alley was lined with doors. Doors, and gates, and arches, and stairs climbing up to still more doors higher up in the walls, a spiderweb of routes crawling across the face of the brick. Some of the doors were short and fat, looking as if someone had installed them sideways, others so tall and thin they appeared to have been squeezed out of true. Some were ornately decorated, all filigreed frames and metal detailing, others were barely clinging together, the wood crumbling from its fastenings. Some had viewing ports, others were all glass with net curtains like her gran's, and she spotted a disturbing amount that had been nailed shut using great slabs of two-by-four or sheets of plywood or, in one particularly alarming case, metal panels. They were every sort of size and colour and design, and they had *not* been there before.

Adams turned on her heel, looking in the direction she'd been headed. More doors. Doors *everywhere*. It was a *wilderness* of doors, an entirely excessive amount of them, and the one thing they all lacked was a sign to indicate where they led. That, and any trace of life other than her and the metal cat.

"*Mrrraow?*"

She turned again, looking back at Fergus. "Did you make them appear?"

"*Mmmip.*"

That didn't seem like a cat noise, but he wasn't entirely a cat, so maybe it was simply a Fergus noise. She looked at the key in her hand, and at the doors again, then put the key on the ground.

"*Mmmrrr?*"

"One second." She didn't have much time, she'd wasted too much in here already, but she *had* to know. She looked back at the walls. No doors, not in either direction, just brick. "*Huh.*" She picked the key up again, keeping her eyes on the walls. The doors were there. They didn't reappear, didn't surface out of the brick. They were just *there*, defying her to think they ever hadn't been. Her head gave a little throb, and she pushed her fingers into her forehead. When she'd stepped into the alley from Ash & Yew, had she had the key? No. She hadn't. She'd left it in the gate, and she'd seen nothing but emptiness.

"*Mrrraow!*" There was a surprising amount of impatience in the noise, considering it came from a metal cat.

"Coming," she said, and hurried after Fergus.

"*Mmmip,*" he replied, apparently satisfied, and trotted off again, the soft rain bouncing off the hard shell of his body.

Adams followed, the key clutched firmly in her hand and her eyes drifting from door to door, looking for movement. There was no knowing what was hiding behind them.

THEY DIDN'T HAVE FAR to go. Adams wasn't sure how long or far she'd walked before, but they couldn't have covered half of it before Fergus came to a halt in front of a familiar, metal gate. The viewing panel was shut, and, just as with all the others, nothing on the outside marked it for what it was.

Adams looked at Fergus. "I suppose if you have a key to any of these, you can see all the doors?"

He looked at her blankly.

"Right," she said. "Worry about all my missing bods first, shall I?"

"*Mmmip.*"

"Glad you approve." She slotted the key into the lock, keeping one hand on it as she grabbed the handle, in case they both vanished on her and she couldn't find them again. She rolled the lock and opened the door a crack, just enough to peer around it, but all she could see was the same jumble of metal as had been there before. Wilfred didn't come galloping across the garden to deal with the intrusion, and nothing else stirred. She looked down at Fergus. "You first?" she suggested.

"*Mmm.*"

She wasn't sure what that meant, but it seemed to be the same sort of non-committal noise as she might've made herself. She took the key out and opened the door wide enough to step inside, still braced to run if the old VW with the shark's fin charged her, or she was assaulted with a rain of rebar. The garden just dripped sadly in the damp, the sound of the drizzle a melancholy symphony on the different metals, and she could almost hear it rusting. Fergus followed her in as she closed the gate and locked it again, then just stood there looking at her.

"What?"

He looked around, as if unsure himself, then abruptly bolted up the path, his jerky movement surprisingly fast, and vanished into the metal undergrowth.

"Fergus! Fergus, *wait!*" But he was gone, and Adams sighed. At least she was out of the alley, and the shop should be at the other end of the path. She started up it, her baton back in her hand. It might not do much against whatever metal beasts could surface, but it made her feel better, at least.

The garden had shifted since the day before, and Wilfred wasn't in his previous spot. He wasn't anywhere she could see, in fact, and she scanned the jumble of pipes and drums and offcuts as she walked, wishing Fergus had stayed with her. She didn't fancy Wilfred going all guardian on her. She still hadn't spotted him when an explosion of barking broke the hush of the garden. She stopped short.

"Dandy?"

The barks didn't sound right, though, rapid-fire and overlapped, as if there were two dogs. *Two dogs.* She covered her face with one hand. "Oh, you're kidding me." She dropped her hand and shouted, "Midge! Pinto!"

The barking redoubled, bordering on hysterical, and she swung toward it. It seemed to be coming from somewhere off at a bit of an angle from the path, and she regarded the jagged garden dubiously. It was *toothy*. The dogs were still barking, though, and she tucked her baton back into her pocket, pushing her sleeves up.

"Tell someone to stay out of it, and what do they do? Get eaten by a metal garden." She picked her way off the path, and quickly decided her sleeves were better down. "As if I don't have enough to worry about. Landed gentry getting munched by old cars." She detoured around a jagged bloom of raw steel strips, bleeding rusty water into a puddle. The barking was starting to make her ears hurt. "I'm *coming.* Settle down!"

The dogs didn't settle down, but they eased from a clamour to more regular barking, and she followed it, doubling back here and there where she came up against the flat wall of a container, or sharp sheets of tin unfurling threateningly toward her. Everything was shifting at the edges of her vision, but nothing attacked her, and eventually she discovered an enclosure formed from corrugated iron, round at the bottom and twisted at the top like the wrapper on a sweet. Adams knocked on it, and the dogs set up such a noise she winced.

"Okay, okay, I'm here." She edged around the enclosure, looking for a way in, and finally found a seam held together by metal clips, not hefty, but impossible to remove by hand. Well, impossible if she hadn't had her multitool on her keyring. It was small, but more than sufficient to get a good grip on the clips with the pliers and twist them off. She peeled the corrugated iron back to be met by two eager, wet noses, the dogs licking her hands and jumping at her legs.

"Yeah, yeah." She peered past them, but there was no Rory inside. "Where—" she started, but the dogs suddenly howled, and fled. She spun, heart hammering, and looked up at a vast metal leg that had appeared immediately in front of her. It definitely hadn't been there when she'd arrived at the enclosure, and she stared up at Wilfred, his blank eyes glaring down at her and his other front leg raised above her head. It would've been blocking out the sun if there had been any, but as it was it kept the rain off. She looked at it, and back at Wilfred.

"Hi," she said, and from somewhere around Wilfred's belly a shout went up.

"Adams! Adams, is that you?"

"*Collins?*"

"Yes! Bloody hell – can you get me out?"

"On it," she called, hoping she sounded more confident than she felt. She turned back to Wilfred. His raised hoof – if that was what it was – seemed closer. "We seem to have a misunderstanding," she said, and showed him the key. "I'm allowed to be here."

Wilfred cocked his head. Or it appeared in a cocked position without her seeing it move, and she was getting thoroughly sick of things that should be inanimate doing that. It was much worse than Fergus. At least he got on and behaved in a way metal shouldn't be able to right in front of her, with no sneakiness.

"Put Collins down," she ordered, pointing at the ground. Another not movement, and Wilfred's vast snout was snuffling the metal-encrusted earth she'd indicated, one of his blank eyes staring at her from very close quarters. She stared back at him, managing not to stumble away, and put her hand slowly in her pocket, searching for something, *anything* she could offer up to distract him. Not the duck. Not her phone, or her baton. She came out with a wrapper from a Yorkie bar, the inside shiny and metallic, and crumpled it in her hand. Wilfred was suddenly *touching* her, nose to her fingers, and she swallowed a yelp.

"Do you want it?" she asked, and it was gone. She fumbled back in her pockets. She'd been shoving them in there automatically as she fed the rabid gerbils back in the tunnel, and she came out with a handful, keeping a good grip on them. "I need that human back first."

Wilfred tipped his head. He'd sprouted the wrapper among his antlers, like a wisp of hair. Another unseen shift, a *thud* accompanied by a clatter of cans falling, and Collins yelped.

"Collins? Are you alright?"

"Well, I'm out."

"Good. Head for the house." She kept her eyes on Wilfred. "Thanks," she said to him. "Is there another silly human about here anywhere?"

That unseen shift again, and Wilfred's snout was pointing at the house, then back again, intent on the wrappers.

"Cheers." She opened her hands, and she thought she felt something, a rough brushing across her fingers, then the wrappers were gone and Wilfred was no longer in front of her. There was only the jumbled landscape of rust and corrosion, running all the way to the house, where Midge and Pinto were apparently trying to chew through the door. She hadn't really needed to ask Wilfred. She could've just followed them.

"Where did it go?" Collins asked. He hadn't started for the house, but was standing on an uneven bed of old paint tins and drinks cans, his baton in one hand, his jacket torn, and scratches on his face.

"Not sure," Adams said, and pointed at her own face. "That okay?"

"Fine," he said, touching the scrapes lightly. "You need to answer your phone."

"I was in the middle of being attacked by a junk shop. And I tried to call back."

"I really don't think that's a good enough excuse. Plus, I lost mine." He looked around the garden. "Somewhere."

She grinned, unable to help herself. She *desperately* hadn't wanted to drag him any further into this with her, but it didn't seem she had a choice. And there was something reassuring about having someone else around who was ready to take on a metal monster with a baton. It probably didn't say much about either of their senses of self-preservation, but it was nice anyway.

She looked at the barking dogs, then back at Collins. "Rory inside?"

"I guess so. I didn't get much of a chance to look around before that … that …"

"Wilfred."

Collins looked at her blankly for a moment, and she could see him wanting to ask all the questions she couldn't answer, then he just said, "Yeah. I heard the dogs, but *Wilfred* got me before I could find them or look for Rory."

"What were you doing out here in the first place?"

Collins grimaced. "Rory called me because he couldn't get hold of you. I couldn't either, so I said I was going to check out Ash & Yew. He said he'd been having a pint with Charles and they had a plan. I told him to wait, but he wasn't having it. Said he had an opportunity and was going to take it. By the time I got to the shop he wasn't answering his phone."

Adams rubbed her face, and started for the path, Collins angling across the garden to join her. Rory had been *having a pint* with bloody Charles. Wonderful. "How did you end up back here?"

"I went in the front and talked to Heather. She told me I needed to talk to Charles, and said he was in the garden. As soon as I was out here she shut the door on me and wouldn't open it. I heard the dogs, so went hunting for them, thinking Rory might be with them, and the next thing I knew I was in the belly of Wilfred, which is nowhere near as dramatic as the belly of the beast."

"But it's much more polite, and we should be polite to the giant metal Wilfred."

"I can't argue with that." Collins looked around warily. They'd reached the path mostly unscathed, although Adams had some mysterious cuts on her hands which she suspected might be from Wilfred taking the wrappers. Not that it was surprising. She'd expected a lot worse.

"How did you get in here?" Collins asked.

"Through the gate. There's an alley out the back, and I got in there from … I actually don't know how any of it works, but I have a key now." She showed it to him, and he nodded.

"Where did you find that?"

"A sort of cat gave it to me."

"A sort of— You know what, never mind."

"Probably best." She still hadn't seen the sort of cat, and kept checking the garden as they headed for the building, wondering where he'd gone. It didn't make sense that he was trying to trap her in here when he could've just left her wandering the alley until she collapsed from exhaustion or sheer frustration. But she didn't know why he was helping her either, and unless he turned up again she wasn't going to.

Midge and Pinto were still leaping at the door, if with a little less enthusiasm now, their barking hoarse and panicked. Adams clapped her hands at them.

"Midge! Pinto! Come on, pups."

They ignored her entirely, refusing to allow themselves to be pulled away, and eventually Collins said, "Here, girls. Here we go." His voice was warm and soothing, but it was the dog biscuits in his hand that really got the border collies' attention. They crowded around him, whining, and he doled out the biscuits then fussed over them until they calmed down.

"Dog biscuits *and* cat biscuits?" she said to him.

"I decided it was good to be prepared." He looked around vaguely. "Does Dandy want one?"

She had to clear her throat before she answered, the metal dust heavy on her skin. "I lost him. And Joe."

"Ah. Any leads?"

"Dodgy copper called Jasper, no last name known. But Joe was grabbed, and I think it was Heather."

"She took Dandy too?" Collins sounded doubtful.

"Dandy might've followed. I told him to watch Joe."

Collins nodded, giving the dogs each another treat. "Well, we'll find them. Nothing a little police work won't fix."

"I don't know. I'm starting to wonder if I'm going about this all the wrong way. If I should be raising sodding ... I don't know. An army of attack ducks or something."

"As appealing as that sounds, I doubt it. It's still just police work, Adams. Run down the leads, look for the motives, figure out the how. Slightly different angle of approach, is all."

She wished she could be as calm about it as he seemed to

be, but she just made a vague noise that could've been agreement as Collins tried the door handle.

It turned easily, and he said, "Look at that. Things are going right al—" He stopped, and they both stared at the bland alleyway with its bins on the other side of the door. Adams looked up at the building, but they definitely *should* have been going into the workshop. She spotted Fergus peering out at her from the window.

"Some help you are," she said.

"Sorry?" Collins asked.

"Not you. Him." She pointed at Fergus, and Collins peered in the window.

"*Huh.* The sort of cat?"

"The very same." Fergus mewled, the sound swallowed by the glass, and Adams pointed at the door, through which she could see someone had dropped an apple next to the bin. "How do I get past that?"

Fergus vanished behind the door without appearing in the alley, and a moment later she heard scratching from somewhere, as if he was clawing at the wood. She hesitated, then reached out, closed the door firmly – the noise of the scratching intensifying – then tried the handle again.

It turned easily, and she pushed the door partway open to reveal Fergus standing on the workshop doormat, looking at her in what could only be an *I told you so* manner.

"*Huh,*" Collins said again.

"Yeah," she said, and led the way out of the metal garden and into a house in chaos.

17

FIND ONE, LOSE ONE

THE LAST TIME ADAMS HAD BEEN IN THE WORKSHOP, IT HAD been chaotic, but there had also been organisation to it. The middle bench with its offcuts and half-finished sculptures had certainly been messy and jumbled, but around the edges of the room everything had been relatively neat, tools in their designated places and the surfaces clear, if not clean. Now, she had to put her shoulder to the door to force it wide enough to get through, Fergus watching her curiously without moving from his spot on the mat. Behind the door things crashed and clattered and ground across the stone floor, and when she finally stepped inside she found the middle bench keeled over, its contents strewn from one end of the workshop to the other.

"This doesn't look good," Collins said from the doorstep. He was still holding Midge's and Pinto's collars, and they seemed torn between rushing inside to search for Rory and fleeing back into the inhospitable garden.

"It was all fine when you were here?" Adams asked, picking her way carefully through the debris and trying not to stab herself on a slightly flattened frog rendered in glossy metal.

"Just looked like a normal workshop." He leaned inside. "We can't let the dogs walk over this."

Adams sighed and turned back, crouching to pick up Midge, who licked her ear enthusiastically, wriggling with delight. "*Ugh.* I did not sign up to be a dog porter."

"You're very suited to it, though," Collins said, picking up Pinto, who stared at him with alarmed eyes. "It's alright, pup."

Adams thought that seemed a bit optimistic, but she just made her way cautiously over the cluttered floor to the hall door, where she set Midge down. The corridor was clear and dark, no lights on and no sound coming from behind any of the other doors. She tried the light switch, but it just flicked uselessly.

"Power's out," she said to Collins as he joined her and put Pinto down.

"Not surprising," he said, nodding at the workshop. "Looks like a massive magnetic surge."

Adams looked at the debris, her head on one side. There *was* a pattern to the fall, now she looked at it.

"*Mmmraow?*" Fergus asked from by the back door.

"I'm not carrying you," she said. "You've got wings."

He shook them out, but only one extended, the other shivering with effort but not doing anything more than sliding off his shoulder. "*Mmmip?*"

"Well, you're not going to cut your paws, are you?"

He snapped his good wing back into place, whiskers trembling, and glared at her.

"Oh for—" She clattered back across the debris and picked him up, surprisingly light despite his metallic workings. He had to be all but hollow inside. She tucked him under one arm and headed for the hallway again, scowling at Collins. "He's useful."

"I didn't say anything," he said, grinning.

Adams huffed at him, set Fergus down, and pulled her multitool out. "Wing," she ordered.

Fergus extended his wing as far as it'd go, sending Midge and Pinto bolting to the other end of the hall, snarling and giving little alarmed yips. Adams ignored them, examining Fergus's injury. The mechanism had come unhooked where the wing joined his shoulder, and it looked like nothing more than a spring that had disconnected.

"What happened?" she asked, using the pliers on her multitool to seize the end of the spring and hook it back into the wing's frame. "Did you get caught up in all that back there?"

"*Mmmip.*"

She glanced at him. It *felt* like a negation, but it was hard to tell. She squinted at the injury in the low light, then found her phone and put the torch on. His shoulder was scuffed and scratched, the marks still shiny and new, and they weren't from her pliers. It looked like he'd taken a glancing blow from something, the gouges showing a path of impact sliding off his shoulder and catching the wing on the way past. She frowned.

"Did someone do this deliberately?"

"*Mmmip.*"

Now it felt like an affirmative, but she wasn't sure how much she was reading into it. He'd definitely still been able to fly after the master charm had been stolen. Why try to deactivate him now, if that was what had happened?

"Are you done, Doctor Dolittle?" Collins asked.

"He talked to animals," Adams said. "I'm talking to …" She waved vaguely, looking for a description. "Him."

"Either way. We should get moving."

She straightened up, nodding past him at the door to the jewellery shop. "Is that open?"

Collins shook his head. "Locked."

She looked at Fergus, who just stared at her blankly, then she fished the garden key out of her pocket and tossed it to Collins. "Try that."

He checked the door. "No, it's an actual lock." He held up the gate key. "This is a child's drawing of a key."

Adams snorted. It did look that way, a bit. "Alright. Worry about that later. Check the other doors."

With the workshop at one end of the hall and the shop at the other, there were four other doors, including the one that led to the apartment stairs. Adams found a cleaning cupboard behind one, revealing nothing more interesting than a mop bucket and a vacuum. Across the hall, Collins found a small toilet with an old-fashioned, chain-pull cistern high on the wall, spotless and smelling faintly of spring blooms. Next to it was an office, the shelves lined with file boxes, everything relentlessly labelled and the desk clear of even a stray post-it, the computer mouse and keyboard aligned neatly with the edge.

"I'm guessing the office is not the domain of whoever does the workshop," Collins said.

"That'll be Heather," Adams said, thinking of her lining up the charms in their displays. It felt contradictory, that Charles worked with the hard, unforgiving lines of metal yet was all chaos, while Heather was some sort of nature witch but embraced such precision. People were contradictory, though, and she had an idea that was less a human trait than simply what it was to be alive.

She tried the door to the apartment, not surprised to find it locked. But it seemed more likely that, if Rory was anywhere, he'd be upstairs rather than dumped on the shop floor, where anyone could look in the window and see him. She looked at Fergus. "Key?"

He tipped his head at her, then walked to the door with his jerky gait, putting his front paws up on it. Adams waited for him to pick the lock with his tail, or bite it out with those formidable teeth, but all he did was look from it to her, then drop back down again.

"Why are all you magical beasties so much less useful than you could be?" she asked, taking her own lock picking kit from her pocket. "Collins, some light?"

He pulled a torch from his pocket, angling it at the lock while she worked. "It is disappointing," he said. "D'you think we were mis-sold in childhood by all the woodland creatures who seemed to like housework?"

"Only if you base your knowledge of the world on cartoons," she said, as the lock gave a satisfying *clunk*. "Although, to be fair, I also expected a lot of different things from faeries and fauns."

"Less teeth on the former, for a start," Collins said, and grabbed the dogs as she eased the door open. They'd evidently forgotten their fear of Fergus in their eagerness to get past.

The stairwell was unlit, but grey light drifted down from the apartment above, painting the plain wooden treads and dark metal of the spiral staircase in dull shades. Adams could smell green, earthy tones, like rain on spring growth, and the air was cool without being chilly. She stepped inside and put one hand on the banister, staring up to the floor above and listening for movement as Fergus trotted to join her.

"I think he's up there," Collins said, and she looked back at Midge and Pinto, who were just about choking themselves on their collars.

"Keep hold of them," she said. "We don't know what else there could be."

"Bollocks to that. I'm coming with you," Collins said, and wrestled the dogs out of the doorway, joining her in the tight confines of the stairwell. Midge and Pinto immediately started barking, scratching at the door furiously.

"Well, there goes the element of surprise," she said, and Collins shrugged.

"Given everything else around here, did we ever have it?"

"Fair point." She started up the stairs, her feet seeming too loud on the hard wood. She was vaguely surprised it didn't collapse under them, or burst out in impaling shards of wood, or sprout clinging vines. But nothing happened, and she walked steadily up, the silence heavy and breathless, Fergus jumping clumsily from one step to the next beside her.

She emerged into the same apartment as the one she'd been in the day before. She'd half expected it to be transformed into a greenhouse, given the rich scent of plant life and soft earth. A greenhouse, or maybe a rainforest, dripping with vines and poisonous life.

But the main room was still as sleek and lofted as before, the plants constrained to their pots and the wall of herbs in the kitchen, the breakfast bar clear except for an abandoned mug, and the floor warm, glossy wood. What *had* changed was the view.

Where before there had been red brick buildings, staid and recognisable, if perhaps a little *off*, there was now a bewildering cityscape, full of wooden towers and spiralling stone keeps, put together with apparently very little thought for city planning, safety regulations, or physics, for that matter. Trees burst through the middle of them, and the humped backs of earthen keeps, and the wooden masts and carved prows of Viking ships and old steel barges. Century after century of the land's life were layered on top of each other, tangled and confused, human and Folk, chimneys vomiting coal smoke at swerving dragons, marauding invaders pouring up the river's banks past fauns in three-piece suits sipping cocktails under parasols, unseen things erupting out of pits in the earth while above them tourist buses trundled cheerily on, frequented by goblins wearing flat caps and sneers.

"What—" she started, but she couldn't even form the question. *What was this? What did it mean? Was it even real?* Just, **what?**

"*Adams!* Help me!"

She hadn't even realised Collins had rushed past her to the double doors that opened onto the little balcony. He was struggling to get them open, and as she finally tore her attention off the bizarre cityscape (a jigsaw puzzle, that was what it reminded her of, one of those ones that was jammed with every possible tiny detail, designed to be as difficult as possible, every feature and landmark of a city squeezed into 3,000 pieces) he abandoned the doors, searching the windowsills to each side for a key. For a moment she couldn't understand his urgency, wondering if he wanted a closer look at the inexplicable world beyond, then she saw Rory, and it jolted her out of her shock, sending her sprinting for the doors.

"Fergus! Is there a key?"

"*Mmmip!*"

"What does that mean?" Collins demanded, abandoning the windowsills and running to the kitchen, ripping drawers open and pawing frantically through the contents.

Adams didn't bother answering. She was on her knees by the door already, trying to keep her hands steady as she attacked the lock with her picks. Beyond the glass, Rory dangled off the edge of the balcony, over the jagged-edged garden below (or whatever was there now. Adams didn't know, and she didn't have time to look). He was trussed in slender, twisted limbs that bloomed out of the plants on the balcony, like one of those ficuses or money trees or whatever the hell they were that everyone always had, the stems usually twining elegantly around each other and capped with a head of foliage. The foliage was still on these ones too, obscuring Rory's face, but she could see grazes on his forearms where the sleeves of his jumper had been pushed up, and a tear in the knee of his jeans. He looked like he'd been trying to fight his way free despite the drop beneath him, and she shouted as she worked, "Hold still! We're coming!"

Rory shouted something back, nothing she could make out properly, just an exclamation of relief or fright or both, and she grunted with frustration as the lock picks slipped. She was rushing. Calm. She had to be calm. The plants had held him this long. There was no reason to think they'd drop him now.

"I can't find the key," Collins called. "You getting anywhere?"

"Trying," she said shortly, ignoring Fergus as he head-butted her arm.

"I'm going to get some tools from the workshop," he said, already starting down the stairs. "We're not kicking through that."

"Okay." She kept on with what she was doing anyway, hearing Collins clattering down the stairs, then an explosion of barking from below, and the scrabbling of two sets of paws as Midge and Pinto charged up. Fergus head-butted her again. "*Wh—*" She swallowed her impatience. He was a helpful little automaton. "Sorry. What?"

He looked up at her, unfortunately without any keys in his mouth (again, the helpfulness of magical critters was exceptionally variable), and put a paw on the door.

"You want to try?"

"*Mmmip.*"

Well, she wasn't getting anywhere. The lock was new, and

not easy to pick at the best of times, let alone when she couldn't seem to catch a breath, not with the combination of that jarring glimpse of all the realities of York, and Rory dangling like a fishing lure above it. Collins' sledgehammer or whatever he came back with was likely to be their best option. "Go on, then," she said, and rocked back onto her heels, giving Fergus some space. He stood up on his hind legs, pressing both front paws against the glass. Midge and Pinto were hanging back, still nervous of the metal cat, and she hooked an arm over each of them, keeping them clear. Something crashed downstairs, as if Collins had fallen over in the workshop, and she yelled, "You alright?"

A shout came back, but before she could decide if it was an *all good* or a *help* type of shout, Fergus reared back and slammed his front paws into the door, the wickedly sharp blades of his claws fierce and unyielding. For all his compact size and lightness, he hit hard, and the smack of his claws was followed by a sharper crack as fine lines spiderwebbed across the glass. He drew back and hit it again, and Adams smelled hot metal. This time the pane turned to a collage of shattered pieces, and she jumped up.

"Let me have a go," she said to Fergus, and he dropped to all fours, stepping back. His claws left little scorch marks on the flooring. Adams turned away from the door, found her balance, then kicked back as hard she could, driving the sole of her boot into the crazed glass. It gave up with barely a whimper, the inside pane falling to the floor. "Bloody double glazing," she muttered. "Not very *other*, is it?"

Fergus didn't answer, just attacked the outer pane, and a moment later Adams was kicking through that one too, clearing enough of a gap that she could step through, pulling the hood of her coat over her head to protect it from the last of the glass. Midge and Pinto tried to follow her, but Fergus stood stolidly in the gap, and neither of them seemed willing to brave him.

"*Adams!*" Rory shouted, peering through a fringe of ficus leaves. "About bloody time. Do you never answer your phone?"

"Do you want to stay out there?" she asked him, eyeing the plants warily. They could evidently move pretty quickly, if they'd grown around Rory, and the last thing she wanted to do was have them drop him while she was trying to get him in.

"I'm only out here because I was helping you out."

"And who told you to go home?" she asked, tugging one of the twisted trunks experimentally.

Rory bounced in its grip, and he gave a yelp of alarm. "It's slipping!"

"Sorry." She stepped back, checking the balcony. She needed rope, but there was none to be found out here. "Back in a sec."

"*Adams!*"

She ignored him, stepping over Fergus and yelling for Collins, but there was still no reply.

"*Adams!* Bloody *hell*—"

"I'm looking for something to tie you off with," she shouted back.

"I've got the dogs' leash! It's here, I just couldn't get enough space to use it!"

"Oh." Adams winced slightly, and hurried back onto the balcony. Rory's face was still mostly hidden by the foliage, but she could definitely feel him scowling at her. "Where?" she asked.

"Here." He wriggled a hand at her, the knuckles skinned and bleeding, but the dogs' retractable leash clasped in it. "I was trying to figure out how to hook the rail or something, but I can barely move."

"Good plan," she said, and leaned dangerously far over the balcony's metal railing, holding on with one hand. With the other she managed to grab the leash's plastic reel, but even as she took it, unreeling from wherever it was attached, the plants shuddered and Rory slipped, bouncing in their grip.

He swore, clutching the slender trunks. "I don't think they like that."

"It's alright. We'll get you out." *We*, but she had no idea what was happening with Collins, and she didn't like to think. Bloody men meddling in her case and getting themselves into trouble. "Have you got it tied off under your shoulders or something?"

"Yeah. It's made for walking a dog, though, not for sodding abseiling."

"It's just insurance." The plants shuddered again, and a length of trunk withdrew, slithering back on itself like an eel retreating into a hole, and one of Rory's legs fell free. He didn't swear again, just tried to reach the balcony with his foot. It was still too far.

"How do we do this?" he asked, his voice steady.

Adams hurried down the balcony a little, then took a turn around the railing with the leash to give her some purchase. "I'll pull you toward me," she said. "That should bring you side on, then we can work you over the—" She was cut off by the plants. They didn't so much retreat as collapse on themselves, concertinaing back into their pots so fast she barely had time to react. She hauled on the leash, both cursing the fact that the turn around the railing slowed her down and knowing it was the only chance she had of holding onto Rory. She'd never have kept her grip otherwise. Rory dropped straight out of the clutches of the plants like a skydiver, but he still had both hands locked onto the trunks. One ripped away from him, sliding out of his grasp, but he kept hold of the other, and with the pull of the leash to guide him, it turned what should've been a helpless plunge into a Tarzan-style swing toward the balcony.

Rory hit so hard the railing shuddered in fright, and he gave a grunt, losing hold of the plant while the dogs barked hysterically, the noise feeling like it was shaking the last of the broken glass from its anchors. Adams leaned hard against the leash as it took up his weight, hoping he'd gone for a fancy brand and not one from the local pound shop. Rory scrabbled wildly, managing to grab the bottom of the railings with both hands, then just hung there for a moment. Adams could hear him panting, her own breath coming far too fast, but the leash had held. The railing was holding. And, for now, nothing else seemed to be attacking them.

She looked at him. "Coming up?"

"Well, I don't know. Dangling from a balcony is such a joy." He'd evidently eased his impact with the wall by use of his face, and blood trickled from a cut over his eyebrow, a large red mark blooming on his cheek. Adams tied off the leash hurriedly and leaned over the railing, offering him her hand.

"Come on."

"Where's Collins?"

"I don't know. Come on."

"I don't know why I asked. You could probably beat him in an arm wrestle anyway."

"I did, once," she said, and locked her hand over his wrist as he matched her grip. "Now shut up and climb."

Rory shut up and climbed, Adams getting his hand onto the top railing then grabbing the back of his jacket to help heave him up and over. He collapsed to his back on the wet floor of the balcony, and the dogs finally overcame their horror of Fergus and launched themselves over the metal cat, rushing to Rory. He grabbed one with each arm, hooking them around the necks as they barked and fussed, tails wagging furiously. Then he didn't move for a moment, eyes closed and face turned up to the rain, while Adams frowned out at the city. All those bewildering layers had vanished again, and it was just red brick under grey skies, still not quite *right,* but certainly not as impossible as it had been.

"Adams?" Rory said, and she looked down at him watching her with level eyes and his hair dishevelled and damp with rain and sweat.

"Yes?"

"I really do owe you dinner now."

"Why is everyone so obsessed with owing each other dinners?" she demanded, and walked back inside, giving Fergus a grateful little tap on the head as she went. "I need to find Collins."

"Why?" Rory called after her. "Does he owe you dinner too?"

She made a rude gesture over her shoulder and he laughed. She didn't look back as she clattered down the stairs, Fergus losing his footing and sliding past her with a startled *mmmip!* Rory could sort himself out. Besides, she didn't want to let on she was grinning. He'd think it was about the dinner.

18

HELP IS INEVITABLE

The hallway was empty, and Adams called Collins again as she headed for the workshop. Fergus had recovered himself, trotting alongside her, and she glanced at him. "Not so good at the stairs, are you?"

He looked up at her, his eyes pinwheeling down to half-closed.

"Embarrassed? You are quite cat-like."

"*Mmmip.*"

"Adams, are you talking to the robot cat?" Rory called, and she heard him hurrying down the stairs after her, accompanied by the rush of dog paws.

"*Brrrip!*"

"I think you've offended him," she said. "That's a new noise." She stopped in the doorway to the upended workshop, looking around with a frown. It was empty. "Collins?" There was no response, not that she'd expected there to be. Not unless he was hiding on the floor behind the capsized centre bench.

Rory joined her, peering over her shoulder at the sea of metal on the floor. "What happened?"

She stepped to the side so she could look at him properly. "This wasn't you?"

"What, throwing over the giant workbench? I mean, I'm flattered, Adams, but no."

She waved impatiently. "I don't mean you *did* it. But this didn't happen when you were here?"

He shook his head. The bruise on his cheek was still an angry red, but his eyebrow had stopped bleeding, at least. "No. I may not have exactly gone straight home when I left you."

"You don't say."

He grinned, easy and warm. "I figured I could walk around, ask some questions. I ended up going back to the pub, and Charles was there. I got talking with him—"

"Played some cards with him?"

"Maybe. Anyhow, he told me he'd talked to you, and you were chasing down a couple of suspects, but there was still the question of how anyone could've got past this one, even if they were inside." He nodded at Fergus. "So we decided to try it."

Adams narrowed her eyes at him. "How many beers was this after?"

"Whiskies. A few. Totally sober now. Being dangled off a balcony'll do that."

"So what happened?"

"He let me in, and we sat here having another drink, talking about how to recreate it, then I went to the loo. Next thing I knew, someone bopped me on the head and that was it. I came around hanging over the balcony like a bloody chrysalis." He tipped his head toward her, touching it where she could see his thick hair was matted with blood.

"*How*, though?"

He shrugged. "I don't know. I never saw anyone."

"You didn't see anything after?"

He hesitated. "Not inside."

"You saw the city?" she asked, meaning not simply York, but *the city*, its layers of myth and history all tangled up together and impossible to separate.

When he just said, "Yes," she knew he'd understood the question, and she sighed inwardly. She really could've done with someone who was distinctly less landed gentry to share these things with.

But there was no point worrying about it. Instead, she just picked her way across the workshop and tried the back door. It opened to reveal a large, dully gleaming eye aimed right at her. She yelped and slammed the door again.

"*Mmmip.*"

"That's not helping," she said to Fergus, and he twitched his ears.

"You know you could go to the RSPCA," Rory said, finding an old length of metal pipe and bouncing it in his hands experimentally. "Adopt a visible dog and a non-robot cat."

"*Bbbbbrrrrrrip!*"

"Stop calling him a robot. He doesn't like it. *And* I've not adopted anyone. Dandy just turned up and never left, and Fergus is only helping out." She hoped. Walking into the station with a metallic cat in tow wasn't going to do anything to dispel the notion that southerners in general were a strange lot, and she in particular was less than well-adjusted. She looked around the room. "Collins can't have gone out that way." She hoped, anyway. Otherwise Wilfred had pounced on him again, and she was out of chocolate wrappers.

"Where is Dandy?" Rory asked, looking around curiously.

"Don't know," she said shortly. "Tracking a suspect, hopefully."

"Okay." Rory took his pipe with him and retreated back

into the hall, to where the dogs were waiting. Adams followed, clattering back through the mess in time to meet him coming back down the hall from the shop door.

"Locked," he said. "I mean, we could try busting it down …"

"There's no reason he'd have gone that way," she said, and turned back into the workshop. Fergus had waited at the door, and he looked up at her expectantly. "Alright, I want the alley," she said, although she couldn't have said if she was talking to the cat or the door itself. Whoever was listening, perhaps.

She put a hand on the handle, imagined the alley, and opened the door.

Wilfred glared back at her, his snout almost touching the doorframe, and she slammed the door again.

"*Alley,*" she insisted, and tried once more.

This time Wilfred had turned snout-on, and a great seam had opened like a gaping jaw. There were no teeth, but an awful lot of hefty gears and she closed the door firmly, putting one hand flat against the wood.

"Is there a key?" she asked Fergus, and he just stared at her.

"What're you trying to do?" Rory asked.

"Sometimes it opens on an alley," she said. "I'm thinking maybe that's where Collins went." And now she'd mentioned a key, Collins had the one Fergus had given her. Maybe that had tipped the door in a different direction. Which made her wonder what *sort* of alley Collins might've emerged into, or what might've grabbed him when he did. She looked at Fergus. "Key?" she said again, and he looked around the clutter as if hoping to spot one.

"Here," Rory said, coming to join her while the dogs whined in the hall. He held up a small key, a plain thing wrought from cheap metal, that looked more suited to the lock on a young teen's diary than a door.

"What's that for?" she asked, as he put a hand on the door handle.

"No idea."

"What? Where did you get it?"

He screwed his face up, a reluctant sort of grimace. "I found it a long time ago. If you're talking about *the alley*, you don't need a key to a specific door. You just need *a key*."

Adams didn't ask any further. *A long time ago* meant it was probably when he was hunting his mum, or for help for his mum, or whatever he'd been doing here, and that was a question for another time. One she was going to have to ask, if he was going to keep popping up in her cases, but not one that she needed answering now.

Aloud, she just said, "Alright. Try it."

She had her baton at the ready as Rory opened the door a crack, peered around it, then slammed it again.

"Not that one," he said.

"Wilfred?"

"Who?"

"Giant metal stag-type thing?"

"I don't know. It was too close to see properly."

"*Mmmip.*"

They both looked at Fergus, who blinked lazily.

"What does that mean?" Rory asked.

"No idea." Adams waved him back. "I gave Wilfred some chocolate wrappers earlier. He might be less likely to eat me."

Rory considered it. "Chocolate *wrappers?*"

"Nothing makes sense," Adams said with a shrug. "I've decided the best approach is to just handle what comes up and worry about if it makes sense or not later."

"How very illogical of you. I like it." He gave her space at the door, brandishing his metal pipe. "Ready when you are."

Adams didn't point out that she doubted the metal pipe was going to do anything – she was still gripping her baton, after all – but just muttered, *"Alley,"* under her breath and opened the door again.

She was barely quick enough to catch Collins as he rushed the door, apparently intent on trying to break it down. He yelped, trying to stop, but still stumbled into her, both of them wobbling on the threshold while she fought not to fall into the metal flotsam on the floor. Getting herself impaled on a half-finished rabbit wasn't going to help matters.

Rory grabbed Collins, helping steady him, and the big man straightened up, clutching the doorframe.

"Sorry," he managed. "Didn't mean to try and flatten you."

"Never mind that," Adams said, examining him. The rain had rendered his short-cropped hair thin, and his waterproof coat had expanded its collection of tears. There were also what looked like coffee grounds stuck to his cheek, and some chewed orange rinds caught in his scarf. "What happened?"

Collins looked at Rory. "Got you in, then, did she?"

Rory touched his cheek. "Damaged, but whole."

"Aren't we all." Collins turned to look warily back down the alley, then stepped into the workshop properly.

"Don't close the door," Adams said sharply. "It's our only way out, unless we fancy trying to bust out through the shop, and if this is what the rest of the place is like, I hate to think what protection Heather's got on her jewels."

"Sooner we're out of here the better, then," Collins said. "I heard something outside, opened the door, and that was there." He waved at the alley. "I stepped out to have a look, the door slammed, and I couldn't get it open again."

"And this?" Adams asked, pointing at the orange rind.

He fished it out, grimacing. "I got set on by a bunch of rabid kids and they threw me in a bin. I mean, I didn't even *do* anything. I'd been around to try the shop door, then decided I was going to have to try and break this one down. I just popped my head into a bar to ask if anyone had some tools I could use, and they rioted."

"Poets," Adams said. "You got set on by a bunch of poets, didn't you?"

"Maybe," Collins said. "They were spouting a load of rubbish. I don't mind a bit of Wordsworth, but any poetry that leads to me being thrown in bins is not my sort of thing."

Adams nodded, looking from him to Rory. "Right, well. You two need to pack yourselves off. I can't be picking you out of gardens and off balconies every five minutes."

They both just looked at her, and she crossed her arms.

"You do realise that other than one – or technically two – foot pursuits and a minor rumble in a junk shop I have been *fine,* and you two are here five minutes and I've lost my two main contacts, plus you've gone and got yourselves caught up in what I think might basically be some fancy automated security systems?"

"I'm pretty sure an automated security system didn't knock me out," Rory said, touching his head.

"That's not an argument for you staying. You've probably got a concussion as well as being over the limit."

"What about your suspects?" Collins asked. "Violet and Joe?"

"I'll deal with them."

"I'm sure you will," Rory said. "But considering Dandy's evidently missing, even if you're calling it tracking someone, don't you think a little help might be handy?"

Adams scowled, trying to ignore the swoop in her belly at the mention of Dandy. She'd expected he'd come back at some point, to lead her to Joe. But maybe he didn't feel he could leave the lad. That had to be it. *Had* to be.

"Anyway, I've got your key," Collins said, dangling it from

his fingers. "And I'm missing the football for this, so you're stuck with me."

"*Fine,*" she said, with a sneaky little thread of relief running beneath the words. She looked at Rory. "You can go home though."

"No, you're right, I'm probably over the limit. Plus I shouldn't drive with a head injury," he said, clambering back over the mess to pick up Midge, leaving Pinto giving an unhappy, wavering howl. He picked an unsteady path back to the door and deposited the dog on the doorstep, then grinned at Adams. "I think you'd best monitor me. That's what you do with a concussion."

Adams' scowled deepened, and she looked at Collins.

He nodded. "It's true. Can't leave someone alone when they've got a head injury."

"Not helping," she said, watching Rory ferry Pinto across the room.

"Losing battle, Adams," Collins said. "You can't stop people helping you, you know."

"I can if I arrest them," she muttered, but pushed past the dogs and onto the old cobbles of the alley, checking for rogue poets. There was no one nearby, just the drizzle building into a ceaseless rain.

Rory and Collins followed her, leaving the door to the workshop open and Fergus on the threshold. He looked at her with glossy black eyes.

"*Mmmip?*"

"Thanks," she said to him, then shot a sharp look at Rory and Collins. Neither of them was laughing, though. Collins was checking his scarf for more orange rind, and Rory was busy examining the dogs' paws, presumably for metal slivers. She watched Fergus for a moment longer, thinking. Heather and Charles both gone. Joe snatched, almost certainly by Heather, given the way the once-living materials of The Shop had suddenly revolted. Violet's location unknown. The dodgy copper still out there on their trail.

"What's next?" Collins asked.

"We need to find Joe. I'm almost certain Heather's taken him, presumably because she thinks he has the master charm."

"You don't think it's him, though."

"He says he was set up, and I kind of believe him."

Collins nodded. "Where would Heather go, then?"

"I thought she'd be here," Adams admitted. "And the way the place has been turned over …" She looked at Rory. "No one else came back with you?"

"No."

Adams thought about it, her fingers tapping on her thighs. The plants, here and in the growth at The Shop. Heather as a near-goddess, steeped in earth and wood. If she thought she was going to be facing down someone with the charm, she'd want to be somewhere she could touch the raw ground. Not the concrete-y bits, as Charles had put it. Aloud, she said, "Is there a good park near here? Somewhere a bit wild still?"

Collins and Rory looked at each other. "Museum Gardens?" Collins suggested, and Rory nodded.

"Near enough. Hardly *wild,* but they're old."

Adams frowned. "I was at the museum before. There's the green in front of Clifford Tower, but it's a bit obvious. Not much other than grass, either."

"Oh, no," Rory said. "Different museum. This one's all river and trees and that."

"*River,*" Adams said. "Fantastic. Come on." She turned down the alley, automatically looking for Dandy. Her breath caught in her throat a little painfully when she realised he wasn't there. Collins was, though, still fussing with his scarf and muttering dire threats as they passed the poet's bar, plus

Rory with the two dogs trotting calmly at his heels, his hands in his pockets and the gash on his eyebrow standing out brightly against his pale skin. He grinned at her when he caught her eye, and said, "Bit of excitement, isn't it?"

She didn't dignify that with an answer. She was missing something, she could feel it, something to do with the complicated entanglement of Jasper, and Joe, and Eddie, and Heather's furious hunger for action. But it'd surface. The answers always did. One just had to be patient, and keep pulling the threads until everything unravelled.

Or start arresting people. That often worked, too.

YORK SEEMED TO HAVE STEADIED, that glimpse of multi-layered reality she'd had from the apartment fading to leave just the shadowy presence of Folk and Folk businesses, no longer remarkable in light of everything else she'd seen. Something was off, though, and she couldn't quite place it as they wound through the tourists and pedestrians toward the park.

It was Collins who said, "Have you noticed the plants?"

"The plants?" She followed the direction he nodded in, spotting long planters outside a cafe, early spring blooms crammed in with ivy and bulbs, glossy in the rain. "What about them?"

"Look at the size of them."

She frowned. The planters looked like a usual size to her, but they were overloaded, bursting with wild growth, their bases splitting as roots searched for the ground. A young woman outside the cafe was using a pair of scissors to cut back a froth of vines that were choking the window, and she gave a sudden yelp, dropping the scissors and snatching her hand back, clasping it to her chest. The shears vanished, and the young woman looked at the plant suspiciously, then turned and hurried back inside, examining her injuries.

Adams slowed. Hanging baskets on lamp posts had sent invading shoots racing down the poles and expanding across the pavement, and the old wood on the leaning buildings was cracking in places, a fuzz of green growth sprouting out of it. Dandelions blossomed in pockets between the cobbles, and a very small yet very identifiable oak tree had taken root in the middle of the lane like a waist-high bonsai, pedestrians detouring around it with faint puzzlement, as if waiting to see a street performer demonstrate how it had come to be.

"Connected?" Collins asked.

"Heather," Adams said. Heather and her plant-based charms. She'd started, whether deliberately or in some sort of preparatory phase. They were running out of time and it felt to Adams like she'd barely even found the trail, let alone begun the chase. She picked up the pace, jumpy and unsettled, thinking over and over, *wood and metal, metal and wood.* Everywhere she looked there was both. And while the lamp posts and metal bollards weren't uprooting themselves in fury, there seemed to be an endless parade of overflowing plant pots and rogue weeds, ivy devouring the fronts of buildings while shopkeepers stared up at them in bewilderment, and saplings springing out of gutters and between cobbles. In one cafe bamboo had busted out a window in an effort to reach the sky, and as they walked past it Adams heard a man with one hand tugging at his hair yelling into his mobile, *"They're bamboo sticks in vases! That's not inappropriate use of plants! What do I pay my insurance for?"*

"You think this is all Heather?" Collins asked, walking next to her with his hands tucked into his pockets.

"I don't see what else it can be."

"Should we go in with weedkiller?" Rory asked. "Or a chainsaw?"

"We're just going to talk," she said, although a chainsaw was quite a tempting idea.

"And if she doesn't listen?"

"Then we'll think about the chainsaw." *And hope whoever has the charm doesn't start waking the metal up too.*

They wound their way out of the Shambles and into wider shopping streets, past old department stores and pubs, restaurants and cafes, florists and the ubiquitous newsagents. Adams found herself more wary of seeing other coppers than she was Folk, searching for a flash of high-vis yellow in the crowds, the glimpse of idling cars as they left the pedestrianised areas. She didn't spot anyone, but that didn't mean she wasn't seen, of course, by Jasper or whoever he was working with. It was an uneasy feeling. Not that she'd ever been idealistic enough to think her colleagues were beyond reproach – or herself, for that matter, even if that was limited to looking the other way when it seemed sensible, especially when it came to Folk and ladies of a certain age – but she'd never felt threatened by them. Not like this.

The gardens lay across one final road, a grey gatehouse standing behind a mix of old stone walls and metal fencing, the gates themselves lying open. A jogger ran past, heading into the wide smooth paths of the park, and a small man with a very large dog sat peacefully on a nearby bench, an umbrella held over both their heads while they shared a bacon sandwich. Otherwise there wasn't all that much foot traffic, the damp and fading day not conducive to garden strolls. A handful of tourists in sturdy shoes and disposable waterproof ponchos scurried out of the gate, fleeing the shadows, and Adams took a steadying breath, slowing as they passed the park's threshold. She could feel the ground beneath her changing, a tingling sensation travelling up her legs as if she'd stepped onto a ship's deck, vibrating with vast and hidden engines. She stopped, blinking at the gardens, dim and lush, alive with spring growth and old stories and scuttling, hidden life.

"Adams?" Collins said. He'd kept walking, and now he turned back, looking from her to Rory. He'd stopped as well, his hands on the dogs' head. They were looking up at him with anxious eyes. "Right, I'm not happy with this. What're you two seeing that I can't, and is it going to eat me?"

"Um, no," Adams said, making herself start walking again. "It's more a feeling than anything else." She glanced at Rory, and he nodded.

"Something's going on in here," he said. "Energies, or whatever." He waggled his fingers in an *ooh, magic* manner.

"Right, well, if any of the energies have big teeth, let me know," Collins said, and continued into the gardens, Adams and Rory following. He raised his eyebrows at her, and she nodded. It was fine, as far as she could tell. Just deeply *alive*, and she wondered if it always felt like that, or if it was Heather.

They didn't go far before the path split into two, one route heading down toward the river, the other up, to where Adams could glimpse the corner of a substantial building that was probably the museum. Collins stopped. "Which way?"

"Up," Adams said, at the same time as Rory said, "Down."

"Up," she insisted. The road they'd crossed definitely led to a bridge, which meant the bridge would border the garden. She wasn't going to deal with that unless she absolutely had to.

"Up it is," Rory said, and Collins headed that way, following a couple of students with umbrellas dawdling up the gravel path.

The museum came into view, a single-storey building with a grand, colonnaded entrance, the yellow stone stained with rain. The windows were lit with warm light, and discreet signs on the door gave little clue as to what was inside. Adams examined it, but Heather wasn't going to be in there, she was sure of it. Instead she kept walking, passing Collins as he paused to survey the museum and the green directly in front of it. It was still quiet up here, but in summer she could imagine it crowded with picnickers and lunchtime walkers.

The abbey lay just past the museum. Or rather what remained of the abbey did, a free-standing wall like the spine of a sleeping, skeletal beast, rising above the grass in a two-storey, slender fin. The lower half was solid, arches detailed onto the stone, while above it the same arches were echoed in open form, graceful and high, and looking far too delicate to still be standing. There was a larger, full height arch to the righthand end, and from here she couldn't see anything more substantial. The rest seemed to consist of clumps of stone, the remnants of pillars and foundations.

That was what Adams saw, on one level. On another she saw the sweeping lines of the original building, tall and luminous and imposing. Beyond that still she saw a wooden structure, well-made but victim to fire and flood. And still deeper, trees. Vast stretches of them, proud tall trunks and heavy branches and vibrant green foliage, trees that had persisted and persisted, offering shelter and silence and protection, just as the buildings that replaced them sought to do.

And standing in the middle, pinning the layers together, was Heather, barefoot in the grass, watching Adams approach with her arms crossed over her chest. She was still in her long skirts, a shawl over her shoulders in a nod to the rain and the chill, a faint smile on her lips.

"Detective Inspector," she said. "You're a very hard woman to shake off."

"That's the idea," Adams said.

Behind her, she heard Rory say to Collins, "You wanted to know if anything was going to bite?"

"Oh, I see this one," Collins said. "And I think you're probably right."

And in the still, grey damp of the day, the gardens all but deserted other than the four of them, Adams thought so too.

19

DUCK, CHOCOLATE, MAYBE NOT A STICK

"So how can I help you?" Heather asked. "Do you still want my fingerprints?" There was a vibrant humming coming from somewhere, hot and summer-toned despite the distinctly chill rain.

"I want Joe, for a start," Adams said.

Heather frowned. "I don't even know who that is."

The humming was getting louder, and Adams raised her voice slightly to be heard over it. "A friend of Violet's. Have you seen her?"

"Why would I?"

The noise was coming from behind the standing wall of the abbey, rising and falling as it grew closer, turning into a melody that Adams didn't recognise, but made her shift uneasily. There was something wild in the notes, something that spoke of deep forest and fast waters, rich earth and old growth being renewed. The abbey ruins and the trees felt solid, real, but she had a feeling that if she turned around she'd find the paths that led to the museum lined with strange stalls and old huts, remnants of another world.

She didn't turn, though, just said, "You grabbed Joe."

"I didn't." Heather sounded puzzled. "How would I know where he was to grab, especially when I don't know who he is?"

It was actually a good question. "Through Violet?" she offered. Maybe she *had* been at The Shop, and Adams just hadn't seen her.

"And how would I know where *she* was?"

"I heard you could track her."

"How? Am I meant to have put a microchip on her?" A smile crept over Heather's face, a gentle sort of amusement.

"No. Ah …" Suddenly Joe's story seemed a lot less believable than it had. Heather had power, that was clear, but she wasn't some movie demon, demanding contracts written in blood. "I heard you had ways of tracking the apprentices. That it was in the contracts."

"But *how?* Am I meant to have location tracking on all their phones or something?"

Adams gave up. "Contracts written in blood."

Heather stared at her, the smile widening. "Are you serious?"

"Unfortunately." The music was now accompanied by gentle, rhythmic clapping, and the soft sound of bells being rung at regular intervals. Its wild notes had slipped, and it now sounded very New Age-y and soothing, and made Adams want to arrest whoever was doing it.

Heather was raising her voice to be heard over it now, too. "Blood magic is rather frowned upon in civilised circles, and besides which, it's against my ethos." She gestured at the damp world around them. "I'm more interested in green things than bloody things."

"Right. So you haven't been looking for Violet? Or Joe?"

"I'm looking for the charm, Detective Inspector. If one of them has it, then I shall be looking for them. But my focus is on uncovering *it*, not an individual. The guardians are moving. I am readying myself."

Adams nodded. Charles had evidently not kept his secret from Heather for long, or she'd found out for herself. "Where's Charles, then?"

"If he's not at the shop, he'll be drowning his sorrows, I imagine."

"About what happened at your place?" Adams could hear chanting joining the humming now, and it wasn't improving her disposition toward the musicians.

"Obviously." Heather looked away, toward Rory and Collins, her fingers tapping her forearms restlessly.

"Who turned it over?"

"What?"

"Who turned the workshop over?"

Heather's attention snapped back to Adams. "What are you talking about?"

"The workshop? Everything thrown about? Is that why you knocked Rory out? Did you think it was him?"

"I haven't knocked anyone out. What do you mean about the workshop?"

Adams inclined her head at the two men lingering on the path. "Rory went back to the shop with Charles. Someone knocked him out, and he ended up dangling off the balcony. Did you do that?"

"No. *What's happened to the shop?*"

"You don't know?"

They stared at each other, the humming and chanting and bloody bells filling the space between them, fizzing on Adams' skin like the constant mist of the rain. She assumed Heather was in the midst of some pre-citywide-destruction ceremony with her disciples, until the other woman turned her head slightly toward the wall and yelled, "*Would you bloody well shut up?*"

The music cut off with a couple of final, slightly nervous claps, and the noise of the city rushed back, cars and horns and the general, endless heartbeat of humans and Folk moving restless and ceaseless through the world.

"What happened to my shop?" Heather asked, and the rain whispered and sighed around them. The grass reached for it, growing long and fierce around her feet, and one of the trees flushed with blossom, an explosion of furious growth.

"I don't know about your shop itself," Adams said. "But something's gone on in the workshop. Bench overturned, stuff all over the floor."

Heather didn't answer for a moment, and a daffodil bloomed near her feet, rising fast and luminous out of the earth. "And you said this Rory was on the balcony?"

"All trussed up in your plants."

"Did he do it?" Her voice was cool and smooth.

"No," Adams said firmly.

"How did he get in? How did *you* get in? What's *happened?*" There was a flicker of fury in the words now, less question and more disbelief. She took a step forward, as if to grab hold of Adams, and Adams held one hand up in a firm *stop* gesture. Heather looked from the hand to her, her face pinched with anger and indecision.

"No one here is responsible," Adams said, her voice level.

"But you've been in. You've been *inside my shop.* Without permission, if you're saying Charles wasn't there. *How?*"

Some tentative singing had started up behind the wall, half a dozen voices intermingling, as Adams said, "Fergus helped us."

"Fer—" Heather stopped, closing her eyes, and shook her head. "That bloody thing needs dismantling."

"He was very helpful. If it wasn't for him, we wouldn't

have found Rory, and you'd have had a manslaughter charge on your hands when he fell."

Heather made a small, impatient gesture that suggested she was concerned by neither Rory's plight nor the possibility of being done for manslaughter. Adams had an idea that might be down to Wilfred and however he dealt with intruders. Aloud, Heather said, "And you're sure Charles wasn't there?"

Adams spread her fingers. "From what I saw of your place. You might have extra dimensions to check in."

Heather shook her head slightly, seemingly more in disbelief than negation, and took a mobile phone from a pocket in her skirt. Seeing Adams' raised eyebrows, she said, "Local designer. Pockets in everything. I'll give you his number if you want."

Adams nodded, but she'd been thinking more about the phone. The grass was growing so steadily she thought she could hear it over the whisper of the rain, sprouting wildflowers all over the smooth lawns, and Heather's hair was misted with damp, her shawl slipping to reveal bare, softly tan shoulders as smooth and strong as old growth. The phone seemed deeply incongruous, even if it did have a case that looked like moss.

Heather poked the phone, listened for a moment, then shook her head. "Straight to messages." She scrolled through it, evidently searching for a number, then glanced at the wall again. *"I said shut up!"*

The singing straggled to a stop, and a young woman in bare feet and a drenched, pale dress that was probably rather ethereal in the sunlight, but which reminded Adams of a wet hanky right at that point, leaned around the wall. "Are we displeasing you?" she asked, her eyes wide. "We're only trying to sing the summer in on your behalf!"

Heather pointed a finger at her. "That racket couldn't sing in a warm breeze. And I'm busy."

"That's why we want to help," a second woman said, emerging from behind the wall. She had a crown of flowers in her hair that looked suspiciously perky and were likely fake. A man followed her, matching flowers in his beard. "We only wish to learn from you."

"I'm not a bloody online tutorial," Heather snapped. "Sod off, can't you?"

The first woman folded her arms over her chest. "Don't be so rude! You're our *queen.*"

"Yes, and queens chop people's heads off *all the time.*" Heather snapped her fingers, and the ground surged, sprouting spindly shoots of gorse that rapidly solidified into vast, gnarled bushes, crowding toward the wall. The trio retreated rapidly, and a moment later the music started up again, with more energy this time.

Adams looked at Heather. "They your followers or something?"

"*No.* I used to have a very nice little coven. We'd do midnight rites and summer rituals, that sort of thing. They learned a bit of base magic, I got to have a little fun, and everyone was happy. Now it's all Instagram snaps and TikTok reels. No one's interested in *actually* learning, just in looking like they are." She peered at the phone. "There." She tapped it, and waited as it rang.

"Violet must've been a good follower, then," Adams said. "She was more interested in your area of expertise than Charles's."

Heather gave her a look that suggested she was trying not to roll her eyes, then said into the phone, "Kaz? It's Heather. Is Charles there? No? Can you ask his ridiculous friends if they've seen him?" There was a pause, and Heather lowered the phone for a moment, looking at Adams. "Violet wasn't *interested.* Not really. She was a magpie, collecting knowledge like postage stamps." She winced. "Trading cards. Furbies. Pokémon— *Ugh.* Honestly, one does try to keep up, but sometimes …" She went back to the phone as someone started talking on the other end. "No? Damn. Alright. Let me know if he turns up."

"He's not at the pub," Adams said as Heather hung up.

"No." She shoved the phone back into her pocket.

"Rory saw him at the shop last, but that was a good hour ago, it seems. When did *you* last see him?"

"This morning." Heather adjusted her shawl. "I need to go back and take a look around the shop."

It sounded reasonable, and of course anyone would want to check on their place if there had been a break-in, but Adams doubted that was all it was.

"Where else would Charles be?" she asked.

"Nowhere I can think of."

"No other pub he frequents? Friends he might go to?"

"I said no." She turned away, starting toward the path.

"Wait."

Heather paused, looking back at Adams with her eyebrows raised. A single, very thorny rose snaked out of the ground next to Adams, its passage rocking the heel of her boot.

She moved her hand away from the rose's sharp bits and said, "Where's Violet?"

"Why would I know where Violet is? I already told you, no contracts in blood around here."

"Joe was with me, and we ended up with a whole shop's worth of junk tipped all over us. He vanished."

Heather turned back to face Adams properly, crossing her arms over her chest. "And why would that have anything to do with me?"

"There were plants overgrown all over the place after.

And the police tracked us there. The same copper I saw at your shop, which seems like a large coincidence."

Heather sighed, looking at the sky then back at Adams. "The *copper at my shop*, as you put it, was checking in because he knew we'd had a problem. You're not the only police officer that knows about Folk, you know."

"So why was he chasing down Joe, if you know nothing about him?"

"I have no idea. Police are your area."

Adams nodded. "And the plants?"

"You might've noticed plants have been overgrown everywhere."

"I have. Why?"

"Because, DI Adams, the guardians are no longer safe. They are *moving*. Charles did his best to hide it from me, but I'm not blind. And I can't wait any longer. I will either find the charm, or I will tear the guardians apart before they can become a problem."

"You really didn't grab Joe?"

"I know nothing about him. And now, if you don't mind, I have a missing husband *and* a missing master charm to deal with."

"Maybe we could help each other," Adams suggested.

Heather looked her up and down, a deliberate, dismissive look. "I fear that would be distinctly one-sided. Stay out of my way, Inspector. I haven't bopped anyone on the head yet, but I won't hesitate if I need to." She turned and strode off, her long skirt swirling around her legs and the wildflowers turning toward her as if following the sun. Adams watched her go, then turned back to the two men. They were huddled together, both peering at Rory's phone and apparently ignoring the exchange altogether. She went to join them.

"What're you looking at?"

"How did asking nicely go?" Collins asked in return, looking around for Heather. "Where's she gone?"

"Off to start a war against the guardians, or find Charles, or both."

"She wouldn't help?"

"She thinks we'll get in the way."

Collins nodded. "That's not the woman I met at the shop."

"Really?"

"Really. She was much younger, blonde."

"Violet," Adams said, rubbing her face with one hand. *"Dammit.* She and Joe are in on it together, aren't they? How the hell do we find them?"

Rory turned his phone toward her. "This might cheer you up."

"What?" She took it from him, frowning at the map on the screen. There was a pin tagging it neatly, near the river, but she couldn't tell much else. "What's this?"

"So, say you want to raise an army of metal guardians. You'd want a big space, right?"

"I imagine."

"And out of sight, because, you know. Giant metal sculptures flocking about the place."

"Yes."

"And then," Collins put in, "knowing Heather would be throwing trees about and all that, you'd want it to be fairly, well, *dead*, wouldn't you?"

"Can you two get to the point?" Adams asked.

"That's the point," Rory said, pointing at the phone.

She looked back at it, zooming in on the pin. "You think they're here?"

"It's part of the regeneration project for the rail museum," Collins said. "That building's an old goods station, so lots of soot and traffic and general nastiness, which means not much has grown there for a hell of a long time. Now they're rebuilding the whole area, and it's full of metal scaffolding and fences, old brick, old rails—"

"And not much in the way of wood or living things," Adams said, staring at the map. "But wouldn't it be full of workers?"

"It's Saturday, after five already," Rory said. "Besides, we all know not everyone sees things the same way, don't we?"

"Might even be part of what makes it good cover," Collins pointed out.

Adams stared at the pin, mired in the satellite image of what looked like a bit of carpark and a whole bunch of tarmac. "We still don't know they're definitely here," she said. "Why bring them so close to Heather when they know she'll be looking for them?"

"Get ahead of the problem before she gets up to speed, maybe," Rory said.

Adams looked from him to Collins. "We've got no Dandy. No Heather or Charles. No one at all."

"*Rude*," Rory said. "You've got me and the dogs."

"You were stuck in an overgrown Venus flytrap. Forgive me for not being entirely convinced."

"Your call," Collins said, rocking on his heels. "But we should probably decide soon, before the police come sniffing after you again."

Adams grimaced, looking for Heather. She'd already vanished in the direction of the city centre, no doubt to check the shop then continue her hunt for the master charm. If she found it before they did, there was no telling what might happen. The re-wilding of York by the sound of things. That, or if things went the other way the city would fall to the guardians and whoever was controlling them. She looked at Collins and Rory, then nodded. "Alright. Let's do it."

THEY HEADED out of the park the same way they'd come, but turned right onto the street instead of crossing it, following it toward the river as the night chased along the edges of the grey day. Adams folded her fingers over the duck in her pocket, her breath tight. The city was *slipping,* or her grasp of it was, the other versions of York bleeding through everywhere. It wasn't just the hunched form of a faery filling jacket potatoes in a food truck, or the long yellow car slouching down the street that wasn't actually a car, although she couldn't have said what it was, or the glimpse of towers and chimneys that didn't belong to any building code she could imagine. She could *feel* it, feel Heather's deep-set, earthy magic thrumming in the bloodlines of the city, waking roots and shoots and dormant seeds, setting them heaving toward the surface, hungry for light and water and territory. She peered over the stone parapets of the bridge as they crossed it, spotting a platoon of ducks and a few swans cruising in the brown water.

"No fog," she muttered. "It's fine if there's no fog."

"Where *is* your dog, exactly?" Rory asked, apparently mishearing. "Who was he following?"

"Joe." She hoped.

"And Heather claims she had nothing to do with snatching him?" Collins asked.

"That's what she says. That the plant growth I saw after everything went pear-shaped was just the side effect of whatever she's doing."

"She's doing plenty," Rory said, nodding at the riverbanks, where the trees were blooming furiously, all the usual caution of a Yorkshire spring entirely abandoned.

"And if not her, who?" Adams asked. "Violet, if it was her at the workshop? If she's already got the master charm, why go back there and risk being caught? Did she do it to get hold of Charles?"

"That seems possible," Collins said. "Maybe the charm has more safety guards on it, or perhaps she doesn't know how to work it as well as she thought."

Adams nodded. "That seems plausible. What about Joe in The Shop, then?"

There was a pause, as they finally crossed the bridge and returned to relatively safe ground, then Rory said, "Could you have been the target? Dandy was with him, and so they thought he was you?"

"I don't look much like him," Adams pointed out.

"Not to another human. But if it was sort of a smash and grab, maybe all they were going on was *human plus dog.*"

Collins and Adams looked at each other, and she rubbed the back of her neck. "Fantastic."

"At least it's not weres. Bit of variety," Rory said, grinning, and she shook her head.

"You're having far too much fun."

"I am. I really am."

She wanted to tell him that this wasn't meant to be *fun,* that there were monsters under bridges and beasts in alleys and much worse things than faeries and goblins and ravenous bins, that the uneasy twist in her belly was telling her they'd barely seen a fraction of what the world held, but she had an idea she didn't need to. He'd probably worked that out a long time before she had.

"Here," Collins said, holding Fergus's key out to her. "You'd be better with this."

She took it, not arguing, and put it in her pocket, her fingers bumping into Fergus's other gift, the duck. She took it out, examining it, then offered it to Collins. He took it, raising his eyebrows at her.

"I don't know," she said. "But mine helps."

"Fair enough," he said, and pocketed it. "What else do we need?"

"Chocolate," she said.

Collins nodded. "Ducks and chocolate. Obviously. We'll go past the train station anyway, so we can get some there. Anything else?"

"A very big stick."

"Baton do?"

"Mine does," she said.

"Well, this is unfair," Rory said, and looked around as they headed down the riverside path. It was lined with trees, all in rich green shades, and the fading day left the shadows deep and dank, the river itself dappled with raindrops. "I should've kept the pipe. Maybe I can get a stick instead."

"I wouldn't go with wood," Collins said, as the trees shivered. "Seems risky, that."

"Isn't your baton metal? That seems risky, too."

The two men were still discussing the relative risks of their choice of weapons when they reached the train station, and Adams hurried into WHSmith to stock up on Yorkies. Her Leeds DCI had favoured Lion bars, and in London it had been Freddos, but Yorkies had worked for her, and she wasn't about to change now. As far as the very big sticks went, she doubted it mattered if they were metal or wood. Neither seemed to have much of a chance against giant guardians and aggressive undergrowth, so they were going to have to figure things out as they went along.

Somehow.

THE SPOT RORY and Collins had decided was ground zero for the guardians was just on the other side of the train station, the footpath leading through an underpass to reach it. It reverberated with an incoming train above and the passage of cars next to them, fended off only by a low metal fence. Adams kept her hands tight on both the duck and the baton, but there was nothing more scary than a teenager on an electric scooter, forcing them to almost flatten themselves against the walls to let her pass, and some vaguely unpleasant graffiti.

They emerged into the same damp day they'd left, not that she'd thought the underpass might be some sort of portal, but … well, she had, a little. Ahead of them, the rounded prow of a red brick building on the corner of a street held a large sign pointing to the Railway Museum, and to the left was the organised carnage of a works site, fenced off with low metal fencing and warning signs. There were no works vehicles visible on the streets, no one wandering about in high-vis vests. They had the site to themselves. Other than the inevitable CCTV, of course, but she'd just have to deal with that when they came to it.

She examined the area, frowning. There was nowhere to hide anything. There were works going on, definitely, but where she'd imagined high, solid fences behind which people could get up to nefarious dealings unseen, this was all open. Nothing could be hidden here, and it looked more like new car parks were going in than anything else. She turned on her heel, examining the tangle of fencing. It split the road into sections, the part they were on apparently heading parallel to the railway, two others splitting around the building on the corner with its sign, and the others forming some complicated navigation around existing car parks. There was nowhere to hide.

"Is this the right spot?" she asked.

"It's what we were thinking of," Collins said. "Not quite what I was expecting, though."

"No," she agreed, narrowing her eyes at the scene, trying

to force something to resolve itself out of the bland mess of roadworks and tarmac. Nothing did. It was the most dull spot she'd seen in the whole city, which should've been rather nice, but wasn't what they needed right now.

Midge and Pinto were whining, and she glanced at them, Rory trying to persuade them to heel without the help of his missing leash. They weren't listening, their eyes on a large hall that could just be glimpsed beyond the roadworks. She clicked her tongue, and they both looked at her, ears pricked.

"Dandy?" she asked, and Midge tipped her head to one side quizzically, then both dogs went back to staring at the hall, only the strength of their training holding them in place. "The useful ones never talk," she muttered.

Rory looked at her, then gave a low whistle. The dogs' head snapped around, eyes intent on him. "Seek," he said, and they bolted across the lane, sprinting for the half-seen hall.

Rory launched himself after them, and Adams gave chase, ignoring Collins shouting, "Running? *Really?*"

Her fingers were tingling, the world outlined in brighter edges. Here it was. They'd found the thread.

20

HABERDASHERY
& LADIES' SHOES

THE DOGS RAN STRAIGHT FOR THE HALL, PAST A SMALL, FLAT-roofed building with a frozen clock above the door, and Adams and Rory sprinted after them, Collins trailing behind. The hall was two storeys, with elegant, curve-topped windows and a large, arched front door. A double-sided set of stairs led up to the door, and below floor level were a series of smaller arches, as if the building had once had three storeys, and the bottom one had quietly sunk out of sight, until only the top of the window frames were visible. They were shuttered, the metal painted in a vibrant red that matched the door and the window frames, luminous in the dull day. There was no sign of life, no lights behind the windows or museum-goers wandering through the doors. To their right, though, was another building with a large sign for the National Railway Museum, and a glass-fronted shop, the interior brightly lit and peopled by a smattering of browsers.

Midge and Pinto surged up the stairs to the front door of the big hall, almost falling over each other in their eagerness to get there, snuffling the frame and whining, and Rory whistled to them. They looked at him, eyes bright, and he pointed at the ground by his feet as he came to a stop at the bottom of the stairs. They left the door reluctantly, slinking down the stairs with backward glances, and Adams caught up to them as Rory gave them each a biscuit.

"We can't just walk in there," she said, nodding at the glass-fronted shop. "We'll be seen." Collins had slowed to a walk, looking in the same direction.

"There's something in there, though," Rory said. The dogs were standing at attention by his sides, eyes still on the door, Midge giving a plaintive little whine.

Adams tapped her fingers against her thighs. Any other time, she'd have just walked over to the shop, shown her warrant card, and demanded to be let in, but the last thing they needed was the staff calling the York police.

She looked at Collins as he joined them. "Don't strain yourself," she said, and he grinned.

"Running's only for emergencies," he said, and nodded toward the left corner of the building, away from the shop side. "That way."

"There's another way in?"

"Should be. This is Station Hall – it's part of the museum, but last time I was up they'd closed it for a redo. Looks like it's still going. If I remember right, though, there's a play area out the back, and we can try going in that way."

"I have many thoughts about you choosing to travel to York to look at a railway museum," Adams said. "But since that's also really useful, I'll save them for later."

"I like museums," Collins said, tucking his hands into his pockets. "And trains."

"You would." She waved him on, and he led the way around the building, the rain intensifying and soaking into her hair. A fenced car park for rail employees butted up against the wall, secured with a high gate and sharp points to the fencing. There was no one monitoring it, and only a handful of cars inside. A line of large industrial bins rested next to the fence rather invitingly, suggesting no one was too worried about people getting into the car park, only about them getting cars out. Adams boosted herself up onto the lid of one, the black plastic slippery in the rain.

"What about cameras?" Rory asked, looking around.

"I doubt they're monitored," Collins said, choosing the bin next to Adams' one. It bowed under his weight but held, and he and Adams looked at each other.

"I'll go over first," he said, taking his jacket off and using it to cushion the spikes on the fence. "Then you can pass me the dogs."

"This is a very calm break-in," Rory said, hefting Midge up to Adams. "You two are consummate professionals."

Adams started to answer just as an "*Oi!*" went up from the direction of the shop. They looked around to see a man in a security guard's uniform jogging toward them through the rain, and Adams swore. Collins tried to heft himself over the fence, then yelped as he jabbed himself in the chest with the spikes. He fell back onto the bin, which gave a loud crack, and he rolled off it to the ground before the lid could give way under him.

Adams looked from the fence to the oncoming security guard, hesitating, and Rory said, "Go! We'll deal with this."

"*Now* we run," Collins said, already starting for the road. The security guard yelled again, waving wildly for them to stay in place, and Collins put on a turn of speed.

"*Go on,*" Rory said again, and Adams looked at the face of the great hall, at the little arches pinned to the ground like hidden doors, narrowing her eyes. They made no sense. There was a slanted hatch below the front entrance that would've been how things were dumped into the basement, coal or supplies of some sort, so why the arches? It was a nice building, but it was a *working* building. They wouldn't be there just for decoration.

They didn't need to go around the back. They just needed to find the right door.

"This way." She jumped off the bin, landing easily and already starting to run back toward the front of the hall. "*Circle left!*" she yelled at Collins, and watched him swerve, heading to loop around the little building in the intersection of the roads.

"*Oi!*" the security guard yelled again. "Stay put, the lot of you!" He altered course, aiming for Adams, and Rory whistled, sharp and imperious. Midge and Pinto shot across the tarmac, heads and tails down, and circled the guard, who came to a stumbling halt. "Hey! Call off your dogs!"

Rory whistled again, the noise close behind Adams, and the dogs closed on the guard, driving him backward with little darting movements, eyes intent and determined. Collins emerged from around the flat-roofed building, keeping up an impressive pace, and Adams stumbled to a stop by the hall, pulling the duck from her pocket and shining it across the little arches. Rory whistled again, and the security guard yelled that he was calling the police out *right now* and doing them for dangerous animals as well as attempted break-ins.

"Hurry up," Rory said. "He's going to realise any moment they won't bite."

Adams ran along the front of the building, the light of the duck showing nothing but red paint and old brick. One arch, two, three— *There.* Stairs bloomed in front of her, leading down to a full-sized archway that wasn't even blocked by a door. It simply loomed onto the darkness beyond, and she grabbed Fergus's key, just in case it helped, then trotted down toward it.

She had one disorientating moment, when her brain

kicked in and tried to assure her she was falling onto the tarmac and about to smack her nose into the ground, but her body carried her forward, legs vanishing into the earth. She could see it on both levels, the old stone steps worn into a dip in the centres, and the flat surface of the tarmac drifting above, then her brain caught up with her body and the entrance sharpened in front of her. She looked back, and Collins came to a stumbling stop, looking at her in utter bewilderment.

"Grab my shoulder," she said to him, and he leaned forward uncertainly, his feet still mired in the rainy car park, placing a large hand on her arm.

"Close your eyes," Rory said behind him, then whistled again, sharp and final. The dogs abandoned the security guard, darting back to join them and flying down the steps past Adams as Rory grabbed Collins' shoulder. "Go!"

Adams plunged into the darkness, Collins' grip tightening on her as Rory propelled him forward. The security guard's shouts went from outraged to a splutter of confusion, then Adams was through the arch and they cut off altogether. The light of the duck lit smooth, old stone walls, driving deep under the building, and she took her baton from her other pocket, walking on until they were all safely inside, the dogs dropping back to join Rory.

She looked at Collins. "You can open your eyes now."

He opened one, and peered around, then released her shoulder and opened the other. He looked back, past Rory to where the archway revealed the flight of stone steps leading to the surface, rain falling softly to dampen them. There was no sign of the security guard, and they couldn't hear him, either.

Rory patted Collins on the shoulder, then let go. "Alright?"

"I'm not sure how to answer that. It looked like solid

ground to me." He looked at Adams. "You walked into *solid ground.*"

She held up the duck. "Things show up under this."

"Invisible ink doors?"

"Pretty much."

He nodded, and took his torch and baton out of his pockets. "Well, my torch isn't that fancy, so I'll just trust you. Lead on. No knowing if our lad out there is going to call the local coppers in or not."

Adams looked at Midge and Pinto. "Was it Dandy? Can you find him?"

They looked back at her, eyes wide in the pale light of the duck, but they didn't seem to be in a rush to head into the dark.

She tried not to think that was a bad sign.

THE NARROW PASSAGE with its dusty floor and raw stone walls didn't run for long before it turned abruptly right, running parallel to the front of the building even as it dived deeper beneath it, the floor sloping down at a gentle angle. There were no doors leading off, no junctions or signs, and it switchbacked on itself twice, still heading steadily deeper beneath the hall. They didn't speak, just walked on steadily, and every now and then Adams glanced back at the dogs, but they were neither trying to run forward nor hold back. No giant dogs or glittery toilet monsters or weird ravenous rodents made their presence felt, so she just kept going, the duck casting a pool of light that filled the tunnel ahead of her, backed up by the men's torches.

When the wall to her left fell away, darkness rushing to meet them, she almost stumbled, pulling away from the edge. No banister had appeared to replace the wall, and a gulf of nothingness yawned where it had been. She almost cut her light, feeling pinned in place by it, drawing any inhabitants of the void like moths, but freezing here on the stair would get them nowhere, and going back would likely get them arrested. So she just said, "Mind the gap," and kept going, while Rory chuckled and Collins said, "Really? *Really?*"

The gap was full of softly moving air, brushing against her cheeks, and the echo of their footsteps drifted out into nothingness, little scuffs and the chatter of dislodged pebbles. But nothing came rushing to attack them, and she kept going steadily, trying to remember how many steps each stretch of passage had been between turns. She wasn't sure, but it didn't feel like this one was any longer than the others had been when she arrived on flat ground, tiled with large stone flags dusted with dirt and grit. She shone the duck around without revealing much, and looked at Collins.

"Anything in your museum knowledge about big spooky underground chambers?"

"No," he said, stepping out into the dark and trying to spot the ceiling with the torch. It didn't reach. "This is *massive.* What's the construction? There's a bunch of trains sitting on top of us here, which hardly seems safe."

"Oh good, I can worry about that now," Rory said, giving the dogs each a treat. He didn't actually sound as if he was worrying about much, and played his torch over the ground, venturing away from the stairs.

Adams examined the walls, which seemed to be solid stone, and spotted a box mounted on a column of brick not far from the steps. She made a small *hmm* sound, and went to examine it. Painted red metal outside, with a fading *Danger* label on it. Closed with a key of some sort, but hardly secure. She took her multitool out and opened the blade, wedging it into the side of the box's door while Collins called, "There's platforms here, and rails. It's a whole bloody train station I've never even *heard* of. And it's so deep! With the river just over there, how does that make sense? How did they build this? When?"

"No idea," Rory said. "Look, is that a tram?"

Adams popped the door off the box and revealed a circuit breaker inside, a big, old-fashioned contraption with a dramatic handle, the sort of thing the evil scientist would throw when powering their dastardly experiments. She looked at it for a moment, then shrugged. They weren't going to find their way out of here with torches. Not in time to stop the city being torn apart, anyway.

She grabbed the handle and threw the switch, jamming it into place with a crunch that spoke of old wiring and hungry corrosion, but the response was immediate, lights flickering on in the darkness, washing across the stone floor and outlining the fingers of plat-forms poking out into a huge cavern. It narrowed down to a passage at the far end, still large but not as vast as where they found themselves. The walls grew up around the platforms, curving overhead, a vast and natural hollow deep within the earth that had been outfitted with all the trappings of a station, old destination boards and a shuttered ticket office and even a little newspaper stall, all empty and swept clean. It had been closed up rather than abandoned, everything tidied away and left to its own devices.

More importantly, a large sign next to the ticket office pointed to a door that simply read, *Higher Platforms*.

"That way," she said, pointing to it.

Collins was still staring around at the walls. "How's there still power? There's been flooding here, you can see. Look, watermarks on the wall. What *is* this place?"

"Collins, come on," Adams said, already heading for the door. "There's no one down here."

"Lots of metal, though," Rory pointed out, falling into step with her.

"And a great big hole. Good way to ensure Heather can't send trees after them."

"Where do you think that connects to?" Collins asked, pointing down the tunnel. "We're not bloody London! We don't have hidden stations all about the place!"

"*Come on*," Adams said. "Come back and do your urban exploring later."

"What if I can't find it again, though? And why abandon it? The flooding? It's dry now, so evidently it's able to be contained." He still wasn't moving, playing the torch over the walls. "I'd be really interested—" He stopped, and turned the light on the tunnel where it plunged deep into the earth, dark and impenetrable. "What was that?"

"Collins," Adams started, then she caught the sound. A rustling, rushing susurration, not unlike the toothy little gerbils that had mobbed her when she left the dungeons, only bigger. Much, much bigger. "Okay, we need to go."

Collins took a step back, his torch still on the tunnel. "I really don't like that noise."

"It sounds like the reason this place was abandoned," Rory said. Midge and Pinto were staring at the tunnel, ears back, as the noise grew from a whisper to a rumble.

"*Move!*" Adams shouted, and Collins spun away from the platform, running to join them as the rumble surged closer, a stampede or a flood of *something*, washing out of the dark to devour the light. They sprinted toward the sign, Adams swerving into a stone archway that offered up a lift and a set of metal stairs, switchbacking all the way up the height of the cavern in an open metal enclosure. It was *far* too exposed, but there was no way she was trusting a lift in here. She grabbed the gate to the stairs, shaking it furiously as the roar of the oncoming attack surfed toward them. *Locked.* She grabbed for her lock picks, fumbling them out, and Rory shouted, "*Lift!*"

"That won't be safe!" She had to shout back to be heard over the rising din.

"Neither's that." He jabbed a finger at the caged stairs. Collins was already at the lift, hitting the buttons frantically, and Adams wanted to point out they couldn't possibly trust it, it'd be older than they were and probably not serviced for decades, and what if they got stuck? What then?

But the protests died before she could utter them, because the wave of invaders had reached them, pouring out of the tunnel and scampering toward the platforms, all long, silky white hair and giant eyes squinting at the light, claws scratching and tearing at the stone. Their limbs were angular and multi-jointed, and a hissing song swept in with them, a chorus that sounded horrifyingly familiar, a *chugga-chugga-choo-choooooo* that evoked the ghosts of steam trains, calling to each other in the deep darkness beneath the earth.

Midge and Pinto were barking, regular and horrified, trying to back away, but Rory had both their collars, his own face pale and set. Adams stepped in front of him as the creatures swarmed onto the platform, peering around curiously and chattering long, jagged teeth, then the lift *dinged*, improbably cheery. The beasts swung toward the sound in one hideously synchronised movement, and Collins hauled the door open.

"In!" he shouted.

The dogs just about pulled Rory over as they shot inside, cowering against the back wall, and Adams backed up hurriedly, then dived into the lift as Collins grabbed the outer door. He slammed it closed, the glass window giving far too good a view of the beasts racing across the stone floor, their *chugga-chugga-choo-choooooo* cries cranking up a notch, filling the air with echoing, frantic calls.

Adams stared at the controls as Collins wrestled the folding metal interior gate into place, the first of the creatures colliding with the door with soft, almost wet *thuds*. The dogs were still barking, the noise deafening in the tight space, and Collins gave a shout of triumph as the gate latched.

"We're in!" Even as he said it, the outer door flew open again, and he staggered back from the gate. Long talons with wickedly sharp points slashed at the metal, paws trying to force their way into the lift, and Adams grabbed the handle of the controls. It was all old, tarnished brass, and there were buttons as well as the large handle, mounted on a circular dial, but the writing was greened out and there were no lights to guide her, so she just jammed the handle over and hoped for the best.

The lift lurched, gears grinding and growling, and the lights outside dimmed for a second, then came up again. The car shuddered, and Adams almost fancied she could hear the cables twanging under the unexpected load, then they stopped dead and a steady beeping started. The creatures moaned, and their attack on the cage intensified. Collins had his baton out, slamming it into their paws, but for every one that let go another took its place, more and more of them piling up, blocking out the view of the cavern.

"The outer door!" he shouted. "It needs to be shut for the lift to work."

Adams swore, and rushed to join him. The creatures were massed around them. There was no way they were closing the door in that.

"Jam the latch," Rory said by her ear, and she jumped, looking at him. "It'll be a circuit that's completed when the latch is in," he almost shouted above the insistent *chugga-chugga-choo-chooooo*–ing, and the clash of talons on metal. "We just need to get something metal into it."

"Like what?" she demanded.

"Duck," Collins shouted, and she did, then looked at his outstretched hand, holding the small metal duck Fergus had given her. She snatched it off him.

"Keep them back," she said, handing her baton to Rory. He gave it a concerned look, then grabbed it and readied himself, and Adams took a breath, eyeing the teeth of the beasts warily. The two men attacked them, jabbing the batons through the gaps in the gate, forcing the creatures back, and she shoved her arm through, fumbling for the notch the door would latch into. She could see it, when she dared get her face close enough to the door, but there were still too many claws in evidence. One set swiped across the back of her hand, making her hiss in pain and almost drop the duck, then Collins was driving it away. Teeth snapped at her jacket sleeve, snagging the fabric, but she ignored them, forcing the duck into the latch, jamming it in place as hard as she could then snatching her arm away. Rory was already back at the controls, hefting the handle over, and this time there was no buzz of alarm. The car lurched, sending her stomach flip-flopping, then they were staggering upward at the pace of a worn-down stairlift, but they were *moving*.

As if realising, the creatures redoubled their attack, but the lift ascended inexorably, the gap closing until the paws could only manage to claw hopefully at the floor, then the last one fell away with a plaintive *choooo*.

Adams leaned back against the wall, panting unevenly, and looked at Collins. He looked as wide-eyed as she felt, and after a moment he said, "Well, the duck was handy while it lasted."

"We'll get you another one," she said, resting her head against the wall and closing her eyes for a moment.

No one spoke until the lift came to a creaking, unsteady stop, and *dinged* politely.

Rory released the controls. "First floor. Haberdashery and ladies' shoes."

Collins looked at him. "Haberdashery was ground floor."

He nodded, and offered Adams her baton. "I wasn't a fan of the ground floor."

"I think that was sub-basement level," she said. "I just hope it's secure."

"Does explain the big *danger, no entry* sign," Rory said, and she stared at him.

"There wasn't one."

"There was. Outside. You ran straight past it. But, upside, we didn't get arrested."

"Only almost eaten," Collins said, and put his hand on the gate. "Ready?"

"Probably not," Adams said, dabbing blood off her scratched hand. "But let's go anyway. And tell me if you see any more signs, alright?"

"Where's the fun in that?"

21

KIDNAPPING FOR THE FUN OF IT

COLLINS HAD TO FORCE THE GATE OPEN, THE METAL squealing unpleasantly and far too loudly for Adams' liking. Evidently the combined assault of the cavern creatures and the batons had been a bit much for it. But he got it wide enough for them to step through, then looked around at Adams and Rory. She shifted her stance slightly, baton already in her hand, and raised her eyebrows. "Well?"

He stepped away from the gate, waving at the door. Or where the door should've been. Instead there was a solid sheet of plasterboard. She stared at it, then looked at Rory.

He pointed at the controls. "It won't go any further."

"Are you sure?" Collins stepped over to them, and tried shifting the lever. The lift jolted, dropping enough that the plasterboard wall gave way to smoothly finished metal frame, and both Rory and Adams yelped.

"Don't go back *down*," she said. "I'm not doing that again."

Collins didn't answer, just forced the lever the other way. They rose again, but only to the level of the plasterboard, then stalled out.

"See?" Rory said.

Adams sighed, examining the blank wall. "This has got to be the least subtle break-in ever."

"And to think I called you consummate professionals."

"To be fair, we are meant to be *stopping* break-ins," Collins pointed out, joining Adams.

"I hope you're better at that," Rory said.

Adams turned her back to the door, steadying herself with one hand on the closed gate, and booted backward, her foot driving straight through the board and exploding it outwards with a clatter of tiles. She dropped into a crouch, shining the duck's light through the hole, and revealed an expanse of glossy white surfaces beyond. A whiff of stale water came through, not dirty, simply untouched for a while, and she spied a row of sinks. "Toilets," she said, straightening up and kicking the edges of the hole a little more circumspectly, opening it up further.

"Wait," Collins said. "Didn't you two have a glittery toilet monster issue before?"

"That was the pub," Adams said, then paused, looking doubtfully at Rory. "Were those creatures after a toll? Was that all it was?"

"My guess is no, and I'm not going back to ask."

"No," she agreed, and crouched down to peer through the enlarged hole again. "Looks all clear." She didn't wait for them to answer, just crawled through, trying not to put her free hand on any of the broken tiles, still wielding her duck. It didn't reveal any hidden doors or mysterious angles, and the toilets remained resolutely silent. She checked them anyway, finding nothing more threatening than the same stale water stench, while Rory and the dogs followed her out, and Collins knocked the hole a bit larger, muttering about no one being of a decent size around here. She waited until he was through before going to the door, lit in the soft glow of an emergency exit sign, and taking hold of the handle, swapping the duck for her baton. She could see well enough in the light from Collins' and Rory's torches.

The door swung open with a creak, and she stepped onto a smooth concrete floor, lit only by a trickle of grey light from the fading day that spilled from translucent panels in the low roof overhead, supported by a gridwork of metal frames. The room within was long and dim, divided into wide fingers of rail platforms holding old-fashioned wooden benches, although the drop to the rails had been covered over, presumably to prevent unwary museum-goers from vanishing into the gaps. There were still train carriages slumbering in neat lines along the length of the hall, protected by scaffolding from whatever repairs were being carried out around them. Plastic drop cloths covered some of them, and the locomotives peered out from underneath like trapdoor spiders.

The whole place was silent, cars distantly audible on the road outside, and rain whispering on the high roof like static. Adams looked around, her belly curling with a dull sort of disappointment. There was no one here. Of course there wasn't. How ridiculous to think there would be. It had been nothing but a guess, and she'd put them all at risk on the off chance of finding Dandy and Joe here, with nothing more to go on than there being nothing green in the place. She looked at Collins, wondering how they were going to get out without the security guard rumbling them, and he gave her a rueful sort of smile. She wondered what the next step was. Back to Heather, she supposed, if they could even find her.

"We may as well check the carriages," she said aloud. "Since we're here."

They spread out, not bothering to stay quiet, the building so clearly empty (other than the monsters in the basement, but she was hoping they'd stay there) that Adams' only concern was to get the sweep through done as quickly as possible so they could move on. So when she heard a bark, she assumed it was Midge or Pinto. She glanced toward it, but saw nothing, and was pawing aside the dust sheet from one of the carriages when the bark came again. She frowned, and called, "Rory?"

"Yeah?" he shouted back, from the opposite direction to where she'd thought the bark had come from.

She dropped the plastic sheet, stepping back from the carriage slowly and looking up at the scaffolding, prowling along the unseen tracks like predators. Like *guardians*. She closed her eyes, wrapping her hand around the duck, and took it from her pocket, clicking its wings a couple of times as if she could switch her way of seeing as easily as she could turn the light on. The bark came again, closer this time but still annoyingly directionless, and she opened her eyes.

The scaffolding was still in the same place. Nothing had moved. Nothing had materialised, and she all but kicked the carriage in frustration. "Where *are* you?" she yelled.

"Here?" Rory called, sounding confused, and Collins shouted from further over, "Are you two *trying* to get that security guard in here?"

The next bark was almost lost under Collins' voice, but Adams heard it anyway. It wasn't Midge or Pinto, not unless they'd suddenly got really good at climbing. She spun around, spotting a shaggy form standing on top of a carriage.

"*Dandy?*"

Dandy gave a joyful yelp but didn't move, tail wagging wildly, and she frowned, then sighed. She had told him to stick with Joe, hadn't she?

"Here! Come on!"

Dandy leaped from the roof and bounded toward her, tail wagging and dreadlocks flying. She dropped to her knees, grabbing him as he crashed into her, almost knocking her over.

"Good boy," she said, scruffing his ears. "*Good boy.* A bit too literal when you decide to actually listen, but you're a good boy."

Rushing paws distracted her as she kept petting Dandy, and Midge and Pinto raced up to her, each of them trying to be the one to greet him first. Adams looked around to see Collins and Rory watching her, Rory with a grin and Collins looking faintly bemused.

"Very odd, watching you pet an invisible dog," he said.

Adams straightened up, looking at the carriage while Dandy panted at her cheerily. "I told him to watch Joe," she said, her voice low. The curtains were pulled on the long windows, allowing no glimpse of the interior. It *could* have been to protect the insides from whatever light did manage to sneak through the skylights during the day, but she didn't think so.

"Where are they?" she asked Dandy, and he turned, padding back along the platform with Midge and Pinto flanking him. Adams adjusted her grip on her baton, duck at the ready in her other hand.

Rory shone his torch down the platform. "I'd quite like a very big stick," he said. "I'm feeling a little bit underprepared, what with no duck and no very big stick."

"Well, I lost my duck," Collins said, looking at his baton. "I hope the very big stick is enough."

They both looked at Adams, and she shrugged. "You two should be better prepared," she said, then fished in her pockets and threw them each a Yorkie bar.

"You've already given us some of those," Collins said.

"It's to make up for the loss of the duck," she said, then headed down the platform after Dandy, who'd stopped outside the carriage doors. His ears twitched, and he looked from the doors to Adams.

She checked on Collins, who nodded, adjusting his stance

and raising his baton. He'd given his torch to Rory, who had both beams trained on the door, Midge and Pinto standing to attention at his side. Adams waved to him to step back a little further, then knocked on the door sharply.

"Joe," she said. "Come on out."

There was silence inside. No lights visible through the curtains.

She knocked again, quick and sharp. "We know you're in there, and you're only making it worse for yourself. Out you come."

Silence again.

Adams stepped to the side and tested the handle gently. It felt like it was going to move easily enough, and she checked on Collins and Rory again, then turned the handle and threw the door wide in one quick move, ducking back as she did so. Movement flashed inside, glimpses of airborne colour, and she raised her baton to fend off the missiles as they resolved themselves in the light of the torches into huge dragonflies, half a dozen of them, each with a wingspan as long as her arm. They swung toward her and she ducked again, yelping more in surprise than alarm. She sent one spinning away with a swing of her baton, Collins running forward to take on the others, and another hit her on the shoulder, bouncing off again harmlessly. They were nothing but thick wire and plastic, and she swatted a second away with her hand, puzzled.

More movement in the carriage, and a metal cockerel with flaking green and red paint charged out, missed the step, and plunged to the platform with a clatter. A skittering selection of rusting squirrels and hopping toads, oddly proportioned rabbits and oversized, flattened lizards tumbled out after it, moving with jerky, poorly coordinated haste. None of them were sporting claws or fangs or anything at all risky that she could see, and she knocked a squirrel away, Dandy pouncing on it with a yelp of delight.

"Leave it," she said, wincing at the thought of his teeth on the old metal, and looked up just in time to see both Joe and Violet rushing out of the carriage's shadows toward her. "*Stop!*" she shouted, not expecting them to listen. They didn't, leaping the staggering garden ornaments and trying to dodge past, aiming to sprint off down the platform.

Adams snagged Violet almost casually, twisting her hand into the back of the young woman's jacket and jerking her to a halt as Violet gave a breathy little scream. Collins caught Joe with one arm around his waist and a hefty shoulder driving into his chest, as if he were about to rugby tackle the young man to the ground, but given the difference in their sizes, Joe just gave a startled "*Oof*" and crashed to a halt.

"Let us go!" Violet shouted, twisting and lashing out at Adams. "You don't understand! You need to let us *go!*"

"Easy now," Adams said, and when Violet didn't stop struggling she twisted her around, quick and efficient, forcing the young woman's arm up behind her back and pressing her to her knees.

"*Ow!* This is police brutality!"

"Violet!" Joe shouted, trying to pull away from Collins. "Violet, are you okay?"

"Let me *go!*"

"Shut up, the two of you," Adams said sharply, as Collins shifted his grip on Joe, holding him in the same manner Adams was holding Violet, but letting the young man stay standing for now.

"No, we have to go!" Violet said, straining to look up at Adams. Her face was even paler than it had been previously, eyes wide and darting toward the distant doors. Rory ducked into the carriage, leaving one of the torches propped on a bench to light the scene, and it gave Violet awful shadows, turning her face into a terrified mask.

"Are you going to behave?" Adams asked. Some sort of giant metal ladybird was bumping determinedly into her foot, and she nudged it away. "And what the hell are these things?"

"Please," Violet said. "We were only—"

She was cut off by Rory shouting, "I've got someone!"

"Is it Charles?" Adams demanded, and Violet nodded, the motion jerky.

"We didn't hurt him, we weren't going to, but he won't help, and there's no *time*—"

"Get him out here," Adams called to Rory, then turned back to Violet. "Calm down, alright?"

"No," Joe said. He was hanging in Collins' grip, his face raw with fright. "No, we have to *go*."

Collins shuffled toward Adams, bringing Joe with him. "Can we call off the menagerie? There's a snail trying to run my foot over."

"Terrifying," Adams observed. This was hardly on the scale of Wilfred. She looked at Violet. "Seriously, what are these meant to be?"

"We were *trying*," she started, and Charles came staggering out of the carriage, making straight for Violet. Rory emerged a step behind, grabbing Charles's shoulder and pulling him to a halt. The metalworker's grey hair was even more dishevelled than usual, his jumper stretched at the neck, and his mouth was red and sore-looking. Adams was willing to bet he'd had gaffer tape stuck over it, and he was still massaging his hands, scraps of silver tape clinging to his cuffs.

"You *brat*," he snarled at Violet.

"I'm sorry! But I didn't know what else to do!"

Charles stared at the wobbling garden art, circling the

platform a little helplessly now Violet wasn't concentrating on them "And what the hell is this? You stole the charm for *this?*"

"I don't know! I don't know why it's not working!" Violet was almost sobbing, and Adams exchanged a puzzled look with Collins.

Charles nudged a lizard with one foot. "This is *worthless.* You're better than this, or I'd never have apprenticed you." His tone was flat and furious, as if he were angrier at her for not making decent guardians than he was about being kidnapped.

"You *were* kidnapped, weren't you?" Adams said, just to check. The tape kind of indicated that, but one never knew what consenting adults got up to.

"*Yes I was sodding well kidnapped!*"

"We needed help," Violet said. She was still on her knees, and she'd stopped trying to get up, staring miserably at the ground. "*I* needed help."

"Then why didn't you just ask?" Charles demanded.

Violet blinked at him. "Uh …"

"You realise she stole your charm?" Adams asked him.

"No, I thought she kidnapped me for the fun of it."

Rory made a strangled little sound and disguised it with a cough.

Adams let go of Violet, since she didn't seem to be going anywhere. "Someone better explain to me why we've been hunting for this sodding charm all over the city if you weren't even bothered it was stolen."

"Of course I'm *bothered,*" Charles snapped. "But I was *bothered* because Heather's going to tear the county apart unless I get it back, and because I thought someone dangerous had got hold of it. It's Violet!" He waved at her. "She's *fine.* And usually decent with charms and metal."

"She is," Joe said. "She gave me really cool hedgehogs." He

shot Adams an embarrassed look. "That's what I was throwing at those cops."

Adams looked at two of the bumbling rabbits, which had somehow got themselves into a rather compromising position, just like some hedgehogs owned by another woman with curly blonde hair. "You stole them from your aunt's pub," she said aloud, looking at Violet, who grimaced.

"Yes. I mean, I gave them to her in the first place, but I was practising and the animation wouldn't come off, so I couldn't exactly leave them."

"But why steal my charm?" Charles asked, crouching down in front of Violet. "Why *kidnap* me?"

"I needed to make guardians," she said quietly. "Or steal some and reassign them, whatever. But I needed the master charm for any of that. Without it, this is about the best I can do." She nodded at a rhinoceros beetle that had got its horn stuck under a bench, stiff legs peddling sadly. "So I took it. It wasn't meant to be for long, I promise. But when it wouldn't work, I panicked."

"What did you need the guardians for, Violet?" Adams asked.

She didn't answer, and Charles said, "You were really going to steal guardians?" He sounded almost bewildered. "But what *for*? Are you after what they're guarding?"

"Not if making new ones was an option," Adams said, when Violet stayed silent. "It sounds more like thieving to order, to me. Don't you think, Joe?" She looked directly at him as she spoke, and he shifted in the fickle light of the torches. It wasn't definitely a flinch, but Adams had an idea that if she'd been able to see him more clearly it would've been. "How much were they paying you? It's a big bloody risk, considering Heather's about to pull the city apart to find you. I hope it was a sodding footballer's salary."

"It wasn't for *money*," Violet spat. "As if I'd do this for *money.*" She stopped short, shooting a look at Joe. He stared fixedly at the floor.

Finally Collins said, "If you've got yourselves in a mess, we can help. But if you don't talk, you're both getting nicked, and that's the end of it."

"You can't," Violet said immediately, her eyes wide. "You *can't.*"

Adams examined her, then said, "Is it Jasper? He realise you were robbing more than basic stuff and start putting pressure on you?"

Violet looked at Joe again, and he shook his head slightly.

"Wouldn't be the first dodgy copper around," Collins said. "Tell us what happened, and we'll sort it out."

Adams wasn't sure they could, considering neither of them should even be there, and this was about a magical bloody amulet or whatever, but she didn't share that. She just said, "We can look after you."

Joe gave her an evaluating gaze, one that made her think he was maybe rather less clueless than the impression he gave. "Like you did at The Shop? I got away right under your nose."

"Except for my invisible dog trailing you," she pointed out, and he looked around warily. She frowned. "Wait – you *got away?* No one grabbed you?"

"I've got skills," he said, lifting his chin.

"You *trashed* The Shop."

"Yeah." He looked at the ground. "I didn't say they were good skills. Eddie's not going to be happy."

"Never mind *that,*" Violet said impatiently. "He'll be here any minute, and he wants guardians. *Proper* ones. And not … not for guarding, really." She gave Charles a pleading look. "Will you help?"

"Not with that," he said. "That's not something we do."

Violet clutched the back of her neck with both hands.

"You see? *You see?* I had no choice. He's going to go after Joe's mum if we don't do what he wants. He'll send Joe to jail, put her in some horrible hospital—"

"She doesn't need a hospital," Joe said, his voice harsh. "She needs *me.*"

"But no one gets to have *attack* guardians," Charles said. "That's … that's unthinkable."

Violet was almost rocking on the floor. "I knew you wouldn't do it. I *knew* it. I thought I could do it myself – you know, like I did the personalities – but it won't work. I had to do something!"

"Alright," Adams said. "We can sort out the details later. For now—"

"For now you can stand down," a new voice said, and she spun on her heel. She hadn't heard any door open, but as Collins shone his torch into the dark it spotlighted Jasper advancing down the platform toward them. Adams thought he was alone at first, but as he got closer the light caught the dull, dark edges of a pack of creatures flanking him. Rory turned his torch on them, illuminating great metallic beasts, dog-like, their shoulders as high as Jasper's waist. She counted half a dozen, each a little different from the next, depending on what materials had been used to create them, but all equipped with sharp teeth and long claws and sharp crests running down their spines. They moved twitchily, with the same jerky, stop-gap motion Fergus had, but with distinctly less impression of friendliness.

"Who the hell are you, and where did you get those?" Charles demanded. "Those aren't my work."

"Oh, no," Jasper said, his hands in his pockets as he surveyed the little group. "I built them. And then I got your girl here to charm them for me."

"When?" Charles demanded, looking at Violet. "You said the charm didn't work!"

She grimaced. "It used to. I was doing them in the work-shop when you were at the pub. Fergus let me take the charm whenever I wanted, after the whole personality thing."

"And Heather didn't know?" Adams asked.

"I used to wait until she was doing a ceremony. But then she made me leave, so I couldn't get to the charm anymore."

"Unfortunate," Jasper said. "But Violet here hadn't finished fulfilling her end of the deal, so here we are. And, to be honest, I prefer the idea of exclusive access anyway." He clicked his fingers at Violet, his face lean and hungry in the torchlight. "Come on, poppet. Everyone stays safe as long as you do your job."

"I don't think so," Adams said, stepping in front of Violet. Dandy came with her, his head down, but she grabbed a handful of his hair, stopping him, and pointed back behind her. She didn't want him anywhere near those dogs. He ignored her, and she sighed inwardly. She had to work out how to make him listen when *she* wanted, not when he did.

Jasper examined her. "Detective Inspector Adams. The detective from down south, thinking she can come up here and tell us how to do things."

"You've got no reason to have creatures like this." Adams gestured at the metal dogs. "Plus this is extortion."

"It's not going to work, anyway," Charles said. "Violet lacks technique."

"Evidently she doesn't," Jasper said, looking at the dogs. "They're not perfect, I admit, but they are biddable. A little practice, and we'll be there. Now come on, Violet. Let's go."

Adams felt the young woman getting up slowly behind her, and said, "Stay where you are."

"You really want to take on these pups?" Jasper asked.

"I really want to see you explain your little racket to your chief," she said. "You know, the missing CCTV footage, which will be from every night you went near the shop, I imagine. The stolen goods you'll no doubt have in your home, because that's all this is, isn't it? Some petty little scheme, because you realised Joe was thieving in more than one version of York, and you wanted a piece. Wonder who else you've been leaning on? It'll be interesting to know."

Jasper nodded, his grin fixed and toothy. "Heard you left London for mental health reasons. Sad you couldn't get it under control before you had a full breakdown and turned on your partner after dragging him up here. I mean, an old train station? Bit like your bridges in London, I suppose, isn't it?"

"It's *nothing* like London," she said, but even as she spoke she was thinking of the creatures in the depths beneath them, and the things weren't the *same*, they weren't *bridges*, but they were something. Something spun from deep places and old secrets and forgotten ways of the world. She'd felt it.

"Well, it doesn't have to be particularly similar," Jasper was saying. "The inquiry only has to think it is."

"You're a right nasty little piece of work," Collins said, stepping forward, and Jasper raised a hand. The dog-things surged forward, launching into an attack, and Adams forgot all about London and all about the bridges.

"Train! Now!" she yelled, grabbing Violet and throwing her almost bodily into the carriage, as the beasts charged and the night thickened, and the world rang with the sounds of metal on stone under the high roof of the old station.

A SMALL TECHNICAL HITCH

They barely made it, Adams hoisting Violet into the car just ahead of Rory and Joe, then turning to help Collins drag Charles in, who was still so outraged by the unauthorised, not-up-to-standard guardian-type creatures that he appeared not to have realised that while they might not meet his approval, they were still distinctly dangerous.

"You can't use them like this! They're not designed for it! They're not *robots!*" he was yelling, as Collins hauled him into the carriage and Adams slammed the door shut, jumping back as the first of the beasts slammed into it, shaking the car bodily. Metal tore under the thing's claws, and another hit the glass expanse of the window, sending cracks singing across it.

"That's not going to hold them for long," Collins said.

Adams gestured at Charles and Violet as the carriage continued to shake under the assault of the beasts, the scream of metal on metal sounding like death cries. She raised her voice to be heard over it. "Can't you use the charm to shut them down?"

Violet scrabbled in her pocket, coming up with something clutched tightly in one hand. "I can try."

"Hurry up, then," Collins said. "This is one of the Royal Carriages. Queen Elizabeth's, I think."

Adams looked at him. "What?"

"It's a classic!"

The window glass gave a deeper, more ominous crack, and she said, "Not really my biggest concern."

"Still," Collins said, sweeping the torch over the tidy, beige interior, which Adams thought looked as if a house robot from a fifties sci-fi sitcom should pop out and offer tea at any moment. "Irreplaceable, this."

The door screeched and juddered as one of the creatures got its claws into the seam, and Dandy growled, deep and furious. "Violet?" Adams said.

"I'm trying!"

"Give it here," Charles said, trying to grab it off her.

"No, I made them, I know the charm—"

"It's *my* charm! You think I can't override whatever you've done?"

"Adams!" Rory called from the far end of the carriage, leaning in the door. "We can get through to the next car from here."

The glass in the window shattered under another blow, still in place but spiderwebbed with cracks, and Adams nodded, grabbing Violet's and Charles's arms. "Move. Come on!"

"I just—" Violet started, and was drowned out by the glass collapsing out of the window. Adams pushed them both ahead of her, Joe and Rory already vanished, presumably into the next carriage, and Collins bringing up the rear as the first of the beasts struggled to get through the window. They were big and toothy, but not particularly agile, it appeared, and Dandy rushed the thing, snarling.

"Dandy!" Adams shouted, but she needn't have worried. He just slammed into the beast's snout and it tumbled back out of the window. Another took its place, clawing determinedly at the frame while the door creaked and groaned, but it gave them time.

Through the door at the end of the room, past a closed door that likely led to a bathroom, then Adams held Violet and Charles back as she stepped into a narrow gap between them and the next car. The creatures were pursuing them on the outside, but the gap was small enough that as one tried to shove its head in to get them its shoulders simply wedged into place. Adams expected it to snarl, could hear the noise in her head, but the thing was horrifyingly silent, the only sound the squeal of metal as it strained to reach them.

"Come on," she said to Violet and Charles, waving them through. Rory and Joe had already vanished into the next car with Midge and Pinto, and a moment later they were in what looked like a misplaced living room, all high-backed armchairs and generous sofas, lamps with fringes and thick carpet on the floors. "Seriously?" she said as Collins joined them. "A classic? This looks like my gran's idea of luxury."

"Your gran knows quality when she sees it," Collins said, as the attack resumed, the carriage shuddering. The curtains were drawn in here too, and Adams had the unsettling sensation of being in a submarine, under attack by unseen monsters in the deep.

"Is there another?" she asked Rory.

He shook his head. "Last car."

Adams nodded. So it was out onto the concourse, and hope they could run faster across the vast hall than the beasts could, or sit here and wait for the train to be torn apart around them. She looked at Violet. "You need to get that thing working."

"I'm trying. It just doesn't *feel* right," she said, as the first of the windows cracked.

"*Give it to me*," Charles insisted, and Violet handed the charm over with a huff.

"Roof," Collins said, pointing up at a skylight. "Buy us a bit of time, if nothing else."

"Good call," Adams said. The creatures seemed to be concentrating on the windows on both sides now, the weakest points on the cars, and a chorus of splintering glass and tearing metal rose all around them, making her raise her voice.

They moved fast, Adams scrambling up onto one of the armchairs, Collins steadying her as she fumbled with the latches on the skylight. It wasn't locked, but the levers locking it down were stiff with disuse, and she wrestled with them for a moment as the volume of the attack swelled around them, still empty of any sounds that one expected, no swearing, no shouting or snarling or anything living *at all*, just the screams of tortured metal and dull crack of safety glass giving up, ominous and inhuman. She dropped down, waving Collins up in her place, and he fumbled with the locks, swearing as they resisted, until Dandy surged up and past him. Collins yelped and almost fell, clinging to the frame with one hand.

"*Adams!* Restrain your monster!"

"He's not a monster," she snapped back, as the skylight blew open under the impact of Dandy's passage. He'd evidently decided to interact with physics in a more useful manner for the moment. "And he's got us out. Move!"

They moved, fast, to a soundtrack of the windows falling in. Collins scrambled out to pull the others through, Rory hefting Midge and Pinto out after them, until only he and Adams were left in the carriage as the first of the beasts charged clumsily toward them. Adams whipped out her baton and snapped, "*Go!*"

Rory didn't argue, just hauled himself through the skylight as Adams scrambled onto the armchair, feeling like a cartoon maiden fleeing a mouse, although the mouse in question was huge and metal-toothed and lumbering toward her with single-minded fury. She braced herself, baton raised, and Dandy charged out of the shadows, colliding with the thing's shoulder. It staggered but kept coming, and above her Collins shouted, "*Here!*"

She didn't hesitate, just jumped for the hatch, grabbing the edge. Hands grasped her arms, pulling her bodily up and through as the beast ploughed into the armchair, upending it, and she jerked her knees up to her chest like she was about to do a bomb into a swimming pool, narrowly avoiding kicking the thing's spines.

Collins and Rory deposited her on the roof, and she dropped to her knees, peering into the carriage. "Dandy!"

She got a wet nose in her ear for her efforts, and jerked back, twisting to look at him. He stood on the gentle curve of the roof next to her, tail wagging softly.

"Right. Well done." She petted him, looking around the roof, dimly visible in the pale light trickling from the ceiling, the day almost entirely gone. Joe was on all fours, peering over the edge, while Violet and Charles were huddled over the charm, sitting down with their heads almost touching. Midge and Pinto wobbled across the curved surface, growling steadily at the ongoing assault below them, and Collins fished his torch out of his pocket to shine it on their little group.

"Well," he said. "No one eaten. Good start."

"I don't think they'll eat us," Rory said, peering over the edge. "No stomachs. Just tear us limb from limb, maybe."

"Oh, not so bad, then."

Adams ignored both of them, and went to crouch next to Violet and Charles. "Well?"

"It doesn't feel right," Charles said, both hands cupped together. He frowned at Violet. "Are you sure it was working before?"

"It was when I was at the workshop," she said. "But it hasn't since I took it." She looked at Charles. "Is it a failsafe of some sort? It won't work outside the shop?"

"I never put anything like that on it," he replied, and held the charm up to the light of Collins' torch. "It doesn't feel right. It feels *empty.*"

Adams stared at the charm, her stomach rolling into a tight knot that sent her knees abruptly weak. The carriage shuddered, and she staggered, but didn't look away from the charm. "That's it? *That's* the master charm?"

"That's it," Charles confirmed. "Lovely, isn't it?"

She took a shaky breath. "It's a *duck.*"

"That's just its shape," Charles said, as below them the carriage shook and juddered, and metal creaked and groaned, and the beasts began to throw themselves against the sides hard enough to set the car teetering on the edge of balance.

Adams got up, and took her own duck from her pocket, shining it into the darkness until it landed on Jasper, who was sitting on one of the benches, one ankle propped on the opposite knee and an arm flung along the back. "Ay-up," he said. "Ready to hand the charm over yet?"

"I thought you needed Violet to make it work."

He shrugged, squinting against the light. "Not so much. Easier with someone who knows their way around it, but by no means vital. The power's in the thing itself, after all. I can find another magic-worker. They're common as muck."

The thing itself. The little metal duck, textured in places, smooth in others. Bloody *ducks.*

"What if I could get it for you?"

"You have it there," he said, nodding at the carriage.

"You think Charles wouldn't have turned your own beasts on you by now if that were the case?" Adams asked, and he frowned.

"True. I was hoping our Violet would keep hold of it, since she knows the consequences if she doesn't behave herself. What's happening?"

"Call off your dogs," Adams said, as the carriage lurched and she staggered again, dropping into a crouch to stop herself falling.

"How about you tell me what's happening with that charm, and *then* I call them off?" Jasper asked, as the carriage shuddered once more.

"*Company!*" Collins called, and Adams looked around to see one of the creatures levering itself slowly onto the roof, claws digging trenches into the metal panels. "The Queen would *not* be amused at all this damage." He straightened up and swung his baton at the creature like a golf club, but the baton just bounced back, making him yelp and shake out his hand. The beast kept climbing.

Adams looked back at Jasper. "She doesn't have the real charm."

"*What?*" Charles demanded, scrambling over to join her. "What're you talking about?"

"That's why it won't work. It's not the real one."

He held the duck up, shaking it vigorously, then peered at it again as if that might've reset it. "It doesn't feel right," he admitted. "It doesn't feel of *anything.*"

"Exactly."

"Where's the real one?" He looked from her to Violet. "*Where's my charm?*"

"I don't know! I thought it was the real one! It was in the

tin!" Her eyes were wide as she peered down at Jasper. "I swear I didn't know!"

Adams checked on Collins. He, Joe, and Rory were attempting to shove the metal monster back off the roof without getting themselves too near its teeth. Rory had acquired a coal shovel from somewhere, and as she watched the dog-thing snatched it off him, splintering the handle in its teeth. Dandy appeared from somewhere, dropping a piece of scaffolding next to the scuffling men, and Collins snatched it up to resume the struggle. Neither they nor the monster seemed to be gaining ground, and the carriage was shaking with ever more enthusiasm. The whole thing was going to go over if this kept up.

"I know where the master charm is," she said to Jasper, and he raised his eyebrows, smiling slightly.

"Aren't you handy?"

"*How?*" Charles demanded. "How do *you* know where it is?"

"Fergus."

Charles threw his hands in the air, almost overbalancing on the edge of the roof, and Adams grabbed his shoulder to steady him. He pushed her hand away. "Bloody *Fergus!* Bloody *personality!*" He glared at Violet. "This is all your fault!"

"You agreed to try the personality!"

"And look where it got us!"

Adams ignored them both, looking at Jasper as the entire carriage keeled abruptly toward one corner, something vital giving way in the structure. She grabbed the edge of the roof to keep herself in place. "Call them off."

Jasper examined her for a moment, then clasped a pendant hanging from a chain around his neck and muttered something under his breath. Abruptly, all was silence other than the men still scuffling to get the creature off the roof.

Adams glanced at it, but it had frozen in place, a clockwork monster whose mechanism had run down.

"Adams?" Collins said, stepping back and looking warily from it to her. "What's happening?"

"I need to go and get the duck," she said, adding hurriedly as he opened his mouth to argue, "from where we left it for safekeeping."

"Where we—" Rory stopped as Collins kicked his foot. "Right. Ah … need a hand?"

"No, you'll all stay right there," Jasper said. "Anyone other than Adams here moves, the dogs'll tear you to pieces, alright?" He gestured at her. "Come on, then."

Adams got up and walked to the end of the carriage, where she could climb down into the gap between the cars, Collins joining her at the edge of the roof.

"You can't go back down there," he whispered, as she crouched to swing herself down. "Those things'll be waiting."

"We're not getting past the dogs without the charm," she replied, her voice low. "Just see if Charles and Violet can do anything after I've got Jasper out of the way. Maybe, since Violet charmed them in the first place, she can break it down if he's not here."

Collins didn't answer, just watched her as she clambered down to the little platform at the back of the carriage, then squeezed past one of the dogs to step onto solid ground. The beast didn't move, and she shivered as she bumped into it, the metal cold and dead under her touch. It definitely wasn't Fergus.

"Well?" Jasper said to her, and she nodded at the main doors.

"There's a way down to a lower level. I left the charm down there."

"Why?"

"Like I said. Safekeeping."

He examined her, then shrugged. "Alright. Drop the baton." He looked at the carriage, where the others were peering over the edge of the roof, the whole car canted sadly over to one side. "On guard," he said, touching his pendant again, and the creatures shifted slightly, not much, just enough to remind one they weren't lifeless sculptures, but things with teeth and claws. "Anyone thinks they can leg it, they're going to get those legs torn off, got it?"

"Bit hard to miss," Collins said.

Adams passed her baton up to Rory, then turned and headed for the main doors, her duck in one hand to light the way. She had no idea if the underground creatures would still be about, or if they could get past them if they were, but there was no other way she could see to get Jasper away. With him gone, it was possible the others could get past the dogs and get out. The metal beasts definitely didn't seem to be able to think for themselves, so it was worth hoping.

Jasper followed her, staying slightly behind and to one side, and when she glanced back she spotted one of the vast metal dogs trudging along next to him, head heavy and low. Dandy prowled the shadows just beyond it, teeth bared, and she tried to will him not to attack. It wouldn't matter how big he got (and he was currently Great Dane size, which seemed to be just under the visibility threshold), he couldn't compete with the knife blades of the creature's claws, or its impervious metal hide. They'd need a bloody steamroller to make a dent in the thing.

They walked silently, the only noise the echo of their footsteps in the vastness of the hall, so when the door at the far end, where Collins had said there was a picnic area, smashed open, Adams spun around, convinced the carriage had collapsed. Jasper's thoughts must've been in another direction, though, because he clutched the charm around his neck, yelling, "*Attack!*"

Adams threw herself at Jasper, snatching the brief moment while his back was to her, hooking him around the neck with one arm and trying to grab the necklace with the other. She missed the pendant, and he drove an elbow into her gut. Even though she was ready for it he still caught her a glancing blow, and avoiding the worst impact meant she loosened her grip. He twisted away, grabbing hold of her arm, and they wrestled back and forth, each trying to land a punch as the beasts resumed their assault on the carriages, and Dandy came barrelling out of the shadows, slamming his shoulder into the metal beast as it snapped for Adams. He pushed it off-course, so all its teeth did was snag her coat, just as the doors to the front of the building crashed open. Both Adams and Jasper paused, looking around to see Heather striding in, an uprooted sapling dripping dirt in each hand, Pip hurrying after her with a large planter clasped to his chest, looking slightly bewildered.

"*Charles!*" Heather shouted, and the plants whipped in her hands, roots and leaves straining to break free. Pip was already almost engulfed in greenery, and he dropped the planter with a yelp as a particularly eager ivy wrapped itself around his neck. Adams wrenched herself away from Jasper, staggering back a step as a piercing battle cry went up from the far side of the station. Byx came into view, sprinting for the besieged carriage with a cutlass in one hand and a hurricane lantern in the other. Dartmoor ran after her, long knives in both hands, and he hurled one with ferocious accuracy at one of the beasts. Unfortunately all it did was bounce off the thing's metal shell, but it was a good throw anyway.

"*You,*" Heather said, pointing at Jasper. "It's *you!*"

"Call them off," he snarled. "I've got your hubby there pinned down."

"The necklace," Adams said. "The charm's on his necklace."

"Anyone *touches* me, my creatures'll tear this place down," he snapped, but even as he spoke a slim, swift form whipped through the door and lunged at him, snarling furiously. Jasper stumbled back, crying out, and the whippet danced away again, teeth bared and skinny legs shaking in fright. The smallest, mangiest wolf Adams had ever seen limped in the doors behind it and set up a wavering howl, and Jasper burst out laughing, already backing away. "This, Heather? *This* is your cavalry?" He turned to look at Adams, as if expecting her to share his amusement, and Heather's plants snapped toward him, wriggling across the concrete floor. They were too slow, though, no earth to lift them, and Jasper merely retreated a few more steps. The big metal beast was ignoring all Dandy's attempts to dissuade it from advancing on Pip, who tried hitting it with a piece of the shattered planter. Deeper in the hall, Dartmoor and Byx had joined the others on the roof of the carriage, the creatures once again working to tear it down.

"Oh, this is *hilarious,*" Jasper said, looking back at Heather. "And everyone's so scared of you. Time moves on, doesn't it? What's your plant magic worth now?"

"I will set your bones in the earth to rot," Heather said. "Feed your organs to the crows and your eyes to the snails, raise flowers from your flesh and—"

"Yeah, yeah. You'll be giving me the charm first, though." He jerked his head at Adams. "Come on, then."

Adams met Heather's eyes, giving her a very small nod which she hoped communicated, *I'm on it, try to stop this muppet following me*, and broke into a sprint.

"*Oi!*" Jasper yelled, and metal claws tore into the concrete as the beast launched itself after her.

Adams didn't stop or slow, even when she heard a dull thump of impact behind her and a yelp that had to belong to Dandy. She kept going, straight out the doors, sliding on the rain-slicked steps and almost losing her footing, then she was taking them three at a time. She stumbled as she hit the tarmac, recovered, and ran hard across the front of the building. One arch. Two. Clattering metal feet on the steps behind her, and the softer tread of human pursuit. Third arch, the hidden stairs glaring under the light of the duck, and this time she vaguely glimpsed a warning sign as she pelted past it, but really, if people were serious about such things they needed to secure the entrance, lock it down properly, otherwise it was just an invitation to kids and—

She clamped down on the thought and focused on the sloping passageway lit in the bouncing light of her torch instead, plunging deep into the earth. Dandy surged up next to her, matching her pace, his grey fur darkened on his neck but his pace unfaltering, and she had a sudden surge of hope. She had Dandy, and she had her duck, and she ran still harder.

Back to the pit. Back to the monsters.

This was *nothing* like London. But she'd beaten the monsters there, and she'd beat them here, too.

There was no other option.

23

DUCK AROUND & FIND OUT

ADAMS RACED THROUGH THE PASSAGEWAY'S SWITCHBACKS, booted feet sure on the smooth, dry ground, Dandy panting next to her. She could hear pursuit, silent and swift, the scuff of feet that weren't hers, the scratch of a hard body bumping into the walls, but she didn't have time to think about it. She needed the master charm. If she could get to it without the monsters getting in the way, maybe even call the lift down and make it in, then get it back up to Charles so he could deactivate the metal creatures … there were so many steps, so many ifs, but no other options. It was this or Jasper's beasts would tear everyone apart. Even if he didn't get the charm, he couldn't risk any of them carrying tales now they'd seen his hand. They were only leaving here alive if they took him down first.

The wall fell away next to her, opening to the yawning gulf of the cavern. The lights were still on, a couple of them flickering unsteadily, but Adams didn't see any of the crea-tures. She didn't slow until she hit the floor, where she pressed herself against the wall with her heart loud in her ears, trying to control her breathing. The monsters had come when they switched the lights on, so why would they have left? She looked around warily, aware the sounds of pursuit were closing, but not ready to rush out of cover until she was sure it was safe. Dandy whined, and she put a hand on his back, then glanced at him. His snout was lifted to the ceiling, and she hesitated, then followed his gaze reluctantly.

The underside of the cavern roof was covered with the monsters. Their long, silky fur made it look as though the place had grown a hide of pale hair, some strange fungus blossoming out of the rock, and she bit the inside of her cheek, her grip tightening on the duck, for all the good that would do. There were hundreds of them. *Hundreds*, all shifting and trembling with fierce breath and old, cruel life, clustered around the lights without touching them, a blossoming of threat.

But they were up there, and she was down here, with Jasper almost on her. She pushed off the wall, moving in an almost exaggerated tiptoe as she scuttled toward the lift, Dandy hurrying behind her. She glanced back to see him moving with the same delicate, high step she was, and scowled at him. That was all she needed, the invisible dog taking the mick out of her. Beyond him, though, she saw torchlight bouncing along the passageway. There was no time. She had to get the duck before Jasper brought every single one of the underground nightmares down on their heads, quite literally.

She picked up the pace, not worrying so much about noise as the sounds of pursuit built up behind her. She didn't know how many beasts Jasper might've brought with him, or if any of the others had followed, but they were making no effort to stay quiet. The lift was straight across the platform, and she hugged the wall as she ran for it, as if that might hide her from the creatures on the ceiling. She thought she could hear them, a soft, rumbling sound, the purr of an idling engine.

She was almost at the lift when Jasper shouted, *"Hey!"*

Adams whirled around, holding a finger up to her mouth in a *shhh*, her other hand out in a *stop* gesture.

"I don't think so," he snapped, striding toward her with one of the great metal dogs pacing alongside him, its claws scraping the concrete so loudly Adams winced, and Dandy whined. She glanced at him, finding him almost spaniel-sized.

"That's not going to help," she hissed, and he whined again, his tail tucked between his legs and his gaze on the ceiling. She pointed at it wildly, still trying to hush Jasper.

"What?" he demanded, glancing up. "Bats? You scared of bats, Adams?"

She didn't know what sort of bats he had around the place, but she'd never seen ones as pale and hairy as the creatures currently stirring above them. A questioning *chugga-chugga?* drifted to her. "Not bats," she said, barely above a whisper. "I'm getting the charm. Just *quiet.*"

He scowled at her, taking another look up at the creatures. They were definitely moving more than they had been, and Jasper looked uncertain for a moment. "Hurry up," he said quietly, and muttered something to the metal dog that brought it to a halt.

Adams ran for the lift, pawing at the door, her breath catching as she thought for a moment the duck was gone. But no, *there*, wedged so firmly into the latch it had just about vanished. She scrabbled at it, but she couldn't get any purchase.

"Come on, come on," Jasper said. He was standing well back, the metal beast between Adams and him, and he played his torch over the creatures on the ceiling.

"Don't do that!" Adams hissed, pawing her keys out of her

pocket and fumbling with her multitool. She didn't wait to see if he listened, just pulled the blade out and forced it into the latch, levering the duck out. It made a nasty scratching sound on the metal, far louder than seemed reasonable, and she glanced fearfully at the creatures.

"*Chugga-chugga?*"

"*Chugga-chugga-choo?*"

"What the hell *are* they?" Jasper asked, but Adams didn't bother answering. The duck popped out abruptly, and she caught it in her free hand, almost dropping it immediately. It was hot to the touch, raising a shivering flood of saliva in her mouth as if she'd just bitten down on foil with a metal filling. She swallowed hard, sure she could feel every knuckle fizzing with the thing's power, and wondered why she hadn't felt it before. Why it had just been a *duck.* Unless it was reacting to all the chaos in here. Or she was imagining it, but she didn't think so.

"Adams?" Jasper demanded. "Do you have it?"

"Dandy, *take it to Charles,*" she said, and hurled the charm across the platform toward the passageway out. Dandy wheeled after it, and Jasper spun on his heel.

"What the hell are you doing?" he snarled, as the duck bounced on the edge of a platform and catapulted into the dimness of the tracks, Dandy right behind it. Jasper didn't wait for her answer, just plunged in pursuit, even as Dandy bounded up onto the platform again and took off up the passageway. Adams sprinted after him, not bothering about being quiet now, while above her the creatures' mutterings turned into a chorus.

"*Chugga-chugga-choo! Chugga-chugga-choo!*"

"*Chugga-chugga-choo-chooooooo!*"

They surged into motion, swarming down the walls, drawn by the shouts and Jasper's bouncing light, and Adams hesitated as she reached the passageway. The metal beast was standing stolidly in the middle of the platform, unable to act without direction, and its master was still scrabbling in the gravel between the rails.

"Adams!" he shouted. "Help me find the damn thing or I swear to every old, low god in existence I'll let the dog eviscerate you!"

The creatures were dropping off the ceiling and launching themselves from the walls, landing softly on the platform, huge eyes glittering and teeth gleaming in the glow of the old lights. The passageway was still clear. Adams looked from it to Jasper, and swore softly to herself.

"Jasper," she hissed, running to the edge of the platform. "Come *on!*"

"I'm not going without—" He'd straightened up as he talked, and now he stared past her at the slowly massing creatures, prowling forward with their long claws scratching the concrete. "What the *hell?*"

"*Come on!*" She stretched out a hand to him, and he lunged forward, grabbing it. She hauled him up, helping him scramble onto the platform. "Go!" She turned to sprint for the passageway, and he seized her around the waist, heaving her back toward the edge. She tried to recover, wobbling wildly and flailing for balance as Jasper bolted, but she couldn't quite make it. She slipped off the platform, landing heavily on the old, soot-stained gravel, one foot catching a rail and her ankle twisting painfully. It sent her to her knees, the stones biting into her skin. She inhaled sharply, clamping down on a cry, and hunkered where she was for a moment, cursing herself for not just running after Dandy.

"*Chugga-chugga?*"

"*Chugga-chugga-choo-choooooo!*"

The noises were far too close. She looked up, and found the platform edge crowded with round, white-eyed faces, teeth chattering softly. In the yellow light drool gleamed on the soft fur around their mouths, and she could see their big ears twitching one way then another, sensitive as a cat's. Distantly, she heard a shriek drift down the passageway, and she wondered if the things had caught up with Jasper anyway.

"*Chugga,*" one said, almost conversationally, and licked its chops.

"*Chugga-chugga,*" another agreed, and a soft *choo* passed among them, faintly amused.

One reached out toward her, its paw five-fingered and eerily human under the coat of long fur, and she pushed herself upright, stumbling back with her ankle smarting but holding.

"Alright," she said. "Enough of that."

Another chorused *choo,* and she scowled at them.

"I've had about enough of bloody monsters laughing at me in the dark." She reached for her baton, but she'd abandoned it back in the main hall. She had the duck and the Yorkies, and she pulled one out of her pocket, unwrapping it slowly while the creatures watched her, still *chugga-chugga*-ing to each other. "Chocolate? Good stuff, right?" She broke a piece off and hurled it into the mass of beasts.

She was rewarded with a small, "*Ow,*" and some more *chugga-chugga*-ing, sounding rather put out.

"Sorry." She hurriedly broke the bars into pieces and tossed them onto the platform, trying to be a bit more gentle. Still nothing.

"Wrapper?" she offered, holding it out to the nearest of the creatures. It snatched it off her, then dropped it without even examining it, and she watched it flutter to the ground. "Dammit."

"*Chugga-chugga. Chugga-chugga. Chugga-chugga.* **Chugga-chugga.**" The chorus built louder and louder, like an entire pub intent on a drinking game, and she found herself fighting not to cover her ears, stumbling away from the platform as if being further out in the mire of tracks and old gravel would somehow save her when they came.

And they did come, with a final bellow of *chugga-chugga-choo-choooooo!* rising from a myriad of furry throats, pouring off the platform in a flood and washing toward her while she snatched her multitool out of her pocket and pulled the blade open, brandishing it at them as if she could hold back the hordes on will alone.

"*Chugga-chugga* your own sodding selves!" she roared. "Come on you train-sotted *freaks!*"

The first ones were almost on her, crouching to leap, and she tightened her grip on the multitool, her other hand out in a furious gesture of *halt*. Not that the tiny blade was going to make any difference at all, but it was *something*, she couldn't just do *nothing*, even if the something was so small and so pointless as to be not even a blip in their charge, it *mattered*, something *always* mattered.

She lashed out with the blade, screaming something wordless, braced for teeth and talons to tear into her skin, but instead of hitting flesh or fur she hit hard steel, the blade sliding off with an impact that jarred her joints. For one bewildered moment she thought Jasper's beast had joined the attack, then her perspective simply *changed*, and she was abruptly above the mass of creatures, who stared up at her, apparently as startled as she was.

"*Chugga-chugga?*"

"Um ..." She put one hand on the heavy metal body that had appeared in front of her, but it was already moving. *She* was already moving, on the platform without being aware of any sort of actual motion, and she grabbed at the joins in the casing. "*Wilfred?*"

"*Mmmip.*"

Adams almost fell off, twisting violently to see Fergus perched behind her on the guardian's broad back. "*Fergus?*"

"*Mmmip.*"

He couldn't have said *obviously* more clearly if he did speak English, and Adams took a shuddering breath as Wilfred continued his strange locomotion, into the passage now and heading upward. She strained to look back into the cavern, and discovered a comet trail of the creatures pouring after them, gaining ground fast. One dropped straight onto Fergus, who gave a startled squawk and vanished off Wilfred's hindquarters.

"*Fergus!*" Adams swung herself around, wishing she'd ever tried riding a horse in her life, although she had a feeling not even that would have prepared her for Wilfred's strange motion. It might've made her feel a little more comfortable being so bloody far off the ground, though. Another of the creatures landed on Wilfred's back, and she slapped it straight off again, heart pounding in her ears. "*Fergus!*"

"*Mmmip!*" He was behind her again, his whiskers looking a little more bent as he crouched on Wilfred's neck with its fluttering mane of Yorkie wrappers. He seemed to have sped up, the light lost behind them now, racing through the darkness, and Adams ducked down a little, conscious of the roof above her as the walls sang with the thunder of Wilfred's hooves and the scratching and *chugga*-ing of the creatures' pursuit. She snatched her duck out of her pocket, risking flashing the light around for an instant, then immediately wished she hadn't. It reflected off the eyes of at least four of the creatures scrambling over Wilfred's hindquarters to get to her, and she leaned back, fingers wedged into the joins of the guardian's broad back. She kicked out with one foot, gratified to connect with at least one creature, which fell away with a wailing *chooooo*. A wind of motion and the clatter of metal on metal told her Fergus had leaped over her, landing on one of the others, and there was some sort of scuffle going on. She flashed the light on quickly, spotting Fergus with his claws in one creature and another apparently trying to rip his wings out. She snatched it by the scruff of the neck, pulling it off him and flinging it into the tunnel.

"Wilfred, *faster!*" she shouted, then yelped as he surged forward and she was almost thrown off. Fergus gave a startled *brrrip!*, but when she flicked the light over Wilfred's hindquarters he was still there, claws puncturing the guardian's back. Another couple of the creatures threw themselves at the light, but Wilfred was moving too fast now, and they tumbled away into the darkness. She gave up on the light and just concentrated on hanging on.

They exploded out into the car park so fast Adams barely had time to register that she could see again. "Hall!" she yelled, and Wilfred swung toward the door. It was open, but she still ducked, covering her head as he plunged through the frame, which seemed *much* too small. Shouts and crashes flooded the hall as Wilfred charged toward the battle, and Adams, still riding backward, strained to see what was happening. Someone had found the lights, flooding the place with colour, but it didn't show anything good. Jasper had evidently made it out of the cavern, as the metal dogs were at war with the tunnel creatures, which scuttled and surged across the platform, pouring through the scaffolding and heavy frames of the hall's structure. The wooden benches were in bloom, chattering across the floor, and trees punched through the roofs of the carriages where the furnishings had taken root. Everyone was fighting from high ground, the carriages islands in the wash of tunnel creatures, Pip swinging a coal shovel with deadly accuracy, Collins and Rory laying about with lengths of scaffolding, and Violet and Joe hurling her garden animals into the fray, while they crawled back like animated boomerangs. Byx was wearing the whippet around her neck like a scarf, and Dartmoor had the scrawny wolf over one shoulder while he roared, "Bloody pixie experiments! It's always *bloody pixie experiments!*"

"Where's Charles?" Adams shouted, and Rory looked around at her, a grin lighting his face.

He started to say something, and Collins yelled, "*Duck!*"

Adams didn't even think about it, just threw herself off Wilfred's back just as one of the metal dogs surged out of the mess of tunnel creatures and landed where she'd been sitting. She scrambled to her feet, ready to run, but Wilfred was already gone, taking the beast with him. Adams whistled, ignoring the creatures scuttling toward her, and Dandy came surging off the platform, running hard.

"*Charles,*" she yelled at him. "Where's Charles?"

He skidded to a stop and spun back along the platform, the answer underlined in the form of a shout and the shriek of tearing metal. Adams sprinted toward it, Dandy racing ahead of her. Scaffolding shuddered and twisted, and one of the carriages hefted itself off its fixings and flexed like a caterpillar, then froze in place as another yell went up, this one agonised. She raced around the head of the platform and found Heather unconscious on the floor, one of the metal dogs with a hefty paw on her chest, and Jasper standing over Charles, hand outstretched.

"Give it to me or I'll gut her," he snarled. His face was bleeding, the back of his jacket shredded, so he hadn't made it up from the cellar unscathed.

Charles was on his knees, hands pressed to his chest. "You *can't,*" he whispered, and Adams didn't know if he was referring to Heather or the charm.

She opened her mouth to speak, then stopped. She'd tried to do things the right way in the cavern, and he'd left her to be devoured. Not just left her, *pushed* her. She looked at Dandy, his teeth bared and his head lowered as he waited at her side, and wondered if she could just sic him on Jasper. Of course she *could*, but would she?

As if hearing her, Dandy looked up, and offered her something. She took it, discovering the fake charm. Or she assumed it was. It felt like plain, dull metal, and she bounced it once in her hand then said, "Hey, Jasper?"

He lifted his head to look at her, almost comically surprised, and she hurled the thing straight at him. And maybe it *was* just a little bit charmed, or maybe (almost definitely, she thought later), Charles gave it a little twist as it went past, because it hit far harder than it had any right to, smacking Jasper right between the eyes with a solid *thunk* that made her wince. He didn't even protest, just collapsed bonelessly to the floor, and Charles looked from him to Adams, then scrambled to Heather's side, patting her face anxiously.

"Heather? Heather, love?"

Adams grabbed his arm, hauling him up. "Can you get those dog-things under control now he's down?"

"Yes, but—"

"Do it, and get the bloody tunnel monsters out of here, or we're all screwed, alright?" Even as she spoke, half a dozen of the creatures scampered toward them, and Dandy stepped forward with a snarl.

"Okay." Charles stood, looking out over the hall, the charm clutched in one raised hand. The metal dogs ground instantly to a halt where they were, but that just meant the tunnel creatures had even less resistance, and they surged toward the carriages, their *chugga-chugga*-ing giving away to *choo-choo*s of excitement.

"Charles," Adams started, looking around for something to arm herself with, and he silenced her with an imperious gesture, the high lights shining on his thick grey hair and his face etched in grim, ancient lines. He raised the charm higher, muttering words Adams didn't recognise, and the shattered carriages hunched themselves up like a caterpillar, sending everyone still perched on the roofs sliding off in a chorus of yells. The floating spots of small lanterns, made to look like old oil lamps, came on in the front of the locomotive as the overhead lights went out with the angry snap of a breaker going. With a snarl of twisting metal, the whole train's worth of engine and two carriages lifted itself onto the platform, every interior light blazing. The creatures swarmed toward it, and the locomotive gave an echoing whistle, so loud Adams clamped her hands instinctively over her ears and Heather sat up with a scream.

The creatures roared back as one, "*Chugga-chugga-choo-choooooo!* **Chugga-chugga-choo-choooooo!**"

The locomotive whistled again, and the creatures piled into and onto it, turning it pale and furry, glowing within from the lights visible between the press of bodies. It ploughed across the platform toward the main door, slowly picking up speed.

"Where—" Adams started, and Charles silenced her again with a curt gesture.

"Heather, love?" he said.

Heather didn't answer, just pressed one hand into the concrete, grimacing. Stone rumbled and cracked somewhere deep in the bowels of the building, and the whole place shuddered. Byx appeared at a sprint, dragging Violet with her, the others following. She didn't slow, just kept running for the back door.

"Adams," Collins shouted as he raced toward her, and she waved him on.

"Get everyone out! Hurry!"

The whole place was shaking now, the ground treacherous beneath her feet, and Fergus appeared next to her. "*Mmmip,*" he said, ears back, and she picked him up, tucking him under one arm, where he hung docilely. Dandy pressed himself to her other side, but he was too big to pick up, so she just put her free hand on his head and watched as the ground shuddered and heaved, then gave a roar and split apart like a knife had been driven into it, yawning wide in front of the main doors. The locomotive didn't slow, racing toward the chasm, and for a moment Adams thought it might leap the gap in some spectacular movie escape. But it wasn't fast enough to reach the other side, and instead, without slowing, simply tipped over the edge and plunged into the depths, pulling its carriages after it. The creatures went with it, still *chugga-chugga-choo-choooooo*-ing enthusiastically, and they were gone so fast she almost wondered if she'd really seen it happen at all. Behind them the earth poured into the crevasse, filling fast, gravel and broken concrete knitting rapidly together with steel and earth. The place shook once more, then stilled, and all was dark and silent other than the uneasy creak of destabilised scaffolding.

Adams put Fergus down, found her duck and clicked the light on, shining it on Charles, who was helping Heather up.

"Is that it?" she asked.

"I have my charm back," Charles said. "Thank you, Inspector."

"But the creatures ..." She shone the light around the hall.

"Sealed back in place," Heather said. "And there they'll stay, unless someone else ignores the warning signs."

"Should be better secured," Adams muttered, and turned the torch on Jasper. Or, rather, where Jasper had been. There was nothing to be seen but the metal duck, sitting innocuously in the middle of the platform. "Oh, *come on*."

"It's all taken care of," Charles said, turning toward the exit with one arm around Heather. She pulled away and went to pick the duck up, holding it out to Adams.

"Souvenir," she said, and Adams took it automatically. She

was still standing there in the dark, staring at it, when Collins shouted from the door, "Oi, Adams! You want to explain all this when the York coppers turn up?"

"No," she shouted back. "Coming!" But she still lingered a moment longer, looking around the hall, with its missing carriage and devastated floor and gently nodding blooms growing out of the wooden benches.

"*Mmmip?*" Fergus said.

"Agreed," she replied, and jogged for the entrance, Dandy loping next to her and the metal cat trotting ahead. Nothing made sense, but order had, in some way, been restored. It was going to have to be good enough for now.

24

CLOSE ENOUGH TO A WIN

They trailed through the heavy doors of the Blighted Basilisk, a tattered little group. With the others to guide them, there was no need to detour through the human side of the pub, and while Collins said he wouldn't have minded encountering the glittery toilet monster, Adams thought he was probably joking. They'd had enough monsters for the foreseeable future.

Kaz looked them over as they walked in, set up drinks for the regulars without comment, then looked at Adams. "What'll it be?"

"Whisky," she said.

"Figures." She poured a generous measure into a glass and slid it across the counter, then did the same for Rory. Collins opted for a pint of something called *Cackle o' Crones*, and before long they were back at the corner table, another pulled over to expand it and extra chairs gathered around. There were a few other tables occupied in the pub, one by a heavy-drinking man in a fluffy purple robe, who kept pulling rabbits out of a top hat and sobbing softly. Another held what appeared to be a hen party with literal hens sitting on the women's laps, and a third was occupied by two old men sharing a takeaway container of hot chips and giggling to each other.

Adams watched one of the rabbits chewing on the man's shoelaces, then said to Joe, "Talk."

"Is this off the record?"

"I can't exactly bloody arrest you for a crime no one's admitting happened," she said.

"There is no crime," Charles said. "Violet just borrowed the charm."

"And just about brought the whole damn city down," Heather said, touching the side of her head delicately. "Kaz, dear, do you have some ice? I've got quite a bump."

Kaz, who'd been leaning on the wall listening to them, pushed herself off and went to find some ice, picking up a rabbit and depositing it back on the magician's table as she passed it. "Stop it, Steve," she said. "I'm not rehoming a dozen rabbits again."

Adams gestured impatiently at Joe, then took a sip of her whisky.

"*Mmmip?*"

"No," she said, to both Fergus, who had his front paws on her lap, and Dandy, who had his head on it. "Neither of you can have any."

Rory handed her two dog biscuits. "Told you you needed to start carrying them."

"The metal cat doesn't want a dog biscuit," she said, but Fergus took it anyway, then gave it to Dandy and went back to staring at her whisky. "Look, never mind that—"

"Got a spare one of those, lad?" Snoop asked. He'd been wearing trousers by the time Adams had left Station Hall, but he still had his shirt off, his chest sagging and pale. Rory handed him two biscuits without comment, and he gave one to the whippet and dipped the other in his pint.

"Are we done?" Adams demanded, and when no one answered she said, "Right, then. Where did you all come from, anyway?"

"Find my phone," Kaz said, giving Heather some ice wrapped in a tea towel. "Charles got me to do it ages ago, because he kept leaving his mobile about the place and didn't want to tell Heather."

"As if I didn't know," she said.

"Ah, but did you know *how often*," Charles said, winking at her.

"I probably don't want to," she said, pressing the ice gingerly to her head.

"It was clear he was in trouble," Pip said. "So we could hardly ignore it, could we?"

"I could've handled it just fine," Heather said stiffly.

"None of us could've handled it without the inspector," Charles said, raising his glass to Adams.

She just looked at him. "Where's Jasper?"

"Maybe the beasties got him."

"*Beasties,*" Dartmoor snarled. He had four parallel scratches on his cheek that looked very much like claw marks. "Pixie experiments, I'm telling you!"

"Everything's a pixie experiment to Dartmoor," Byx said, leaning over Rory so she could whisper to Adams. "He has a thing about them." She tapped the side of her nose and settled back as Dartmoor hissed at her. She hissed back, then took a gulp of her Guinness.

"That's what they were?" Adams asked, directing the question to Heather and Charles as the most sensible people in attendance, although she wasn't sure what her scale of that was.

Charles shrugged. "Maybe. Or maybe they were once but changed into something else. Or maybe they're simply unknown beasties. None of us know everything, DI Adams.

There are many more layers to the world – and many more things that inhabit them – than we're aware of."

"Great," she muttered, and had another sip of her whisky. It was good, smooth and peaty, and she made an appreciative noise.

"You two, then," Collins said, pointing at Violet and Joe, who had tried to slip away at the hall, but had been firmly shepherded along by Dartmoor and Byx. They were still flanking the two now, trapping them in the chairs closest to the corner, where they couldn't get out. "Start talking."

They looked at each other, and Joe said, "It was my fault."

"I stole the charm, though," Violet said. "And made guardians for Jasper."

"But only because I needed you to," Joe insisted.

"It's still my fault!"

"Adorable, I'm sure," Heather said. "You're both guilty as far as I'm concerned, and only the fact that Charles is far more forgiving than I am is stopping you from ending up as compost in the Museum Gardens. Explain yourselves."

Violet sighed. "So I discovered the other York—"

"*Yours* is the other York," Snoop snapped. "Speciesist."

"She's not speciesist, she's just human," Pip said, petting the whippet heavily on the head. "Carry on, Violet."

"I'm really not speciesist," Violet said. "I just didn't know there *were* other species."

"Never seen a bird before, *hmm?*" Snoop demanded, and Violet looked bewildered, taking a hefty slurp of her vodka orange.

"Um …"

"Ignore him," Pip said.

"Right. Well. I discovered *true* York—"

"Oh, no one else had come across it before?" Snoop asked. "*Discovered* it all by yourself, did you?"

"Snoop, shut up," Pip said. "The detectives are trying to complete their inquiries, and you're derailing everything."

"I'm just saying."

"I went into true York first," Violet said, speaking quickly. "With the help of some, um, maybe not entirely legal substances." She shot Adams a wary look.

"Wouldn't be the first," Pip said.

"Right. Anyhow, I showed Joe, and we figured out how to access it, through the tolls and so on. And I started really exploring it, you know, trying to experience everything? And I went to a load of your ceremonies, Heather."

"Did you?" Heather sounded faintly startled. "I didn't recognise you."

"I'm not sure you pay that much attention to the humans that attend," Violet said. "You're very dismissive."

Heather lowered the ice to glare at her. "*You're* very rude."

Violet made a non-committal noise, and continued, "I wanted to learn more, but you were really clear that the only teaching you did was at the ceremonies, which wasn't even teaching. It was like, burn this, drink this, dance around and chant a bit, then off you pop."

Heather sniffed. "You could've learned more from a book if you tried."

"That's not the same, though, is it? It's not experiential."

"Swamp goddess save me from young people and their need for *experiences*," Heather muttered, taking a sip of her own drink, a murky liquid over ice.

Adams tapped the table. "So when you couldn't learn more from Heather ...?"

"Oh. Then I persuaded Charles to apprentice me. It was pretty easy. I just turned up here and annoyed him until he agreed to see me, then when I got to the shop I told him he'd already promised me an apprenticeship."

"You *tricked* me?" Charles asked, sounding horrified.

"Only a little bit."

"*Huh.* But you were quite good with metal, really," he said, taking a swig of his beer. "Does explain some of your funny ideas, though. Like Fergus. What was the whole personality thing about? Was it part of your plan?" He gestured at the metal cat, who had climbed onto Adams' lap and was sitting there with his ears pricked, while Dandy whined.

"No, not at all. It just seemed so unfair, having him *look* like a cat but never get to *be* a cat," Violet said. "And people really do like personality. You've sold more, haven't you?"

"Well, yes," he admitted. "But what about Wilfred?"

"Oh, I don't know why he's got a personality all of a sudden. Maybe it's catching."

Everyone looked at Fergus, who gave a thoughtful, "*Mmmraow.*"

"Alright," Adams said, petting Dandy, who was trying to push Fergus off her lap with his snout. "So you got yourself apprenticed. How did Jasper come into it?"

"My fault," Joe said. "I could see the … business opportunities of accessing the different levels of York. On my own at first, then I started working with Eddie. I did a few jobs for him, and he gave me an easy way to get between the layers. We weren't after anything *bad*, you know. Just insured stuff, not family heirlooms or anything from people who really needed it."

"Positively Robin Hood," Collins said.

"Yeah, well, Jasper picked up on it. He found out my mum was struggling – that's why I needed the money, for her – and started demanding I get things for him. *Then* he realised where Violet was working, and started leaning on her too."

"Joe's mum was basically my mum for ages," Violet said. "We grew up next door to each other, and my mum wasn't … his mum was just really cool."

"How did he know about the guardians at all?" Adams asked, and Joe and Violet looked at each other doubtfully.

Charles spread his hands. "They're common knowledge for those who're immersed in this world," he said. "Some humans are as deep in it as you, for better or worse."

Adams opened her mouth to protest that she wasn't *deep in it,* then looked at Fergus and Dandy, and just sighed. "So he wanted the guardians? Or what they were guarding?"

"Guardians," Violet said. "But to use for attack rather than protection. I was making him the dogs, but they weren't great. I don't have Charles's skill."

"Practise," Charles said comfortably, and Heather snapped, "*No.*"

"Then you fired me as an apprentice," Violet continued.

"I didn't," Charles said. "You wanted to leave."

"Heather told me to tell you that."

Charles looked at Heather, and she shrugged. "I'll just point out that my instincts were right, shall I? I didn't know what she was doing but I knew something was going on."

"Then why didn't you point me straight at Violet?" Adams asked Heather. "You made it sound as if it couldn't be her."

"Well, I rather thought I'd deal with her," Heather said. "I doubted she really had the skill to take the charm, and I doubted *you* had the skill to help us."

"Wow," Rory said to his glass, and Byx whistled through her sharp teeth softly.

Heather just raised her eyebrows. "I'm willing to admit I misjudged things."

This time it was Charles who said, "*Wow,*" and patted Heather's knee. "Well done, love."

"I will plant toadstools in your hair."

"Once was enough," he said, and looked at Adams. "How did you end up with the charm?"

"I'm going to guess that Fergus realised something was

up," Adams said, looking at him. His eyes pinwheeled down to almost closed, then opened again. "He gave it to me when I was at the shop, and I didn't even realise I'd picked it up until later. I imagine he hid it somewhere when he realised there was a threat to it, and thought I was safe to look after it."

"Clever," Charles said admiringly, and Heather made a doubtful sound but didn't argue.

"Finish your story," Adams said to Joe.

"Right, well. We couldn't see a way out of Jasper's demands. Violet was making the dogs for him at the shop, but once she couldn't do that and he *still* wanted more—"

"I was going to try and stop him," Violet said. "Once I realised he was just going to keep asking and asking and never let us alone. I was going to turn the guardians against him when I had the master charm, but, well." She shrugged. "It all went pear-shaped."

"I still don't understand how you got the fake one," Charles said. "You didn't have a key, Violet."

"No," she agreed. "We planned it. You didn't know *I* knew Joe, so he got himself invited back to an afterparty at the shop. Then he let me in, and Fergus let me take the charm because he likes me."

"*Brrrip*," Fergus said, tail twitching.

"I think he may mean, because he knew what you were up to and had already hidden the real charm," Adams said.

"*Mmmip*," he said, slumping against her belly. Dandy had his head in her lap too, and it all felt very crowded.

"Anyhow, that's what happened," Violet said.

"But you handled the box," Adams said to Joe.

He grimaced. "Schoolboy error. We did it while Charles was in the loo, and he came back too quick. I panicked, and grabbed the tin off Violet to put it away."

"Then you tried to make new guardians, but no luck," Adams said.

"Exactly," Violet said. "And Jasper was getting more and more insistent, and I couldn't even try to fight him without the real charm, so when Charles and Heather were out today I went to the shop to see if there was something else I could use, or if I did the charms in the shop they might work. Then you came in," she said, nodding at Rory and Charles. "I panicked and hid, then when you went to the loo you surprised me. I hit you with a spanner."

"*Ow*," Rory said. "Unnecessary."

"Sorry. Like I said, I panicked. Charles had gone upstairs, and the shop just sort of … took care of things. I guess it still recognised me from the apprenticeship because it left me alone, but next thing you were gone and the dogs were gone, and the other detective was knocking on the shop door." She gave Collins an apologetic look. "I didn't want Charles coming back down, so I let you in and shoved you into the garden."

"The shop needs to be better at taking care of things," Heather muttered.

"It doesn't," Byx said. "I've woken up hanging from your balcony before."

"And now you don't come back after hours, do you?"

Byx sniffed, but didn't answer.

"And then you jumped Charles?" Adams said.

Violet winced. "Yes. The workshop kind of exploded when I did, but I got him out."

"And Jasper told us where to meet him," Joe said. "But then you turned up."

"He evidently knew enough to think the hall would be safe from me," Heather said. "Luckily I can make at least some of my charms portable."

"With help," Pip pointed out, grinning, and she scowled at him, then smiled.

"Yes, with help. Thank you."

He raised his glass, and she tapped hers to it.

"Did anyone actually see what happened to Jasper?" Adams asked.

"There really were a lot of beasties," Heather said, running a finger along the rim of her glass.

"Or he just ran off," Charles said. "But he didn't get the charm, so that's what matters."

Adams scowled at him. "What about Wilfred?"

"No idea where he came from. I assume Fergus brought him." Charles nodded at the cat in question. "He's rather taken to you."

"*Personality*," Heather muttered.

"Another round?" Kaz asked, from where she'd been leaning against a neighbouring table.

"Why not?" Rory said.

"I thought you had a concussion," Adams said to him.

"Probably. But the whisky's for the shock."

She shook her head, not quite smiling at him. They were all in one piece. The charm was safe. The guardians had been stopped, and no one had torn the city to pieces.

It was close enough to a win for her.

"Go on, then," she said to Kaz.

THE SPRING SUN WAS THIN, and a sharp, inquisitive wind whipped around the outside table they were sitting at, Adams with her scarf pulled up to her chin and a hat pulled down to her ears.

"Soft southerners," Collins said to Rory, who grinned.

"I'm not *soft*," Adams said. "It's bloody freezing."

"It's positively balmy," Rory said, but he had his shoulders hunched deep into his Oxfam coat, and his nose was running.

"Why are we sitting outside?" Adams asked. "Just because the sun's out? The sun comes out in the Arctic too, you know."

"*Soft*," Collins said again, unzipping his jacket and stretching his legs out.

The fourth chair at the table was taken up by Thompson, his ears flattened against the wind. "Can I sit on someone's lap? This is unacceptable."

"For once I agree with the cat," Adams said.

"About the lap?" Rory asked, and Collins choked on his pint.

Adams ignored him and said to Thompson, "You can sit on my lap if you don't make it weird."

"I'm a *cat*," he said, jumping from his seat and scrambling up to curl onto her. "*Ugh*. You stink of dog."

Dandy whined, and shoved his nose at the cat, who hissed and batted his snout with one paw.

"Oh, sod this," Adams said, getting up and tipping Thompson off. "I'm going indoors."

A few minutes later they were huddled around a table inside the pub, Adams rubbing her fingers together to get some feeling back into them. The bartender had looked at Thompson, started to say something, then just shrugged and walked off again. Midge and Pinto were sprawled out under the table, flanking Dandy, and Adams looked at the cat.

"What's happened with the missing guardians?" she asked. "Raised any flags with the Watch?"

"No," the cat said, accepting some biscuits from Collins. "They didn't get up to much, in the end. The crab's just been hanging out on the beach, burying itself in the sand and blowing bubbles at donkeys, and the boar's been wandering about the woods. No idea where the bat went, but humans all think they're art installations, so I'm not too bothered."

"That's something."

"Any sign of Jasper?" Rory asked, and Adams looked at Collins.

He grimaced. "Body turned up in the river. Internal investigation's pending, but Farzana tells me he was known to be crooked, and the assumption is something caught up with him."

"I suppose it did, at that," Adams said.

"You think Charles and Heather did it?"

"Wilfred," she said. "And given the quirks going on with the guardians, I'm not sure anyone told him to."

"Are they going to deprogram them or whatever?" Rory asked.

"I think they'd like to," she said. "But I know they can't even get near Fergus to try it. Heather called me to tell me she was gifting him to me as a thank you, but I got out of her rather quickly that he's driving her to distraction and they can't get him under any sort of control, and she's trying to find any way to get rid of him."

"Told you," Thompson said. "Can't go giving things a semblance of life and thinking they'll just stop there."

"Are you going to take him?" Collins asked.

"No. I've already got an invisible dog."

"I think Kaz has taken him," Rory said. "Good for clearing the pub at closing, apparently."

Adams looked at him. "You hanging out in the Blighted Basilisk still?"

He shrugged. "It doesn't seem I can hide from that part of the world, even when I try. May as well embrace it, right?"

They were silent for a moment after that, the pub filled with the quiet murmur of Saturday afternoon drinkers, a week after the chaos at the station had unfolded. Adams had been keeping an eye on the news, but Collins told her he'd asked Farzana to look into it, and there had been no reports of any damage. She supposed if one knew how to twist metal and earth to one's will, it was easy enough to rebuild when literal tracks needed covering. She didn't like to think of the creatures still scuttling around their tunnels in the deep, *chugga-chugga-choo-choooooo*-ing in the secret ways beneath the city, but Charles said the entrances were sealed now. Maybe that would be the end of it.

Jasper wasn't the end of *that* side of it, though. Adams still didn't know why he'd been trying to get himself an army of guardians, any more than she knew who'd been trying to dose half the population of Yorkshire with enchanted beer, or who in Leeds was quietly trading Folk artefacts. There was something larger behind all these things, something moving beyond Folk and humans, something full of threat and desire, and she hadn't found the thread to pull yet, the one that would begin to unravel everything.

She would, though. She just had to keep going. Keep asking questions. Keep following trails. Keep poking things until something gave. It was how every investigation worked, and this one would be no different.

"Want to grab a curry?" Collins asked, startling her, and she looked at him.

"I'll never say no to a curry," Rory said.

"I'll just take straight fish," Thompson said.

"No one asked you," Collins pointed out.

"Excuse me, I am a *vital* source of information, and you should treat me better."

"I carry cat biscuits for you! I don't even like cats!"

"You do. Everyone does, unless they're a dog."

Collins sighed, and looked at Adams. "Coming?"

"No," she said, getting up. "I owe someone dinner."

"I thought that was me," Rory said.

"Next time," she said, heading out of the pub with Dandy ambling next to her, out into the cold crisp air, breathing in the scent of damp earth and fresh growth, old stone and clandestine cigarettes, car exhaust and spring blooms and the cool waters that raced down from distant fells, peopled with spirits and sprites and old secrets, human and Folk alike.

The world was so full of strange, wild, and inexplicable beauty, none of which made sense yet *all* of which mattered, and all she could do was navigate it the best she could, protect it even if she never understood it, and hold back the chaos with her duck, her chocolate, and her very big stick.

She tapped her phone as she walked, and when it was answered she said, "Isha? Be there in about an hour." She didn't bother with small talk, just hung up again, looked at Dandy and said, "Come on."

They ran for the car together, not because they were late, or because the trip was urgent, but because it was spring, and the world was wild, and running with an invisible dog seemed like the most important thing in the world, right in that very moment.

And that was enough. *That* was a win, for whatever might come next.

THANK YOU

Lovely people, thank you once again for joining the eternally over-caffeinated Adams and her slowly expanding network of not entirely helpful friends and allies in the treacherous reaches of Yorkshire. I hope very much that you enjoyed this latest jaunt, and are as concerned as I am about just what's behind the door of the last toilet cubicle in the row. (Seriously, what's with the *glitter?*)

As ever, I appreciate your support so much. The fact that you trust me to be your tour guide on these increasingly treacherous expeditions is beyond wonderful, and I hope we have many more adventures ahead of us (even if Adams would likely prefer we didn't).

Adams and Dandy will be back later in 2025, and this time I suggest you invest in a good pair of running shoes to go with the Yorkie bars. We're going to need them …

Finally, if you did enjoy this book, I'd very much appreciate you taking the time to pop a review up at your favourite retailer or on Goodreads (or both, if you're feeling particularly generous).

Reviews are as good as caffeinated beverages to writers.

They makes us all happy and bouncy and productive, and less likely to crawl under the desk when confronted with Wilfreds. Plus, reviews tickle the retailer's algorithms, and encourage them to show our books to more readers. Which hopefully means more sales, which means writers can buy more caffeine to fuel more writing, and then we will have *all the words! Muahahaha!*

Ahem. Look, we just really like reviews, and they really help, so if you fancy doing one, I would appreciate it very much. :)

And that is all from me. Thank you again so much for reading, lovely people. If you'd like to send me a copy of your review, photos of pubs you suspect of being Folk-run, or anything else, drop me a message at <u>kim@kmwatt.com.</u> I'd love to hear from you!

Until next time,

Read on!

Kim

CROSS-SPECIES
MISCOMMUNICATIONS
& OTHER CONCERNS

As if the toilet monster wasn't bad enough ...

DI Adams already has an invisible dog.

She does not need a clockwork cat.

Fergus, however, is not quite as convinced of this fact …

Head back to York to find out just how 'useful' a metal cat can be in this free short story download!

Scan above or head to https://readerlinks.com/l/4754590

There's more than one way to get to Faery. It's getting back that's the problem...

DI Adams is not having a good summer. Her house has been hexed. Her DCI's muttering about mental health breaks. Her invisible dog keeps disappearing at inopportune moments. And now her parents have turned up for a family holiday.

Which was tricky enough even before the Fae Lord went and kidnapped them.

But if Faery wants to fight? Come on and give it a go. Adams still has her duck and her very big stick, and this is her *family* ...

Get Adams' next adventure today!

ACKNOWLEDGMENTS

Every time I do this section, I *know* I am missing so many people out, and I am truly sorry. Please feel free to write me a passive-aggressive note, or send a disapproving duck. I will do better next time.

But, for now, I need to thank as always my fantastic beta readers, particularly Jon, who I sometimes think understands my stories better than I do. Thank you all for your patience, accommodation of my erratic schedule, and general wonderfulness.

My beautiful friends, online and off, who forever remind me that there's a world outside my stories and I should go out and experience it once in a while. Well, other than my writer friends, who point out the opposite is also true. You all keep me in balance more than you know.

The utterly fantastic members of the The Toot Hansell Auxiliary, plus my *amazing* Ko-fi supporters, who show me over and over again that I know the best people, and who make me want to write *all the things,* just so I can share them with you.

Of course, Lynda, the most wonderful of editors, who is patient, hilarious, and the best of friends (I never expected editing would involve me laughing loud enough at her comments to scare the foster cat). As always, all good grammar praise goes to Lynda, while all mistakes are mine. Find her at www.easyreaderediting.com for fantastic blogs on editing, grammar, and other writer-y stuff.

And finally, with all my heart, thank *you,* lovely reader.

Without you, there would be no stories at all. Thank you for trusting me, thank you for adventuring with me, and thank you for being here. I'm sorry about the toilet monster. The glitter's *such* a pain.

Until next time,

Kim x

ABOUT THE AUTHOR

Hello, lovely person. I'm Kim, and in addition to the DI Adams tales I also write other funny, magical books that offer a little escape from the serious stuff in the world and hopefully leave you a wee bit happier than you were when you started. Because happiness, like friendship, matters.

I write about baking-obsessed reapers setting up baby ghoul petting cafes, and ladies of a certain age joining the Apocalypse on their Vespas. I write about friendship, and loyalty, and lifting each other up, and the importance of tea and cake.

But mostly I write about how wonderful people (of all species) can really be.

If you'd like to find out the latest on new books, learn about giveaways, discover extra reading, and more, jump on over to www.kmwatt.com and check everything out there, or join me on Ko-fi for monthly short stories and weekly updates.

Read on!

amazon.com/Kim-M-Watt/e/B07JMHRBMC

goodreads.com/kimmwatt

bookbub.com/authors/kim-m-watt

facebook.com/KimMWatt

instagram.com/kimmwatt

youtube.com/@KimMWatt-yd1qb

ALSO BY KIM M. WATT

The Beaufort Scales Series (cozy mysteries with dragons)

"The addition of covert dragons to a cozy mystery is perfect … and the dragons are as quirky and entertaining as the rest of the slightly eccentric residents of Toot Hansell."

– Goodreads reviewer

The Gobbelino London, PI series

"This series is a wonderful combination of humor and suspense that won't let you stop until you've finished the book. Fair warning, don't plan on doing anything else until you're done …"

– Goodreads reviewer

The DI Adams Mysteries

"… will grip you within its story and not let go so be prepared going in with snacks and caffeine because you won't want to put it down."

– Goodreads reviewer

The Hollowbeck Paranormal Cozy Mysteries

(With Amelia Ash)

"It's a no-brainer to recommend this one to anyone who enjoys cozies. Or laughing. Or paranormal stuff. Or sarcastic wit. Or great writing in any form."

- Amazon reviewer

Short Story Collections

Oddly Enough: Tales of the Unordinary, Volume One

"The stories are quirky, charming, hilarious, and some are all of the above without a dud amongst the bunch …"

– Goodreads reviewer

Need more stories?

Join the Ko-fi membership site for monthly, member-exclusive short stories, behind-the scenes content, early access to ebooks, and more!

Free stories!

The Cat Did It

Of course the cat did it. Sneaky, snarky, and up to no good – that's the cats in this feline collection, which you can grab free by signing up to the newsletter. Just remember – if the cat winks, always wink back …

The Tales of Beaufort Scales

Modern dragons are a little different these days. There's the barbecue fixation, for starters … You'll get these tales free once you've signed up for the newsletter!